STORM OF CHAOS AND SHADOWS

A FAE FANTASY SERIES

BOOK ONE

C.L. BRIAR

Storm of Chaos and Shadows

First Edition published March 2022

Map Design © 2022 by C.L. Briar

Cover Design © 2023 Artscandare Book Cover Design

Edited by Second Pass Editing

Identifiers:

ISBN: 978-1-956829-00-6 (ebook)

ISBN: 978-1-956829-02-0 (paperback)

ISBN: 978-1-956829-01-3 (hardback)

ISBN: 978-1-956829-06-8 (special edition)

❀ Created with Vellum

To those of us who struggle with our own darkness: You are not alone.

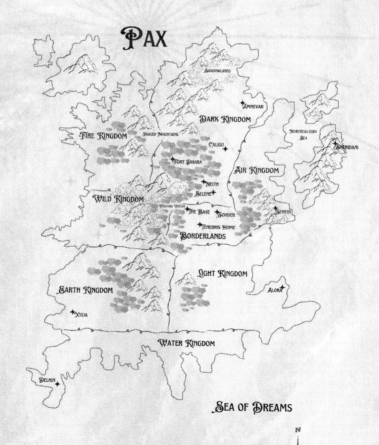

PAX

SHADOWLANDS

AMNEVAR

DARK KINGDOM

JAGGED MOUNTAINS

FIRE KINGDOM

NORTHEASTERN SEA

SHERIDANI

CALIGO

FORT DHARA

AIR KINGDOM

NEITH

SELENE

WILD KINGDOM

WESTERN MEADOWS

THE BASE

SONDER

SEREIN

TENEBRIS HOME

BORDERLANDS

LIGHT KINGDOM

EARTH KINGDOM

ALORA

XYLIA

WATER KINGDOM

DELMIN

SEA OF DREAMS

N

W

E

S

CHAPTER 1

THE FLUTTERING WINGS OF ROGUISH PIXIES WHIPPED AND whirled around me, celebrating their freedom on a brisk, winter breeze. They hovered over my head, iridescent wings and pale skin swirling between escaped strands of my chestnut curls. Mischievous grins met my glare as their agile forms darted into the branches above.

Shielding my eyes, I shrieked as snow tumbled down. The sting of sleet pierced my neck, jerking my body upright as the icy chill slid down my spine. I leapt up, shaking off the frost-covered pine needles with a slew of curses on the tip of my tongue, but before I could give life to the words, the pixies were gone.

Already off on their next adventure.

How I envied those beautiful, wicked creatures. No larger than my smallest finger and yet granted with the power to choose their own destinies. While I was stuck trudging through mine.

Sighing, I turned back to the task at hand.

"How is this possible? No wonder we haven't had any meat this week," I grumbled, scolding myself while I hunched over the tangled lump of rope. I knew better than to trust my Will to help. He was a quick study, but my younger brother shouldn't have been trusted with something as important as this.

The chill of snow pressed through my worn, oversized boots as my numb fingers pulled and stretched the jumbled mess to no avail. Without the snares set properly, we would be dependent on the limited amount of vegetation peeking through the melting snowbanks, which wasn't nearly enough.

My sisters had gone foraging the day before last but had found only a measly handful of winter roots. We had agreed to save the remaining bits of dried hare for young Will, but if I didn't manage to bring something back tonight, we'd have to split what was left between the four of us. Even then, it would only last another night or two.

My stomach twisted as I considered the alternative. I could venture north, just outside of the human village where I knew other hungry families had snares set. It wasn't ideal, stealing food from others who were in situations just as precarious as mine, but if I had to sacrifice another sliver of my soul to ensure my family survived, I would.

I'd done it before.

I hated these woods. Hated the time I was forced to spend trekking through them. It hadn't always been that way. There had been a time when I'd begged to join my older brothers and father in the forest—a time when I had yearned for the adventure that came from stalking through the thick trees, reveling in the scent of pine, knowing I was safe within the Borderlands.

But that was before. Back when we had enough strength to defend our borders and offer respite to other humans fleeing the innate brutality of the fae. Before humans had started dying.

We were left with only a fraction of the force we once had. Our government was in ruins. There simply were not enough humans left to sustain it. What remained of the military force had pulled together, attempting to keep the scraps of our civilization alive, but their power was limited. Especially with the human death toll continuing to climb.

The world had changed the day that terrible storm ravaged our land, claiming nearly half of all human lives. Attacks against human villages started soon after and had been growing ever since. Entire towns—destroyed.

Most thought a rogue group of rebels from the vicious Dark Kingdom were responsible, intent on ridding this world of us— humans—once and for all. Others thought it was the coming of days, foretold by the ancient prophecies that had somehow been lost over time, only circulating in bits and pieces of sacred text.

But me? I didn't care what had brought about this fate, prophecies or otherwise. The outcome was still the same. My parents, my older brothers... they were dead. And *that* dreadful reality would never change.

My fingers pulled and twisted, but the tangled heap of rope didn't loosen. I'd had enough of hunting, enough of the constant hunger gnawing my belly, enough of the guilt that raked me at not being able to give my family a better life.

The days of carefree happiness were at an end. This forest had become a prison, one that was capricious with her blessings, begrudgingly offering the minimum amount of nourishment to keep my family from starving.

A few choice words issued from my mouth as I launched the useless ball through the forest. I'd have to make do with the other snares, poaching or otherwise, or risk delving further into the treacherous lands of the west. My stomach twisted at the thought of going into the Wild Kingdom. At least if I ran into one of the beasts, it would serve as a good distraction.

The hairs on the back of my neck stood on end as a huffed surprise pierced the surrounding silence. My head shot up, eyes combing through the trees for the source, but I kept my kneeling position, not wanting to give away more than I already had.

A hulking figure emerged from the still lingering morning shadows, untangling itself from the mess of rope I'd tossed. Closely kept sandy blond hair reflected the rays of the late winter sun, as did the white of his winter-issued military uniform.

My stomach lurched at the sight. Men from the base didn't normally stray this far south. Most were said to be honorable, but I was well aware that even the most adored beings had a dark side. I had no intention of being at another's mercy.

My hand reached for my dagger on reflex, only to find the sheath along my boot empty. A curse flew from my lips. I knew better than to be unarmed in these woods. Yet another careless oversight on my part, but it was hard to think straight when you hadn't had a proper meal in weeks.

Get it together, Elara.

I stood and took a cautious step backwards, toward the large pine tree where my blade sat tucked within my pack. It was nestled among the gnarled roots, just beside my bow and quiver.

The crunching of dried leaves and twigs grew louder, snapping my attention back to the looming figure. No weapons were visible upon quick examination, but I was smart enough to know there were probably a few tucked beneath his clothes.

His lofty frame shifted as he worked through the maze of branches. A broad chest gave way to thick, muscular arms, one holding the twisted rope, and the other supporting the swaying weight of two juicy hares dangling from his left shoulder.

Just one of those animals would keep my family fed for the next week. My mouth watered at the thought of fresh meat and the feeling of a full belly. I wouldn't have to steal from other families, not today, at least. There was only one obstacle blocking that future from being fulfilled, and he was walking right toward me.

My fingers twitched, eager for the familiar weight of a blade in my hand, but if he were truly from the base, he would be difficult to defeat. Only the best fighters were accepted within their walls. What he didn't know was that I had spent countless hours hovering on the outskirts of the military base, probably the very one he resided in. I knew it was an unattainable dream, the last of my childhood hopes, but I couldn't find it within myself to relinquish the desire to one day join them.

He stepped through the last of the trees, pausing in a patch of soft sunlight. Astonishment flashed across emerald eyes as he took in my appearance, eyes sweeping the length of me.

I kept my chin dipped. I was grateful for the encompassing hood hiding me from his curious gaze, but I couldn't hide the tips of my hair from tumbling past its cover. His lips slanted up, easing his strong jaw line dotted with the hint of what promised to be a full, golden beard. His once-sleek nose had a small kink, probably from a previous break, but rather than stripping an ounce from his beauty, the irregularity added to it. How annoying.

"Hello," his deep voice soothed. "I must confess, I am surprised to find anyone out in the forest, let alone a young girl. Was that you I overheard?"

It took all the self-control I had not to scoff. I was twenty, the eldest of my family and hardly a 'young girl'. But if I were going to have a chance at those hares, I needed to use every advantage I had.

Content to let him think I was an abandoned child, I chose not to answer, and instead crept further toward my pack.

His lips quirked as he took a hesitant step in my direction. "Such strong language for someone so young. Can I be of assistance with something?"

Strong language, indeed. As if he hadn't heard worse living at the base. I chanced another step back. His eyes tracked the movement, drifting along the oversized coat dwarfing me with its bulk.

"It's okay. I mean you no harm, little one," he soothed, his voice dropping as if to calm a skittish doe. "Is your father nearby? Or perhaps an older brother?" My gut twisted with the unintended blow as the memories of their ghosts surfaced. There was no one else in these haunted woods but me. And the unsuspecting man before me.

My ravenous eyes tracked the hares as they swung forward with the soldier's approach. They were thick; large despite the ruthless frost still lingering. I hadn't yet needed to kill for our survival, but a cold, rational part of my mind knew it was only a matter of time. My foot crunched across bare, brittle branches littering the frost-covered floor as I cautioned another step away. A few more and I'd be in reach of my pack and the blade within.

His green eyes narrowed at the movement, darting from the gnarled mess of rope and my retreat. A calculated look crossed his features as he inspected my clothing once more, as if trying to decipher a clever puzzle without having all the pieces.

My spine straightened under his gaze, knowing what those intrusive eyes of his would find and refusing to be ashamed by it. The coat, which had only been waist length on Papa, dropped to my knees. It was worn, with fraying material along the hem, but it was the warmest item of clothing I had. Likewise, the leather boots had once belonged to my older brother, Jem. The toes were scoffed with small holes that let in flakes of melted snow, but the balled-up bits of material I used to stuff the tips blocked most of the cold and helped to keep my balance.

"Is there no one with you?" he questioned in a soft, worried tone.

A quick shake of my head was my only answer.

His shoulders dipped, as if my response imparted an added weight to his already heavy shoulders. Voiced laced with pity, he spoke, "Do you need help learning how to set a snare, little one?"

"I don't need your assistance. I'm quite capable of handling things on my own," I snapped, irritation overwhelming my better judgement. I hated pity. It was a worthless emotion, used only to differentiate the strong from the weak. And I refused to be weak.

I wasn't helpless. And I wasn't little. I was a perfectly reasonable height. In fact, most would consider me tall, at least by human standards, though I suppose nearly everyone would seem insignificant to a person of his stature. My eyes flickered over his ears, half expecting him to be fae based on his size alone. Rounded tips. So, he was human.

With a condescending tilt of his head and a twitch of his lips, he resumed his approach. "Come now, is that any way to speak to your rescuer? I may even share one of these juicy hares with you, if you ask nicely."

To my utter humiliation, my stomach chose that moment to issue a raucous grumble. Maybe there was a chance he hadn't heard it.

A capricious laugh rumbled from him. "It seems like your stomach is in agreement with me."

Hating the amused glint lingering in his eyes, I groaned as I risked a glance over my shoulder. The tree was further away than I had anticipated, and he was approaching quicker now, at ease with the knowledge that I was alone.

I wouldn't make it to my blade before he was upon me. Shifting my stance, I staggered my feet, readying to defend myself. I'd heard horrific stories before of young women bewitched by handsome strangers only to be deceived, but I refused to buy into the noble rescuer ploy.

The agonizing truth was there were very few decent people left in this world. Not after the storm that rocked Pax to its very foundations. I'd been the naïve girl once, and my family had suffered for it. I refused to fail them again.

This last year had been harder than the rest. The creatures of the forest were growing bolder, flushed out from the dark corners of the world by the mounting attacks. Though humans appeared to be the primary target, all of Pax was suffering. It was as if the earth herself were unsettled, as if she were trying to warn us of something worse looming nearer.

Not that any of that bothered the approaching man. Handsome, confident, and if the thickness of his legs and the strength displayed across his forearms were any indication, he hadn't been forced to skip meals. He looked happy.

The thought spurred my anger, igniting it into a deep-seated rage. He looked light, content with his life, while my family struggled to make it through each night.

"Don't be upset. I can help. I know it may seem like a complex task for someone such as yourself, but snares are actually quite simple."

Quirking a brow at his arrogance, I watched as his powerful legs propelled him forward. The insignia of the guard flashed in the corner of his bulky, white coat. His boots were smudged with mud, but his outfit was otherwise in pristine condition.

I wondered if this was the man the others had spoken of at the trading market some months ago.

I'd retired to the local bar, sipping on a pint of honey-flavored ale when a rowdy cluster of swaying men chatted about a military influx. They had praised a renowned fighter, a general, who was to join their ranks, sure to strengthen the human resistance and fortify our grossly under prepared defenses against the increasing fae attacks. They spoke of him as if he were a legend. As if the gods themselves had delivered him to us.

My eyes drifted over the man before me, noting the self-assured strides and the cocky tilt of his lips, the very man who still thought me an ill prepared, silly girl lost in the woods. If this was the savior of humanity, we were surely doomed.

"I've taught many. I'm sure instructing you will be no different. Though, really," he reprimanded. "You'll never be successful if you can't keep your rope organized. The snares should be checked every few days and adjusted as needed."

Heat flooded my cheeks as I fought to keep a response from flying off my tongue. Did he really think I was responsible for that tangled mess? That I didn't know how to set a simple snare? Gods, every surviving being, human and fae alike, knew how to set one. You learned or you died. And here was this arrogant prick acting like I had less knowledge than my eight-year-old brother.

He continued with confidence, the type that only self-assured males were capable of. "It's okay to be embarrassed, little one. Not everyone has the same skills in life. The important thing is being willing to learn."

His height caused me to arch my neck as he took a final step toward me. He deposited the hares alongside us as he held the would-be snare up. "This bit may be too tangled, but I'd be willing to show you how to place a simple one. It would be something basic. Even the most inexperienced of people should be able to pick it up."

He gave me an empathetic smile. My jaw clenched. "Do you happen to have more rope?"

Lifting my chin, I met his question with a mischievous smile, the movement causing my hood to fall back. I paused, just long enough to appreciate the confusion blossoming across his face, before striking.

I spun, one leg sweeping out against his own. He crashed onto the ground, gasping for air as he landed in a puddle of muddy sleet. Taking advantage of my opening, I snagged the hares and my pack before dashing toward the thicker part of the forest, sending up a prayer he'd leave the bow and quiver for me to retrieve later. I couldn't waste the time securing them now.

Running away may have made me a coward, but I wasn't

stupid. This guy was huge, and I didn't feel like testing my luck with him in a proper fight.

I sprinted through the trees, chest heaving, feet hitting ice-slicked earth in a maddening dash. Each stride carried me toward freedom. A laugh bubbled through my lips, the hares thumping against my back as I dashed through the trees. I'd done it. I'd bested a soldier and secured weeks' worth of food in the process. Greer and Lannie would be relieved, and little Will —I could already picture his eyes widening at the sight of food.

A gasp tore from my lips as a rock-hard mass slammed into my back, tackling me to the ground. I landed face first in a frosty pool of dense mud. The hares went flying and my pack landed just out of reach. Despite his thick frame, I was able to wiggle forward through earth and ice, stretching until I reached the edge of my tattered bag.

My hand plunged inside, searching. Sending up a quick thanks to the gods, as my palm found the iron hilt of the dagger. A sinister smile stole across my lips. His larger size proved to be a hindrance, but I was quick and used to being outmatched. With the blade secured in my grasp, I twisted beneath him, swinging the sharpened tip up, toward the soft flesh of his neck.

The silver of the blade gleamed across tanned skin. It would be so easy. If I tilted my wrist just a hair further, his flesh would split. A bit more, and the great vessels beneath, the ones thrumming with pulses of rushing blood, would rupture. I could almost see it, could practically taste the metallic tang that would coat the air in the aftermath.

With unexpected speed, he jerked away a moment before the fatal blow could land. Large hands cupped my own, slamming my wrist down against the ground, the force knocking the dagger from my grasp.

His murderous glare bored into me as his solid body pressed against mine. I bucked and strained, searching for a weakness— for anything that would allow me to escape—but found none.

Firm thighs held me in place as the force of his arms restrained mine. With another swift jerk, both my hands were pulled up, secured in place with just one of his.

A lump formed in my throat as I realized there was no way to overpower him. I needed to be smart, bide my time until he let his guard down, but judging by the angry glint in his eyes and the taut pull of his body, that wasn't likely to happen anytime soon.

"What is wrong with you?" he growled. "I was trying to help!"

"I don't need your help. I'm not some child and I definitely don't need some arrogant jerk thinking he's a hero. Now, get off me!"

His livid glare eased, diluted, as a hint of curiosity flickered over his features. Emerald eyes moved down my body, taking in my brown curls and hazel eyes, before traveling down to snag on the disheveled opening in my baggy coat. The thin cotton clung to my chest, heaving with rage and exertion.

Eyes widened, his pupils dilating with something dangerously close to desire. It wasn't the distraction I had planned for, but as his eyes dipped lower, his grasp lessened slightly, affording me the opening I needed. Bucking my hips, I planted my feet, throwing him off balance enough to tear my hands loose.

But his thighs still held mine, grounding me to the earth. I pushed and shoved, leaving grimy smudges across his once pristine uniform, but only solid unmoving muscle lay beneath.

He threw his head back in a laugh. "Is that all you've got, little one?"

I hissed in rage. If only I had my dagger, I'd be able to put an end to his laughing once and for all. My body twisted with all the force I could muster, allowing my arm to spring back before snapping forward. A splintering crunch echoed through the forest as my fist connected with his nose.

Ignoring the sting of pain across my knuckles, I shoved against him again. This time, he fell. Scrambling up, I launched toward the forest, pausing at the edge to search for the hares. With this pissed off prick, it would be several days before I could chance hunting.

A strangled chuckle drew my attention back to the muscular frame kneeling in the snow. He was holding his nose, a thin streak of scarlet mixing with the muddy stains across his chest. But rather than angry, he looked at me with a bemused smirk, his eyes roving across my form as he stood.

"Well done, little one. That was impressive." He swiped an arm across his nose, unbothered by the crimson streak slashing through his sleeve and glanced to his left.

I cursed, following his line of sight toward my pack and the pair of hares beyond it. In the time it took for me to start forward, he'd already swung around and gathered my belongings.

"What do we have here?" he said, rummaging through my things.

"That's mine!"

With a quick leap, he managed to avoid my swing, moving closer to the hares and my discarded knife beside them.

"You know, when a gentleman offers to help a lady, she normally accepts." His head tilted. "And most are grateful."

I snorted. This guy was so full of himself.

"I'm impressed that you bested me, even if only for a moment, little one."

A flush crept across my cheeks as my temper flared. "I am not little."

His pacing halted as his bright eyes surveyed me once more, his attention snagging on my exposed undershirt. A chilling breeze licked across my chest, the chill pebbling my skin to draw taut against the damp fabric.

"No. You most definitely are a woman." His lips twitched as

my blush deepened. "Though I find you still come off as rather small. And inexperienced."

I blinked.

"Had you been a little quicker, you could have gotten away, and with my hares too, I might add."

My fists clenched as I thought of all the ways to end his life. If only I had my dagger. He continued unaware of the grisly pictures flashing through my mind.

"That being said, I do think your efforts deserve a reward."

Stooping, he gathered the hares, weighing his decision a moment longer before holding them out for me.

I snatched them away with a wary glare. This may be a trick, but I would have to risk it. My family wouldn't survive without the food.

"Thanks," I mumbled, uncertain what was in it for him.

"It's a gift," he said, answering my unspoken question as he handed over my pack. "No catch. It has been a while since someone's surprised me."

"You say that like it was difficult."

His lips twitched. "For most, it is. It's extremely challenging to surprise a general."

My spine stiffened with his acknowledgement. I had suspected him to be the one they spoke of, but having it confirmed felt different somehow... more foreboding. Being a general was always a position of power, but with the fall of our human government, he was practically the equivalent of a human royal.

"Well, this has been fun," he said into my answering silence. "I could escort you home—"

"No," I swallowed. His shoulders pulled back. "No, thank you. I live just south of here and can take care of myself. Your services won't be required."

His lips tilted up with some unknown jest. "Yes, I can see that."

I gave him a wide berth as I stepped around him. He was courteous enough to respect my wishes and maintain his distance.

"Be sure to stay safe. If you find you are in need of anything, I've just returned to the base, Camp Bellum."

"Returned? I thought the renowned general was a transfer from the south, having faced the horrors of the Earth Kingdom, fighting for human equality, and now graciously agreeing to protect our small, crumbling corner of the world."

A tick in his jaw hammered at the mention of the Earth Kingdom. "That's me." He shrugged, crafting a dazzling smile full of charm. I had no doubt that smile alone had earned him the hearts of ladies across the realm, perhaps men as well. "I apologize. Let me introduce myself. My name is—"

"That's not necessary."

His confident smile faltered at my blatant refusal. I nearly laughed at the sight. It was clear he wasn't used to being denied. Still, it would be best not to test my luck.

"There's no need for formalities. Our lives are grossly different. I doubt we will see each other again."

He dipped his head, though remained quiet.

"Thank you, again, for the hares," I muttered as I slipped past him.

"You earned them. I'd be careful, though. It is not our place to presume what fate has planned for us. Perhaps, we'll be seeing each other again."

"I am the bringer, bearer, and executioner of my own fate. Unlike some, I do not expect the gods to hold my hand through life. They have far more important things to do."

He chuckled, the sound vibrating through me. "I'm beginning to understand that."

Narrowing my eyes, I looked him over, deciphering and memorizing as much information as possible. If I did encounter him again, I'd be better prepared. Though, I doubted any amount of preparation would save me from the strength contained within the span of his shoulders, or the tightly coiled bands of muscle adorning his arms.

"Do you see something you like, little one?" Amusement glittered in his eyes.

My jaw clenched as I spun away, refusing to let him see the blush flaring across my checks. Deep laughter chased me as I dashed through the trees, clutching the hares as I ran.

CHAPTER 2

My stomach clenched with hunger, waking me from sleep. It had been nearly two weeks since the encounter. The tender meat of the hares had proven a welcome reprieve to the scraps we had been surviving on, but food had once again started to run low.

Greer braved a late winter storm yesterday. Frost had coated her wild platinum curls, creating a silver glow against her fair skin. Her light pink lips had paled with the cold, nearly as blue as her crystal eyes. Despite her efforts, she had only a handful of roots to show for it, placing the responsibility on my shoulders to provide for us.

I grumbled as I tossed and turned in bed. We needed this winter to be over. Summer offered such a lovely retreat from all of this. Both my sisters adored venturing into the surrounding forest when the weather was nice. Greer would focus on gathering seasonings to use for dinner, insisting that even the poorest of beings could enjoy tasty meals if they only knew where to find the proper herbs. Lannie would tag along, her sleek dark hair typically secured in a neat tie, with her sketchbook in hand.

It had been a gift for Yule in her sixth winter, my favorite holiday. Fae and humans alike enjoyed the longest night of the year under a blanket of stars, the darkness lit with bonfires and warm conversations celebrating the return of the light. I could nearly smell the hot, spiced wine Mother used to make, the clove and ginger aroma comforting and excited all at once.

Since then, Lannie had catalogued every plant she came across. It had started with rough sketches, but her interest soon evolved into robust depictions with accompanying purposes, poison level, consumption methods, and habitats of the plant.

Not wanting to et out of bed just yet, I allowed my mind to wander back to the weeks before the storm—the one that had changed everything.

Mother had been so proud of Lannie, insisting that at least one of her daughters had a chance of securing a match within the esteemed Light Kingdom, a land overflowing with medical advancement and riches. Light fae were said to be a gentle, refined group, focused on crisp, clean living with an over-whelming sense of propriety. Rather than brute strength, like the fae kingdoms of the north, the light fae prided themselves on intelligence.

Seven years had passed since that summer. Lannie would have loved it; studying in the capital with the most talented healers of Pax. I wonder whether Greer and I would have changed our minds.

Not that any of that mattered now. Reaching for the pile of clothes next to the bed, a long sigh escaped me. I donned my dead brother's pants, frayed and tattered along the seams, and secured them with a worn belt across my hips. The memories of the past slipped away as I trudged down the stairs, toward the light chatter of my siblings in the kitchen.

What remained of our meager cooking supplies were laid across the once white kitchen countertops, now worn with age. They were chipped and stained into a dull grey, but that didn't stop Greer from imagining this was a grand workspace, one in which she could craft beautiful feasts and extraordinary presentations.

Lannie's melodious voice sounded from the living room. She was seated with Will on the faded blue rug, the edges rumpled and bunched from years of use. The light of the fire warmed their backs, casting a faint glow over the pages of the book Lannie was reading. Will was sprawled out on his belly, his curly blond head cradled in his hands, limbs thin from his recent growth spurt, as he gazed up at her with wide eyes.

I smiled as the words of the story took hold. He'd heard this tale dozens of times, but he somehow continued to find it enchanting, always eager for the next part of the adventure to unfold.

Greer's smile reflected my own, her shorter frame joining me as we paused to appreciate the peaceful perfection of this small moment. She retained her feminine, curvy figure despite our lack of steady food. Though she was two years my younger, our shared clothes grew tighter across her chest and hips, while they stayed disappointingly looser along mine.

A few silver-blonde curls sprang free of her large messy bun as she tipped her head in Lannie and Will's direction. "It's the one about the selfless queen who embraces her ruin to save the world. The one where nobody ever realizes her sacrifice. Such a morbid tale, but he loves it."

Greer shook her head, love blooming across her face as she watched Will. He pressed up on his knees, entranced as Lannie's voice pitched and dipped.

"I think it's supposed to be a moral thing, Greer. You know, teach him to do the right thing whether he gets rewarded or not."

She rolled her eyes. "Who wants to give up their life for nothing? I mean, I get that she's saving the world and everything, but can't a girl get some credit?"

I laughed as her hands came to rest on her hips.

"Speaking of credit for tasks well done, I'm not sure what I can make for dinner tonight. We still have the roots I gathered, and a few dried herbs left hanging in the barn, but it seems a shame to waste them on anything other than meat."

My spine stiffened at the implication. "I'm heading out now."

It's not like I could force the snares to fill with meat. They'd been empty for the past two weeks—longer, actually. I'd have to chance poaching if they were empty again.

I looked over my shoulder, making sure Lannie and Will were still distracted, before lowering my voice. "Did you tell Lannie about the general?"

Greer matched my tone, keeping her voice barely above a whisper. "No, I didn't want to worry her. I know she's sixteen now, but we've had to deal with so much from a young age. I figured it would be another topic we dealt with on our own."

Our own. Greer's and mine. I nodded my agreement.

Lannie helped us with Will often, more so when he was younger, but we still viewed her as our little sister. The two of us had silently decided over the years to try to preserve what semblance of childhood she and Will had left.

The two of us didn't have time together often. When one of us was hunting, the other was busy conducting lessons with Will. It was Greer who had insisted he be given as close to a formal education as we could manage. She believed just because our world had ended, it didn't mean we should stop learning. We needed to prepare for the future, whatever that may be.

"I've been out every day for the past week and still no sign of an attack, soldiers or otherwise," I soothed.

"Any plans for heading to the trading market?" she asked, relief washing through her features. Her eyes darted to the fireplace and back, her voice lowering further. "I've heard rumors of human infants dying, most not gaining enough strength to attempt life outside of their mothers' wombs. If that's true, if humans really are dying before they're even born... add that to the number of us killed in the storm and the increasing attacks on outlying villages... It's like humanity is dying, El."

Worried ice-blue eyes searched mine, begging for a contradiction that I couldn't give. The storm was one thing, cutting the human population in half within a matter of weeks, but it was the growing strikes against human settlements that worried me.

The Borderlands remained safe, for now, under the protection of the military. We had carved out a place among the fae, demanding a section of Pax that was entirely our own. It was only a small strip of rolling hills and thick, untamed forest wedged between the Light and Dark Kingdoms, underdeveloped and unwanted by both, but it was ours all the same.

The truth was, the strength of humans was failing. Most had relocated within the Borderlands where our forces still held sway, but there were no laws forbidding us from settling elsewhere.

Some were either too brave or too stupid to heed warning and chose to live along the less populated outskirts of the fae kingdoms. Those had been the towns to fall. They had proven easy to destroy, their obliteration complete without so much as a whisper until it was too late.

Humans *were* dying, triggering a chain reaction that I feared couldn't be stopped... But my sister was still looking to me for an answer, fear swirling in her eyes. "Perhaps it's an exaggeration. Probably nothing more than town gossip."

I gave her hand a tender squeeze, choosing to offer comfort rather than the truth. Because even though she was the closest thing I had to a best friend in this world, it was still my job to protect her.

She gave me an exasperated glare, her hand pulling away from mine with a huff. "I'm serious, El. We're dying off. The fae already severely outnumber us. Human death tolls continue to climb, while fae, especially the pure royals, remain largely unaffected. Tell me this isn't the beginning of the end."

I held her gaze a moment longer before I forcing a laugh from my strangled chest. "Humans can't just die off, Greer. We are tied to the land, just as the fae are. They may be stronger than us and live longer, but humans are needed to maintain the balance of this world. We prevent it from falling into chaos. Our humanity feeds the land, which in turn feeds us all. There's nothing to worry about. Pax will reestablish balance. It always does."

The tension in her body eased as my words settled around her. Giving her a quick hug, I turned and slipped through the door before she could sense the lie.

CHAPTER 3

MY FINGERS YANKED THE TIE AROUND MY HAIR FREE AS I STEPPED into the brisk morning air. Frosted earth crunched beneath my boots as I combed through the tangles of my curls, marveling at how long it had grown, the tips nearly reaching my elbows. Rays of early morning sun danced across my loose tendrils, reflecting the dark chestnut undertones that always intensified with winter. It would lighten in summer, but in the colder months, it reminded me of Papa's hair.

My hair was the only feature that reflected his influence. My eyes were a hazel blue, darker than Greer's, and yet, still not the deep brown of Lannie's or the twins. I had Mother's small, pointed nose and high cheekbones with my lips being the same full shape, but they were a few shades darker, more consistent with a dusty rose her pale pink.

But my hair—the dark, loose curls—those had to have come from Papa. My fingers worked to divide it into even strands before weaving the silken threads into a thick braid.

Strange, pale birds flitted across the narrow clearing as I bent to check and reset another empty snare. An overhanging branch bowed with the weight of one of them as sharp, black-tipped talons gripped the rough bark. Lingering winter sun shimmered over translucent wings streaked with icy-blue veins. The creature cocked its head to the side, revealing bright red eyes studying me, inquisitive and intelligent in their assessment. A sharp click sounded from its obsidian beak. It was hooked at a dramatic angle perfectly shaped for the tearing flesh from bone.

Judging by its stature and calculating look, it wasn't resting, as I had first thought—but hunting. Those scarlet depths simmered with hunger, seeming to consider the amount of force required to slice through *me*, the time it would take to sever my skin and muscle, and feast on the tender bits beneath.

A shrill avian call sounded from deep within the forest. The creature's head jerked toward it, breaking our stare. It paused with one last ravenous look before pushing from the branch.

Repressing the nerves clawing their way to the surface, I forced in a deep breath. There would be no room for error, not when braving the Western Woods. Not when I dared step foot within the Wild Kingdom. It was a risk—a big one—but I'd already checked half a dozen snares that weren't my own. All were empty and my family needed to eat.

I was the only one decent enough with a bow to attempt it. Besides, neither of them knew how far I dared travel. Setting off toward the next trap, my eyes scanned the surrounding trees, but it wasn't humans that worried me, or even fae for that matter. I had studied the soldiers at the base, and continued to hone those skills throughout the years, with the help of my late brother's fiancé.

I'd been surprised the first time he'd returned after the storm —after Jem died. They would have been married the following spring and Evander was the only person in this world who missed Jem as much as I did. I knew it pained him to be near us, to be near the ghosts of the past, but he insisted Jem would've wanted us to be safe. Well, as safe as we could be.

He was a soldier of the renowned Legion of the Light, the

highest-ranking class of warriors among the light fae. Knowing he'd be called away often, Evander had insisted on teaching us the basics of combat. He thought it'd be easy instructing three girls after serving among some of the most lethal of fae. He had been wrong.

I worshiped those lessons, hanging on every word he said, but dealing with my sisters had proven a little harder for him.

Greer had been surprisingly skilled at picking up techniques, but her heart wasn't in it. After countless afternoons of her laughing and Lannie crying, of endless sessions of Evander's face flushing as scarlet as his fiery hair in frustration, he conceded I would be the only warrior of the house. I had secretly delighted that title and had worked at earning it every day since.

I *was* confident, but even the most skilled warriors wouldn't stand a chance against the monsters lurking in these shadows. The hairs on my neck stood on end as I trudged on, wiggling my cramped toes in an effort to prevent them from going numb.

Bare branches scraped against my shoulders as I bent to check the last snare. Empty, just like the others. A slew of curses left my lips as my stomach twisted with hunger. A pair of juicy hares flashed in my mind, followed closely by a pair of green eyes and a sinfully sweet smile. Images of broad hands and thick arms followed after, unbidden and unwelcomed. Inwardly groaning, willed thoughts of the general from my mind. I doubted he had spared a second thought for me. Men like him had their pick of partners. What was I compared to all that was offered to him?

I needed to stay focused on figuring out the best place to hunt. It wasn't like a second crushingly gorgeous man would appear with a bundle of food, saving me from yet another fruitless morning.

As the thought filtered through me, I noticed the forest had gone quiet, the wind itself seeming to hold its breath. I scanned my surroundings. Nothing but trees, but I felt it—a growing presence.

Crouching under the pretense of resetting the snare, I unsheathed the dagger from my boot, and concealed the blade along the sleeve of my oversized jacket. Forcing my footsteps to remain light and unhurried, my eyes darted across the horizon, picking up on the small shifting of fallen leaves toward my right. I was being tracked.

Heart hammering, I veered toward the path leading to the ruins of a fallen temple. It was nothing more than massive chunks of rock said to have been the remnants of a fierce battle from long ago, but not many knew of its location. Maybe it would an advantage.

Tips of broken columns came into view, reflecting soft blues and dazzling silvers, so bright it looked as if starlight had been captured and crafted into stone. The altar remained nearly unblemished by time, the center stone stretching up toward the clear skies beyond and borders by two large pillars collapsed toward each other on either side.

Dashing through the last of the trees, I stepped into the inner circle, joining the swaying grasses that dared to thrive among the alluring stones. A wash of warmth enveloped me, generated from the same unforeseen power that kept the bite of winter from claiming this piece of land.

Sending a quick prayer to the gods to not strike me down for desecrating one of their ancient sites, I leapt onto the altar, swinging myself over to one of the massive, slightly tilted pillars. I scaled the ruins until I was perched on top and able to peer over the side. Willing the frantic beating of my heart to calm, I exhaled as I waited to glimpse my prey.

The shifting of earth grew nearer. I peered through the trees, spotting a streak of grey and a flash of silver. A sword.

A wave of adrenaline cascaded through me as I worked my way to a crouching position, silently stalking my would-be hunter. It was clear I had only one pursuer, meaning my attacker had hoped for an easy target. My lips curled as my pulse ignited. I would enjoy disappointing them.

The final branches snapped, depositing the large, hooded figure below me.

I leapt, blade in hand.

His head snapped toward me as his body rolled to the side. My knees slammed onto the ground, my blade slicing deep into hard dirt rather than the soft give of muscle I had been aiming for. A hiss tore from my lips at the impact, but I forced myself to regroup.

Spinning, I slashed with my dagger. His blade met mine, halting my attack as his hood fell away. Emerald green eyes met mine, blazing with the near-death encounter, his soft, pink lips twitching into a bemused smirk.

"That was impressive. I was starting to wonder how long it would take for you to realize I was tailing you. I should have known you'd figured it out and were luring me into a trap. Had I been any less aware of your movements, you would have killed me."

"If only," I muttered as I pulled my blade back, not completely ruling out the possibility.

He barked out a laugh. "Such pent-up anger. Surely, you could find a less violent way to relax?"

"Maybe I find stabbing would-be-predators to be cathartic," I snarked, flashing a toothy grin.

"Predator I may be, but I assure you my prey has never minded the pursuit. In fact, most enjoy the chase." I narrowed my eyes as he chanced a step closer. "Though, I've been told the capture is even more enjoyable."

My cheeks flushed, drawing another laugh from him.

"What do you want?" I snapped, my fingers twitching with the urge to stab him.

"I thought you'd be happy to see me. I've been checking in on you, you know."

"You've been spying on me?" My fingers tightened along the hilt of my dagger.

He shot me an incredulous look as he noted the movement. "Well, not me in particular. I've had my men do most of the work, but the reports have been impressive." His playfulness waned, shifting into the disposition of a man used to being answered. "You have a routine of sorts, working through various training exercises, nearly identical to those completed at the base."

I blanched as icy fear wrapped around my throat. What else had he uncovered? If they'd tracked me home, they knew of my family, but of Evander? It wasn't innately obvious he was half human. For the most part, Evander appeared as any other light fae, but with a human mother and fae father, he suffered unwarranted hatred from both groups.

Lifting my chin, I met his steely gaze with my own. "Why follow me?"

He eyes narrowed at my deflection, taking note of my tense stance and the dagger still poised in my hand, before his voice shifted into a low, steady tone. "I mean you no harm, or your family. I've had the men circulating to ensure nothing... unsavory happens."

My eyes widened at that. How had I not noticed? "For how long?"

He seemed to read my mind. "They're my best men, the Select Guard. Nobody knows of their presence unless I want it known."

I lifting a brow in challenge. "That might be, but their presence has undoubtedly kept animals from drawing near, leaving my snares empty and my family hungry."

"Oh."

"Yes, 'oh'," I scoffed, suppressing the urge to roll my eyes. "I suppose for someone like you, the thought of not having enough food seems preposterous."

"I'm sorry about that. I only meant to help." He had the decency to look chagrined. "We started badly. I know I can come off as a bit of an ass sometimes—"

"A bit?"

His lips tilted at the corners. "Forgive me. You were an unexpected treat, a momentary reprieve from the ordinary."

I lifted a scornful brow at the word *treat*, but kept silent, choosing to glare at him instead.

"I *am* sorry about the food. I'll deliver enough some to make up for it."

His promise eased some of the tension across my shoulders. With a heavy exhale, I asked again, "What do you want from me?"

The general drew himself up to his full height. "I am in need of an informant."

I blinked.

"You've already impressed my men, and have basic knowledge of how to defend yourself. This was my final test. You detected my presence quickly." He shrugged as if that was not something all too difficult. "But the winning moment was how you reacted. You flipped the tables, becoming the hunter rather than reacting as the prey. Then luring me into a territory familiar to yourself, using the rocks to shield your position—that was remarkable.

"You would be compensated, of course." A wave of his hand beckoned me to follow as he walked toward the trees, ducking beneath branches, and returning a moment later with a pair of hares.

"Are you serious?"

He smiled back, confident that I'd agree. I hated that smug grin of his, and yet, I couldn't deny the allure of having a steady flow of food. It would be nice to have enough meat to dry.

Perhaps a sack or two of grain and flour for bread. Maybe some fresh seasonings for Greer. Weighing his proposition, I narrowed my eyes. "What type of informant?"

His delighted grin almost made me change my mind.

"Nothing too terrible. I require help gathering intelligence."

"In regard to what?"

"Attacks on human villages have been increasing. I would like to know why. There are barely any of us left. We can't pose much of a threat to the fae, so why would they be eliminating us? I'm good at acquiring information, but being a woman affords you the ability to go undetected in places where I can't. Most would assume you were harmless."

I quirked a brow, unable to prevent sarcasm from staining my words. "Yes, it really is amazing how a person can be under-estimated based on something as trivial as their sex."

The crisp winter breeze chose that moment to swirl around us. It wove through the stones, their ancient forms seeming to pulse with its frosty caress. We were along the tree line, outside the span of the swaying grasses, but I didn't like the prickling of unease that was growing.

"I suppose that would make them fools indeed," Alarik grinned. "Though, to be fair, the clothes you wear really do make you look small."

"What, this perfectly tailored outfit?" I replied with mocked seriousness. His eyes widened before I smiled, releasing him from his unease.

Soft, lighthearted laughter sounded from both of us, receding into a comfortable silence. His lips parted as if to speak, but were cut short by the thundering of the earth. It was a brief rattling, passing through us with unsettling swiftness and racing toward the ancient temple. The skin along my spine pebbled as the wind licked the stones. I could have sworn they flashed a brilliant white, flaring brightly before returning to the muted blue-grey.

The general locked eyes with me, holding a hand out as he slung the hares across his shoulder. "Come."

I heeded the command, pushing past his outstretched palm, as I fled. Echoing footfalls mirrored my retreat as the reality of his proposition settled over me.

It was an unparalleled opportunity. I'd be in the employment of the general, not as a soldier, but the closest I would ever come to being one. My family would be provided for, and maybe I'd be able to bargain for some training time down the line.

The only question left was whether I was up for the task. It sounded like the agreement would take me beyond the safety of the Borderlands and into the unscrupulous kingdoms of the fae, all to provide this arrogant general with information. I'd be put in danger, perhaps even expected to venture into the brutal, bloodthirsty realm of the Dark Kingdom.

I couldn't remember the last time I had felt so excited.

CHAPTER 4

WE MADE QUICK WORK THROUGH THE TREES, OUR PACE SLOWING only once the branches thinned and the menacing presence passed.

"I would need to test you first." He panted, sucking in deep breaths as he repositioned the pair of hares. "To make sure you could handle it before I send you on a mission."

"Why would I do this, again?" I questioned, feigning disinterest. It was a vulnerability to show what you cared about. I desperately wanted to train at the base, to be a part of a mission, to experience *anything* outside of my monotonous routine, but he didn't know that. I peered over at him with one brow raised. "I don't even know your name."

"Whose fault is that? I was more than happy to—"

"Shh," I warned, holding up a hand while my other pulled a blade free.

The scrape of dried brush and hardy leaves thick enough to survive the frost of winter rustled in front of us.

His relaxed position jolted as he dashed in front of me, body angled toward the approaching sound. I gritted my teeth at the chauvinistic move, my jaw aching from the clench of my jaw as his arm lifted to the side, preventing me from advancing further.

I *could* stab him. If nothing else, a good stabbing would remind him I wasn't helpless.

A curly-blond head came into view, bobbing among the trees with small, unencumbered footsteps.

"Will, what are you doing here?" Pushing past the general, I rushed to his side. "You're supposed to stay with Greer and Lannie."

My reproach pulled him up short, a guilty flush blooming across his small brow as he gathered the courage to respond. He drew himself up to his full height, which was only a head-length shorter than me, with a stubborn gleam in his blue eyes. "I know, but I'm old enough to check the snares with you. I want to help. Soldiers help, Ellie. How am I supposed to become the greatest soldier in all of Pax if you won't let me?"

I couldn't prevent the hint of a smile as his brave tone gave way to a boyish whine. "I have the snares covered for now. Why don't you head back to the house and I'll catch up?"

He took a step back, battling the urge to argue. Just as he was about to turn for home, his face lit with wonder as he caught sight of the man behind me.

Releasing a long, measured breath, I turned to find the sandy-blond guard had eased into his cocky, carefree countenance once more. He extended a hand toward my little brother. "Hello. Will, was it?"

Will nodded, speechless, as his eyes landed on the military insignia. His small hand wobbled in the general's steady one.

"My name is Alarik Holt. How do you do, Master Will?" I scoffed at the formal title, but Will ate it up, his spine straightening with pride.

Alarik's eyes drifted over Will's too thin limbs and weathered clothes. Sparing a glance toward me, Alarik continued.

"Your sister and I have just concluded a business agreement and were about to celebrate with a tasty meal."

Will's eyes grew wide with hunger, and as Alarik lifted the hares, a loud rumble sounded from his belly. "What do you say? Think you can help me prepare them?"

"Yes, sir! I can, sir." Shaking with eagerness, his eyes feasted on the hares as he licked his lips in anticipation.

"Wonderful. How about you start toward the house and prepare for the feast. Your sister and I will be right behind you." He jerked his head in my direction, holding my eyes to see if I would accept his offer.

Will's stomach growled again.

"Will, please tell Greer that Alarik has kindly supplied us with two additional hares, the same size as last time." I swallow the lump in my throat. "And will be joining us for dinner."

His boyish features lit with joy as he flung himself into my arms. "Thank you, Ellie. I promise to go straight home." The words were nearly lost as he took off through the trees.

Alarik sauntered toward me as I watched Will disappear. "Ellie, huh? I suppose that has a nice ring to it. Though I think 'little one' is more fitting."

A flush crept up my spine. Turning, I fixed my gaze with his. "If you must refer to me at all, you will address me as Elara and nothing else. 'Ellie' is reserved for my friends and family. We are neither. We have an agreement, which still needs the details worked out, by the way. I'll play spy only if you help expand my training and keep my family fed. And protected," I added after a moment.

"I agreed to replace food." He gestured to the hares. "Guarding your family indefinitely was not part of our bargain."

"Well, it is now. I don't see many women lining up to help you, especially not any who have combat training."

He snorted. I ignored him.

"I'm also guessing that you need a human, or at least prefer one. As you mentioned earlier, humans are being killed off. So, I would imagine that your options are limited. It looks like I'm quite the catch, *Alarik*." I flashed him a sanguine smile, the sound of his name tasting foreign and sweet on my tongue. His eyes dipped to my mouth as if willing me to say it again. Refusing to be distracted, I pressed forward. "If helping my family is a deal breaker, then you can leave. No agreement."

I prayed to whatever gods were listening that he wouldn't call my bluff.

"It's not that I don't want to help. It's more that you live miles away from camp." A mixture of irritation and hurt flashing across his face.

"Your men have already been stalking me. What's a few more weeks?"

"Sparing their presence for two weeks is very different from committing them here for what could be months."

I blinked. *Months* of working at the base? My heart gave a hopeful stutter.

Careful to keep a disinterested look on my face, I forced my body to remain relaxed. I needed him to agree. My family had to be cared for if I had any hope of committing to his proposition.

He ran a hand through his hair, turning to face me as he came to his decision. "I'll train you. I'll provide food *and* protection for your family, so long as you complete whatever tasks I ask of you without question."

I couldn't help but roll my eyes. "Without question is not going to happen. That's just unrealistic."

He nearly growled. "Fine. Gods. If there are things you need clarification on, you can ask, but you *will* complete the missions I send you on. No combat will be needed. All assignments will be recon only."

"Fine," I breathed. How bad could it be?

As much as I hated to admit it, he was right. I *had* gotten rusty. This would afford me the ability to brush up on my combat skills while being privy to the inner workings of the strongest remaining human military base, all under the blanket of relief that came with knowing my family was safe.

Memories of running through early morning drills with Evander sent a thrill through me. I fought to suppress the tell-tale signs of excitement.

What others failed to realize—what I had become all too skilled at hiding—was that there remained a deep restlessness prowling beneath my skin, a looming presence lurking in the dark.

Yet in those few moments of training or hunting, when my focus was dimmed to the movement of muscles, and the beat of my heart pumping through my veins, the stalking beast quieted. It was as if a tight band pressing across my chest had been cut, allowing me a moment of uninhibited air in an otherwise constricted existence.

My morning routine of exercises kept it at bay. Hunting helped as well, particularly when I was placed in more precar-ious situations, but that twisted part of myself wondered how liberating it would be to have a real challenge.

Flashing Alarik a smile, I turned toward home. "Dinner awaits."

~

I THOUGHT WE'D CATCH UP WITH WILL, BUT HE MUST HAVE sprinted the entire way back. The thought of him practically skipping through the melting snow and barreling into Greer's arms brought a smile to my face. I could only imagine the state of him as he tried to explain to my sisters that he had met a general.

Who knows, maybe he *would* become a soldier. I'd caught him following me a few times over the years as I made the half-day's journey toward the base. Last year, he had gone nearly an hour before I caught him. It was unprecedented—the agility and stealth he could accomplish at only seven years old.

Sparing a glance over my shoulder, I realized that Alarik having dinner with us was a dream come true for Will. If nothing else, I was grateful for that. Will had already been through enough in his short life.

"What type of information will I be gathering for you?" I asked, cocking my head to the side as I scrutinized Alarik.

His eyes flashed to me before switching back to the forest ahead. "Nothing too dangerous. I need to make sure I can trust you, first. I've seen your skills with a blade, and while they are better than I had anticipated, you still need work."

I scoffed. Cocky jerk. "I managed to get the jump on you, didn't I?"

His brows arched. "I didn't mean to offend you, but I can't afford any loose ends. We'll start at the beginning."

"I can handle myself."

"We'll see, little one," he said, amusement fading into seriousness. "Soon, in fact. I've had whispers of a future meeting taking place. It's being held at the trading market, just north of here. Are you familiar with its location?"

"The one in Sonder, the human village?" I'd grown up visiting and knew most of the families in that town.

"That's the one. I figured you would stop by regularly for supplies. I need you to arrive in three days' time. I've been informed there may be dark fae present. I'd like you to listen for any information on military movements, particularly those involving the northern kingdoms.

I willed my features to remain neutral as my heart increased in tempo.

"Listening only," he emphasized. "You lack the training and the skills for anything further."

Condescending bastard. My mind was already working

through the underlying unrest of his earlier questions. Why would the fae be targeting us now?

There was a time centuries ago when the power of humans rivaled that of the fae. At one point, we had gone as far as joining forces with some, blending primal magic with the temperament of humans, crafting power into a force of not only strength, but precision. We had come together to stand against the harsher kingdoms who sought to annihilate the human race, or, at the very least, enslave us.

It had been a dark period of history, one in which the world learned that the complete destruction of humans was not possible—not without all of Pax suffering with us. But now? We were weak, too insignificant to be bothered with.

"There are hardly any humans left," I mused out loud. "We have, what, a handful of villages remaining within the Border-lands, another handful scattered across the Seven Kingdoms? We are barely tolerated by the docile kingdoms, and openly scorned in others. We have no power, not compared to the fae."

He bristled at that but remained silent.

I shook my head, unable to find an answer to the nagging question scratching in the back of my mind. "What could the fae possibly want with irrelevant, feeble creatures such as us?"

White teeth flashed my way. "If you do your job correctly, Elara, you'll be the one answering that question. Now, let's catch up to that brother of yours. I'm starved."

CHAPTER 5

ALARIK HAD THE HARES SKINNED AND SKEWERED WITHIN MINUTES upon arriving home. He insisted on completing the task himself in order to show Will the 'proper' way to prepare the meat. I shook my head, not bothering to hide the roll of my eyes as the two of them dismissed me with a wave.

Will was attached to his side, like a duckling with its mother, asking as many questions as he could. Alarik let him assist with the safer tasks, listening intently as Will prattled on. I was worried, at first, cautiously watching to see how Alarik responded, but his eyes sparkled with warmth at Will's pestering, answering each question with exaggerated interest and well-thought-out answers.

Despite his easy-going façade, I had seen the ease with which Alarik had disarmed me. I wouldn't be letting my guard down anytime soon.

Neither of my sisters bothered looking in my direction as I stepped through the door, choosing instead to continue gawking at Alarik through the kitchen window.

"Who is *that* beautiful creature and why have I never seen him before?" Greer exclaimed, pulling a giggle from Lannie.

Their eyes tracked Alarik's every movement, widening as he stripped out of his jacket. Though he wore a long-sleeved cotton top, the bulk of his sculpted chest could be seen shifting beneath the fabric.

I swallowed, eyes snagging on how the taut bands of his arms flexed. He chose then to turn toward the house, his cocky smirk stretching into a wicked grin as he caught the three of us staring.

Greer let out a shriek. "Good gods, El. You are so lucky you saw him first." Lannie's quiet snickers sounded as he approached, with Will trailing behind.

"Don't you have a boyfriend, Greer?" I snapped as an unfamiliar sourness coated my throat.

Her brows rose at my tone.

I turned toward the fireplace, under the pretense of adding another log in preparation for dinner. "Sorry. I don't know why it came out like that. He offered me a job and we need the income right now. That's it."

"Wonderful." Greer nodded, not in the least bit concerned I had only just met this man. She'd always been more trusting than Lannie and me, able to see the good in a world filled with misery and death. She pulled her silver-blonde curls into a messy bun atop her head before grabbing a stack of mismatched plates.

"And no, I don't have a boyfriend," she said as she set the table. "John and I broke up last week, remember? All that talk of marriage and us moving into the village once he saved up enough money. He *actually* said I'd look beautiful in a painted sitting room."

Her mocking tone caused a giggle from both Lannie and me, her voice dipping to mimic his. Moving across the room, she gathered the worn silverware, setting them alongside the plates.

"I explained multiple times that I don't want that type of life—the one with parlors, and fancy brandy, and being expected to wait on him while he drones on about the newest trade agreement." She slammed the last of the forks down, whirling around to face me, her hands coming to rest on her hips. "I'm only eighteen, for gods' sake. I definitely don't want to be stuck living among boring humans my whole life."

Greer's eyes found Alarik's through the window, tracking his movements as he approached. "Though, I could make an exception for that yummy morsel of meat."

"Did I hear someone mention meat?" Alarik asked, stepping through the door. "They're all ready." He held up the two skewered hares coated with herbs and spices. The aroma of thyme and sage licked the air. "I know I'm hungry. Will, can you help me place these across the fire?"

Will beamed, eagerly joining him beside the hearth. His small hands shook with the offered end of the skewer, placing it clumsily across the flickering flames. Alarik steadied the teetering hare before adding the next, bending low, as he settled the hares evenly across the spit.

"Delicious," Greer hummed as she took in Alarik's thick backside, her assessment having little to do with the hares, and everything to do with the view of the man cooking them.

I shot Greer a glare, urging her to keep her remarks to herself, which earned another laugh from Lannie. A satisfied smirk was Greer's only response, her crystal blue eyes widening as she lifted her hands in mock surrender.

Once the hares were secure, Will and Alarik joined us in the dining area. Much to my annoyance, Will ushered him into Papa's seat at the head of the table. The vantage point allowed his curious gaze to sweep the house.

I refused to cower, but couldn't help the twist in my stomach as his eyes roved over the worn sofa and chairs. The furniture was once vibrant, though practical material, with soft patterns of blues that Mother said reminded her of the open sky. Various tears and repairs of the years left numerous patches stitched together by unskilled hands.

The wooden staircase led to the overhanging banister and the rooms beyond. It was meager now, but the foundations remained strong, grand even. The paintings, along with most of our precious items, had been sold. It had pained me to do so, but food and clothes were more important than luxury.

Alarik's gaze returned to the wooden table, sporting chips and dents from the carefree days of our childhood. His eyes snagged along the four empty seats, before shooting me a questioning glance.

I gave a subtle shake of my head. There would be no others joining us tonight.

Greer slipped out the front door, returning a minute later with the last of the wintergreens. She prepared a salad, mixing the bitter strips of kale and thinly sliced cabbage, before starting on a honey-dressing.

Alarik pushed from the table, joining Greer at the counter. "Would you like some help with that, miss...?"

She flashed him a dazzling smile, increasing her tempo of whisking the dressing after having just added a few dried herbs. "I'm Greer. Thank you for the offer, but I enjoy cooking and, if what El tells us is correct, we wouldn't be having much of a dinner without you. Please, relax." Her eyes roved freely across his chest, down his pants, to the still frosted tips of his boots. "Warm up a little."

An amused smile tilted his lips. "If you insist."

"I do," she beamed. "It will only be a moment."

Her eyes met mine as I shook my head, trying to contain the laugh threatening to bubble forth. She shrugged, the picture of innocence, before turning back to the dressing.

"What is your name?" Alarik's deep voiced shifted my attention back to the table as he extended his hand toward Lannie. A creeping blush started at her neck and advanced shamelessly to her cheeks as she placed her petite hand in his large one. Her dark brown eyes hid beneath a curtain of black lashes as she fought to find her voice.

"That's Lannie," Will answered, deciding she was taking too long to respond. "She's shy and normally doesn't talk much—until you get to know her. Then she will go on and on about all the different plants and which ones are safe to eat and which ones can kill you. She even knows how to make healing potions.

"One of them saved a man's life once—cured his fever and everything! The people in the village had given up, but Lannie said it was our responsibility to help if we could. And then, whoosh! A few days later the man was able to join his family again."

Lannie was practically purple as she slunk in her chair, letting a wave of sleek, dark locks spill forward.

"It's very nice to meet you, Lannie. Most are frightened of illness, especially these days without the light fae nearby to provide healing remedies. You must be very brave." He gave her an encouraging smile as she muttered a 'thank you'.

"I heard the words 'light fae'. Have you seen any locally?" Greer said as she sauntered over to the table. "I've always wanted to escape the human settlements and venture into the fae kingdoms. When I was younger, used to think the souther kingdoms were boring, but I'm smart enough now to stay away from the northern territories. Wouldn't want to come across any dark fae." She placed the salad in the center of the table before returning to the fire, shifting the hares to coat the underside and ensuring an even roast. "The Light Kingdom sounds wonderful. Did you know there's supposedly one or two of their royals who specialize in light bending?"

Alarik shook his head.

"It would be nice to learn a few techniques for healing," Lannie conceded, her cheeks still slightly pink from the social interaction. "I know a lot of their healing comes from being fae and their connection to Pax, but maybe there would be something I could learn."

"An adventure?" Will turned beseeching eyes on me, the same shade of blue as Greer's. "I want to go! Can we, Ellie? Please?"

"That's not a possibility," I said, hating the way his smile dropped. "I know you were too young to remember Mother's stories, but it's dangerous."

Greer shot me an angry glare before turning back toward the flames "You sound just like Mother used to, full of hate."

"Hate?" Alarik's voice cut in. "As in, your mother hated fae?"

"No—"

"Yes—"

"Greer! You know Mother didn't hate fae. Gods, her best friend was a light fae. Things just..." I shook my head, recalling that night when she returned, angry and distraught. I grimaced. "Things did change a little, in the end—"

"Exactly."

"But, overall, she didn't have anything against fae. It was more wanting us to be smart when around them."

"I guess," Greer admitted, though I could still hear the skepticism in her voice.

Alarik's gaze swung between us, a calculating glint lurking beneath his gaze as Lannie and Will looked on.

I didn't like his keen interest, or the amount of knowledge he was gaining about my family. He had already revealed my first task involved gathering information on fae, and I wasn't sure where he stood on the matter.

"She used to help Papa deliver healing potions from the Light Kingdom to the human villages of the west. She even insisted some of the northern kingdoms could be trusted, despite Papa's resistance. She didn't hate fae."

I hoped that would put an end to the conversation, but

Alarik lifted a brow in my direction. "So, she was an advocate for fae-human relations?"

I studied his features, unable to detect which answer he hoped to find. Shifting my feet, I searched my mind for what I knew about him. He supposedly traveled north from the Earth Kingdom, advocating for human rights. It wasn't a lot to go off of, but he didn't seem like a man prone to hatred.

My chin lifted. "Would it be a problem if she was?"

He held my gaze a moment longer, but I refused to blink. If he despised fae it would be better to learn now, before we risked Evander being discovered. The poor treatment of humans throughout the kingdoms did very little to cultivate good relations. Most humans loathed how much power fae wielded over us but growing up with Evander had opened my eyes to the fact that not all fae were bad.

Just as I was about to demand an answer, Alarik said, "Of course not. I just find it interesting. There aren't many humans who realize we need to work with fae toward a better future."

Greer had taken the hares off the fire to cool. She stood, arms crossed, as she glared at me. Her voice was low, but firm. "I don't remember anything like that happening, El. If it's true, why didn't you tell us?"

My eyes darted to Lannie and Will, pleading they would forgive me for withholding such information. Realizing it was too late to turn back now, I looked away from the hurt in Lannie's eyes and chose to meet Greer's fierce glower, instead.

"I overheard them one night. Lannie was just a child at the time and Greer—you had already gone to bed. I wanted to prove that I was old enough to join the twins on one of Papa's trips. His answer was no, of course. He said I was 'too little and too loud'. So, I snuck out of my bed and made it all the way down the stairs, right in front of their door without being heard. I doubt I would have remembered at all, but Mother and Papa were arguing."

"Really?" Shock coated Greer's voice.

"Yes, Mother was trying to convince Papa to trust someone. She must have been referring to a fae because he said, 'Those twisted spell-casting bastards can't be trusted, Adara! Did you forget what they did? What we went through?'"

Greer gasped as she settled into the dinner chair. "I never saw Papa angry, never even heard him raise his voice."

"I know. That's why it struck me as odd." Shaking my head at the memory, I continued in barely more than a whisper. "And then Mother mentioned a prophecy. She said something about going to the north for help. Something about a spell. I'm not sure what she meant, but it was clear she trusted the fae to help her with something important. If anything, Papa was the one who was suspicious."

Greer seemed to weigh this new bit of information. "Why didn't you tell us?"

"Because that was all I heard of it. Mother had a visit from a friend, and a few weeks later, she started telling us those legends about awful things happening to humans who wandered deep into the fae kingdoms, not to mention that dreadful lullaby she insisted on singing every night. Do you remember it?"

Greer snorted. "Of course, well the sentiment of it, anyway. Why do you think I thought she hated fae?"

Alarik shifted with an inquisitive stare. "What lullaby?"

"Just a twisted bit of nonsense meant to scare us, I'm sure," Greer soothed, turning back to the hares.

Alarik reached for his water as Greer transferred the meat to a platter for carving. He licked his lips, eyes capturing mine as he swallowed the chilled liquid in a slow gulp. "I know it's nothing more than a story, but I'd like to hear it."

Greer looked up, her knives stilling under his gaze. My skin pebbled as I watched a curious glint flare to life in Alarik's eyes.

He tilted his head, water-slicked lips splitting into a dazzling smile. "If you wouldn't mind."

Greer glanced to Lannie in question before swinging her gaze to me. I shrugged, not at all comfortable with his interest, but unable to see a way to decline without raising suspicion. "I don't remember much," she answered. "But it was an awful song of brothers plotting war and death coming for us all."

"There were happier parts about a dragons and phoenix," Lannie added.

"Yes, but wicked forces arrived in the end, and everyone died," Greer said, her brows pinched as she tried to recall forgotten words.

Alarik's face was a mask of cool enjoyment, as if he found this bit of our childhood amusing, but the tension in his shoulders told a different story.

"Are you familiar with the lullaby, Alarik? Perhaps you could fill in the blanks for us," I asked, careful to keep my tone light.

"I'm afraid I'm unfamiliar with that particular one." He flashed a bright smile toward my trusting sister. "Thank you for carving the meat, Greer. It smells delicious."

His smile was warm, and just like that, any remnants of lingering friction were dispelled. Easy conversation filled our home as we feasted but I held back from joining in. Alarik swirled his glass once more, throwing his head back in a laugh in response to something Will said.

Greer was in her element, topping off glasses of water and offering seconds. I knew she hated the idea of being a lord's wife, but she really would've done well. Alarik had already won her over, which wasn't surprising with her open heart. She wasn't naïve, per se, but hopeful that humans and fae alike would live up to her expectations.

Lannie preferred to keep to herself, normally, but even she looked relaxed, not finding the conversation very stimulating but content to let it wash over her all the same. Will was completely enamored. His rounded face, still clinging to the softness of childhood, was dripping with grease as he shoveled another bite of meat into his mouth. That didn't stop him from talking, though, and Alarik met each of his questions with a smile.

The general was one of those rare breeds of people, gifted with carefree banter and easy smiles. It was up to me to keep suspicion at the forefront—to keep our family safe. Even though I knew it was foolish, even though I knew I needed to keep my guard up, it was hard to not let my walls crumble—just a bit—as I looked around the table.

It had been a while since I had seen each of them with such lightness.

I shifted my gaze to Alarik, watching his seamless flow. We had stumbled into a mutually beneficial deal for now, but that was all it could be. In this world, the strong ruled and the weak were either used mercilessly, or killed. Nobody left was altruistic; not anymore. There was always a cost to kindness.

Alarik's eyes flicked up, capturing mine, as if he heard the thoughts echo through the space between us. He continued to laugh at Will's tale as he tilted his cup in my direction. It was small, just a whisper of a smirk, a subtle nod of his head, as if in toast, before he brought the glass to his lips.

Nobody else had noticed the exchange. It was flawless, delivered solely for me, in a silent challenge: Let the games begin.

CHAPTER 6

GREER'S GIGGLES CARRIED ON THE BALMY SUMMER AIR AS SHE RACED between the twins. Torin, the larger of the two, chased after her, doing his best to mimic a dragon. She dashed between Jem's lean frame, hiding behind his legs for cover, but Torin found her, sending her small body crumpling to the grassy ground in a fit of laughter as he tickled her mercilessly.

Our brothers doted on Greer, enraptured, like everyone else, by her daring personality. Even at an early age, she was set on escaping our little corner of the world in search of her next adventure, much to Mother's horror.

I giggled as I watched their fun, envious of her carefree nature. I wasn't like her. I didn't know how to be like that—always happy, always able to focus on the good and ignore the bad. Everyone had a darkness inside of them, but perhaps my sister was the exception.

Setting my practice snare down, I made my way over to the rest of my family.

"Greer, honey. Don't you think you're getting a little old for this?" Mother called from the house, her crystal blue eyes tracking Greer's movements. It was comical how the two of them could be so similar in looks but opposites when it came to everything else.

Papa's deep voice sounded from behind. "It's okay, my love. She's only eleven." His strong arms wrapped around Mother, her scowl softening immediately with his presence. They watched as young Will crawled among the soft grasses near Lannie, his chubby legs not quite strong enough to hold his weight. "The years pass far too quickly as it is. Let her be a child for a little longer."

He leaned forward, pressing a gentle kiss to the top of her platinum hair. Mother dropped her head back to rest upon his chest, looking lovingly at our family, with only a hint of worry as the twins hoisted Greer toward the clouds.

The carefree moment was short lived. The subtle buzzing of wildlife around us quieted as an eerie feeling crept through the air. Even the rush of leaves seemed to pause.

Mother dashed to Will, pressing him close to her chest, as her piercing gaze swung to Papa. Worry flashed across their crystal depths as we waited, not daring to move—hardly daring to breathe.

Papa's voice rang clear and low, breaking the spell. "Torin, Jem, Greer. Step back from the forest." He studied the muted trees, starting forward as my siblings heeded his command. Papa managed a few more steps before the ground beneath our feet began to vibrate, the intensity increasing into a crescendo of chaos. Then the screaming began.

I jolted awake, chest heaving with the dream—the memory. My eyes darted around the dimly lit room, the lightening deep purple sky indicating that sunrise was not far off.

It was just a dream. I willed my heart to calm as I slid out of bed, trying to convince myself there was nothing to be afraid of. I hated that feeling—of being small and helpless. Of being weak. I pulled off my damp shirt, tossing it aside as I yanked on the clothes I'd laid out the night before. Bile rose in the back of my throat as I reached for Jem's coat, my hand stilling over the soft, brown fabric.

It was just a dream.

Ignoring the clench of my stomach, I pulled the coat over my black leather pants. Somehow, my trembling fingers worked through my hair, securing it back into a tight braid.

It was just a dream—just a horrible nightmare. I repeated the lie over and over again, but the chant had worn thin over the years.

Hating myself, I stepped into Jem's shoes. They were every-where—all of them—my brothers, my mother, my father. *Every-where*. And irrevocably, unbearably absent at the same time.

I needed to get out of this house.

Thank the gods I had already planned on leaving for the trading market this morning. Greer had wanted to see me off, but I knew she would understand. I wasn't the only one who suffered from nightmares.

Pausing only long enough to jot a hastily scrawled goodbye, I rushed out the door, refusing to spare a glance for the ghosts that chased me.

THE EARLY MORNING AIR WAS CRISP, BUT THE BITE OF WINTER WAS lessening. The slanted rays of sleepy sunshine were beginning to peek through the still-bare branches of the forest as the sounds of life woke around me.

Dried leaves crunched under Jem's old boots—not my boots —not really. I grimaced as a wash of unwanted memories flooded back. I was normally able to rein them in, but this time, it was like the dream had punctured a hole through the carefully crafted dam in my mind. The fissures grew until the waters refused to be contained, hurling wave after wave of repressed anguish.

It had been Papa who'd shown the first signs of illness, with the twins following soon after. A part of me had known what would happen, but I hadn't wanted to believe such a thing was possible.

I had refused to acknowledge the grim reality around me and instead, snuck into the twins' room that terrible night. I had climbed into Jem's bed—just as I had done dozens of times before—and fallen asleep, thinking myself safe in my big brother's arms.

Mother's bloodcurdling screams wrenched me from sleep, flinging me into a reality I wasn't prepared for. They echoed through my mind, even now. I had tumbled to the floor in alarm, my mind not understanding what the crimson stains along Jem's bed meant. I remember thinking someone had draped sheets of tanned ribbon over him, the edges curling up with scarlet tips.

Bile rose in the back of my throat with the memory. It hadn't been ribbon, but strips of skin—*his* skin that had peeled off in the night, clinging with thin, sticky fibers to the mangled body that had once been my brother.

I hadn't realized I was coated in it. Not until I lifted my arm to wipe the vomit from my mouth. The cotton sleeve of my nightgown had left bits of flesh and blood and hair—all of it—streaked across my face.

I don't know how long I stood there, screaming. I screamed and screamed—until my lungs ached and my lips were cracked —until the broken fragments of my voice could muster sound no longer.

"Snap out of it, El," I grumbled to myself, desperately trying to dispel the memories. It had been Greer who had finally convinced me to leave the room, Greer who'd helped peel off my soiled clothes, who'd cleaned my body as I sat curling on the shower floor, stunned into silence as the scalding water ran over me.

I hated that I was forced to wear their clothes and I hated all the memories that came along with them. But I had to be practical. All of our extra funds went to purchasing clothing for Will. The three of us had decided long ago to not waste the coin on ourselves. Most of Mother's gowns had fallen to Greer, Lannie having taken what remained of our childhood wardrobes due to her willowy frame, which left my brothers' and father's things to me.

Pants were more comfortable than dresses anyway, but last night had me reconsidering. I'd seen the way Alarik's eyes landed on Greer and her womanly curves. It had only been a moment or two, nothing more than a glance, but my gut had twisted, nonetheless.

I couldn't blame him. Greer was beautiful. Her unruly moonlight curls paired with her pale-pink lips and piercing light-blue eyes painted the picture of perfection. Even the splash of freckles across her cheeks added to her allure. I had expected Alarik to be drawn to her, as most were, but I hadn't expected the vicious slice of envy that followed.

He was a cocky, condescending ass—I knew that—but that weak, wicked part of myself couldn't help but wonder what it would be like to have those emerald-eyes captivated by me.

I mentally chided myself for the idiocy of the thought. Love was foolish. Perhaps there had been a time for it before, but now? Love was nothing more than a naïve illusion.

Adjusting my pack, slightly heavier with the allotted coin Alarik provided for food and lodging, I veered north, turning down the path that would take me to the market.

It had been nearly four months since my last trip to the trading market. By arriving a day early, I hoped to have dinner at the inn, catching up on town gossip and listening for anything useful before the mission started.

Alarik had assured me he would return within the week for a report. He had gone, but not before reminding me this was a test—one that, if I didn't pass, would void our contract, leaving me with nothing but empty snares and the annoyingly, ever-lasting sliver of hope to fill my family's bellies.

CHAPTER 7

INHALING A DEEP BREATH, I RELISHED THE PINEY SCENT OF THE outer edges of the forest as I crested the hill and stepped onto the narrow path that would take me to Sonder.

It was deep enough in the forest to be protected from the thieves that preyed upon travelers of the main road, but it stuck close enough to the main path that it hardly added travel time. It was a narrow road, little more than a trail, but several merchants had taken to using it in recent years. Tendrils of grass lined the worn edges, always one step away from reclaiming the exposed earth and hiding its presence from the world.

I wondered how many other paths had been lost to time, how many other temples were overgrown, unrecognizable—

Shouting cut through the churning of my mind, snapping my attention to the twist in the road a few paces north. My body tensed as I came to a standstill, listening.

A gruff shout pierced the air, slightly east of the point I had first thought. Slipping the dagger from my boot, I dashed along the trail, pulse racing as I rounded the corner and skidded to a halt.

Flashing shadows darted across the path, swarming a thick, burlap sack at the foot of a lopsided wagon. The sack had been sliced open—no, not sliced, clawed—with chunks of cured meat littering the ground around it.

The shifting darkness enveloped the sack once more, before dashing to the shade of the trees. The shadows solidified, pooling among the twisted roots until two large, violet eyes peered back at me. A sleek, feline form emerged with a hunk of meat between its paws. Ebony fur was slicked back across an arched spine before blossoming into a swaying tail of black flickering flames.

My lips parted in a gasp. *A vulpling.* They were said to be guardians of darkness. Most believed them to be borne from the first shadows to grace this world, cast from Erebus himself, the God of Night. Though I had heard whispers of their presence in the deepest corners of the Dark Kingdom, a skeptical part of myself had thought them myths—until now.

Bright eyes held mine, its head tilting to the side in inquisitive evaluation. The midnight tail flared with life, flames bristling across its spine, but I felt no hostility from the creature. Only a deep-seated, resonating familiarity that sent jolts of electricity coursing over my skin.

A gruff voice cut through my trance, issuing a slew of curses from the damaged wagon.

The front wheel of the wagon was twisted at an odd angle, spilling grain across the soft green grasses. The breeze shifted, bringing with it the scent of fresh herbs and the distinct smell of ale. Angry mutterings grew in volume as a stout body rounded the front of the wagon, fist raised as he stomped toward the vulpling.

The curious creature cocked its head to the side, unperturbed by the promise of vengeance. Its front paws stretched forward, releasing all tension as it got comfortable, before sharp fangs ripped into its procured meal.

Conceding, the man turned back toward the wagon, only to stiffen as he became aware of my presence. His balding head came only to my shoulders, the bits of remaining grey hair sticking up at odd angles. His mouth was missing a few teeth, and the remaining ones looked like they wouldn't last much longer, but his smile was warm and the joy at seeing me had his slightly cloudy, brown eyes sparkling.

"Is that you, Ellie?"

"Mr. Sapo?" My eyes narrowed, taking in the disheveled figure. It had to be, what with that thick accent, I should have recognized him sooner. He was a bit wider than I remembered, but I suppose being wealthy allowed one to indulge.

Mr. Sapo had more money than the entire village put together, but you would be hard pressed to figure out what he did with it. He wouldn't buy new clothes despite the numerous tears and stains riddling his current ones. His shoes were straining to contain his plump feet, the fibers nearly splitting from the combination of wear and tension. He even insisted on residing in his small, crumbling cottage. His only indulgence remained the finest food and drink money could buy.

"Oh Ellie, it is you! It's been too long, near an age since I last laid eyes on ye." He gathered me into a hug, the roundness of his belly preventing him from embracing me fully. Smiling, he held me back with clammy hands on my shoulders. "Well, look at ye! You're all grown up!"

"Come now, Mr. Sapo. I saw you a few months ago, just before winter set in. I was as grown then as I am now. It's a good thing, too, because it seems you require some help."

"Aachh." He waved a hand. "It's nothing. Just a busted wheel. I didn't see the hole when I was rounding the corner. I've already sent the lad ahead to fetch the second wagon. He should be returning soon."

Ignoring his assessment, I knelt to conduct my own. The wheel was indeed wedged in a deep pocket. The force of the drop must have caused the wooden beam holding it to snap. "I'm afraid the whole axel will have to be replaced."

"Aye, and at a pretty penny. Would you mind keeping an old man company until the cavalry shows up? That there wraith has already snatched away a hefty amount of my wild boar. I'd hate to lose anything further."

"It would be my pleasure, Mr. Sapo."

"Aachh, lass. How many times do I have to tell yea to call me Archie?" With a tilt of his head, he had us moving toward the front of the wagon. One of the horses had been unhitched, most likely for the boy to ride for help. Mr. Sapo gestured for me to help unhitch the other, allowing the horse to graze while we waited.

"How have you been? Still caring for that family of yours?" he asked in a huff, settling himself on a small boulder lining the path.

Sparing a glance to see that the vulpling was content with her breakfast, I joined him. "Yes, we're still looking after each other. We're doing well. I'm on my way to the market to sell these." I brought my bag around to reveal the two hare pelts.

In addition to the coin Alarik provided, he had insisted I bring something to barter with, if only to maintain my cover. The pelts had proven a perfect solution.

"Those are nice, lass. You should get a decent return on them."

"I hope so. How have things been going here? There are rumors of attacks growing more vicious, possibly even some involving the dark fae." I kept my voice light, despite the grave topic.

Mr. Sapo may look like an easy target, but his mind was sharp. Sometimes I thought he purposely went around in little more than rags to have his competitors underestimate him.

His cunning eyes searched my face a moment before matching my carefree tone. "There's been talk of a new batch of guards up at the base. Swanky folk. Real high-ranking fellas. It should come as no shock, though. We are the largest human village left, with a trade market to boot. I wouldn't worry yourself."

Careful not to let my frustration show, I leaned against the side of the wagon. We both knew he was holding something back. I considered forcing the information from him, but quickly thought better of it. Fear wouldn't sway him, at least not without destroying the relationship we had, and I liked Mr. Sapo.

"That does make sense, Archie," I said, purposely using the informal title he liked. "It's just, well you know how it's been for us. This winter has been harsh, and Will's a growing boy. Did you know he's eight already? It's important that I'm able to continue hunting. If there are dangers in the forest, I need to be aware of them."

He shrugged his shoulders, dismissing my concerns. I ground my teeth, forcing a calming breath in through my nose and out through my lips as I gestured toward the vulpling, already halfway done with her feast. "The fact that a vulpling has ventured this far south is just the beginning. That sly, cute-looking creature would be able to rip through the throat of a man in a second, and we both know there are other, far more dangerous creatures prowling through the woods of late."

I followed his gaze as his eyes washed over the swaying shadows. The vulpling's violet eyes flicked up, holding his, as she licked her paws clean, polishing the sharp, smooth claws. "The world is growing restless. Something or someone is flushing out monsters that have remained hidden for decades—centuries. I'm grateful we encountered a vulpling today, and not something like a wyvern or the cú sidhe."

He studied me for a few moments, no doubt picturing the ferocious flying creature, or the monstrous, malevolent hound, before looking away. Still not taking the bait. Feigning disappointment to hide my annoyance, I turned toward the south, looking past the trees.

"Mother was going to take me to the Light Kingdom before everything happened. Did you know that? I was going to be a proper lady before all of this." I sighed loudly, as if dreaming of a better time.

"Those damn light fae, stealing everything from us. They're the real beasts here, you mark my words. Walling themselves up in their castle, leaving us all to rot as they swim in riches." Mr. Sapo's face had taken on a purple hue, his anger bubbling forth. "Makes me sick."

I knew it was low of me to use his hatred for the light fae for my own advantage, and normally I wouldn't stand for such prejudice, but I needed information. "Come now, Mr. Sapo. The entire world knows the light fae are the only hope we have left of figuring out why the storm was so deadly. They're the best chance we have to stop the lingering effects, as they have the greatest affinity for healing. They walled themselves up to protect the brightest minds of the realm. If they all died, nobody would be left to work on a cure."

He rolled his eyes. "Humph. The storm was ages ago. Where are they now when humans could do with a bit of healing? Or better yet, protection wards from the attacks? All this talk of the dark fae wiping out entire human settlements, leaving nothing but bits of charred remains—I think it's all a distraction, you see? The light fae are behind it all. They used the storm as an excuse to hide and then started wiping us out. And there they sit. Just watching the world fall to pieces, looking down their noses at us, never having to worry about their next meal."

I gave a pointed glance at his belly. He had the decency to look chagrined, but continued with his rant, nonetheless.

"I'm telling you, the dark fae are not attacking humans. This is all the light fae's doing! I don't care what that git Alderidge says."

"Alderidge?" My brows furrowed at the unfamiliar name. "Is he new in town?"

"Aye. New, but already making an impression. Trying to get everyone to march on the dark fae. But I told him, I told the whole lot of them in Sonder, that it's not the dark fae. That's just what the light fae want you to think, the clever bastards. But they won't fool me, no, sir."

The crisp clip-clop of horse's hooves interrupted his rambling. The squeak of wagon wheels grew louder as an older man with the same colorings as the young boy beside him came into view. The man hopped down with a bag of tools when they reached us, getting to work on the repairs as the boy started transferring Mr. Sapo's cargo to the new wagon.

"It looks like you'll be up and running in no time. I should be on my way. It was nice running into you again, Archie. I'll see you tomorrow?" Everyone knew Sun's day was the biggest day for trade.

"No, I'll be sending one of my men in my place. I'm making a trip south beyond the Borderlands before venturing north to the town of Neith, but you be visiting me soon, you hear? And bring young Will with you next time."

"Of course." I smiled.

He extended a broad hand as we parted, but instead of the scrape of his palm, a small leather pouch met my skin. It shifted heavily, the sharp clattering of coins echoing from within.

I shook my head. "I couldn't possib—"

"Ach, now. Don't start. You can and you will. I see how hard you work to keep that household running. I may be old, but my mind is young." With a gentle, but firm nod he muttered, "Take it."

The hint of tears stung my eyes. Before they could fall, I threw myself forward, embracing him in a fierce hug. We would be able to purchase food for the winter, clothes for Will, maybe even a pair of my very own boots.

"Thank you. Here, at least take the pelts. They aren't worth a tenth of this, but it's something." He refused at first, but conceded after a little coaxing.

Muttering thanks and broken promises to visit soon, I turned, starting off down the road to see what secrets the market might share.

CHAPTER 8

THERE WASN'T MUCH TO SEE AT THE MARKET. BY THE TIME I GOT there, it was well past lunch. Vendors were setting up for the next day, but only a few buyers were present, mainly the local villagers. I was able to meet up with a few acquaintances and learn that Mr. Alderidge only ever arrived on Sun's Day in order to gather the biggest crowd. His stand was along the back wall, near the center, where he would be sure to gather a lot of foot traffic. Based on Mr. Sapo's rantings, I figured that would be a good place to start my investigation tomorrow.

I left the market as the sun started her descent, heading to the inn for an early dinner. Smiling at the thought of seeing Liam, I pushed through the door. It had been months since we'd last spoken. He had been one of my brother's closest friends, and though we only saw each other a handful of times throughout the year, we remained close—our conversations effortlessly picking up where they'd left off.

A frown marred my face as I drew up short. A glance toward the bar revealed a young woman whom I didn't recognize. Wisps of hair fanned out around the tie desperately trying to secure the dark brown tendrils away from her face. Exhaustion sank beneath the surface of her skin, leaching the color under her eyes.

Unease tugged at my chest as I took a seat, sliding onto a chair at one of the wooden tables in the corner. I hoped Liam was all right, but the weight of coin was heavy against my side, begging to be used. My stomach rumbled, eager for the delicious tastes of a well-prepared meal. The weary barkeeper met my gaze. She stepped around the bar to the edge of my table in a flourish of long skirts and a stained apron.

I splurged on a plate of sautéed chicken and roasted potatoes with a pint of ale to wash it down. She nodded at my order, but I stopped her as she was turning away. "Is Liam here? I'm a friend and, last I knew, he was working here."

A kind smile met my question. "Liam still works here. He was supposed to be on tonight, but I'm not sure he will make it in." Her eyes darted to a group of men flagging her down.

"Why would he not make it?"

A chime sounded as another group walked in. The door slammed shut as they headed straight for the bar. "He's been tending to Lucy. I'm sorry, but I have to see to the others."

"Yes, of course. Sorry for delaying you."

She gave a tight nod before rushing off. I pulled my bottom lip between my teeth, hoping both Lucy and Liam were well. More selfishly, I needed Liam to show. As the barkeep, he heard every line of gossip that passed through this town. He would know if there was something of importance involving the dark fae.

The ale arrived first, followed soon after by the plate of food. As I leaned forward, the weight of the coins shifted against my stomach, secured within an inner pocket of my coat. It had been ages since I'd last felt the comforting weight of a leather pouch. Tearing into the juicy meat, I was hardly able to contain a moan as the spices danced across my tongue.

Most of the coin would be spent on necessities. I had to be

practical, but tonight, I would allow myself a moment to be greedy—to enjoy this meal, savoring each delicious bite, without letting myself feel guilty about it.

Greer would love this—the market, the food, the rowdy cluster of humans slurring crass bar songs. I had no doubt she could cook a meal just as tasty if we had the supplies. Lannie would be happier away from all the noise, but she did enjoy trying new food.

A sigh pushed its way through my lips as I relished another perfectly seasoned bite. Maybe one day, we'd have more. Accomplishing this mission was the first step toward that future.

Time fell away as I settled into the flow of the inn. Conversations prattled around me, some discussing love interests with promises of marriage, while others were intent on securing passionate affairs for the evening. There was talk of who would be at the market tomorrow and even mention of the young, talented general—the savior of us all.

A sour taste built in the back of my throat as a woman with a particularly high-pitched voice gushed over her encounter with the great General Holt.

"Giant, nearly as tall as a fae, with all of the hard planes to go along with it." She wiggled her brows as the gaggle of girls surrounding her giggled. My jaw clenched. "Hair like sunshine, eyes as green as fresh clovers." She made a show of glancing around as if to ensure nobody else could hear, but her voice hadn't dipped. "And I heard his reputation for skill and endurance isn't just in reference to the battlefield—"

A round of squeals drowned out the rest of what she said. I arched my neck, gulping down the last of the ale, the food feeling heavier in my stomach than it had a moment ago.

The hour chimed from the wooden clock above the old bar as a lean male with shaggy brown hair pushed through the side door. The barkeeper's eyes lit as she yanked off her apron, dashing into the night with little more than a wave.

Placing my napkin on the table, I made my way over. "Liam," I breathed, my smile reflected across his face as his eyes caught mine.

"Ellie! I was hoping you'd come to the market. It's been too long. Come here, little sis." He reached across the bar for a one-armed hug before securing a worn apron across his torso. Small crinkles formed at the corners of his eyes with his smile, lines that had gotten much deeper over this past winter.

"Are you selling or buying?" he asked, his clothes shifting, looser than they had been a few months ago.

"Buying, if the prices are right."

He nodded as he whirled around the bar, filling up fresh glasses and clearing away old ones. "This winter has been bad. Sales have been slow, which means less clients for the inn and we need the money now more than ever." He furrowed his brow as if trying to solve a difficult problem but coming up short.

"Why?"

"What?" he asked, my question pulling him from his thoughts.

"Why 'now more than ever?' Did something happen?" I took notice of the dark circles under his eyes. "The other barkeep mentioned she wasn't sure if you would make it to your shift tonight. Something about Lucy. Is everything okay?"

"Oh." He paused mid pour, shooting me an awkward glance.

I narrowed my eyes as he finished with the customers. He returned, face breaking into an uncomfortable smile. "Gods, I'm so sorry, El. I should have told you. I sort of... forgot you didn't know, but how would you? It's not like we've talked the last few months." He fidgeted with the tie of his apron, looking anywhere but my eyes.

"Liam, what's going on?"

He took a deep breath, his sheepishness fading into a proud, gleaming smile. "Lucy's pregnant."

My mouth dropped. "That's... that's wonderful! Congratulations. Gods, you had me worried—but this is great. You've always wanted to be a father."

His smile faltered. "That's just the thing. I *have* always wanted to be a father. Luce too. She can't wait to be a mother, but things haven't exactly been going well these past few years, have they? At least, not for humans."

The heavy grit to his words weighed on me. Liam was the hopeful one—easy to love and easy loving. The rawness of his despair caught me off guard. I blanched, realizing what was plaguing him. It had been a while since I thought about children... and all the risks that came along with them.

Most of what I knew involved avoiding children. Greer brewed the tea to prevent pregnancy, sure to drink a prepared glass at the first of each month. I hadn't talked to Lannie yet, but I walked in on Greer going over the basics when she had her first cycle. It was something along the lines of welcome to the club of monthly suffering and irrational food cravings. And oh, by the way, if you need it, there's tea we can make. It tastes awful, can cause irrational mood swings for a time, among other ungodly things, but since we can't rely on anyone else to be responsible, it's best to do it ourselves.

A chuckle nearly tore from my lips as I recalled Greer's words, but things *had* started to change in recent years. I'd heard of more men being willing to consume the tea themselves, which had sparked a new interest in better forms of contraception. The hint of a laugh died in my throat as the motivations behind those actions came to the forefront of my mind.

There was a reason why humans had taken extra care to prevent pregnancy in the last few years—the last seven, to be exact. Ever since the storm hit.

"The babies. Have they—have any survived?" I hated the way his face darkened.

"Not many." My mouth ran dry as his shoulders dipped. "A few dozen or so have survived since the storm."

"Gods," I breathed. I hadn't realized how bad it had gotten—hadn't realized that in just over seven years, a once thriving city had welcomed so few children.

He cleared another glass away, pocketing the tip. "Those that do make it through pregnancy are still weak, barely growing. Sometimes I don't know which is worse: having your child ripped from you before birth or having to watch them suffer in life. I can't even talk to Lucy about this. She's convinced her light fae lineage will protect the baby and is refusing to acknowledge the risks."

"Light fae lineage? I thought she was human."

He growled, running a hand through his already messy hair. "She is. She thinks her great-grandmother was light fae, or half-light fae. I don't know." A long, exhausted sigh left his lips as his eyes swung to mine. "We all know the storm targeted humans. She thinks the baby will be fine as long as fae magic runs in its veins, light fae in particular, as they are the fae closest to the goddess, protected and blessed with healing. She's not even worried." His head fell into his palms.

Knowing it would only add to his fear, I elected not to point out that there were dozens of fae villages also reporting losses. Nothing to rival the volume of human lives, but the rumors said all seven kingdoms were affected.

Trying to stay positive, I suggested, "Maybe she's right." That earned me a glare. "No, really, we know little about the Light Kingdom's death toll. Most of the high fae sequestered themselves behind the walls of Alora within days of the storm."

He looked skeptical, but I could see the hope fighting to take root. He wanted to believe me—needed to.

"Lucy does have a point," I continued. "The light fae *are* the fae most blessed in healing. That could help. Besides, if any baby were going to make it through unscathed, it would be the one with your stubbornness and Lucy's optimism. Throw in the magic of light fae lineage, and your child is all set."

He flashed me a grateful half-smile before offering me another ale. "Care for one more? It's on the house."

I smiled in thanks but declined. "I've been traveling all morning and wanted to check out a few other places in town before turning in for the night."

"Sorry about the inn being so full. I would have reserved a better room for you had I known you were going to be here. At the very least, I can bring your bag up for you."

"Thank you," I said, unstrapping my pack and handing it over. "Though I am surprised at the inn being so full." I glanced around the tightly packed bar as Liam muttered instructions to a young boy. The boy gave a quick nod before dashing up the creaking steps my pack taking up the expanse of his small back.

"It's Alderidge's lot. They come every Sun's day to hear him speak. He's been talking to anyone who will listen about how we need to turn against the dark fae." Liam snorted as he handed me a brass key with a wooden number attached to it. "As if we would stand a chance against them."

Good to know Alderidge would be present tomorrow. Pocketing the key for later, I said, "Mr. Sapo mentioned Alderidge as well. Anything else you can tell me about him?"

"Black eyes and an even blacker disposition. He's against the dark fae, so I want to like him, but there's something that's just... off. He's a few decades older than us. Shows up hours after opening, walking straight to his booth. And then the ranting starts. You can't miss him, or the crowd that he typically gathers. Sorry I don't have more for you, El. I've been focused on Lucy. She's been having the worst nausea, though I'm told it should be ending soon."

"No need to apologize. I hope Lucy feels better soon.

Perhaps this could help take some of the stress away." I pulled the small grey pouch from the inner pocket of my coat, extracting a small fortune and pressing it to Liam's hand.

"El. Gods, where did you get this?" Worry flashed across his features as he tried to push the coins back toward me.

"Don't worry. I ran into Mr. Sapo on my way into town. He must be doing well for himself because he insisted I accept this." I shifted so that he could see the purse.

Liam let out a low whistle. "When is that man not doing well? He probably has more money than the light royals, what with him being the main supplier of grain for the Light Kingdom. Though, you would never know how well off he was based on his appearance. Or his conspiracy theories." He looked down at the coins filling his palm once more. "Are you sure?"

"Of course. You're going to be a father soon."

"Thank you," he said, matching my smile, though it remained tight around the edges.

"Don't wait up." I waved as I slipped from the barstool, pushing through the side door and into the night beyond.

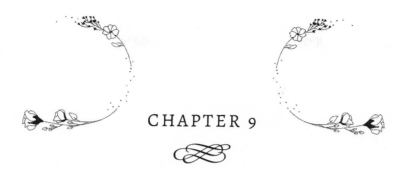

CHAPTER 9

THE BRISK AIR WAS A SHOCK. MY BODY HAD GROWN USED TO THE overheated presence of the tavern and shivered with the stark contrast. I glanced around, filtering through piles of trash and oozing puddles that lined the narrowed alley. My eyes zeroed in on the brightly lit road a dozen yards away, and I hurried toward it, sending a silent thanks to the gods for the frost that kept the rotting stench to a minimum.

My chilled fingers clenched the fabric of my overlarge coat, securing it tight against the cold. The waxing crescent shone overhead, surprisingly bright in the early hours of the cool night. I tipped my head back, basking in the glimmering glow of stars.

They had been a source of wonder for me, even as a child. Stars were resilient, the guardians of the night. Always watching. They blazed with an icy fire that pierced even the endless depths of darkness surrounding them, always refusing to yield to the shadows.

Puffs of heated breath clung to the air in front of me as I turned my attention to the road ahead. Couples passed, huddled close as they walked, while a few others were contently enjoying the peaceful night on the benches lining the boisterous street. I wondered what it would be like having a partner in this life.

The couple nearest the alley were leaning back and gazing at the sky. Her head tilted against his chest as his arm came around her, tugging her close. She giggled. I couldn't hear their shared words from this distance, but the unabashed smile that lit her face—his answering grin, reflecting every bit of love held in hers—it cracked something wide within my chest.

I marveled at it—at them—at the whole idea of love.

This world was on the brink of disaster. Some would argue we had already tipped past the point of no return and were now spiraling toward the wicked, brutal end. And, yet somehow bonds like this still flourished. Despite the escalating chaos and lurking predators throughout the kingdoms, love still managed to ensnare its prey.

The woman sighed, sinking deeper against his body. What would it be like to have that comfort? To feel the heat from another's body emanating into mine, pouring through my veins, seeping into the chilled cracks and frosted fissures of my soul?

A face flashed across my mind, and before I realized it, I was pondering whether his lips would feel tender along the curve of my neck, if the golden strands of his hair would be as soft as I imagined. I wondered what it would be like to watch those emerald eyes ignite with desire for me.

Get a grip, El. I shook my head, appalled by the path my mind had taken.

I knew it was foolish, utterly ridiculous to even think about Alarik as anything other than an employer. But that weaker part of my mind wandered. I had felt the press of his thick, firm body against my chest the first day we met. I'd seen the ease with which he pinned my hands above my head, how he held both of mine with just one of his.

An unwanted stirring coiled in my stomach, drifting lower into my core as my traitorous body remembered. It was infuriating. I didn't even like him. How could I possibly be considering—

A calloused hand clamped over my mouth, stifling the scream that ripped through my chest. My body was yanked back until the cool tip of a blade pressed against my throat. My lungs seized as rancid body odor engulfed me. Bile burned the back of my throat as my stomach heaved with the scent.

"Easy there, girl. We wouldn't want things to slip, now would we." The smell of stale alcohol wafted over me as his disheveled body swayed. "Now, kindly handover that purse of coins you got, and you can be on your way."

His words slurred as he fought to keep his balance. I willed the contents of my stomach to stay in place as I took assessment of the situation. The knife pressing against my neck was a problem, but this was one man, one *drunk* man who had no clue who he was robbing.

Forcing myself to take a disgustingly full breath, I steeled my spine and launched into action. Throwing my body into the man, I slipped one of my palms beneath the blade. Better my hand than my neck.

I winced as the cool metal bit my flesh, but the pain only sharpened my resolve. Gritting my teeth, I pushed out with my bleeding palm, my other arm slipping beneath to disarm him as I crushed his foot with my own.

A strangled screech tore from him. The wet, repulsive heat of his breath grazed my ear as he doubled over. Nausea rolled through me at the damp caress as I slammed my head back. My lips curled into a satisfied grin as a sickening crunch sounded.

He stumbled, freeing me, as his splotched, stained hand grasped the oozing mess of his nose. Bloodshot eyes widened as he looked down, watching the stream of blood add to the grime coating his palms. He blinked, the effects of the alcohol dulling.

A snarl twisted his features as he shouted, "You stupid whore!"

I laughed. He had the element of surprise, a weapon, and still this was little more than a scuffle.

Pushing off the building, he hurled his body toward me. I held my ground until the last moment, slipping to the side as he sailed past. He slammed into the stone wall, eyes glazing over as he fell. The ground shuddered as his skull connected with the disjointed cobblestones.

My body hummed with adrenaline as I dared to check whether he was alive. His eyes remained closed, but the steady rise and fall of his chest continued. The breath that was held tight in my chest released. He was still alive. I knew he deserved worse, but I was glad this pathetic waste of blood and bones was not the reason I would become a killer.

"Disgusting," I muttered, my gaze drifting over the putrid puddle seeping from his pants. He may not be dead, but I wasn't going to leave a weapon waiting around for him when he awoke. I gathered the dull blade, finding nothing worth salvaging. It was little more than a butter knife.

A shadow of movement caught my attention. It was quick, just a flash of dark across the star bright night, but my skin prickled.

I had learned to trust my instincts—they'd kept me alive more times than I could count in the forest. Holding as still as possible, I scanned the area as my ears fought to detect the faintest of sounds, but only the muffled noises of the inn mingling with the carefree conversations of the road reached me.

The sting of the wound flared as my fists clenched. I cursed, opening my palm to expose the angry cut. I'd have to clean it. My eyes snagged on the flakes of dirt and filth mixing with my blood. I'd have to clean it *thoroughly*.

My head tipped back with a groan. I was hoping to stop in at a few other bars tonight to learn more about Alderidge, but fear of an infection urged me back toward the inn. Pressing against the wooden door, I let the warmth welcome me as I stalked toward Liam to request a pot of boiled water.

CHAPTER 10

THE RUMBLING OF THE EARTH RAGED, CHURNING WITH CRIES OF suffering. It took me a moment to understand what the sound was, but the devastating reality crashed through me as the screeching grew, expanding as their agony increased.

Gods, there must have been hundreds of them—thousands of dying forest-dwelling creatures desperately trying to outrun the shadows rushing toward us.

"Everyone to the house! Now!" Papa's voice bellowed.

Heeding his command, I turned, intent on running as fast as my legs could carry me, but as I twisted away from the quivering forest, a force caught me, dragging my thrashing body back, toward the screaming darkness. I was caught in a swift, cruel current too powerful to swim against.

My eyes darted to my family. All were as transfixed as I was, hovering inches above the ground in the foreboding force for a moment longer, before an electric pulse blasted through the world, exploding out and sending our bodies flying.

The charged atmosphere prickled and singed my skin as a sickly-sweet aroma coated the air.

"Now! Everyone, move!" Papa's voice boomed, as he pushed up

from the ground. I felt his arms wrap around me, scooping me up as he sprinted after the others. Torin held Lannie in his arms, racing for home a few strides behind Jem and Greer. Will's blond head peeked out from Mother's shoulders as she tore after them, desperate to reach our house and whatever protection it offered.

Greer made it first, swinging around in the doorway as she paused to look toward the storm of chaos that rumbled around us. Her eyes widened, her jaw falling open as the shadows coating the sky grew deeper, staining the bright blues into a murky grey. Her terrified eyes dropped to mine, my breath seizing with the raw, unwavering fear flashing in their depths—and then Jem was upon her, catching her in the middle to lift her up as they swung inside.

Icy tendrils of dread crept up my spine. I knew I shouldn't look—it wouldn't help—but the clenching of my stomach demanded I peek. My head swung over Papa's shoulder, bouncing with each of his strides, as I fought to comprehend what my eyes were seeing.

A dense cloud thrust into the sky, billowing toward us with a rage to rival the gods. The sun had gone, blotted out by the consuming darkness. There was no light, no hope. Only the promising viciousness —the escalating fury—only the ravenous shadows remained.

Dark, heated waves stretched toward us, forcing the scent of rotting meat into my lungs. Bile singed the back of my throat as my stomach lurched. Their agonizing cries ripped through me. The creatures, the forest itself—the shrieks, the screams—gods, they were all dying.

And it was gaining on us.

"Papa," my voice squeaked as my arms tightened around his neck. His pace somehow picked up, willing us to move quicker as the cloud thundered onward, intent on consuming everything in its path.

Torin and Lannie were almost there, a few more steps and they'd be safe. My eyes locked with Jem's agonizing stare, but he was help-less to stop this. The heat of the raging storm swirled past Papa's legs, climbing up my chest, coating my arms, until the blackness reached my face, cutting us off from the rest of the world. My throat burned with my own screams, mimicking the horrors around us as we were swallowed whole and plunged into an infinite, deafening darkness.

~

A SEARING PAIN SHOT THROUGH MY HAND, JOLTING MY BODY awake with a gasp. My fingernails had dug into the cut across my palm, displacing the bandage. Untangling myself from scratchy sheets, I sat up with an all too familiar sheen of sweat coating my forehead.

Inhaling deeply, I allowed the stale ale-scented air to calm my frantic heart.

Gingerly, I flexed my hand, testing the movement. It was stiff, but not unbearable. Grateful for Lannie's skill with medical herbs, I slipped the small tin out of my pocket, and made quick work applying the honey-based salve, before redressed the wound. With the ointment, my hand should be healed in a few days.

My eyes darted across the narrow, wood-paneled room, the unease of my dream lingering. There was nothing. Silently chiding myself, I made quick work of dressing, and slipped on my black leather gloves before heading to the market.

Banishing the memories of the past, I focused instead on the fresh scent of pine and earth surrounding me as I worked my way through the streets and into the field stretching before the large wooden building.

Nostalgia flared as I stepped through the door. The familiar buzz of the trading market pulsed around me. Each weekend, the locals would gather for a modest exchange, but today was the quarterly market, which meant vendors from across the kingdoms would be present. The enthusiastic energy drowned out most of the nerves working through my body as I recalled my mission: Find the dark fae, learn as much information as I could on military movements, and do not engage.

The words filtered through my mind in Alarik's voice, the image of his full lips and emerald eyes causing a tightening low in my belly. With effort, I banished the scandalous thoughts and the jitters that accompanied them. I wouldn't let the ridiculous fantasy distract me. Was that what he was now—a fantasy?

I gritted my teeth. It didn't matter. This would be like any other market day, only with a bit of spying thrown in. If I could pull this off, I would secure a better life for my family. No more disappointed frowns after turning up empty-handed from a hunt. No more bleak future devoid of options—not because my sisters and I weren't talented enough to seize them, but because we couldn't afford the lives we desired.

We didn't have enough money for Greer to pursue her interest in food, traveling across all of Pax as she discovered new cuisines. Likewise, we couldn't afford to send Lannie to the healer academy in the Light Kingdom. The academy was free to attend for any who qualified, but the cost of housing and supplies alone was a small fortune.

If I could prove my worth by completing this one, simple task, all of that would change. Strengthening my resolve, I started through the rows of vendors.

The noise of shifting packages and the voices of early buyers rattled around me. Chimes of delicate jewelry mingled with the clash of foreign metals and wicked looking weapons. The smells were even better. Fresh bread and pastries scented the air, contrasting nicely with the spiced aroma of prepared meats. Fresh morsels roasted over a low-flame fire just outside the building making my mouth water.

I wove between the tables, recognizing most in the early hours without suspicion. Pressing deeper, I reached the far wall. Two bulky men framed a large wooden table with a hefty assortment of weapons.

Frowning, I looked over the crass and unrefined blades. There was a family of blacksmiths in town, but these couldn't have been crafted locally—not with the lack of skill clear to see. My stomach twisted as I spotted stamped insignias across the handles: A full sun with a blooming peony in front, representing light and life—the Light Kingdom.

A thick wooden sign was coarsely painted: 'Alderidge's weaponry'. I sucked in a breath. My gaze sliding to the two burly men standing guard. I blinked, surprised to find both blatantly glaring at me.

They were young, neither sporting the black eyes Liam had described. Their noses wrinkled, as if my presence left a bitter taste in their mouth. I suppressed an incredulous laugh. I knew it was still uncommon for women to be familiar with war, or anything that went along with it, but most kingdoms had loosened up after the storm.

It was a new world, one in which women had discovered they were just as capable as men. There were even tales circulating of a fierce band of female warriors spanning the northern kingdoms. Despite the slow growing revolution, well-off families—particularly those in the Light Kingdom—clung to tradition.

Not bothering to hide the amused curl of my lips, I took longer than necessary looking through their pitiful collection. Only after my third pass did I afford them a reprieve and move on.

It was better to explore the rest of the market until Alderidge arrived. Perhaps I'd antagonize them more later. Maybe I'd even offer them a demonstration of how deadly a blade could be.

The market was as alive as ever with more vendors showing up by the moment. The hollow clank of shells sounded as a man with a deep complexion and turquoise eyes arranged jewelry and tools that could only have come from the Water Kingdom.

Another stout man unveiled an intricate light-blue crystal tower with glimmering facets and jutting peaks. Smaller, less detailed sculptures surrounded the focal piece, each sparkling in the soft rays of the sun. "Get your protective charms and figurines here!" the vendor called, his curling horns marking him as an earth fae. "Crafted by the Winter Witch herself. Protection from the Dark Queen, long life, and good fortune!"

I hurried past as I recalled the bleak childhood tale of the Winter Witch battling the dark mistress of the night. It was one of Will's favorites to this day—or at least one that he recited often. The Dark Queen was said to be evil, intent on vengeance for being locked away. She was destined to be unleashed by the bringer of the end. The Winter Witch was her counterbalance, light and bitterly cold as opposed to the other's shadowy flames.

Most tales had the Winter Witch defeating the Dark Queen and saving all of Pax, but Mother had taught us a different, more brutal ending—one of only death and pain. Forcing he morbid thoughts from my mind, I continued to wander.

Perfumes and potions, fresh herbs and various roots, even thick pelts and hunting supplies were showcased. It seemed the fae kingdoms hadn't noticed the hardships of winter. Not like the humans had.

I recognized and stopped to chat with many families as I strolled by. Most of the men here had known my father, their sons having been friends with my elder brothers. Jem was known for his formal manners, nearly always accompanied by Evander. He was smitten, even then.

Torin, his twin brother in looks only, never failed to provide entertainment, mostly by getting caught with a daughter or two in compromising situations. People would wave to Papa, Jem, and Evander, while Torin was met with menacing glares from families who had the burden of looking after a teenage daughter —not that their scowls ever bothered him.

A soft tilt of my lips bloomed with the memories, widening as I spotted Mr. Wilson and made my way over. He had the misfortune of being the father to the beautiful dark haired, blue-eyed Sophie Wilson, the most popular girl in the village. It was whispered that she was part wild fae—that she had to have worked some type of ancient magic—because when she set her sights on Torin that summer, he lost interest in anyone and anything that wasn't her. And Sophie, gentle, kind, never-step-out-of-line Sophie, fell head over heels for him, much to the horror of her tenderhearted father.

The summer before the storm, the two of them were inseparable. The well-known sting of grief deepened as my eyes landed on Sophie. She busied herself with arranging fresh loaves of bread and pastries. In another life, we could have been sisters. Shaking off the remaining sadness, I crafted a smile to my face and took the final steps to their booth.

"Hello, Mr. Wilson, Miss Sophie." I dipped my head in greeting. "It's good to see you. Looks like you have a good batch this month." I motioned toward the sugar-glazed pastries and still-steaming loaves of bread.

"Elara." Sophie breathed, a sad smile springing to her face. "It's good to see you. How is everyone?"

I gave her a quick rundown on the family as her father waved a brief 'hello' before turning back to set up. "What about you? How have things been here?"

"Nothing interesting has happened. It's been the same routine. Bake. Sell. Eat. Sleep. Nothing changes. Not since the storm. Not since losing—" Her voice hitched. "Losing him. I miss those days. Things were simpler back then."

The sorrow she still felt at Torin's passing surprised me. We hadn't been particularly close then, and we saw each other even less now, but we had settled into an effortless friendship over the years. Still, I hadn't seen her look this dejected since immediately following the storm and all the death that it had brought.

"I miss him too." I squeezed her hand. "Every day."

She nodded in thanks, pulling away quickly to wipe the tears that coated her cheeks. "I'm such a mess lately. I'm not sure why, but it's like something is hovering in the air. It's the same foreboding feeling I had right before—before that summer. I hope to the gods I'm wrong, but I can't seem to shake it."

Regaining her control, she reached beneath the table, returning with a bag of pastries and two loaves of bread. "The usual?"

Her half-smile faltered as something caught her attention over my shoulder. I turned slowly, cautious to not draw attention.

A middle-aged man with a lean frame and an intricate sword resting on his hip marched through the aisles. His presence created a circle of hushed murmurs as he went. Though he must have been in his fourth decade of life, his tall body was hardened with battle. His once dark hair had flecks of grey along the sides and a sneer looked to be permanently etched across his face. His long, pointed nose was tilted up at a ridiculous angle, causing cold, black eyes to peer down at anyone in his path. It was a wonder he could see where he was walking at all.

"Who's that? I don't recognize him."

Sophie swallowed, her eyes widening as they swung to those nearest us. She leaned forward as her voice dropped, making sure we we're overheard. "That's Mr. Alderidge. He moved down here a few months ago with a dozen or so others."

"Moved down?"

She gave a tight nod, already knowing my concern. There weren't a lot of human-friendly territories outside the Borderlands, and even less to the north. The Dark Kingdom was directly above us, a primal brutal land full of fae that would use humans for their sick, twisted desires just as soon as slaughter them for sport. Everyone suspected they were the ones behind the growing attacks, but only those with a death wish dared to venture into their territory.

"Do you know which north?" She gave a small shake of her head. The Air Kingdom with the winged fae was northeast of here. It was said to be a little better in regard to tolerating humans, but not by much.

Then there was the Fire Kingdom, secluded in the northwestern part of the continent. Legends of ruthless fire-dwelling creatures and lava dragons kept humans away, and most fae as well. Even the bravest men elected to take their chances with the dark fae rather than venture into dragon territory.

I weighed the options. Though he was clearly no stranger to battle, I doubted he would have been strong or quick enough to have survived any of the northern territories. No humans were. It didn't matter where he came from, only that he was here now, and, if rumors were believed, was set on arming the town for battle.

Unease pricked along my skin as Alderidge reached his booth. He made a show of scanning the crowd, the simple act alone quieting the room. Then he started. Something akin to hunger stirred in his eyes as he wove tales of disturbing scenes.

"Too long have we let fae rule, content to live in a world where humans are little more than playthings. They view us as simple beings meant to curb the viciousness of their race. For centuries, we've been toyed with, preyed upon—and now," he paused, lowering his voice to pull the crowd in closer. "Now, they come in the dead of night, slaughtering our women—our *children*—under the banner of the Dark Kingdom!"

He held up a scrap of cloth containing the crescent moon with three stars trapped between its tips.

"These creatures are savages. They have no mercy, no souls." His malevolent gaze swept through the audience, relishing the taut silence that awaited his words. "We must rise against the north. We must put a stop against the gruesome deaths that have befallen dozens of settlements. Join me, brothers, on a quest for justice!"

His voice bellowed, igniting a wave of cheers. He held a blade up, swiping it through the air, demonstrating what he

CHAPTER 10 | 83

planned to do on the battlefield. People cheered, swarming the stand, snatching for weapons as they pledged their allegiance. His lips curled into a gruesome, satisfied smile.

I shot a quick glance around the room, wondering how the southern fae were feeling about his claims. I blinked. They were gone. All of them had packed, leaving glaring, vacant holes throughout the once tightly packed booths.

My stomach twisted as I took in the mob demanding death. Fae were powerful, unrivaled by human might, but I suppose even the strongest of fae could be overthrown by a righteous swarm.

The sight sent tendrils of ice dripping down my spine, but it was clear the little knowledge Alderidge possessed of the dark fae wasn't based on facts. Alarik had tasked me with discovering military happenings of the dark fae themselves, not a trivial human revolt.

I turned away to meet Sophie's wide eyes. "Wherever Alderidge came from, it looks like it hardened him. I need to be heading home. Thank you for the bread and the pastries."

Her body sagged as she exhaled, and I couldn't help but think her relief had something to do with not being asked further questions. "Give my best to Lannie, Greer, and little Will."

I nodded, offering a small smile as I slipped into the crowd.

Alderidge's stand of Light Kingdom weapons had all but confirmed he was against the dark fae. His speech had proven it. It should have been a relief knowing humans were taking a stand against fae brutality. Everything he said about the dark fae had been said before. And said often. They were vicious, blood-thirsty savages. Alderidge should be an ally. So why did I get the feeling that he would prove to be more of an enemy than a friend?

CHAPTER 11

I MADE ANOTHER PASS AROUND THE MARKET BEFORE WANDERING through the village. If I could find where the southern fae had gone, perhaps I would be able to overhear something more pertinent to my mission. While Alderidge was set on revenge, it wasn't quite the military details I'd been hoping for.

After another hour of scouring the village and turning up empty, I called it quits. I leaned against a large oak tree, just off the main road, and stripped the dressing from my hand. The wound looked great. The edges were slightly pink and already knitted together. I made quick work of applying a fresh bandage before heading toward the inn to say goodbye to Liam, trying to ignore the disappointment blooming in my chest..

I hadn't completed Alarik's task, not really. I hadn't seen a dark fae present, had no further knowledge on what the dark fae's plans were, and I'd learned nothing that would help quell the growing attacks against humans. If anything, it sounded like things were about to get worse.

A weight settled in my stomach. I hoped the information I had would be enough to satisfy the general. I couldn't bear the disappointment that would follow if he dismissed me—both my family's and my own.

I realized then that I needed this. I didn't just want to be a part of this, the base, the human resistance, I *needed* to do this. My life had boiled down to a monotonous routine of getting through another winter, passing another night without food, waking to another day without hope.

My jaw clenched with resolve as I pushed against the wooden handle of the inn. I hovered in the doorway, letting my eyes adjust to the dim light. A familiar laugh cut through the clatter of the inn, snapping my attention to the bar.

My body tensed as I saw Liam flashing a smile. The person he was talking to was facing away from me, but the width of his shoulders, the golden shade of his hair—it all stirred recognition. The casual brown jacket and dark pants were the only reasons I didn't make the connection right away, but as Liam waved hello to me, the man's head turned.

The force of his emerald eyes stilled my thoughts as that playful, arrogant smile tilted at the corners. "Good morning."

My jaw dropped as my mind fought to catch up to what my eyes were seeing.

"Oh no, Liam. I think I may have frightened her," Alarik teased.

It took a moment to dislodge the lump in my throat. "What are you doing?" The words sounded harsh, even to me. Liam's eyes snapped to me, thinking the question was meant for him.

"Mr. Holt is a friend of mine," Liam chided. His stern tone killed my snarky response. It was so like a rebuke Jem would've given me, delivered in the same disapproving tenor. "He moved to the military base recently after earning a promotion and we were catching up. Is that a problem?"

"No, not at all," I said in a formal tone. "Nice to meet you, Mr. Holt. My name is Elara Tenebris. I'm sorry for my rude behavior. I must have confused you with someone else." He shook my extended hand, merriment dancing in his eyes.

"Not a problem, Miss Tenebris. While I'd be delighted to get to know you better, I'm afraid Liam and I were just parting ways. I'm venturing south before returning back to base."

"That's perfect! Ellie lives a few miles south of here. I'm sure she would appreciate the company." Liam beamed with what he thought was his brilliant idea.

Alarik's eyes widening in mocked surprise. "Is that right, Miss Tenebris? Am I to believe you are headed there now?"

Stifling the urge to punch him, I plastered a smile on my face. "I must decline. I wouldn't want to distract you from your duties."

"Nonsense, El," Liam cut in. "Just last night, there was an attack, right behind the inn. I'd feel better if Alarik would see you home."

Damn Liam and his brotherly concern.

I opened my mouth to respond, but Alarik clapped before I could speak. "It's settled then." He placed a few too many coins on the counter, pushing past Liam's protests. "I won't take no for an answer. Besides, children are expensive." I quirked a brow at that. Alarik cleared his throat. "Or so I've heard," he muttered, the faintest blush brightening his eyes. He flashed me an awkward smile before excusing himself to use the facilities, affording Liam and I a chance to say goodbye.

Liam held my gaze a moment before darting around the bar to wrap me in a tight hug.

"Liam, you're squishing me."

He squeezed tighter.

"I know, little sis. I know." He released me with a huff.

Gods, I missed my brothers. The hollowness was always there. Most days it stayed buried deep within, but there were times when it felt like a gaping chasm of sorrow—one that could swallow me whole.

Blinking back the sting in my eyes, I reached into my pack to pull out his favorite pastry. "It's cold now, but it was baked fresh this morning. Got it from Sophie." His answering smile was all I needed. "You know, Liam, if you and Lucy ever wanted to slip away from here, you could stay with us."

"I know." The smile didn't reach his eyes this time. "Even if I could get away, there are too many memories there."

I nodded, understanding all too well. Our home had been the place the boys had stayed most often. It made sense ghosts would linger there for him, too.

"Ready to go?" Alarik asked, appearing behind me with a thick pack across his back. I threw my arms around Liam in one last brief hug, pulling him tight, before donning my own bag and joining Alarik.

His teeth were gleaming in an obnoxiously full smile as he held the door open for me. Swallowed, I stepped through and into the afternoon sun. I had planned on having finding a way to spin my shortcomings with the mission, but the present had caught up to me and time had run out.

CHAPTER 12

THE SUN HAD BEGUN ITS DESCENT IN THE WEST, ITS SOFT RAYS heating the surrounding forest. Most of the snow had thawed, staining the earth in damp, muddy patches. Only dwindling icy clumps lingered in the shadows, refusing to yield to the changing seasons. The scurrying of wildlife and melodies of birds brought an energy to the budding forest. It looked like winter might finally be ending. *Thank the gods for that.*

"What's that smile for?" Alarik asked.

"I was thinking how wonderful it will be when this winter is done. Spring is near. I can feel it." My arms opened wide as my face tilted up, soaking in the heat as we walked down the dirt road.

It was a different route than the one I had traveled, but Alarik insisted it would save us time. Normally, I would have argued, but this way allowed us more time on the road, which meant more time basking in the beauty of the clear, crisp skies and warm sun.

"Spring will be nice, but it is not here yet. It will be at least a few more weeks before this winter breaks."

I rolled my eyes, shooting him a contemptuous glare. He

chuckled, the sound only antagonizing me further. With a brief flick of my wrist, my dagger could be free. But then I'd be out of a job.

"How would you know?" I gestured to the grass surrounding us. "Nearly all the snow has melted, and the sun has shone brightly the last three days. How could we not be on the eve of spring?"

He pinned me with that arrogant smirk before nodding to the road behind. "Do you feel that breeze?"

Of course, I did. That was a stupid question, and stupid questions didn't deserve answers. The bite of the wind was the only reason I was still wearing my heavy jacket. I refused to look at him, choosing to continue walking in silence.

He laughed, shaking his head. "Gods, you're stubborn. The breeze is cold, painfully so, and has been picking up speed since this morning. It's at our backs, meaning it's coming from the northwest, most likely from the Jagged Mountains."

I blinked. I hadn't picked up all of that.

"I'd wager the clouds will roll in by nightfall, bringing with it an ice storm." He shrugged his shoulders like it was the most obvious conclusion. The simple movement brought out a boyish quality in him, softening some of his sharpness.

"I only have a standard bedroll and a tarp. I stayed at the inn last night and the weather has been getting warmer… I thought I wouldn't need it."

Glancing to the road behind, I considered turning around, but we'd been walking for a few hours now, and wouldn't make it back to Sonder in time. "I have a tarp that we could use, but it's small, only meant for one person. It'd be a tight fit for both of us."

"Miss Tenebris, are you suggesting what I think you are? Because if so, I have to warn you, I'm quite fond of snuggling." That seductive smirk was back, his eyes dancing as he shot me a wink.

My traitorous cheeks flushed, causing his eyes to zero in on the pink stain. "Mmmm. It seems you are made of flesh and bone after all. For a while there, I feared you were nothing more than ice."

Embarrassment dissolved into fury. Who was he to judge me? I pinned him with a fierce glare, savoring the stumble of his footsteps that followed. "Is that so?"

"I only meant that most women are flattered by my attention, my title alone earning me at least some stimulating conversation."

Smashing my worn boots into the softened earth, I quickened my pace, refusing to add to his obviously inflated ego.

A chuckle chased me. "At the very least, most women don't look like I forced them to swallow raw lemons. Is your face always pinched or am I the only one who has the pleasure of seeing it that way?"

I came to a halt, fists clenched, as I rounded on him. "Gods, you're so conceited! Just because you know how to flirt, have some ridiculous title, and mountains of muscles, doesn't give you the right to be an arrogant ass! I'm not some clueless girl that's going to bat my lashes at you every time you crack a smile. It sounds like there are plenty of people who would line up for that opportunity, but I'm not one of them."

I turned, stomping down the road, as I called back over my shoulder. "And I don't need a damn escort, either. I can take care of myself." My chest heaved as I stalked forward, only to have a pair of heavy footsteps sound behind me. I nearly growled. Couldn't he take a hint?

"El, wait. You may not need an escort, but I have a large tent and an extra tarp. You at least need my supplies." His voice was strong, but an undertone of uncertainty bled through. "Let me travel with you."

I blinked, eyes darting to the sky. It had darkened considerably with looming clouds, meaning I *would* need more protection tonight. Taking a steadying breath, I met his waiting gaze. "I need your supplies. Not you."

His eyes lit with amusement. "As much as I like the idea of you being in my debt, I wouldn't make it back to Sonder before the storm hit and I wasn't lying when I said I have business to attend to before heading back to base. I will share them, as long as you stop shooting daggers my way."

Shoving down the scream ready to burst from my lungs, I released a deep breath slowly. "Fine, but there's no way I'm calling you General."

His lips twitched as he tried to keep a straight face. "I wouldn't dream of asking you to call me General, though it does roll off your tongue nicely."

A pink glow tinged my cheeks. "It's been three seconds."

"You keep setting me up. I think we both know you find me attractive and just don't want to admit it."

Arrogant prick. I stalked forward once more, refusing to continue the conversation.

"Fine, Fine." He relented, allowing the silence to stretch as the wind picked up around us.

Our steps drifted nearer to one another, our bodies subconsciously craving warmth as the temperature dropped. My shoulder brushed his, causing his eyes to drop to the contact, before rising to mine.

"So, you really think my muscles look like mountains?"

I lifted my chin and pulled ahead of him, refusing to let him see the telling flush across my cheeks.

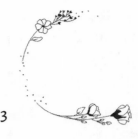

CHAPTER 13

THE SKY BLACKENED AS MENACING CLOUDS BLEW IN, obliterating any remaining traces of warmth from the afternoon. Alarik pointed out a small path along the side of the road, adjusting our trajectory toward my home.

We'd been traveling along it for about an hour, slowly making progress through the dense forest, when I pulled out a loaf of bread, tearing pieces off to placate my growling stomach. I should have stopped for food at the inn before leaving, but at least the bread was fresh. I offered a chunk to Alarik, the two of us eating in silence.

Brown-green leaves clung to most of the surrounding trees, creating a dense web of brambles and sticks to work through. The foliage provided a small buffer from the wind, the leaves absorbing the milder blasts, but the frigid air grew wilder as the sun sank lower. My shoulders rounded and my body trembled as it whipped past, piercing through the thick layers of my jacket.

I kept my head tucked as I dipped beneath a low-hanging branch. The outer layer of its bark had been stripped, exposing the shiny layer beneath—a deer, most likely. Normally, I'd be tracking it, intending for the meat to keep my family alive for another week or two, but as my body shook at another powerful gust, I sent a silent prayer to the gods that the animal had found shelter.

"Are you going to tell me how your mission went?" Alarik asked, the heat of his breath tickling the back of my neck and causing me to jump. "Or are you going to make me wait till we arrive at your house?"

"It was fine," I breathed, annoyed he had surprised me. I popped the last of the bread into my mouth, taking my time chewing. Daring a glance over my shoulder when he didn't respond, I was met with raised brows. "What? It *was* fine."

My gaze drifted to the terrain as I lifted my legs over a fallen tree. The silence weighed on me, growing heavier each moment as I rapidly tried to distill how best to present the information.

"It was all right. There are a few new people in town, but I'm guessing if you're friends with Liam, you already knew that."

"Assume I know nothing. Tell me everything you discovered. Any detail may be important."

"A few people moved to the village recently. I'm not sure from where, specifically, but I was told they moved south, so from somewhere up north."

"Yes, that's typically where they'd be coming from if one says they moved south."

I shot him a glare. "Yes, but it sounded like they came from human settlements in the north. A man named Alderidge is one of them—their leader. He had plenty of weapons to sell and was very vocal about wanting to move against the dark fae."

Alarik's shoulders pushed back as he sucked in a shallow breath. Curious that this bit of information piqued his interest. I would've thought he knew about Alderidge.

"The weapons had the Light Kingdom's emblem. It's possible he could be using it without their knowledge, but..."

"But that would be a death sentence if they discovered it. It's more likely they are aware and support his actions."

We both focused on our footing as we shuffled through a particularly tangled segment of vines in the darkening forest.

The quiet stretched, and just as I was sure he had dropped the subject, Alarik asked, "How did the people of the market react?"

"They were angry. Alderidge said some terrible things. He said the dark fae were responsible for the attacks, for killing families and—and children." I could have sworn Alarik flinched, but by the time I focused, his mask of cool control was securely in place. "He called them monsters, little more than creatures without souls." His jaw definitely ticked. *Curious.* "It sounded like he was trying to start a revolt, or, at the very least, hoping to assemble a dark fae hunting party."

"I was afraid of that. The people of Sonder are mostly farmers. It takes years of training to stand a chance against fae, especially the dark fae. Even with our training, we remain grossly out matched." Alarik exhaled, a piece of that carefully crafted control crumbling.

Squeezing between another set of trees, I pondered his words. Alarik's path may be shorter, but it was definitely more treacherous. "What do you mean by 'especially the dark fae?' I thought all fae had increased strength and speed—well, at least those of the royal line."

There were royals in every kingdom, descendants from an ancient line of fae who possessed certain coveted gifts. Each kingdom had distinct traits, but the royal bloodlines tempered said traits and forged them into something... more.

"They do. The royals more so."

"What sets the dark fae apart? Do you mean their ruthlessness?"

"Something like that. What about the dark fae soldier? Did he ever show?"

"No. Even the southern fae left once Alderidge got started."

"You did well. I'll start the arrangements for your training when I get back to base, if you are still set on joining." His voice rang with approval, dousing the embers of worry that had started to smolder in my chest.

"I still want to join," I said against the wind, hardly daring to believe it. It would take endless hours of grueling work, but I could do it. I'd be training with the world's greatest human warriors. There would be no telling what I could accomplish, what I could defeat, if I kept my ears sharp and eyes open.

"Good, because I have another task I could use your help with, but it will be difficult."

"I can handle it," I said, lifting my chin despite the cold.

He smiled. "We shall see, little one."

I gritted my teeth, hating that nickname.

Turning around, he walked the length of a small clearing, nothing more than a narrow break in the trees. New blades of grass had started to peek through the earth, already frosted with the impending storm. Clusters of what would grow to be tulips shook, despite being nestled among thick roots.

"We should probably make camp for the night. The wind is picking up, despite being in the denser part of the forest. We have maybe another half hour before the sun sets."

I blinked as he slouched off his pack and pulled out a thick tarp barely larger than mine. My eyes narrowed as I watched him drape it across the flattest section, clearing away most of the branches and rocks beneath.

"That better not be the tarp you were talking about."

He grinned. "Yeah, about that. I may have exaggerated its size, and the tent size, but they're military grade."

Crossing my arms, I dropped my voice to a lethal calm. "You assumed I'd rather spend the night cramped in a tight space in the middle of the forest with you than deal with a little rain on the way back to the inn?"

He pulled out a thick canvas material, unfolding it over the tarp as he flashed me a cocky smirk. "Who wouldn't want to spend the night alongside these 'mountains of muscle'?"

My nostrils flared. "You're not going to let me forget saying that, are you?"

"Never. I knew you wouldn't listen, and when you didn't, you would've been trapped with no extra supplies, and unable to make it home before the sleet started." He picked up a set of rods, placing them along small openings in the double-layered canvas. "Judging by how stubborn you've been, you probably would have kept walking, despite the storm, and ended up lost, or worse."

He glanced at the mostly hidden sky before shooting me a glare. Another blast of icy wind whipped around us, bringing with it a few frozen drops. He gestured to the deconstructed tent. "This would go a lot faster if you helped me."

Realizing I had no other options besides freezing to death, I clamped my mouth shut and bent to help. We worked our way around, lifting the heavy edges while wedging the rods through, until all were in place.

"All right. Now, secure your footing and lift."

"I know how to assemble a tent," I snapped, heaving in tandem with him.

He chuckled as we locked the rods in place, our shelter finally looking like something that would provide a respite from the cold. After securing the tent to the ground with a few stakes, Alarik reached for my pack, pulled out the additional tarp, and spread it over the top.

I cocked my head to the side as I took in the dimensions. "That can't possibly fit two people."

"Like I told you before, I like to snuggle." I scowled as Alarik stepped closer. "You can growl all you want, but the storm is here. We need to get inside."

The pace of the falling ice droplets increased, each one

pinging off my body with a mild sting. I crossed my arms, contemplating taking my chances in the storm. Spending a night slowly freezing to death almost sounded better than staying with *him*, but I had siblings to care for. Even if I somehow survived the freezing temperatures, I had no clue how to find the path home and nearly all the light had bled from the sky.

"Don't even think about running," Alarik warned. "I'm not going to let you die in the middle of the woods because you were too embarrassed to share a tent."

"I'm not embarrassed," I snapped.

"Then what's the problem? This is the logical solution, El."

"Fine," I huffed as I pushed past him and dove inside. Slipping my pack from my shoulders, I fumbled in the dark until I found my bedroll and yanked it free.

The tent flap opened a moment later. Alarik moved beside me, locking eyes for a breath, before turning to cinch the opening shut. The effect plunged us into darkness, only allowing me to make out the blurry edges of his form.

"Did you need to relieve yourself before I secure the opening for the night? I figured you were good since you made us stop within the hour."

I was grateful for the dim lighting that concealed the scarlet flush to my cheeks. The only people whom I talked to about my bodily functions were my sisters. "I'm fine, thank you."

More rustling sounded by the flap with the heat of his body at my back.

"Thank you?" he asked in mocked surprise. "Is that you, El? Are you feeling well?"

"Ha. Ha." I snarked as I fought with my bedroll, unable to get it to zip. I growled, shoving against the stalled metal.

"What's wrong?" His voice sounded right behind me, the warmth of his breath tickling my ear.

My breathing quicken as I felt the shift of his body, pulling away from the entrance to graze my back. He must have been kneeling. Waves of heat licked my spine, urging me to lean back, to sink further into him.

When I didn't answer, he pressed forward, closing the gap between us. His larger frame loomed over mine as his arm reached around to see what I was fumbling with. Heat flooded my body, the surge of warmth causing a moan to slip past my lips.

Swallowing, I prayed to the gods he hadn't heard me.

Alarik cleared his throat before pulling away, taking my bedroll with him.

He'd definitely heard me. Fighting the urge to walk right out the tent and into the storm, I twisted around, putting as much distance between us as the small space allowed.

"I think my zipper is broken," I breathed.

The rustling of fabric was followed by the clash of the zipper's metal teeth.

"It's not broken, but it won't catch the track. Let me try something." His form moved, pulling out what could only be more fabric from the lump that I assumed was his bag. I heard a click, and then a zip in the dark.

"You got it?" I asked in disbelief.

"Of course," he scoffed, as if not being able to accomplish something was ridiculous. "Now, step back so I can lay this down."

"Not possible in this tiny tent."

"Okay, *lean* back, then. I wouldn't want to cause anymore moans of pleasure. At least, not yet."

Thank the gods for the cover of night that hid my scarlet cheeks. His dark chuckle echoed around me and I sank further against the cool wall of the tent, willing the hours of the night to pass swiftly.

"Are you done yet?"

"Almost," came his cheerful reply. His form shifted, grabbing two small lumps before returning to the bedrolls. "There. You're on the right."

I moved forward, surprised that he was able to fit both of our bedrolls in the tight space. I felt for the edge, the zipper slightly open and folded back.

"Take your shoes and wet coat off."

I could imagine that annoying tilt of his lips as he spoke, the sparkling of his eyes as he watched me heed his instructions. Sighing, I undid the straps of my boots, setting them near the opening of the tent next to his larger pair before removing my damp coat.

Grateful that I'd selected a rather thick, long-sleeved shirt this morning, I crawled over to the bedroll and slipped inside. The material was softer and thicker than I remembered, welcoming me in a cozy embrace. A moan escaped me as I stretched into the plush fabric. It couldn't be helped, and I wasn't sheepish about it.

"Comfortable?"

"Yes, thank you."

The rumble of his laughter grew closer, slicing through the mounting clatter of sleet hitting the canvas. "Two 'thank you's in one day? If you keep this up, I'm going to get a big head."

The darkness shifted as he moved closer, casting a shadow, until I felt the material of my bedroll shift. "Scoot over, you're hogging all the blankets."

Before I could ask what he meant, a very thick, muscular leg slid alongside my own, coated only in a soft, loose fabric. He shifted until the hardness of his chest grazed my shoulder, his thin, long-sleeved shirt doing little to conceal his sculpted torso.

"What are you doing?" I squeaked, my body going rigid as he rolled closer. I forced myself to take a gulp of air, trying and failing to remember how to breathe.

Daring a glance, I opened my eyes, but could hardly see. Judging on shapes alone, he had, indeed, shifted onto his side, the warmth of his body spilling across the narrowed space between us, allowing the soft whisper of his breath to fan the top of my head. The beat of my heart thundered in my ears, deafening with its intensity. If I tilted forward—if I even took a deep breath—my chest would brush against his.

"Calm, little one. This isn't a big deal. Part of your zipper was broken, but it fit perfectly with my own bedroll. So, I combined them. I really had no choice. Your bedroll was thin already. Without a zipper securing it, you were sure to freeze. Now you won't. You're welcome."

"You should have just left me in the forest," I muttered, rolling onto my back.

"Nonsense," he said, the sound of a smirk ringing through. His body moved down a little more, our sleeping sack shifting as he adjusted. "Now, getting to the important part of this sleeping arrangement. Normally, I prefer to be the little spoon, but seeing how much you enjoyed even the quickest of caresses from me earlier, I figured I would be nice and save you the embarrassment of asking."

My body went taut as one of his thick arms wrapped around my center, pressing the front of his body against the rigid side of mine.

"Relax, El. It's just a hug. You need warmth, and we both need rest. Let your body have both."

I stayed immobilized, as every point of contact between our bodies pulsed with an electric heat, but there was no teasing to his words this time. After what felt like hours, his breathing evened out into a steady rhythm.

Figuring it was safe, I rolled onto my side, deciding it would be less awkward if I faced away from him. Craving the promised warmth, I pressed the back of my body to the front of his.

A delighted sigh slipped between my lips as his searing heat enveloped me. I adjusted my legs to the bends of his body, welcoming the relaxing tempo of the rise and fall of his chest syncing with mine. I thought I felt the twitch of his lips along the bridge of my ear, but his breathing remained even, his grip across my stomach soft but strong.

The storm raged outside, the whistling wind throwing sleet and ice against the tent. He was still an ass, but this was a matter of survival. Under the cover of night, with no one to bear witness, I allowed a soft smile to tilt my lips as I relaxed into Alarik's embrace.

CHAPTER 14

THE SUBTLE CHIRPING OF BIRDS AND GENTLE BUZZING OF ANIMALS created a jovial melody, celebrating the retreat of the late winter storm and easing me from sleep. My body felt... rested. Gods, I couldn't remember the last time I had felt this good.

Squeezing my eyes, I nestled into the warmth surrounding me, refusing to let the blissful sleepiness end. With the subtle shifting of my body, I became aware of a thick, somewhat uncomfortable, length pressing against my hip.

My eyes popped open. An expansive chest lay before me, a thin grey shirt shifting with the steady rise and fall of his chest. I froze, but Alarik remained unaware of my inquisitive gaze. I noted the intimate angle of my body curved into his, the tangle of our legs, of how my face was cradled along the crook of his arm. His other was draped over my middle, holding me close.

I swallowed. *Gods*, I was with Alarik. Arrogant, self-absorbed Alarik—alone—in the middle of the woods, sharing a tent. My breathing hitched, catching notes of sandalwood. The scent gave me pause, curiosity overpowering the fluttering in my chest.

Assuring that he was still asleep, I inhaled deeply. He *did* smell of sandalwood—with a hint of spice. Was that cloves? I stretched forward, intent on identifying the smell, when his body shifted. His arms collapsed around me, pulling me into a tight squeeze, and smashing my face against the hard slate of his chest.

"Good morning to you too." His voice was thick with sleep but that didn't stop the arrogance from bleeding in.

"Get off!" I shrieked, but the words were muffled by his body.

His chest rumbled. "I'm only making it easier for you. You were trying to smell me, weren't you?"

The band of muscle released me without warning. I fell halfway out of the bedroll, a shiver instantly coating my skin, as the chill of the morning seized me.

"Now, you don't have to worry about sneaking a smell. My scent is all over you. You're welcome."

"It's cold."

He lifted a brow.

"And I wasn't trying to smell you. You must have been dreaming."

He rolled his eyes, turning toward the pile of folded clothes along his side of the tent. His blond hair was messy, and slightly flattened where he had been lying on it—while he had been holding me.

He grabbed a pair of military-issued pants, similar to the ones I first saw him in. The tent was too small for him to stand, so he began shimmying out of his sweats while kneeling, not bothering to conceal the lingering effects of morning.

Gods help me with this man. I averted my gaze, fumbling for my own clothes.

"I promise you, Elara, had this been my dream, you wouldn't be trying to sniff me."

The boot I'd been holding tumbled to the floor. Swallowing, I peered over my shoulder to make sure he hadn't noticed, quickly recovering it. I shoved my foot in, before grabbing the second and doing the same. I needed to get out of this tent. A little fresh air would help clear my head. In a silent haste, I laced my boots and zipped my jacket, before snatching my pack, and turned toward the exit. A gasp left my lips as I looked at the rows of twisted knots securing the flap, blocking me from freedom.

"What? No witty come back?"

I didn't answer as my fingers moved with determination. Just a few more hours with this insufferable man, and then I'd be home. I'd be rid of him.

He chuckled, inching closer as he laced his own boots. "Nothing? Not even the 'you're an arrogant ass' comment?"

My fingers freed the last of the ropes, allowing the flap to list inwards with the crisp morning breeze. His eyes widened, taking note of the untied knots.

I smiled back at Alarik, finally daring to meet his gaze now that the heat of the blush had left mine. I leaned forward, as if to whisper a secret in his ear. My smile grew as his hands stilled, his face alight with surprise and intrigue.

The whisper of my lips grazed his ear as I breathed, "You're an ass." I paused for a moment, savoring the confused and disappointed look that washed over his face before dashing outside.

"You know what? You're the ass," his voice hollered from inside the tent, followed by a slew of indistinguishable mutterings.

I chuckled softly to myself. Someone had to knock him down a peg or two.

Wandering a few yards away, I took care of my bodily needs before noting the beauty of the morning. The chill in the air had a refreshing effect. I felt energized and ready to get the day started as I braided back my hair.

A cool, swirling breeze caressed my now bare neck as I

stretched my arms toward the sky, working out the stiffness that followed a good night's sleep. Gods, that was one of the most peaceful nights of sleep I'd had since the nightmares started.

My eyes darted to the rustling of fabric as the tent rattled with Alarik's movements. I sighed. Why did it have to be with him?

He exited the tent, securing our packs as we both got to undoing the tent. One of the lines snagged the rumpled dressing adorning my hand, pinching my still-healing cut. The bandage needed to be cleaned, but I'd finish helping first, if only to be rid of the general sooner.

We worked in tandem, packing away the pieces of our overnight shelter, until there was nothing left but a patch of flattened earth.

"We need to head south for another hour before adjusting slightly west," Alarik said, as he pointed out a narrow path through the forest.

"Okay, but before we do, I need a moment." I rifled through my bag, searching for the small healing kit Lannie prepared for me.

"Do you need to relieve yourself again? It's only been twenty minutes."

"No," I grumbled, really wishing I could stab him. My fingers brushed over the thick fabric of the kit. I pulled out the supplies before tucking the rest back in place.

"Are you hurt?" Concern flashed across his face as his eyes noted the swath of bandages and the small metal tin. His brows knitted together as he searched my body for an injury.

"No, not really. It's just a small cut. As long as I switch out the dressing, I should be fine." Pulling off my left glove, I carefully unrolled the soiled bandage. The last layer adhered to my skin, pulling small scabs with it as I carefully worked the material away from the sensitive flesh.

"Here, let me help you."

"Really, it's fine. I'd feel more comfortable doing it myself."

"Just relax, I can take care of it."

He grabbed my hand with his much larger one, jerking it away as I maintained my grip on the bandage. The material yanked free, haphazardly reopening a small area.

"Great. Now you're bleeding. Give me that," he snapped, reaching for the bandages.

"No," I refused, glaring back at him.

His lips thinned as he extended a hand. "Please?"

Sighing, I relinquished the strips. He took a clean one, dabbing it along the raw spots until the worst of it had stopped bleeding. Had it not been reopened, it would have been good by tomorrow, maybe even tonight. As it was, I'd probably have to keep it dressed for a few more days.

He reached for the salve, opening it swiftly. His caress was surprisingly gentle, securing the bandage with unexpected skill.

I flexed my fingers, balling them into a fist. The sting was still present, but already fading. Alarik lifted my glove, gently slipping it on.

"Thank you."

He only glared. "Any other knife wounds I should know about? Maybe a few arrow punctures, broken bones?"

My scowl was answer enough as I hoisted my pack and stalked past him.

CHAPTER 15

THE FOREST HAD THINNED, GIVING WAY TO PATCHES OF PETITE wildflowers, unearthed by the melted snow. Water droplets sprinkled the trees, the bright rays of the sun dancing across them, transforming the forest into a shimmering haven.

Inhaling deeply, I relished the scent of fresh earth laced with the sweetness of budding blossoms. My eyes drifted toward my left, surprised to find Alarik enjoying the peaceful morning as much as I was. His head was tilted back, blond hair tousled to the side, as he bathed in the sun.

He looked so… calm. A soft smile tugged the corners of my lips as I marveled at this hidden side. His chest expanded with a large breath, exhaling loudly in a contented sigh. Emerald eyes peered down through strands of tumbled golden hair, the top long enough to settle in a gentle swoop as he ran a hand through it.

"What are you thinking, little one?"

"Nothing important."

"Just daydreaming about my good looks?" His lips tilted into a taunting grin.

"Definitely not."

One of his brows lifted into a skeptical arch. I rolled my eyes.

"Does this really work for you? I've heard the rumors of the handsome general sweeping across the seven kingdoms, saving lives and charming maidens. Is *this* really your move?"

"My *move*? I don't need moves. I'm the leader of the last human stronghold. I'm the one the human world has turned to in its time of need—the general who is expected to be the savior, the last bright flame in a world quickly being swallowed by darkness. Women across the seven kingdoms seek me out." He cocked his head. "And a few men. I don't have to seduce anyone."

The last word was drawn out. 'I don't have to seduce anyone,' *especially not you*, my mind finished. Because he was too good for someone like me. He didn't say it, but he didn't have to. It was obvious in how he carried himself, with his chest puffed out, his confident smirk always in place.

I yanked my eyes away from his. "Don't forget to add grotesquely egotistical to that long list of attributes."

He shrugged. "It's just the way things are."

Speaking through clenched teeth, I said, "I can't believe you have such a sense of self-importance. You're no better than the pathetic fae royals lording over us—"

"Stop." It was a low retort, but I continued in a rush as if I hadn't heard.

"—thinking you're some type of gift from the gods. Are you going to wall yourself off, too?

"El," he warned.

"Wouldn't want to risk the precious General Alarik Holt. You could turn the base into your own little mock kingdom, just like the light fae—"

"Stop," he growled, pulling up short and forcing me to do the same.

I knew it wasn't true. He risked his life over and over again to protect humans, but I couldn't help speaking from that broken inner part of myself that had never quite felt like enough. I hated the confidence he had, hated how nothing ever rattled him, how he knew himself so fully. I'd always knew there was a darkness inside me, walled off and just beyond reach, like the final pieces of a puzzle had been purposely removed or locked away. Did he really need to rub how different we were in my face?

We stood there for a moment, chests heaving and neither of us blinking. I refused to yield, even as my eyes burned.

He conceded first. Smug satisfaction coursed through my veins as he stalked off.

We walked in tense silence, neither one of us wanting to be the first to speak. Time stretched, and just as I was sure we'd go the rest of the day without a sound, Alarik's voice rippled through the quiet.

"I'm sorry if I offended you. That was not my intention."

I took a few steps further in stunned silence before I was able to form words. "It's okay."

"No, it's not. I'm normally not like this." He ran a hand through his hair.

It was my turn to pin him with an incredulous look.

"No, really, I'm not. With you I forget..." He shook his head, keeping his eyes averted. "It's nice to forget the pressures of being *the* general. It's constantly there—the responsibility of the base, for protecting every human across the seven kingdoms, but that's no excuse. I'm sorry for making you feel uncomfortable."

The words spilled out of him, as if they'd been pent up for years. My stomach completed an array of acrobatics. Had that been what I was feeling? *Uncomfortable?* I dropped my eyes to the widening dirt path.

"You didn't—I mean, you did—but it's fine. I'm not... upset, anymore." I gnawed on my lower lip as the truth of those words settled over me. Why *wasn't* I still upset? I shook off the confusion. It didn't matter. We would be working together for the foreseeable future, and I needed this to go well.

"You said you had another task for me?" I couldn't stop the thread of hope spilling through.

A relieved smile softened his features. "Just the one looming on the horizon, but you'll start with the basics." I opened my mouth to protest, but he pushed forward. "If you seem sufficient in certain areas, then we will move on, but I need to be fully aware of your strengths and weaknesses if I'm going to send you into the field."

I grumbled, but understood his point. Excitement surged through me. This was really happening.

"Okay. I was thinking we could start with swordplay. I sparred with my brothers when I was younger and sporadically over the years, but it's still one of my weaker points, because I've had to focus on hunting. I'm fairly good with a bow, hence the hunting, so we can probably skip that for now, but I've had next to no exposure with other weapons. It will take some work, but I've studied—"

"Whoa, slow down," he cut in. "I never said we would do all of that. Your missions involve scouting. That's it. Your training will reflect that."

His harsh words cut through me, like a freshly sharpened blade through tender flesh. This was the voice of a man used to others falling in line, but we had a deal, one I intended to hold him to.

"You said you would train me. I don't need lessons on gathering gossip. I expect proper instruction on how to fight."

He laughed, dismissing my dreams with little more than a fleeting thought. "I doubt you'd be able to keep up with physical combat. Maybe some of the beginning classes, but the base houses the most elite human warriors. It would be near impossible for a person of no structured training to match them."

"I told you, I've been training since I was seven with my father and older brothers. I furthered that training after the storm with the help of a family friend." I didn't think it wise to mention that said friend was half-light fae and my late brother's ex-fiancé—not when he had been so angry with the comparison to the light fae earlier. "I've also studied military techniques and know the basics of several genres of fighting. I just haven't had the opportunity to pursue it as thoroughly as I wish."

His gaze was speculative, sizing me up for a moment before turning away with an unimpressed huff.

My fists clenched as ichor coursed through my veins. "Some of us haven't been given the opportunity to train our whole lives. *Some of us* have a family depending on us for survival."

His eyes shifted into steel, his face morphing into an eerie mask of control. "Yes. Not all of us have a family to look after anymore."

I stumbled, mouth gaping as his angry strides carried him ahead. *Anymore.* My stomach knotted. He must have lost his family in the storm—like I had—like so many others. And here I was berating him, envying him, for his accomplishments, the very ones that were achieved, in part, because he had no one left to care for.

Finding my footing, I dashed after him. "I'm sorry. That was stupid of me. I should have realized that you've probably lost people, too. We all have."

His shoulders dipped as he released a long, low sigh. He glanced over, allowing me a moment to read the depths of anguish swirling in his eyes, before fixing his gaze on the forest ahead. "I would give it all up... to have them back."

Reaching for his hand, I gave it a little squeeze of support. His breathing hitched, shock widening his eyes as he looked to where my hand met his. A wave of guilt washed through me. How terrible must I have been that this minute gesture of kindness could jolt him so thoroughly?

I started to pull away, but his hand strengthened the hold, only for a moment before releasing me. Working the strange stiffness out of my fingers, I tucked my hand away in my pocket, hating how empty it felt.

"Did you want to talk about it?" I asked as we fell into a leisurely stroll.

"There's not much to say. They died. Just like most humans." I could see the debate playing out across his features, warring with himself on how much to disclose.

"My sister...her name was Aiyana. She was seven at the time, nearly as tall as your Will is now. She was so full of life. I was ten years older than her and had already been accepted into the military. My commitments required me to train often, but I'd always find time for her. I think she would have found you intriguing."

"Yeah?"

"She was gentle and kind. It bothered her when she learned I'd joined the military. She insisted that having tea parties were more important than 'flinging swords around'." His laugh was strangled, torn between the joy of the memory and the loss of his sister.

"I wasn't aware tea had such hidden powers," I jested.

"She said people talked over tea, and when people talked, they were able to explain their feelings and not be angry anymore. She once told me that would never be a reason for fighting if the world only made time for tea."

A giggle burst through my lips. "Can you imagine a world where warriors from across the kingdoms would meet to enjoy tea parties and discuss their feelings?"

A raw sputter of laughter escaped him as his eyes glistened.

I leaned in, bumping my shoulder into his. "She sounds quite clever."

"She was, just like my mother. All sass and charm, the both of them. Ma used to say it was their fiery red hair that caused it.

She thanked the gods that I was the eldest because it gave her at least one child with the ability to make sound judgments."

"That does sound like you, always with an answer."

He flashed me a toothy grin. "I like to be right."

I rolled my eyes.

"It was just the three of us. My father died when Aiyana was a babe. It was an illness our healer couldn't cure—the light fae could, but they refused. Because we couldn't afford the potion." His jaw ticked. "So, he died. Then the storm came a few years later, obliterating the last working pieces of my heart."

The rawness of his pain sliced through me, igniting my own grief-stricken past. The nightmares hadn't surfaced last night, but I could feel them snaking through my mind, poised to strike again. I flexed my fingers, trying to shake the feeling of phantom blisters—the ones that took weeks to heal after digging their graves. A shiver ripped along my spine.

Alarik's lips tugged into an unfamiliar frown. "I suppose you're familiar with how that story goes?"

Swallowing the lump in my throat, I was fully intent to shutting him out, like I always did, but my lips started moving, spewing words that had been locked away for the past seven years.

"We were outside when the storm hit. I had two older brothers, twins. Torin was the cocky, athletic one, and Jem—Jem was my best friend."

He reached out to squeeze my hand, the small, fleeting gesture giving me strength to continue.

"It was an ordinary summer afternoon, like so many before. Until everything changed. I was moving too slow. Papa picked me up. He ran as fast as he could, trying to make it to the house in time... but the magic of the storm was too powerful.

"The cloud rolled over us, blinding us. And still he ran. He somehow found the house through the darkness, bursting through the door before the worst of it caught up with us.

"We thought the house would protect us. We were wrong. That awful scent—the one of wilted roses and burnt sugar—it coated us. Then the pain started. Like millions of blades slicing their way through your flesh, only for the raw wounds to be doused with alcohol and set ablaze."

Alarik flinched. I should stop. He didn't need to experience my pain, but the words were already bubbling up, simmering with their vicious need to be freed.

"Papa threw his body over mine, my brothers doing the same for Lannie and Greer, trying to protect us even through the torture they must have been feeling." Silent tears slipped down my cheeks. "The pain started to fade after a while. I tried to let Papa know I was okay, but he couldn't hear me. He was still trapped in his internal torment. My sisters crawled out from under the twins, the three of us helplessly watching as their bodies stayed twisted in that bent position. And the animals, the forest creatures... all of them stampeding, just as desperate for an escape as we were."

I clamped my lips together. It had been Will's screams that pierced the shock shrouding me that day, pressed close to Mother's chest as her pale lips moved frantically, whispering— no chanting—as though in prayer. My brows knitted together as I tugged at the memory. She *had* been chanting, her blue eyes bright that day—as though lit with a subtle glow.

"I'm so sorry," he said in a soft whisper. "I know it won't help, but I'm sorry all the same."

I nodded, wiping the back of my hand across my damp cheeks. He was right. Sorry would never make it feel better. Nothing would, but if I could join the base, train, maybe I'd be able to channel this swirling darkness of pain and rage into something useful.

CHAPTER 16

Purpose. The word sounded sweet in my mind. What would it feel like to have a direction in this life? To know I was making a difference, as small as it might be.

"Not everything about the seven kingdoms is as it seems." Alarik's voice cut through my thoughts, a hard-edge creeping through his words. "After nearly two centuries of peace, why would the fae attack?"

"Why do all wars start? Hatred, fear, greed, superiority complexes, the list could go on forever."

A cynical snort escaped him. "Have you been able to learn the history of our world for yourself, or, at the very least, been exposed to books?"

My brows furrowed as I contemplated his question. We had a few books growing up, and there had been a time before the storm when we'd had a formal education, but nearly everything after had been texts of preference—not history. Those stories had been passed down through word of mouth, most involving a life lesson imparted in the end.

"I don't have books referencing those topics, but everyone knows how it was centuries ago. The northern kingdoms prided themselves on their domination over the human race. The Fire Kingdom prized physical strength. Thinking that humans would weaken them, they banned fae-human relations. The Air Kingdom was similar in not wanting to dilute their blood for fear that it would cause the loss of their wings, but the dark fae, they had no trouble using us for whatever they wished."

Bile brushed the back of my throat as I recalled the stories whispered in town. Mother refused to discuss such things, calling it gossip, but we all knew the tales. "Out of all fae, they used us for breeding, finding that humans were the perfect conduit for blending of the bloodlines—and not just with high fae, but with other powerful, dark creatures. They created ruthless monsters, adding to their armies through our suffering."

His lips pressed into a thin line. "Despite what you may have heard, why would the dark fae create the storm when fae and humans were at peace?"

I fixed him with an incredulous stare. "You think someone constructed the storm, and then wielded it like a type of magical weapon?"

He winced. "I know I sound like one of those conspiracy theorists."

"Yep." My eyes widened as I realized this wasn't a joke.

"It's the only thing that makes sense. I believe it was a constructed attack, maybe even a spell, aimed at the human population. It was the first of many strikes over the last seven years." He glanced at me, checking to see if I was buying any of this. I wasn't.

Catching my skeptical glare, he sighed. "Okay, let's break it down from a military standpoint. It's common knowledge that the storm hit humans the hardest. If it was a natural storm, one born from Pax herself, it wouldn't leech life from its creations. Humans are more vulnerable than fae, but every storm, magical or otherwise, has claimed equal lives of human and fae. Everything in Pax is connected. There's *always* a balance."

My brows knitted together as my mind rushed through each historical storm or natural occurrence I could remember. I'd spent my entire life in the Borderlands. Seasons were mostly steady but even I had heard of the great monsoons of the south, and tales of trembling mountains to the north, quaking with a force great enough to split the earth, each one affecting both human and fae.

"Think about it, El. Pax heals herself. She is unruly and fierce, but forgiving. We are bound to the earth, just as she is bound to us."

A faint memory stirred in the recesses of my mind. Mother's voice drifted to the surface, like fitting pieces of a puzzle together that I hadn't realized I was constructing. "Humans are the balance to the primal, innate nature of the fae."

He frowned. "I don't see what that has to do—"

"Say that I agree with the storm being unnatural, or even an attack," I rushed forward, following the breadcrumbs of my mind.

"Okay—"

"Maybe the dark fae regret blending our lines. Maybe— maybe they are trying to return to a time when fae ruled and humans were little more than a thought. By killing off humans or fae with human blood, it would force Pax to swing toward its more primitive state—closer to what this world was before it was Pax."

Alarik ran a hand through his hair. "Maybe."

"You don't sound convinced."

"I don't know. It seems a little far-fetched."

"It's as reasonable as any other explanation," I snapped.

"The human population has been growing steadily over the last century or two, not only in the Borderlands, but in the outlying areas where fae and human cohabitate—where the lines have blended. I know most still find fae-human relations to be taboo, but I've traveled across Pax. It's more common than people realize."

He paused, waiting for me to catch up. "The villages on the outskirts throughout the kingdoms—where most of the attacks have been?"

With his nodding confirmation, another piece clicked into place. My lips set into a grim line. "But that would mean places like the Dark Kingdom, places where human and fae relations are accepted..."

He nodded, finishing out the thought. "It would mean the Dark Kingdom has the most to lose out of any of the seven kingdoms. I've been trying to gather more information on the losses in each kingdom, but it's proving more difficult than I thought. We may need to have you return to the market to see if the dark fae—"

Thwang.

Alarik's arms wrapped around my middle, slinging me against a thick trunk wide enough to conceal our bodies.

"What was that?" I breathed into his chest.

Alarik's body was a wall of muscle shielding me from the world, his dagger somehow already in hand. He passed the small blade to me, unlatching a second, more deadly looking blade from a strap along his forearm. Unclasping our packs, he lowered each to the ground with skilled slowness. As he rose, he held a large stone in his hand.

Sharp green eyes scanned the surrounding forest, but his voice remained little more than a whisper. "That was an arrow. Judging by how wide it was shot, these aren't skilled fighters, but novices can be deadly, as well."

My heart thundered against my chest. "We need to get home. My family—"

His free hand clasped over my mouth, the rough skin scraping the softness of my lips. He nodded toward the right,

CHAPTER 16 | 119

but his body blocked my line of sight. I strained, listening for anything that could be of use.

The snapping of twigs sounded against cold earth, echoed by a second set further back. My eyes widened as a third heavy gait crunched behind us, only a few paces off.

Only three. It could be worse. I sent a silent prayer to the gods that Alarik was right, that these were novices—and human. Because if they were fae, we were already dead.

Alarik's eyes lowered to mine as his head dipped. His thumb brushed the curve of my cheek as he tucked a stray lock of hair behind my ear, causing my already erratic breaths to catch. "Stay here."

He threw the stone behind us before I could answer. The crackling of the branches drew the closest assailant forward into the thicket parallel to us, chasing the sound.

Alarik lashed out, quick as a viper, sinking the blade deep in the man's gut before driving it up. The enemy's mouth fell, gaping at the hilt protruding from his chest. The sickly grey sheen of his skin was growing paler by the second, as death waited to claim his next victim.

Alarik ripped his hand back, yanking the weapon free. The body lurched, the wound forcing a gurgling cough that caused thick, tarry liquid to ooze from his mouth. Cold, black eyes met mine a moment before he collapsed.

Rotten blood coated Alarik's wrist, dribbling down the dagger to mar the earth beneath. Alarik's jaw ticked as he noted the black residue. He knelt, releasing an additional blade from along his calf. It was dazzling, the hilt intricately crafted, the curved blade pulsing with a faint purple hue.

"If we are going to make it out of this alive, I need no distractions. That means you stay right where you are." His eyes bored into mine. "Understood?"

I shook my head. "No—"

"You will only be a liability."

"I can fight—"

"Elara, *please*."

The thumping of footsteps hurtled toward us, growing closer by the second. He was wasting time arguing with me.

Swallowing the thickness coating my throat, I conceded. "All right."

Relief flooded his face a moment before branches snapped behind him. He spun, meeting the attackers head on. They had the same grey decaying skin and cold black eyes as the other, but my attention snagged on the sharp tips poking through their matted hair. We were fighting fae—well, *we* weren't doing anything. I was stuck on the sidelines like some inept fool while Alarik tested their strength.

My heart thrummed, pumping furiously as adrenaline filled my veins, awakening my body further with each thunderous beat. My breaths were deeper, vision sharper. I fought against the growing need to step forward. To fight. To kill.

Snarls shook the air around us as the fae descended. Alarik leapt away from one, narrowly avoiding the jagged, pointed teeth that sought to remove a chunk of flesh. His arm rose, deflecting a thrust from the first, as he slammed his foot into the chest of the smaller one.

The clash of metal screeched through the clearing as the first spun his sword free. He pressed his advantage, bringing his blade down in a swift, forceful arch. Alarik's blade lifted, meeting the sword with a deafening clang. His arm shook, but held long enough for the purple blade to slice forward, imbedding deep in the fae's ribs.

I forced another breath out, trying to quell the growing restlessness inside of me. The urge to *move*—to end them—it was nearly unbearable. Maybe Alarik didn't need me, but *I* needed *this*.

The smaller one had recovered from the kick. He stalked toward Alarik with curled lips, the expression revealing a sharp row of yellowed, pointed teeth. Alarik struggled to rip the blade free from the fallen fae, tugging against the hilt, as black blood oozed from the wound, soaking his tattered tunic. He hadn't seen the smaller one creeping toward him.

A buzzing grew in my chest, the vibrations demanding I step forward. It didn't matter what I had promised—not if the cost of keeping my word meant Alarik died.

I leapt around the tree, intending to intercept the stalking fae, when dark laughter rattled through the air. It froze me in place, my dagger raised, as the sound reverberated off the trees, through the very earth itself, sending tendrils of dread coiling in my stomach.

My head snapped to the fae before me, looking for the source of the sound, but another voice echoed the manic cadence—the one lying beneath Alarik. He was nearly dead, but his face contorted with a warped smile. Frenzied laughter spilled from them both, synchronizing into a harmonious blend of voices.

The one nearest to me turned to Alarik, his lips twisting further into a crazed smirk as he saw the blade still wedged between the bones of the other's ribs. Black sludge bubbled from the fae's grinning mouth as Alarik jerked and shook the hilt, desperately trying to work it free. It didn't budge.

They laughed, a myriad of voices ricocheting off the leaves and branches. A toothy grin split across their faces in tandem, one mirroring the other. "You will die, young general. We know who you are—the leader of the last stronghold of humanity. You will fail."

Perhaps it was the confirmation of impending war, or the color draining from Alarik's face, but what little fear I had fizzled away, leaving only a scorching, unrelenting thirst to destroy.

Gripping the hilt of my dagger, I dashed forward. I knew I was outmatched, that my hunger for bloodshed may get me killed, but I wouldn't leave him. I couldn't. If my choice to fight was the last decision I made in this life, then so be it.

"No, Elara. Stay back. Go—run!" Alarik's piercing green eyes found mine, begging for me to heed his plea.

That look cost him.

The maddening laughter of the fae ceased as the one before me darted toward him. Alarik spun, abandoning the purple blade to meet his attacker, but the impaled fae's claws lashed out, sinking deep into the flesh of Alarik's forearm, holding him in place.

A strangled cry tore from his chest as the fae yanked him back. Alarik slashed wildly with his other blade, the sharp edge cutting through the impaled fae's throat. A gurgle of coagulated black sludge bubbled across the gash before his body went still with a final rattle.

Alarik had slain two, but lost sight of the smaller one. He hadn't realized the blade had already started its descent, angling for the exposed curve of his neck. I wouldn't make it in time. I wouldn't be able to save him.

"Alarik!" His name burst from my heaving lungs, my legs pumping faster.

He thrust his blade up, eyes widening as the much larger sword clashed against his dagger. Alarik's arm shook, body trembling, but he halted the sinking weapon.

The tightening in my chest lessened, just a breath, as I closed the final distance between us, noting how the fae's attention was locked on Alarik. Perfect. Without a second thought, I launched forward, my movements pulling Alarik's gaze to mine.

The fae tensed, reading Alarik's tell. He whipped around, but he was too slow. His black eyes widened a moment before my knife plunged into the vulnerable flesh just beneath his ear. The skin surrendered to the slice of my dagger, giving way to the pool of fluids beneath, as I ripped the steel across his neck with a quick jerk. Bone scraped against the weapon, vibrating through the hilt as I yanked it free. Black fluid burst from the deep gash in a spray of vile warmth.

Forcing a few shuddering breaths through my lungs, I nearly gagged on the putrid stench as the body crumpled to the ground in a lifeless heap. I stared at the fallen—at the first life I had claimed. With one swipe of a blade, I had rendered this being useless—nothing more than a clump of decaying tissue.

I waited for the guilt to wash over me, the shock, the devastation—something—but I felt only an overwhelming sense of relief. Perhaps that made me a monster, but I'd rather be the monster than the prey.

That was the truth of it—my darkest secret. There was a time when I would have cried, when I would have mourned that last untarnished piece of myself being forfeited, but that girl was gone—buried with her parents and brothers. This girl—the one who'd helped dig the graves for her elder brothers, the one who'd then dragged the bloodied bodies of her mother and father into another—*this* girl was something else entirely.

I let the silence of the still forest surround me, focusing on nothing but my ragged breaths, drifting back toward normalcy. I had seen their eyes, endless shadows, devoid of feeling. There was no love, no empathy, in these creatures.

Alarik gasped, snapping my attention back to the present. "Alarik, are you okay?"

He remained kneeling over the fae, ignoring my question, as a dark pool of rotten blood seeped out around them. Alarik worked to pry the last of the serrated tipped claws from his forearm. A stream of curses fell from his lips as he ripped a piece of fabric from his shirt.

"Here, let me help—" He jerked away, green eyes burning.

"I told you to run."

"I heard you."

"They could have killed you," he snarled.

I raised my chin. "They could have killed you, too."

"El."

"Alarik. You can yell at me later, but you're bleeding everywhere, and we need to get your arm dressed." I extended my hand for the strip of cotton.

He held my gaze a moment longer before handing it over with a huff. "This discussion isn't over."

Biting my tongue against the retort, I took his outstretched arm. Holding it up, I could see eight puncture wounds, four on each side of his forearm, all with bits of debris along the edges. "I'd normally insist on proper bandages and washing this out, but…"

"It would delay us, and we need to move as quickly as possible."

I gave a tight answering nod, brushing off as much as I could of the debris before finishing the knot. "What were they?"

He stepped past me, toward the base of the trees to reclaim the packs. "Fae, I think. Or something like fae." His voice was clipped, but at least he was speaking to me.

Questions danced on the tip of my tongue as I joined him in securing our packs, but now was not the time to ask.

"Are you able to handle a swift pace?" His voice softened. "It's nothing to be ashamed of if you need a moment to process everything."

"No, I'm okay. No injuries, just worried about my family. We're too close. What if—"

"There's no point in worrying about things that haven't happened," he cut in, halting my troubled thoughts before they could spiral.

I swallowed, forcing morbid images away. "Ready?"

Without so much as a look back, we sprinted into the trees as fast as our legs could carry us.

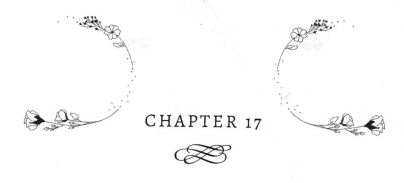

CHAPTER 17

WE RAN FOR WHAT FELT LIKE HOURS, THRASHING PAST BRANCHES
and through thickets, until familiar broad-based trunks of thick
pines came into view. The light grew brighter as we neared the
edge of the forest.

They were safe—they had to be. My legs burned as I pushed
my body further, pulling ahead of Alarik, with a visceral
urgency.

Bursting through the trees, I entered the clearing
surrounding our house. Nickering sounded off to my side and I
jolted to a stop at the sight of a golden-brown stallion, his
saddle already removed.

That meant only one thing: Evander had returned.

I closed the remaining distance to the house, leaving Alarik
to catch up. My palms slapped the front door as I barreled
through, concern still clawing in the recesses of my mind.

"Gods, El. You scared the life out of us." Greer's shoulders
drooped as she released a breath. Lannie peeked her head
around her, the two of them in the kitchen, preparing what
looked like a hearty late-morning breakfast. Will was perched
on the counter, his eyes wide at the abruptness of my return.

"What is it, El? What happened?" Evander's strong, but firm tone drew my attention toward the dining table.

He was here.

Bright copper hair cascaded past his shoulders, longer than the last time I had seen him, and he desperately needed a shave, but he was here. Auburn eyes caught mine, flashing with concern.

I opened my mouth to explain, but before the words formed, Evander's gaze shot over my head to the open-door frame behind me. He flitted to my side, shielding my body with his a moment before Alarik burst into view.

Alarik's chest heaved as his hands came to rest in his hips. "Gods you're fast, El. It's like you've—" His eyes locked on the man before me. "Evander?"

Evander straightened, his defensive position forgotten. "General Holt?"

Alarik blinked, staring at Evander a moment more, before his face split into a wide, boyish grin. "Gods, what are you doing here? I thought we planned on meeting tomorrow."

General Holt? Meeting? My gaze bounced between the two of them. "Wait," I interrupted as realization dawned. "Evander was the 'business' you had before returning to the base?"

Alarik nodded, his breathing slowly returning to normal. My brow quirked. "And just how do you two know each other?"

I could have sworn Evander's cheeks flushed, but Alarik waved off my question. "We've been working together for years. We can discuss the details later."

My mouth opened, a protest ready on my lips, but Evander was quicker.

"Yes," Evander answered, studying Alarik's bloodied clothing before shifting his attention to me. "It would appear there are more pressing matters to discuss. Please, General Holt. What's going on?"

"Gods, Evander, for the love of all that's good in this world, just call me Alarik." Evander muttered something about old habits before Alarik waved him off and continued, "But you're right, there are more pressing matters at the moment. We need to move."

Greer approached us with Will in tow. "What do you mean 'move'?"

Alarik turned toward them, meeting each of my siblings' worried frowns with a grim look. "Three fae attacked us a short distance from the house. The threat is taken care of, but I have no way of knowing if there are other potential dangers lurking nearby. Everyone needs to gather their things and prepare to leave for the base. Take only what you require. Nothing more. I'll give you fifteen minutes to pack, but that's all. We have a lot of ground to cover before nightfall."

Stunned silence met his declaration, the four of them staring with gaping mouths. Will's confused plea broke the spell. "Why would anyone want to kill us? We're just making breakfast."

The sound of his worry snapped Greer out of her daze. She knelt next to him, taking his hands in hers. "Oh sweetie, nobody is trying to kill us. What General Holt means to say is that there are some bad creatures in the forest. He has already made sure the ones they met won't hurt us, but a second group could be close."

"Let's think of this as an adventure. You get to see the base up close." I bumped my shoulder into Alarik's. "General Holt would love to show you around when we arrive."

Will's eyes lit up, the possible threat already forgotten. Content with Alarik's promise to give him a personal tour, Will's small form sprinted up the stairs to gather his things. Greer shot me a concerned look before following.

Lannie remained staring off into the distance.

"Lannie?" I took a few steps toward her, my hand outstretched. "It's going to be okay, but we need to leave as soon as we can. Do you need help packing?"

She blinked, dark eyes focusing on the black stains splattered across my coat before shifting to Alarik. Her gaze lingered on the layer of filth coating his hands and then the dirty strip of cloth across his forearm dotted with bright red blood.

"You'll need to clean that," she whispered, not taking her eyes off the crude bandage.

"I will once we get to the base."

She shook her head, gaze drifting up to meet his. "Before we leave. An infection has most likely already started." Her voice was unusually firm as she studied the black sludge covering his hand. It had started to flake across the creases of his skin. Her swallow was nearly audible, but I didn't think it was the gore. She had tended to far worse injuries.

"Lannie," I said, closing the distance between us. She flinched away.

"I'm sorry. This is a lot to process. We were going to have a proper breakfast today. Evander only just arrived an hour ago with all these supplies... But of course, we must leave."

She shook her head as if to clear it, and then untied her apron, placing it on the flour-coated counter, before starting down the hall. She paused half-way, turning to capture Alarik's gaze. "I meant that, General. You will clean your wound before we leave. You are no use to us dead."

My eyes widened at her candor.

"El, can you get the healing kit for him? I need to bring it anyway."

"I'll get it. Thanks, Lannie."

She headed upstairs, leaving the three of us to discuss the situation. I walked near the door to find Alarik and Evander already in conversation.

"Their clothing was black, but I saw no insignia and no distinguishing features that would point to a specific kingdom." Alarik's brow furrowed. "Their movements were slow for fae, clumsy even. Are you aware of any threat in this area?"

CHAPTER 17 | 129

Evander snapped to attention, arms at his side as if giving a report. "No, sir. I've heard mention of forces moving from the north, with other attacks coming from the west. Most of the newest targets were..." He paused, glancing in my direction before waiting for permission to continue.

Alarik realized and waved a large hand. "Permission granted to continue. She just completed her first recon mission and will join us on a few in the future. This will save me a briefing later."

Evander's auburn eyes widened, but he continued. "The most recent attacks have occurred along the southern border of the Dark Kingdom. There are at least three reported villages. All were known for their acceptance of humans." Evander paused once more, debating with himself to continue.

Alarik sighed. "Out with it."

"There were rumors that these attacks could be the enactment of The Phoenix's vengeance, as mentioned in the great prophecy. Some claim the rogue group of dark fae responsible have joined forces with The Dark Phoenix itself."

The Dark Phoenix? Vengeance? There was a deep pull in the recesses of my mind, like the whisper of a memory straining to break free. The recollection of a long-forgotten melody hummed, incomplete and unable to rise to the surface.

Alarik's pacing stopped, his look silencing Evander in a flash. "Elara, you need to pack."

"What? No. I'll pack after this conversation."

"That is the second time today you have not heeded a direct order." He spoke the words low, but venom dripped from each syllable.

My spine straightened. "A direct order? Let's get one thing straight, *General*. You came to me for help, and we settled upon an agreement—"

"And that agreement," he cut in, eyes narrowed, "means you work for me. As such, I expect you to heed commands. You are not qualified to hear this information."

Keenly aware of how quickly I could have a dagger secured in my palm, I took in a steadying breath. I knew right where I'd position the blade if he didn't get that presumptuous attitude of his under control.

"You may get to dictate what missions I go on, what training I'm allowed to complete, and even what intelligence I receive while at the base, but we are in *my* home right now. I am not speaking to you and I am not asking for your permission."

Not waiting for a reply, I turned toward Evander. "I know it's not official, but you're my big brother. You were there for us in the beginning when nobody else was. I've trained with you for years. You *know* me. I can handle this."

He shifted on the balls of his feet, eyes bouncing to Alarik, before settling back on me. "There's a prophec—"

"Nine minutes, Elara. I won't wait a moment longer."

My fists clenched as rage bubbled within me, but the pained look on Evander's face had me swallowing it down. It wasn't fair for Evander to be put in this position. I'd figure out a way to get the information later. Pausing only long enough to set the healing kit on the counter, I bit my tongue and ascended the stairs. Let him figure out how to clean and dress the wound, and if he didn't, then maybe he deserved the infection that was coming for him.

AFTER CHANGING, I SNAGGED THE SMALL ROLL OF WEAPONS beneath my bed and spent most of the remaining seven minutes attaching various blades to my body.

I shoved a few worn pairs of clothing into my bag before rifling through the twin's closet for a clean coat. The others were already in the front yard by the time I descended. One good thing about not having a lot of money was most of our belongings fit in the packs across our backs.

Alarik was front and center, but I couldn't find Evander.

"Everyone ready?" Alarik asked. "You may have to remain at the base for a period of time. A full sweep of the area will need to be completed and your safety assured." Greer and Lannie shared a worried glance, but Will buzzed with excitement.

"Will Evander be joining us?" I asked in a short tone.

"He's ridden ahead to send a team in our direction. I want the extra force with us if we don't make it to the base by nightfall." His eyes were steel, daring me to question his decision, but I nodded my agreement. It would be nice to have the extra protection of Evander, but we were outmatched if we encountered any more fae. Alarik had made the correct decision to send him for reinforcements.

"Will, want to lead the way with me?" Alarik's voice softened as he motioned for Will to join him at the head of the pack.

My brother's face lit up as he darted forward, eager to please his idol. At least Will wasn't worried. That innocence wouldn't last much longer, but a small warmth filled my chest as I watched him skip to Alarik's side.

I spared one last look at my childhood home as Lannie and Greer started after them. A slew of memories swirled through me: Nights spent with Papa singing as Mother held small Will. The twins would clap, keeping the beat, as Greer, Lannie, and I danced to the chanted songs. But then the others surfaced—the ones filled with blood and pain, and the bitter taste of loss. They were all here, tangled together in a cruel web, the good soiled by the inexplicable horrors of the bad.

"Goodbye," I whispered, parting with the ghosts of the past. I wasn't sure why, but it felt like we wouldn't be returning. I exhaled a deep breath, starting toward the forest and the future awaiting.

CHAPTER 18

WE WALKED IN SILENCE FOR THE FIRST FEW MILES WHILE THE SUN started its descent into the west. Bright rays pierced the surrounding shadows, easing the tension of the group as light illuminated the forest around us in a warm, golden glow.

Will and Alarik remained a few paces ahead, pieces of the conversation drifting toward us on the gentle breeze. Will was his typical self, a vast pool of endless questions and stories. Currently, he was telling Alarik about his plans to become a great warrior and then travel through the seven kingdoms, defeating evil as he went.

"The trees are finally putting out buds. A few plants as well." Lannie said from my left. "Not much, but a few of the seasonal trees should have leaves again in a week or two. I wonder if we'll have a good batch of lavender this year. Isn't that your favorite, El?"

"Yeah. It was Mother's favorite, too. I used to love sneaking in to use her lotion. Do you remember?"

Greer snorted. "You would always deny it, too, but all it took was one sniff."

"I guess I wasn't the most skilled liar back then." The three of us giggled. "I think Lannie is right, though. It looks like spring will be here soon."

"That's good to hear. It will be nice cooking with fresh herbs, again." Greer licked her lips thinking of all the meals she wanted to make. "I was thinking about making a vegetable loaf with seasoned bread. Maybe rosemary? It would be even better if we're able to spare a bit of butter this spring. And I wanted to try something new with chicken. I know we normally go savory, but what about adding a little citrus?"

"Like a bit of lemon?" Lannie asked. The two of them fell into conversation about cooking recipes, which inevitably lead to possible healing concoctions.

A twang of jealousy shot through me as I listened in. Their relationship was effortless, forged from their mutual pull toward plants and herbs. The two of them had created dozens of impressive medical tonics, lotions, salves, and teas. It was their dream to open a small shop one day, and if we ever had the funds, I had no doubt they'd be successful.

I couldn't help but feel like my mind was wired differently. While they enjoyed reading through Mother's journals on healing, I would beg Evander to sneak me another book involving military strategy. I even asked Greer to look over some of them with me, once. While she enjoyed the depictions of shirtless men showcasing various exercises, the actual content hadn't interested her.

To each their own, I guessed. I blinked, looking around to find that while I had been lost in my train of thought, my sisters and Will had fallen back—leaving me dangerously close to Alarik.

His chest was pushed out, fists clenched, as he purposely avoided my gaze. I contemplated ignoring him right back, but we needed to get past this. It was time he realized I wasn't going to compromise on certain things. I would respect him as a superior when it applied to matters of the base, but he couldn't expect me to turn a blind eye to things that could affect the safety of my family.

I had no doubt he *would* understand that, but now was not the time to have that fight. Not with my family steps away and Evander's wellbeing tied to my decisions. Instead, I attempted to lighten the mood.

"I see you made it through Will's endless questioning unscathed."

Alarik scoffed, the movement loosening him up, just as I had intended. "That's what you think. Some wounds can't be detected physically."

I snorted. "I know Will can be a lot, but I find his innocent optimism fascinating. You just wait, when he feels really comfortable, he'll start telling you about his dreams. They are so detailed."

"You mean this was him being *shy*?"

"Yep. Only the best people get to hear his dreams."

A gentle smile played across his lips. "I look forward to it, then." My stomach flipped with the sincerity of his words.

Alarik took a deep breath, glancing behind us to make sure the others weren't listening. He released a long sigh. "We need to talk about what happened."

"Okay. Let's start with your purple blade. What is it?"

"My dagger? It's embedded with shadow crystal. That's what creates the purple hue. It's known for killing wraiths, particularly the wraiths of the Shadowlands to the north. I thought it would kill the fae we fought." He shrugged. "I was wrong."

"The Shadowlands?"

"Yeah, between the Fire and the Dark Kingdoms. How did you kill the fae?" He kept a casual pace, but his voice had a restrained edge.

"What do you mean?" My finger twitched toward the hilt of my dagger, pressing through the layers of my oversized coat until I felt its solid outline. Flashes of thick, black blood flooding from gaping, pale skin shuddered through me. "I sliced his throat, the same way you did for the other one."

"That's not what I'm talking about. How did you develop the skill to approach the fae without him knowing you were there until your blade was buried hilt deep in his neck?"

I shrugged, sorting through the questions, but Alarik's raw suspicion had the words clustered in my throat.

"Okay, how did you undo the knots on the tent? You had the flap opened in, what? Three minutes? That would have taken me at least five, and I'm the one who placed the knots."

"I told you, I've trained."

He rolled his eyes, clearly thinking I was keeping secrets. I was surprised to find how much that small motion stung.

"It's true. I've told you. Even as a little girl, I'd spend as much time with my father and brothers as possible, practicing things like knots and defense moves. It wasn't until Evander brought me military books that I started to understand the fine intricacies of war."

I glanced back at my sisters, currently captivated by another of Will's fanciful stories. My ears pricked as a few lines listed my way. It sounded like the tale about the dragon king who faced an evil darkness and rescued a fair maiden.

Shifting my gaze back to Alarik, I saw that he was not-so-patiently waiting for me to explain, but there was no story to tell. "It was because of Evander that I learned how to work a bow and dagger and the reason I have some training with a sword. He taught me how to hunt properly. He's the only reason my family and I are alive."

It wasn't much, but Alarik must have been satisfied with my answer, because when he next spoke, his voice was soft. "I'm glad he found you. I'm glad he didn't leave after..."

After Jem died.

We walked a few minutes in silence as I gathered the strength to recount the wounds of the past, still raw despite the passage of time. I wanted to be rid of them, to purge the phantoms from my mind.

In little more than a whisper, I said, "Evander didn't make it in time. Jem had already died. The two of them were to be married that winter."

Alarik's eyes cut to mine, but I stared ahead. The memory of their engagement stirred a mixture of emotions. Tears stung the corners of my eyes as I recalled how happy they had been.

"Neither of them particularly liked the winter, but Evander insisted fall colors would clash with his hair and Jem didn't want to wait until spring, so winter it was. But then the storm hit. And everything changed."

"I'm sorry," he said.

"It's not your fault. For the past seven years, I didn't think it was anyone's fault... but now, I'm not so sure."

"It's a lot to take in."

"I guess." I dared to meet his gaze. "I gather you know he's in the Legion of the Light, serving the Light Kingdom?"

Alarik nodded. "He started working for me shortly after. He's been invaluable at understanding the ways of the light fae, but he is gone often. I can imagine that must've been tough for you and your family."

"I was young then, and trying to process the notion of death, but I remember Evander storming through the house, screaming for Jem. My mother was in the twins' room, doing her best to save Torin. Greer and Lannie had Will tucked away upstairs, and Papa—he was digging the grave for my brothers already, despite his own declining health."

My chest shuttered as I forced my lungs to draw air. Not bothering to wipe away the tears dripping along my cheeks, I let the memory surge forth. "Evander flew up the stairs. I tried to stop him, but he wouldn't, not until Jem was in his arms. I thought Mother's screams were bad. I hadn't realized she must have been holding back—not until I heard Evander. His agony, his grief—It was the sound of a soul shattering.

"He wouldn't leave Jem, despite seeing he was gone. He wouldn't accept it. Papa had to force him away from the body. Evander was shouting, cursing the fae of this world for letting this happen to Jem."

I blinked, looking up, seeing my pain reflected in pools of green, but my sorrow shifted to probing curiosity as I replayed his rantings in my mind. "He said he blamed the fae of this world for taking Jem. The *fae*, not the storm. Almost as if—

"Gods," I breathed. Could it be? My eyes snapped to Alarik's waiting gaze. "Did Evander tell you anything about the storm?"

His shoulders tightened, but he kept his mouth closed. My nostrils flared as I dragged him by the arm further away from my siblings.

"If you know something concrete about the storm linked with half the human population dying and the subsequent attacks, you need to tell me."

He shot a quick look over his shoulder before pinning his gaze on the path ahead, chin raised. "I already told you my suspicions. It seems unlikely the storm was naturally born of Pax."

The reality of the situation thundered through me. Could it be real? *Gods.* Maybe the storm really wasn't of this world.

"What type of attack could affect all of Pax?"

He looked at me with equal measures of despair and determination. "I've spent the last seven years trying to answer that question."

Our pace slowed over the next few minutes, allowing my siblings to catch up. Lannie took my hand as Greer linked her arm with mine. Whenever my world felt like it was spiraling out of control, they grounded me, as I did for them. We didn't have to speak. There was simply an underlying energy between us, an unseen link, allowing our essences to flow together. I supposed it was that way with all sisters.

My understanding of this world was shifting. I needed to adapt quickly, because ff any of these theories were true, the twisted fae in the forest were just the beginning.

CHAPTER 19

THE SUN SANK LOW ON THE HORIZON, ILLUMINATING OUR PATH IN a wash of gold. We'd been walking at a brisk pace for hours without a break, and I could feel my little brother growing weary.

Will's stomach gave an audible grumble as he looked toward me with hopeful eyes. "Can we stop to eat?"

"I wish we could," Alarik answered over his shoulder. "But the sun is already setting, and we have a lot of ground to cover."

Will's eyes shot to me, disbelieving that after skipping lunch and being robbed of his pastries this morning, he would also have to forgo dinner.

"I might have something that can help," I said, recalling the loaf of bread and pastries Sophie supplied from the market. Was that only yesterday? My siblings' attention was fixated on me as I pulled free the crumpled paper bag. Even Alarik quirked a brow in my direction.

"Sophie was at the market?" Greer asked, letting out an excited squeal. She knew I picked up pastries and bread for the family each time I visited. The treats were squished by my haphazard packing, but they smelled delicious and would still taste just as good.

My own stomach growled as we partitioned out the food. Greer's croissant had suffered the most damage, having been beneath my roll of weapons. The top layer was nothing more than flakes, but it didn't deter in the least.

Lannie's heart shaped palmiers were next, only sporting a few cracks and she took them with a hungry smile.

"Where's mine, Ellie? You didn't forget about me, did you?" Will bounced around me.

"I could never forget you. It's here somewhere." Praying to the gods that Will's chocolate éclair would be salvageable, I reached toward the bottom of the bag and discovered a relatively preserved pastry."Here you go. Try to eat it from the wrapper so you don't get your hands too sticky."

Before I could finish, Will snatched the pastry away, issuing his thanks from an already full mouth. His happiness was a simple thing: enjoyment of a tasty treat, but it somehow possessed the power to lighten the morbid day despite the growing darkness and dangers around us.

I glanced past him, spotting Alarik lurking conspicuously. Ripping off a section of bread, I extended it to him with a smirk. He muttered a thanks, before returning his attention to the surrounding forest.

At last, I pulled out a small wax-lined bag for myself. It had once held three perfectly round and crisp macarons: Pistachio, chocolate and black tea. My three favorite flavors, and each one of them smashed to bits. I picked out the larger parts, savoring the rich fillings before turning the bag on its side and sliding the rest of the crumbs into my mouth. The merging flavors were odd blended together, but still tasty.

"Thanks, Ellie!" Will said, handing me the crumpled wrappings. I noticed all the chocolate glaze and custard had been

CHAPTER 19 | 141

licked clean, as evidenced by the smears of both across his cheeks.

He looked between the three of us with an excited gleam in his eyes. "Have you heard the tale of the dark-winged bird?"

"That's not one we're familiar with," Greer answered with motherly enthusiasm, brushing back the blond curls springing across his forehead. "Would you tell us about it?"

"Yes!" His eyes shone as he hopped in front of us, walking backwards to better see our reactions. "The dark-winged bird was unlike any other bird. All of the other birds were white, or at least mostly white, with very light brown tufts of feathers along their inner wings.

"The other birds feared the dark-winged bird, but he was actually very nice and wanted to have friends. The mama bird told him that his dark wings were beautiful, and that the other birds would learn to see how friendly he was. The dark wings were a sign the bird was blessed with great powers from the gods. She said sometimes, when there are differences, other birds can become afraid because they don't understand those differences.

"The dark-winged bird tried to listen to the mama bird, but then she got sick, and he was left alone. He didn't want to wait for the others to decide to be his friend.

"So, he decided to hide his darkness. He flew till he found the grove of white poppies. He rubbed the magical petals all over his wings, and the magic covered up the darkness. When he was finished, his wings were as white as all the other birds. He thought, surely, they would be his friends now. But when he tried to fly home, he couldn't. The pollen from the poppies was too heavy."

Will shrugged and turned back around.

"Wait, what happened to him?" Lannie asked. "Did he realize he didn't need white wings?"

Will frowned. "He found a way to return to the other birds

with the petals still hiding his darkness. The other birds were nice to him when they saw he had white wings like them. He was happy for a little while, and decided having friends was more important than flying, even though flying was his most favorite thing to do. But he *would* always get really sad when the other birds would fly off without him."

"That's a terrible story," Lannie snapped.

"That's how the dream went." He tilted his head as if it wasn't up to him. "My feet are sore. Are we there yet?"

A snort caught in the back of my throat. How many times had I heard those words? "When we are there, you will know. Here, hold Lannie and Greer's hands. They will give you some extra strength. I'm going to check in with Alarik."

I jogged a few paces up, noting we have maybe another hour left before nightfall. "Are we going to make it?"

Alarik looked back, seeing the fatigue of my siblings. "Perhaps, but we would need to move faster. See that they keep up." He made to turn away, but my hand snagged his arm.

"Wait. Are you okay?" His whole demeanor had been off today. There was a lot going on, but I was hoping the day traveling together would loosen things up. "Where's the fun, albeit cocky prick I've been traveling with?"

He huffed a laugh before letting out a long sigh. "I'm sorry. It's hard for me to balance being the general and a friend sometimes."

Did he really just say *friend*? Gods, why did it feel like I swallowed lead?

"But we aren't just friends traveling together anymore, El."

We aren't just friends. My stomach did a little flip. Did he mean—

"All of your lives are my responsibility, now."

The silence hung between us. My fluttering heart squeezed, dropping into the pit in my stomach, right beside the lump of lead I didn't remember swallowing. How could I think he meant anything more? Alarik clearly wasn't interested. And neither was I. This was nothing more than an agreement.

"All of this about the storm and the attacks, if it's true, then it means half my family was murdered. I can't sit by while the remaining humans suffer the same horrible fate."

His lips pressed thin. "You will be trained, as agreed, but your tasks remain restricted to recon only. Your education will reflect that."

My fists balled. "I get you have this duty to protect everyone, but I refuse to be another helpless person begging for shelter. I'm going to strike back, hard. If you won't train me, I'll find someone who will. The sooner you learn that, the easier this will go."

He kept his voice low and steady, but fury dripped from each word. "This is not a game, and I am not some piece on a board to be pushed around. *I* am the general of this base—*Me*. Every life that crosses those gates is a responsibility *I* have to carry, no one else. When you agreed to work for me, you became another life that I'm duty-bound to protect. You *and* your family. Until that changes, I will be making the decisions. The sooner you learn *that* the easier this will be. Now, keep up."

He stalked forward, heading directly into the failing sun. The ultimatum was clear, keep up and fall in line, or get left behind.

I'd show him how quickly I adapted, how deep my need for action, for vengeance ran. Now that I finally had a reason for the destruction of my family—now that I could direct all of my darkness and years of pent-up rage to uncovering who or what was responsible for destroying humanity—nothing and no one would stop me.

CHAPTER 20

Time passed quickly in strained silence as the strong rays of the sun transformed into the softer shades of twilight. The gentle sounds of awaking night creatures greeted us as we passed through thickening trees. It would have been beautiful had we not been worried about a deranged group of fae hurtling toward us at any moment.

My mind filtered through everything I'd learned. My family weren't the unfortunate casualties of some unavoidable storm. They were the victims of a brutal attack by an enemy who possessed the ability to concoct a spell so powerful that over half of the human population was wiped out within a fortnight.

The body count only grew when I thought of the fae kingdoms surrounding us. The ongoing attacks may not be crafted through identical means, but the intent remained the same. Those housing the taboo villages of both human and fae offspring had suffered.

Gods. And the children. The innocents like the little baby growing in Lucy's belly. Was the difficulty to conceive and bear a child linked with the unnatural storm? Would Liam get to be a father? Or would he join the countless number of grieving parents?

The sounds of a half-a-dozen galloping hooves thundering against the earth interrupted my morbid thoughts. Following Alarik's command, we dashed for cover, diving behind boulders and tree trunks along the side of the road. He crouched ahead of us, posed to strike, but his shoulders sagged as the figures came into view. Stepping into the middle of the road, Alarik greeted the team of horses and the armor-clad men sitting atop them.

My eyes darted to the flash of copper hair visible even in the early hours of night. Unlike the others who stopped to speak with Alarik, Evander rushed to our sides, his auburn eyes landing on Will's drifting form.

"Will looks like he's about to fall asleep in the middle of the road." Evander said. "Help me get him onto my saddle."

"Thanks, Evander. We've been half carrying him for a while now," Greer answered.

The three of us hoisted Will's wobbly body up, until his small frame was leaning against Evander's chest. Greer and Lannie's shoulders slumped, their own fatigue catching up to them now that Will was cared for. They moved to the edge of the road, resting against a few of the larger boulders. I peeked over to see Alarik still immersed in conversation and seized the opportunity to speak with Evander.

"I need to know about that prophecy."

His russet-colored eyes locked with mine, the curtain of weariness instantly dissolving. He dared a glance to the cluster of men, before meeting my waiting glare. "I'm sorry, Ellie, but I'm not just in the Legion of the Light. I'm also under General Holt's command. I report to him."

"Please, Evander. I've spent my entire life trying to piece together my family after losing them—trying to accept this terrible thing that happened. If anyone understands how little progress I've made with acceptance, it's you."

His resolved crumbled, his voice dipping low. "Recent reports allude to a prophecy of war and fathomless darkness. I've only heard pieces, but The Dark Phoenix has been mentioned multiple times as well as a small town called Neith."

"Neith?" It sounded vaguely familiar, but I couldn't place where I'd heard it before.

Evander gave a lopsided shrug, only mildly inhibited by Will's sleeping form. "From what I've discovered, it's a cozy town just inside the Dark Kingdom's borders. There is a myth involving it, something about the surrounding rocks offering protection from harm, but it's never been the focus of an attack."

"Humans?"

He nodded. "And fae. Those who choose to live there tend not to leave. They lead meager lives and have little possessions."

Frowning, I couldn't understand why a place like that would be of interest. Evander answered the unspoken question. "I'll keep an eye out for any further information."

"And the storm? You think it was an attack as well?"

His shoulders pressed back. "There were rumors circulating in the Light Kingdom a few weeks before the storm hit— rumors of an attack mounting against 'lesser beings.'"

I started to question him, but he silenced me with a look. "It wasn't anything official, only gossip within the inner city. I thought nothing of it. The light royals are notorious for their arrogance, but they lack the will for battle."

That was true. Even before humans were created, the light fae were known for their mental achievements, purposely avoiding physical conflict. Appearances were everything to them. Evander knew that better than most.

He had been accepted into the Legion of the Light only because his grandfather had been a high-ranking light fae. It was expected that any sons would join the ranks and uphold the family's elite status. With fae children being so rare, Evander was claimed by his father's line, despite having a human mother.

Once an oath was made, it was final—at least in the eyes of the light fae. It didn't matter that Evander's grandfather denounced him after discovering his preference for men. Evander would be bound to their army until death.

Of course, that didn't mean his disgrace-of-a-grandfather was above making his life miserable. He encouraged Evander's ostracism, thinking that by publicly humiliating him, the light fae would somehow forget that Evander was his blood. Even when the slicing words had switched to pounding fists, his grandfather refused to put a stop to it—not at the sake of his reputation.

I took in the tick to his jaw the clenching of his fists. "You do think the light fae are responsible, that they need to be punished. I hadn't realized your views had shifted so completely."

Evander had always maintained there were terrible beings in any kingdom, fae and human alike and held no ill will toward the Light Kingdom before, despite his personal experiences.

"Yes," he hissed. "The storm changed it. It changed *everything.*"

I flinched at the raw anguish in his voice. "I'm sorry. I didn't mean to judge. Of course, it changed everything."

Brushing my hand over his, I tried to rub away the sting of my words. Evander had been planning on leaving the Legion after he married Jem, but after her died...

"I went back in." The words were spoken on an exhale, low but urgent. "I've been trying to gather as much information as possible—" He swallowed, schooling his expression as the men started their approach. They were within hearing distance now.

Evander dropped his voice. "He agreed to train you, correct?" When I nodded, his tone returned to a normal pitch.

"Good. I'll be sure to stop by tomorrow. Maybe we can go for a jog, like old times."

I nodded once more. "Thank you. Perhaps in the afternoon? I plan on sleeping through a good portion of the morning, and you know how much of a grouch I can be if I'm tired."

"That I do. Afternoon it is." He jerked his chin toward the sizable, black horse spotted in white that galloped over with a large blond rider mounted atop. "This is Blazer, and the man he is allowing to ride him is Lieutenant General, Vidarr Rafe. Lieutenant General, this is Elara Tenebris."

A cloud shifted in the night sky, allowing the soft glow of the stars to filter through the budding branches of the forest, illuminating the man before me. He was similar to Alarik, the same strong build and square jaw, but his chest was a tad wider, and his hair a touch lighter, cascading past his shoulders in various braids and knots. His thick, well-trimmed beard had the beginnings of silver mixed in with the blond, matching his storm-cloud eyes. This man looked like he would rip his opponents apart and leave the pieces scattered for the crows to feast on.

"Wait, I thought Alarik was the general?"

Evander groaned as the Lieutenant General chuckled, answering openly before Evander did. "He is. Alarik is the general of the entire army. I'm his second in command. You may call me Vidarr. It is my understanding that you've had a very long day. If you would do me the honor, I would like to escort you to the base. Do you feel comfortable riding with me?"

I hesitated for a moment, but the kindness in his eyes quieted my qualms. My dry lips parted into a weary smile. "Yes, thank you, Vidarr." Placing my smaller hand in his larger, rougher one, I carefully swung my leg up and around before settling in front of him.

A quick glance assured me that Greer and Lannie were already seated with others riders and ready to go.

"Hold on," Vidarr said. "We travel fast."

CHAPTER 21

THE REMAINING TIME PASSED IN A BLUR. JUST WHEN I THOUGHT I'd surely succumb to the sleep, our horses thundered through the iron gates of the military base and into a wide, well-lit pavilion.

We continued past various buildings until we reached a beautiful structure in the middle of the camp. White walls stretched three stories high, with large windows, each encrusted with ornate designs framing the glass. Two iron rimmed balconies jutted out opposite each other with the promise of hanging flowers once spring was in full bloom.

Vidarr guided us toward Alarik, the general issuing orders to the rest of the men who'd accompanied us. They darted off, heeding his directions without question.

Alarik's gaze found us, an order rolling off his tongue. "See them to their lodgings. The second floor should do. Make sure they are given adjoining rooms with en suites."

The green hues of his eyes shifted until they met mine. My stomach did a small flip as I watched their harsh glint yield to something softer. There were dozens of unspoken words peering up at me, begging to be shared.

"Are the meals ready yet?" Vidarr had the kindness to ask. "I could have sworn I heard the boy plead for pastries in his sleep."

Alarik's lips twitched, but his voice stayed hard and he spoke to me. "Evander had the foresight to alert the cook. Dinner should be up shortly along with fresh towels. The horses were unloaded upon arrival and your belongings have been brought up. If there is nothing else, I have matters to attend to."

"Thank you, General Holt, for your hospitality." The 'General Holt' title earned me the glare I was aiming. "Vidarr, would you mind helping my little brother? It seems Evander is having quite the time trying to rouse him."

Alarik's brow raised at my informal address to his second in command, but he didn't comment as Vidarr turned toward Will's slouching body and Evander's failing grip.

"I want the Select in the council chambers in half an hour, Vidarr," Alarik bellowed before riding further into the camp, not waiting for a reply.

"What happened between you two? We managed to get everyone home safe without any run-ins and he's still in a foul mood." Vidarr's chest vibrated with deep laughter as he dismounted in one sleek motion. He extended his large, calloused hand to help me do the same.

I shrugged, not sure how to explain my relationship with Alarik. It had started out as a business agreement, but it was more than that now, wasn't it? No... at least not to him. Apparently, I was just another responsibility for him to deal with.

Sliding off the saddle, I shrugged. Vidarr smirked but didn't comment as he handed over the reins to a young soldier waiting to take the horses to the stables. Within moments, he was scooping my brother away from Evander.

Evander released a breath. "Oh, thank the gods. Will has definitely grown since the last time I saw him."

Greer laughed as he shook out his arms and stretched his neck. "He has. You missed his eighth birthday. He was too tired tonight but be prepared for him using that against you to get some training. His heart is still set on becoming a soldier."

"The lad wishes to be a soldier?" Vidarr mused.

Greer nodded.

He looked over at Evander who was gazing down at Will's sleeping form with a proud big-brother grin. Vadarr's gaze swung to me. "Well, I'm sure we can arrange something. I take it you're the woman Alarik found to help with recon?"

"Yes, but he agreed to train me as a proper fighter, once I've proven I can handle it. I *will* be holding him to that." Straightening my spine, I put as much force into my words as I could.

The weight of Vidarr's gaze locked me in place as he took my measure. His eyes had a thin layer of blue surrounding the deep grey of heavy rain clouds. Intelligent, perceiving eyes.

Each word was drawn out with meaning as he answered. "I see no reason why you should be denied training, but be warned, you will find no modifications here. You will be held to the same standard as every other soldier in this base."

"I understand."

"I'll give you tomorrow to sleep and one more day to familiarize yourself with the camp. Training starts the following morning at dawn."

I couldn't contain the smile that burst across my face.

Vidarr led the way into the grand building before us, Will's weight proving inconsequential as he climbed the stone steps. The large cedar door opened, the polished handle shining as the light spilling out from within. Greer gave a small gasp as we entered, clearly taken aback by the finery surrounding us.

The floors were white marble with hints of grey. The foyer was lit by a wide, sparkling crystal chandelier with matching ones spaced throughout the hall, visible along the main floor, but it was the staircase that demanded attention. The marbled steps twisted up with a dark, intricate railing, opening to a wide landing on the second level, before continuing up to the third level.

"Welcome to your new home. Right this way."

Vidarr headed up the steps to the second floor. He took us down a lengthy hall before arriving at our bedrooms. At Greer's urging, Vidarr tucked Will into the bed she claimed as her own.

"This way, he won't be spooked when he wakes in a new place," she whispered. "At the very least, he'll know he's not alone."

I recalled the dark-winged bird story from earlier and agreed that it'd be best if he woke up next to someone who loved him. She worked swiftly, pulling off his shoes and jacket as he grumbled.

"Not a problem, miss," Vidarr said. "The four rooms are yours. You may decide how you would like to use them. Alarik's chambers are on the third floor, if you need anything."

"Alarik lives here?" My voice hitched.

Greer shot me a look as Will stirred at the noise. Grimacing an apology, Vidarr and I left the room. The rattling of silverware sounded as we stepped into the hall, the subtle clash of porcelain drawing my attention.

"This is the general's residence," Vidarr answered. "So, yes. Alarik lives here."

I barely heard his response as a young boy, looking only a year or two older than Will, clamored down the hall pushing a wheeled cart stacked with covered dinner plates. His shoulders drew up as he noticed Vidarr.

"Sorry for the late hour, Lieutenant. General Holt ordered food to be brought up. He didn't say what to bring. So, I brought a little of everything."

Vidarr muttered his thanks as I stared openly at the stacks of trays before me, filling my lungs with a deep breath. The scent of roasted chicken and freshly baked bread were swirling around me, mingling with other unidentifiable spices.

CHAPTER 21 | 153

Lannie peered out from her room a moment before Greer stepped through hers. "Is that for us?" Lannie asked, eyes growing wide as she noted the tower of food before me.

"Even if it's not, I plan on eating it," Greer said, pulling the tray into the room across the hall. I caught a glimpse of two large bookshelves lining the far wall with a deep green velvet settee and low-set wooden table placed in front. An eager smile lit Lannie's face as she hurried after Greer.

"I wasn't sure which food you would prefer, but I'm happy to help you select a plate," the boy offered, following after them.

"That won't be necessary," Greer said as she guided him back into the hall. "We're going to eat all of them. Thank you for dinner!"

The young boy gaped, looking at the three of us and then back to the stack of dishes. He grumbled something about returning in the morning for the plates before trudging away.

"Goodnight, Elara," Vidarr said as he retreated. "Please don't hesitate to ask if you need anything."

My stomach growled as I nodded, before joining my sisters. Greer was setting each of the dishes out as Lannie shifted her weight from foot to foot.

"Greer, I'm hungry," Lannie whined. "I don't care how many options there are. I'll take anything at this point."

"Calm down, I'm almost done. This way we can pick out the tastiest dishes to eat first. Honestly, your stomach will thank me in a few minutes."

"Minutes?"

"Yes," Greer met her with an unflinching gaze. "Besides, El needs to wash up. We all should before we sit anywhere in this place. I only wish I was able to have Will bathed before bed, but there is no way I'm going to risk waking him up."

"She's right, Lannie. You two aren't bad, but I definitely need a shower." I looked down at my body, seeing only the swath of dried blood the debris of travel. My stomach issued a loud rumble as I glanced at the plates of food. "Meet back in ten?"

"Agreed," they chimed, both dashing across the hall to the other bedrooms and the showers within.

Pushing open an interior door, I walked through the bedroom. There was an oak armoire beside a delicately crafted wooden writing desk, the room wash of pale pinks and creams surrounding a large bed topped with throw pillows and an airy rose-colored comforter.

I passed through the en suite and into the washroom, noting the brilliant marble of the halls continued throughout the floor. My eyes snapped to the glass-enclosed, rainfall showerhead. Tossing my filthy clothes into a pile, I stepped inside.

Deliciously warm water blasted against my aching muscles, soothing the soreness while washing away the grime of the last day and a half. I reached for the block of mint-infused soap and got to work scrubbing away the stains still clinging to my body. After three full-body scrubs, two rounds of shampoo and one glorious washing of conditioner, I finally stepped out of the shower.

I had just finished slipping into a pair of worn sweats and a flowing top when I heard the click of the door and my sister's easy conversation filling the sitting room.

"I see you two enjoyed the showers as well," I said, joining them around the food. Their hair was damp, their tops dotted with stray droplets.

"It was incredible," Greer moaned. "I can't wait to just sit under the water all day tomorrow."

Lannie rolled her eyes. "Yes, it really was great, but I'm starving. It's time to eat."

"Agreed."

We joined Greer at the table, piling our plates high with food. There was fresh bread and roasted chicken along with steamed potatoes spiced with rosemary, a spring garden salad topped with fresh fruit with a variety of dressings on the side, and a platter of melted cheese sandwiches surrounding a bowl of steaming tomato soup.

Each of us took a helping of the salad before sharing the main courses. Lannie declined the chicken, preferring to refrain from meat when the supplies allowed.

After working our way through most of the food, we found one last dish tucked underneath the others loaded with sweets. Thick brownies with chunky chocolate chips, cookies, and a few blackberry tarts. Greer and I split a brownie, already too full for more while Lannie helped herself to a sugar-coated cookie.

I was grateful for the idle chatter of the evening, but soon the fatigue of the day caught up with us. My sisters returned to their rooms for the night, leaving me alone with my wandering thoughts. In a futile attempt to escape memories of the day, I headed to bed, slipping between the crisp, clean sheets that awaited me.

Visions of black eyes and grey skin rose to the surface, their laughing bodies surrounded by thick, tarry pools of blood. I had killed him—it—the fae. The adrenaline of battle had waned and still, I felt no remorse.

I sighed as I rolled over, dragging another plush pillow against my chest. There was something wrong with me, but as my eyes drifted shut and my body sank deeper into the soft sheets, I couldn't find the will to care.

The darkness was waiting for me, as it always was. I welcomed the sweet peace it offered, praying the gods were merciful enough to the nightmares at bay for another night. Funny thing about prayers—they often went unanswered.

CHAPTER 22

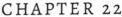

THE WOODEN FLOORS GAVE A FAINT CREEK AS LANNIE MADE HER WAY *over to where Greer and I sat, perched at the top of the banister. Despite being the youngest sister, she would normally reprimand us for eavesdropping, but this time she stayed silent, choosing instead to slide in beside us.*

It had been three days since the storm and her dark eyes reflected the worry pooling in my own. Lannie took my hand, dipping her head to rest on my shoulder as we turned our attention to the conversation below.

Papa paced in front of the fireplace, its flames casting distorted shadows across the room. It was late summer, much too early in the year for fires, but Papa and the twins had been cold since the storm hit, regardless of their climbing fevers.

"The twins aren't getting better," he muttered, as he ran a hand through his dark curls. Every third step of his pacing squeaked with the shifting floorboards. "I had hoped it was a simple illness, but the fever has only gotten worse."

"Jem is beside himself, going in and out of consciousness, pleading for Evander." I flinched.

"I thought Evander was in the Light Kingdom," Mother's voice

drifted from the cushioned chair partially tucked beneath the stairs. "Isn't he serving at one of their outposts a few weeks' travel from here?"

"He is, or at least that's what I was led to believe. Jem seems to think this storm is some sort of attack. Before the fever took him under again, he said there were whispers of an uprising."

The logs shifted in the fire, triggering a loud pop and pulling a gasp from Mother. Greer jumped as well, her hand tightening in mine as the three of us leaned forward, following Papa's strides.

"The Dark Phoenix... The prophecy," Mother whispered. The three of us held our breath, straining to hear. "Oh gods, it's the prophecy." She shifted in the chair, just enough to see the heated glow of the hearth reflected along her smooth golden locks, the light's morbid reflection causing it to appear as if she too were on fire. Greer's ice-blue eyes snapped to mine, stirring with unspoken questions, but I had no answers to give.

Papa kneeled, his large hands gently cupping her face, trying to pull her out of whatever memory she was reliving. "What are you talking about, my love? What prophecy?"

"I thought I could escape it. It seems like ages ago. Before we met. I —I told you when we ran away together, I told you there were things in my past that I needed to hide from. There are things I've done, things that have set certain events in motion. I thought we were saving this world, heeding the warning of the prophecies. I gave up everything."

She stood, turning away to face the flickering flames. "I was wrong. I wasn't preventing death but delivering us to it—to the darkness. It was already too late. Events had been set in motion, ones that couldn't be recalled."

The fire cracked again, but Mother didn't flinch. She didn't seem to hear it.

"It should have been enough," she murmured, barely audible. "It was the most powerful... She's bound, as are the others. This shouldn't be possible. It's not possible."

"What do you mean, Adara? Speak plainly. What have you done?" Papa's voice was low, but the tenor of it snapped her attention to him.

"I fear I may have doomed us all. If this is what I think, it will get worse. Many will die—" Her breathing hitched. "And I fear our family will not be spared."

"No," Papa's hollow voice pleaded, hands gripping Mother's shoulders. "That's not possible, Adara. I heard you when the storm rolled through us. The illness was removed from the twins and me within moments of exposure."

I'd never seen Papa in such a rage, nor Mother so quietly resigned to her fate. Her tears flowed freely, now, transforming into streams of molten lava in the glow of the fire.

"The girls and Will should be okay, but the twins... I used everything left and I'm afraid even that won't be enough to spare their lives—or ours." It was a mere whisper, barely discernible above the cackling wood, but Papa's entire body went rigid, until he was gathering Mother in his arms.

"You didn't. Please say you didn't." But the answer he found in her eyes must have confirmed his fears. He pressed gentle kisses along her hair, letting her collapse into his larger frame as her body shook, the sounds of her cries enveloping the room and snuffing out the last, fleeting embers of hope.

The rapping of knuckles against wood snapped me out of my dream, the details dissipating with the fluttering of my eyes. Unease twisted in my gut. I needed to remember it. It was clearer than my usual dreams, there had been whispers... Mother had been present. Something about the storm?

"El, are you here? Vidarr said this was your room." Evander's head popped through my open bedroom door, scattering the fraying fibers of memory further.

Right, training. I'd completely forgotten. Groaning, I dragged the pillow over my head as I turned away from him and his perky attitude.

"It's too early. Come back later."

"It's past noon." He chuckled, and I batted his hand away as he made to snatch the pillow. Evander wrestled it from my grasp, only for me to wrap myself thoroughly in the blanket.

There was a loud sigh, followed by the sound of his footsteps retreating and returning a moment later.

"I brought something for you."

A delicious scent filled the air. I yanked the blankets away, daring to see for myself. There it was, a steaming, whipped-cream-topped mug of what could only be one thing.

"Gods, is that coffee? I haven't had a proper cup in ages," I said, pushing up into a sitting position.

"This hardly counts as a 'proper cup' with all of this added to it," he teased, gesturing toward the mound of cream.

Smiling, I slipped out of bed and accepted Evander's bribe. I swirled the cup, savoring the caramel flavored brew inside. "Okay, training time it is."

"I thought that would work. I figured it would be a nice way of apologizing for leaving out some key pieces of information these last seven years."

Lowering the mug to my lap, I met his gaze. "About that, I was a jerk. I get that you have an obligation to your commanding officer."

He shrugged, but his shoulders were tense. "It was only a matter of time before you learned the truth for yourself. I'm hoping to prevent you from sneaking around to get the information."

"I won't. It's just, I've felt restless these past few months, like there's something I should be doing, only I can't remember what it is. And then to find out that we've been at war without most of the world realizing it... It's awful knowing I was another clueless human. Learning the truth changed things. It feels right being here. When those *creatures* found us in the forest, I was afraid, but there was this other part that felt... alive.

Like the first stretch after a long sleep. It feels as if I'm finally waking up."

A shadow passed over his face but instead of commenting, he pulled out a small bag of clothing. "Well then, little monster, get dressed. The rest of your uniforms will be brought up this evening. I know you're training with Vidarr the day after next, so we will stick with cardio today. Meet me in the hall when you're ready."

Setting the coffee down with a rushed clatter, I sorted through the clothes, barely managing to contain the excited squeal threatening to escape.

My fingers combed through the soft, stretchy fabric of the pants before shifting to a lighter, flowing material of the top. Both were inscribed with the military insignia. Bits of black snagged my attention. Evander had even thought to include proper undergarments.

A disbelieving laugh bubbled forth. I had clothes. Clothes that belonged to me. They were clean and new, exactly my size, and most importantly, tied to no one and nothing else. No ghosts. No past. Just mine.

There was a pair of running shoes at the bottom of the bag, complete with a few comfortable pairs of black socks. I normally hated running, but I couldn't help but feel excited to try out my new wardrobe. Taking another sip of coffee, I redid my braid, pulling my hair away from my face and securing it with a tie.

I paused for a moment, studying my reflection. My complexion remained light, though still a few shades darker than my siblings. The return of the sun in spring would have it warming to a dark tan. Shadows lined my eyes, as they always did, but there was a spark sizzling beneath, seeming to force the blue edges to retreat, just a little.

This felt like the path I was meant to be on, and for the first time in a long time, I let the kindling of hope grow.

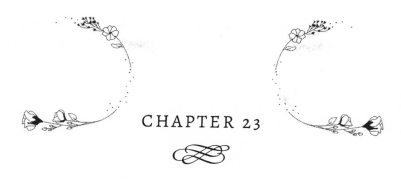

CHAPTER 23

"I KNOW YOU HATE CARDIO, BUT IT'S IMPORTANT TO KEEP UP WITH it. If you don't complain too much, we can head to the stables after. I think I found you the perfect horse." Evander's warm eyes met mine as we stepped through the front doors.

My eyes widened as I gaped, open mouthed at Evander.

"Oh wow. You? Speechless? I didn't think I'd see the day."

Forcing myself to focus, I asked, "You got me a horse?"

"Well, sort of. She belongs to the base. She's my horse's sister. His mother returned two years ago and out came Ember a few months later. She's small, too narrow for any of the warriors here, but she should be a perfect fit for you."

"I'm sure I'll love her. You know I've always wanted a horse of my own. Remember when Torin used to pretend to be my pony?"

He snorted. "He would carry you on his back and gallop around for hours. Torin was always so tough, but he turned into a total marshmallow around you girls."

"Mmm, marshmallows. I remember those. You brought them back for us to try, what two, three years ago? Was it from one of your adventures to the north?"

His smile faltered. "I found them in the Fire Kingdom, actually."

I stumbled as his words slammed into me. "You went to the Fire Kingdom? Were you on assignment from the Legion of the Light or from Alarik?"

"Neither, so there's no need to bring it up, but not all fire fae are ruthless, El. There are a few villages where their people choose to live above ground, similar to how we live. It's not all lava and brimstone, not like we've been told."

What other untruths had I accepted as facts? I pondered this as the buildings thinned out. In the light of the day, I could see the base was far larger than I remembered. The military workings were grouped along the eastern border, sitting upon a small hill. The walls extended past fields, through the tree line, and emerged in the west to loop around crisscrossing streets humming with life. There was a full city below us, complete with multilevel homes and shops, nearly every corner speckled with trees sprouting fresh, green leaves. The outline of recently constructed homes dotted the periphery—those who had sought shelter from the attacks.

Evander followed my gaze as we neared the field. "It's beautiful, isn't it?"

I nodded, taking a moment to find my voice. "It's the largest grouping of humans I've seen. When I would sneak up to watch the soldiers train, I'd camp along the southeastern ridge. It's been years since I've really looked at the city. There must be hundreds of people down there."

"Thousands, actually." He pointed to the stone walls in the distance. "The walls are extensive and have held for centuries. This entire area is said to be protected from the wards placed ages ago when the base was first constructed. With the mounting attacks targeting humans, the city has grown exponentially."

That made sense. Still, seeing the stretch of buildings before me reminded me how powerful this base was.

"On another note," he continued, as the road curved away from the sprawling city and toward the fields, "I overheard Vidarr and Alarik's conversation last night, well more of a disagreement really. It was about you."

"What? Why?"

"It sounded like Alarik wasn't happy with the idea of training you in combat. I'm not sure what you said to Vidarr, but he didn't back down. It was perfect timing on my part, though. I reported the training we've done over the years and seconded Vidarr's opinion that you be allowed to show these men up."

"Thank you for defending me, but I don't understand why Alarik is being such an ass. Learning techniques will only help improve my self-defense skills. If anything, I'll be safer."

We passed the last of the buildings, turning into a smooth trail at the edge of the tree line. Evander started to pick up the pace, easing into a light jog to allow for our conversation to continue.

"You may not want to hear this, but he's only making sure you're safe, like every other soldier here."

A low grumble left my lips, but I understood. I knew what I was capable of, but the men here didn't—Alarik didn't.

Evander's words about the sorting process for new recruits and how to climb the ranks rushed over me until he circled back around to Alarik. "I think he cares for you."

I snapped my focus to his face.

"I've known him for almost seven years," he said, his eyes trained on the path ahead of us. "He has casual flirtations, but nothing serious."

Why did that thought cause my stomach to twist? It didn't matter who he chose to share his bed with, casual or otherwise.

"He's a good man, but he's under a huge amount of pressure.

Each person we lose is another weight added to his shoulders. He lost someone important a few years ago. Alarik doesn't like to talk about it, but he's been through a lot. I guess I'm asking you to be patient with him."

I mulled over his request as our pace quickened. "I'll try. I'm not known for my patience."

Evander snorted. "Fair enough."

Craving a distraction, I increased our speed, following the trail as it stuck to the edge of the forest. If I could just get through the first part of running, I knew my body would switch to autopilot. The beginning was always terrible, but I loved the euphoric numbness that crept over my legs after a certain point. The minutes passed and I felt the beginnings of the transition start in my thighs, the tingling telling me we were about four miles in.

I pushed harder, moving faster, welcoming the burning in my lungs. I felt lighter as my legs pumped, the crisp early-spring air providing the perfect incentive to continue moving. Evander increased our tempo a little more, arching his brow in question. Shooting him a bemused smirk, I raced forward, meeting his challenge head-on.

CHAPTER 24

THE TRAIL LOOPED AROUND, STEERING US BACK TO CAMP BEFORE stopping in front of the stables. I fought the urge to bend forwards, inhaling deep breaths as I walked off the burning of my lungs, my legs blissfully numb from exertion.

After regaining my breath, I followed Evander into the stables, his shirt dark with sweat. He tossed me a small towel and a water pouch before drinking his own. The fresh water was energizing, its icy temperature cooling me from the inside out. I took another gulp, watching as Evander retrieved a young mare from a stall in the back.

She was dazzling. Flecks of rusty browns and auburn spots graced her legs, rising like the glowing sparks from a fire along her thighs and belly against a flawless white coat. Her mane and tail were a deep bronze, with bright oranges and reds woven throughout, contrasting beautifully with her dark brown eyes. She peered down at me with an awareness that had the hairs on the back of my neck prickling.

"This is Ember. Be careful. She may seem small, but she's clever, and the quickest horse I've seen." Evander held the reins as I stepped forward.

"Hello, Ember. My name is Elara." I reached out a tentative hand toward her, hoping she would accept me. Her dark eyes pondered me a moment longer. There was a quick flash, something like recognition in her knowing eyes, before she nudged my hand with the soft tip of her nose. I exhaled in delight.

"I would like us to be partners, you and I. Seeing as how you're the only mare in this troop of stallions, I think we could relate on a few things."

Evander scoffed as he released her reins to me. "It seems like she's already warming up to you. Do you remember those riding lessons from when you were a kid?"

"I'm not sure. There hasn't been much opportunity for riding."

"It's not really a skill you forget," Evander confirmed.

I continued to stroke her mane, running my hand along her spotted neck and chest as she sank further into my touch. "What do you think? Are you willing to let me try?"

Ember huffed, head dipping. She nudged my hand, flipping it up as she stepped forward.

Raising a brow toward Evander, he answered, "You could take her for a ride. The perimeter extends deep into the forest. I could saddle my horse and we could go togeth—"

Ember cut him off with a huff. I tilted my head. Her dark eyes held mine, waiting for me to heed her request. Glancing toward the trees, I felt the addicting promise of fear and adrenaline such an adventure would offer.

"It seems she wishes for it to be just the two of us. It would be safe, right? As long as we stay within the walls?"

"Yes, but only if you are comfortable riding her." He turned narrowed eyes to Ember. "And if she behaves for you."

I could have sworn Ember glared right back at him.

"Do you have a saddle for her?" I asked, but stopped when Ember nudged my hand again, bowing lower.

"We do, but she's never allowed us to put it on her."

Feeling not the least bit foolish for addressing her directly, I asked, "No saddle then?" She huffed.

"Okay, here goes nothing."

Flutters of anticipation swirled through me as I hoisted myself up, sitting directly on her beautiful coat. I had just enough time to steady myself before she started moving, circling the fields around the stables as if to prove to Evander we could handle a short trip through the trees.

Weaving my hands lightly around her neck, I used my thighs and core for balance. She cantered in a loop once more, before coming to rest in front of Evander.

I laughed. "Did we pass the test? Can we go for a ride?"

"Yes, but please be safe," Evander said, giving a begrudging smile.

The rest of his words were lost as Ember tore from the field. My legs clenched, shoulders hunched as I fought for balance, trying to avoid pulling on her mane. Within a minute or two, my body adjusted to the gait, muscles syncing to match hers as we sped into the welcoming forest.

Trees flew past us, the bright greens of spring dotted with the whites and pinks of small flowers all becoming one blurred streak as we move. The wind whipped through my hair, lashing against my neck. I threw my head back, allowing the bright rays of the sun to heat my skin, the warmth was perfectly tempered by the cool, blossom-scented wind.

This was freedom. This was everything.

I drew myself close to Ember, my fingers weaving through her soft mane. Her body hummed with mirrored anticipation, the both of us eager for adventure. Her hooves thundered against the earth as we hurdled over boulders and dodged stray branches. She slowed to an easy canter as the trees started to thin, until we reached a clearing with a stream gently rumbling in the background.

Light filtered through the canopy of trees, creating a vivid haze of green and soft blues. Ember brought us to the edge of the stream where it opened into a dazzling turquoise pool. Bluebell fairies flitted among the clusters of flowers lining the waters, their soft wings too wide for some of the daintier flowers, but unlike their pixie cousins, these were peaceful creatures.

Sliding off her back, I crept to the edge and peered into the crystal waters. Multi-colored guppies floundered about, no bigger than a thumb's length. I took a cautious step back. They were charming and seemed harmless, but so did most things of beauty. Creatures throughout the kingdoms were growing bolder. I wasn't about to test my luck, regardless of being within the confines of the base. Who knew if the wards were still working, or if the protection from harm extended to the beasts of this world.

Instead, I reclined among the wildflowers. Subtle lapping noises sounded as Ember drank from the sleepy stream before she joined me, her back lengthening along my body. I soaked in the beauty of the world around us, allowing the kaleidoscope of colors and shapes to lull me into a tranquil peace.

I'd heard tales of enchanted glens with flowers so large, they spanned the floors of the forest, their scent said to have the power of coaxing their victims into sleep among their cushioned centers. Once their prey was thoroughly entranced, the petals would close as great vines rose, curling and twisting around the bodies until the entire blossom was dragged beneath the earth.

Narrowing my eyes at the tiny flowers beside me, I studied them as they shifted non-threateningly in the delicate breeze. While it wasn't my intention to meander through flesh eating flowers, I couldn't help but acknowledge a deep calling urging me to seek... something.

I'd mentioned it to Mother once, my desire for adventure, this feeling of *other*. The color had leached from her face, and she immediately started talking about the benefits of living a quiet life. She had always been the proprietor of mundane tasks —encouraging us to choose safety over thrill.

My brows furrowed as I tried to recalled the details of my latest nightmare, my hand subconsciously stroking Ember's coat as my thoughts spun. She had spoken of a time before Papa. One of risks.

Had she explored this world as I yearned to? I knew she had ventured to the Light Kingdom. She spoke of it often, describing ornate golden halls, freshly kept flowers, and the grand statues stretching high at the gates of The Walled City of Alora, one clutching a book to represent knowledge, while the other carried a sprouting althea plant, meant to symbolize healing.

Knowledge and healing were the two things light royals coveted above all else. They had closed the gates when the storm had ravaged the realm, and had been working endlessly to discover a way to stop the lingering effects, mainly the inability for humans to conceive. But if they truly were the most skilled, why had there been so little progress after all these years?

Not a storm, I mentally chided myself, an attack.

The vision of Mother in my dreams resurfaced. There was mention of a prophecy, one with a great darkness. Those creatures Alarik and I had faced—the broken fae—they seemed pretty gods-damned dark to me.

There was something else... The edges cleared as I focused, not fully but enough. Mother had mentioned The Dark Phoenix, just as Evander had. My eyes narrowed as I realized Evander hadn't elaborated this morning, not after Alarik had cut off his report yesterday.

This would require careful exploring. I didn't want to push Evander, but I was living at the base now. If I had a chance of learning, or rather *overhearing* anything of importance, it would be here.

Chewing my lip, I attempted to stitch together the remaining wisps of the dream, but it was like water pouring through a fisher's net—I managed to hold on to the larger pieces but the vital details slipped between the woven knots. My dreams, my memories—it seemed there were so many pieces missing, pieces that would shed light on the heavily shadowed past.

A flustered sigh escaped me as I rubbed my temples. Ember startled from her nap. She rolled to stand, giving her body a great shake before her head tilted.

"I guess you're right. We should be getting back." I settled along her back. "Are you up for another sprint?"

She whinnied her agreement, and within moments, we were off.

Ember soared, erasing my worries as I soaked up her stamina, allowing it to bleed into me as we lost ourselves to speed. The world quieted and came alive all at once as I crouched low over her, fading into the pace of the gallop. Wisps of hair whipped against my neck, the cool caresses lashing across my eyes, my cheeks, but I didn't mind the sting.

CHAPTER 25

I awoke early the next morning, eager to spend some time with Ember before the day got started. Last night, Evander had reiterated the need to be cautious but encouraged us to connect. He was right. I knew I had one more mission looming, hopefully more if Alarik wished me to return to Sonder, and having a horse I was comfortable with would only aid me.

After spending the sleepy hours of dawn flitting through the trees, we returned to the stables. Evander's lean, muscular frame was turning out the other horses, letting them graze in the nearby field as the sun rose.

"It's nice to see you smile, El." Evander beamed. "I can't believe how quickly she's warmed up to you. She's been a nightmare to work with."

Ember huffed, her eyes peering down at Evander with clear disdain.

I hopped down beside her, scratching behind her ears. "Or, maybe, those silly men just didn't understand her."

She nickered in agreement, head dipping as if she were nodding.

"Apparently. I'm sorry to break this up, but I thought it

would be nice to see some of the training exercises before you're thrown into the mix tomorrow."

"That would be smart," I admitted, watching as Ember made her way toward the other horses.

He followed my line of sight. "You can visit her whenever you like. I confirmed it with Alarik."

My brows scrunched together as I turned to face him. "Wait. So, he doesn't mind me having a war horse but the thought of me completing basic training exercises stresses him out?"

Evander's laughter rang. "I don't think he considers Ember to be much of a threat because she hasn't let anyone get near her, let alone ride her. The plan was to release her back to the Fire Kingdom if she didn't come around soon. You were my last hope."

My eyes widened, connecting with Ember's deep brown ones from across the flowing grasses. "She's from the Fire Kingdom? I thought you said she was your horse's sister?"

"She is. Half-sister anyway. I can't prove it, but I'm nearly positive she was conceived while in the Fire Kingdom. It would certainly explain her coloring. I'm only glad you two get along. It means she can stay."

My head tilted, watching as the other horses avoided her. All but her half brother. She was too much for the others. Instead of hiding her true nature as I had done, as I still did, she chose to embrace her ferociousness. She was free. Perhaps not the most popular or accepted, but she was *free*.

What would it feel like, to shed these layers?

An exhausted sigh escaped me as Evander led us away from the gently flowing grass toward the center of base. I knew I would never experience that type of freedom. I wouldn't allow myself, because I wasn't a bright, glorious force like Ember. There would be no light if I let others get to know me, let them understand every inch of my mind. No, it would only expose them to the burning, impenetrable darkness that seemed to be growing bolder each day.

I shook my head, dispelling the morbid thoughts, as neared the peripheral training rings. Rows of seats surrounded the center dome open to the clear blue sky above. Despite the lack of clouds, the air swirled with a balanced cool.

Pairs of men punching and spinning came into focus as we walked down a worn dirt path between warped wooden benches. I glanced at the horizon behind them.

"Vidarr said you could stay as long as you want, but no participation."

I nodded. Of course, Evander had already approved my late morning observation. "I'd love to stay, but I have a few pressing matters to attend to."

"You're leaving?"

"No. I'll still be on base, the barracks directly next to General Holt's residence, actually. There are *things* I need to speak to the Guard about."

Evander's eyes bounced from the sparing warriors heeding Vidarr's corrections before meeting mine with a warning glint.

My chin dipped with a near imperceptible nod, but Evander exhaled with it nonetheless. He gave Vidarr a brief wave as he slipped along the curved rows and out into the compact dirt path beyond.

Vidarr's corrections captured my attention as he adjusted a particularly sweaty pair of men. They were all firm planes and hard lines, their dark skin damp with sweat. I swallowed, cheeks heating briefly as I realized Greer would reconsider her disinterest in training if she were here.

Another adjustment. Another correction. I committed every piece of advice to memory. Curious, my eyes quickly combed over the ring, finding only men. I wasn't surprised. The only women I'd seen here had been a few tending to the house or the kitchens. That would change soon enough.

Alarik chose that moment to appear, his scowl deepening as he noted my cheery disposition. He was by my side in moments, causing the sensual scent of sandalwood and cloves to wash over me.

"You haven't changed your mind, then?" he bit out. "Still set on getting yourself hurt?"

"I don't plan on being the one getting hurt," I clipped back, keeping my gaze straight. It was incredible how he could infuriate me within a matter of moments. Vidarr noticed the tense tone and was doing his best to pretend as if he couldn't hear the conversation.

"No, I don't think anyone ever does, but that doesn't stop it from happening," Alarik spat, his unchecked fury snapping the last of my restraint.

"What's your problem? This can't all be some overprotective bullshit because I have a pair of breasts strapped to my chest. I can fight just as well as any person here. I plan to prove that point as soon as I get the training I was promised."

Emerald eyes burned as Alarik met my unflinching glare. "You really think you can handle this, that you won't end up dead?"

His voice trembled slightly on the last word, but I pushed forward, too lost in my own fury to stifle the wave of bitter words.

"Why do you care what happens to me? Oh, that's right. I'm another responsibility. Just another *burden* you have to carry."

"Gods, you are the most frustrating person. Why can't you just listen." He leaned in to meet my glare, hands clenching and unclenching as he desperately chased the control he loved. I didn't let him catch it.

"I don't want a hero. So, stop trying to be one."

"If you used your brain once in a while instead of letting your emotions control you, maybe you wouldn't need one." My nostrils flared, but he wasn't finished. "I want you to be able to defend yourself, Elara. It is up to me to know when you are ready, and right now," he tilted his head, taking in my measure and finding me wanting, "you have a lot of work to do before we can even get started."

I almost flinched. His words certainly felt like a slap, but I focused on my rage and pain, on the soothing shadows within my battered mind, and held his gaze. I refused to blink, worried the watery sheen would pool with the motion and betray my raw, injured pride.

I let my anger speak for me, instead. "I have much to avenge before I let death claim me, most of which was only just brought to my attention. Thanks to you, my closest friend has been lying to me for years."

A few of the nearby pairs had slowed, staring at us, but a quick rebuke from Vidarr had them back to practice.

Alarik shook his head, huffing out a humorless laugh just as Vidarr approached. "You have no idea what you're talking about, little girl. It's all fun and games playing soldier with your big brothers and daddy, but shit is different when it's the real world."

My hand connected with his face, the crack of the blow silencing the entire training area. "Fuck you," I seethed, failing to hide the tears that pooled with his words.

Horror was written on every soldier's face as they saw the red stinging outlines across their general's cheek.

"Shit," Vidarr muttered. "All right everyone, take a lap." A groan sounded as he issued his command. "That's right, the entire loop. Get some food when you're finished."

I was vaguely aware of shuffling footsteps and fading grumbles, but I refused to yield to Alarik's glare.

"What in the gods' name is going on?" Vidarr growled.

Despite the bite of his words, neither of us looked away.

"Hey, this isn't a fucking staring contest." He shook Alarik, forcing him to turn toward away. "You can't pull shit like that in front of the new recruits. Gods, Alarik. It's just training. It's not like we're sending her to the border or anything."

Alarik scowled, tearing his eyes from mine. He dragged a hand across his face, taking in a deep breath before meeting my gaze. "Gods, I shouldn't have said that."

"No, you shouldn't have," I spat, but my words had lost their earlier punch.

"It's just, there's so much more to this than you know." He spoke to the ground, to the empty ring behind me as he paced. "There's a lot more danger than you think."

"If I'm missing vital pieces of information, *General*, that's because you haven't told me. So, fill me in, because plan on fighting in this war one way or another."

Horror and anger warred across his features as he processed this, realizing that I wouldn't stop.

"She has a point," Vidarr defended, pulling an exacerbated huff from Alarik. "The more information she has, the better prepared she'll be." The whisper of a smile faded from my lips as Vidarr turned his sights on me. "You will have to climb the ranks like any other soldier. Until you are qualified for combat, you will remain working under reconnaissance."

"Fine, but once I prove myself, and I will, I'll be sent on missions like everyone else."

Alarik features smoothed, his shoulders relaxing as a sly smile crept up. "Deal. The first requirement is understanding military techniques and the history of our world. Once you have mastered that, you can catch up on current events. Each person accepted into this camp has had to show proficiency in these areas prior to picking up a blade. Do you agree to these terms?"

Hesitating, I looked for a trap. "The terms referred to are just completing some history lessons? The same ones everyone else has to complete?"

"Yes," Alarik grinned as Vidarr confirmed this with a small dip of his head.

"Okay. I'll complete a few history lessons, but once they're done—"

"I know. You'll be included in all areas of training."

"Including techniques with various blades, bows, and hand-to-hand combat."

I expected his face to sour, but his smile widened. "Deal. My days are normally busy, but we can start on your lessons this evening. Does an hour after dinner work for you?"

"Tonight? Yeah, that should be fine." I was still whirling from his sudden change of pace that I barely heard him when he responded.

"Wonderful. Meet me on the third floor around eight o'clock. Do you know how to get back from here or would you like me to walk with you?"

"No. I planned on exploring a bit more." I spoke slowly, still unclear where this was going.

"Okay, I'll leave the door to my chambers open for you. Don't bother knocking," he called over his shoulder, strolling across the now empty training area, and off to the dirt path beyond that would lead into camp.

Vidarr gave me an amused smile before falling into step next to him.

I blinked.

"Wait... You're—what? Alarik! Can't we meet in the library or something?" But the two of them didn't turn around. I could just make out Vidarr's laughter and something that sounded like "smooth" and "she's going to kill you," before they turned toward the armory and out of hearing range.

CHAPTER 26

AFTER ENJOYING THE VIEW OF THE BUSTLING CITY BELOW AS I finished off a light lunch, I spent most of the afternoon exploring the base. I wandered among buildings, peering through windows and down hallways until I was once again at the center of the open square before Alarik's house.

House wasn't the right word. It was more of an estate or a small palace. What had Evander called it? A *residence*. I snorted, startling a young boy who was passing, as I realized I was now living in said residence.

The three-storied building was just as beautiful in the day as it was at night. The bottom floor was larger than I'd realized, extending wide and connecting to great arching glass windows with various shades of green housed within. A green house.

A smile graced my lips as I wondered if my sisters had discovered this treasure yet. I debated venturing through the domed jungle myself, but a swirling breeze had me realizing just how desperately in need of a shower I was.

There was a note on my door when I'd returned. Greer's messy sprawl indicated that the three of them had, indeed, discovered the greenhouse and would be there the remainder of the day. She also mentioned new clothes had been dropped off for all of us and to 'give fashion a chance.'

My smile lingered as I stepped through the bedroom toward the shower. The simple items from last night were still there, but a small container of lavender lotion had joined them. Strange. I turned on the water, letting the shower get nice and steamy while I set out a towel and stripped out of my clothes.

The water pressure was perfect. I lathered my hair, allowing the stream to beat against my back. After a quick scrub, I went in search of the clothes, wrapping the large, plush towel around myself as a makeshift dress.

There were two sets of clothing laid across the bed—one for training, composed of military issued uniforms, and the other for casual everyday use.

It was the pair of military-grade, waterproof boots and an additional pair of black running shoes sitting next to them that had me squealing. The workout gear yesterday had already been more than I expected, but this opened up a level of gratitude within me that was nearly unbearable. I had clothes, plural. That also meant that my siblings—Greer, and Lannie, and young Will —had experienced this same joy, now having their own carefully selected wardrobes.

I didn't bother to quell the surge of tears that pricked my eyes at the thought of their happiness as I decided on a casual outfit for myself. Slipping into a plain white top, I selected a pair of black pants to go with them, surprised to find they were comfortable despite hugging my curves.

After dressing, I headed to the armoire to put the rest of the items away, only to find that it was no longer empty. Two new coats and a handful of dresses were waiting for me. From a brief glance, I saw two formal gowns, one a deep blue and the other black, and a few off-white sundresses for more practical uses.

The jackets—gods, they were beautiful. Pristine, military issued jackets, nearly identical to the ones that Alarik wore. The material of the heavier one was thick and durable, perfect for frigid winter nights. The thinner one had a simple soft lining, less formal, but still carrying the insignia of the military base.

Adding the lighter coat to my ensemble for this evening, I pulled on the black running shoes, loving the way they molded to my feet. After a quick brush and braid of my hair, I headed downstairs in search of my family.

They were still wandering about the enormous greenhouse, which ended up being the entire west wing. Will spotted me first.

"Ellie! Ellie, you have to see this place. It's like from one of my dreams. There are these plants that have huge leaves that are waxy and waterproof, just like a dragon's wings! And then there are these small blue flowers, as blue as the gems deep in the earth. Hurry up, I want to show you."

A smile tugged at my lips as I followed. I would never grow tired of his enthusiasm. Neither would my sisters. We let him pull us around for hours. He really did have the most beautiful imagination. Was there ever another child as clever as him? I didn't think so.

"How have you been? Did each of you get a new wardrobe?" I asked, looking them over. Lannie and Greer were both sporting similar black pants and loose tops. Lannie had selected maroon while Greer went with a light blue that highlighted her eyes. Both of their coats were new, but neither bore the military insignia.

"Yes!" Greer beamed, twirling to show off her outfit. "Isn't it wonderful? Cadoc said this was just the beginning."

"Cadoc?"

"One of those special guards that picked us up. I rode with him into camp. Tall, pale skin, thick dark hair." Her head tilted in thought, her hip cocking to the side. "He sort of resembles a bear."

"Oh, I remember now. He's part of the Select Guard?"

"I think so. He's ranked right below Vidarr, but I'm trying to tell you something, El." The words were a rush of annoyance as Lannie shifted on her feet with a smile. "He asked if there was anything else I wanted. I'm sure he was thinking I'd list shoes or dresses, or maybe some jewelry. I mean, I wouldn't turn any of that stuff down." She paused, lost in her own thoughts. "Maybe I should have asked for more things."

"Greer, focus." I laughed. "What *did* you ask for?"

"This! I asked for as many herbs as we needed and he granted it, didn't he Lannie?" She raised her arms up and twirled around the greenhouse.

"Yes, and he didn't complain when I asked for a few jars and other ingredients, as well. Don't you see, El?" Lannie said. "We'll be able to make our healing supplies. He said the only thing we have to do is get Alarik's approval."

Greer waved that away as her gaze met mine. "I picked up on the tension between the two of you. There's no way Alarik will turn down our request if you ask him, El."

Both peered up at me, waiting expectantly. I frowned, "I think you have things confused. Alarik doesn't like me. He can barely tolerate me."

The two of them shared a look.

"It's the truth, but I can ask," I relented, the words nearly drowned out by their squeals. "Hold on! I said I'd ask, but I can't promise he'll say yes. I'm sure he'll want to know how this will benefit the base."

"You think we should offer them a percentage of the profits or something?"

"Can't we just offer them free supplies whenever they need it?" Lannie rationalized. "I mean, they fight battles, right? Surely their healer would be in need of additional salves. Perhaps I could stop by the healer's building at some point this week and get an idea of what we are working with."

"That is a brilliant idea, Lannie." Greer beamed, pulling us both into a hug. "It's settled. El will talk to Alarik and Lannie will speak directly to the healer. Now, if only we could get Will to calm down for a few moments. I swear our little brother is the most energetic person that ever lived."

"Do you think he'd like to see the base again?" I asked. "I was thinking about taking a walk to become more familiar with the grounds. Today is probably the last day I'll have off for a while."

"Sure," Lannie answered as we neared Will. "It would be smart to learn about this place, especially since we will be staying a few weeks."

"Cadoc said it would be closer to a month or two," Greer said. "Isn't that wonderful? I hope we never have to go back."

Lannie bobbed her head in agreement before turning to the planter nearest us.

"What else did he tell you?" I kept my tone light. If he was third in command, he would know plenty about the inner workings of this base. He was probably smart enough to keep his mouth shut about important things like the growing attacks or what The Dark Phoenix was, but men often forgot common sense when they were vying for Greer's attention.

"He mainly prattled on about himself. It's always the same with his type. All daring adventures and dazzling achievements, but who really wants to hear about the highpoints? I want the dark parts, the moments where you were forced to change, to grow. Give me the raw truth. It can be as gritty and as dirty as it needs to be, as long as it's real." She sighed. "But it seems the truth is sorely lacking these days."

Lannie leaned into her. "I'm sorry, Greer. You'll find your person someday. Or people."

Greer sank into Lannie's smaller form with a soft, sad smile. "Thanks."

"You already did," I said. "It's us, your sisters. We are your people. It's the three of us in this world. Any other being who thinks of joining this group better be pretty amazing."

"Agreed," Lannie chimed, as we started down the rows in search of Will. After a moment, she added, "Will had another dream."

"Nightmare," Greer corrected with a grim frown.

"That bad?"

Greer nodded but it was Lannie who answered. "It was worse, actually. He described the dark swarms, again. He said they were circling an island of power, not ready to attack, but nearly there. This time there was a shadow bathed in red. He mentioned something about it being the leader of the darkness or 'one third of a weapon.'"

"*The* weapon," Greer corrected again.

Lannie glared. "I don't think the distinction between 'a' and 'the' is all that important."

"Maybe, but he kept repeating 'the weapon' like it was something."

"Did he mention anything else?" I cut in, not wanting the small disagreement to escalate.

Both had creases between their eyes, shoulders drawn tight, as we spotted Will at the end of the next row. He was hovering around a plant with wide waxy leaves, each nearly the size of his arm.

Lannie spoke low. "It took him much longer to come out of it. I had to use the smelling salts. He just kept muttering..."

"Almost like he was in a trance," Greer added softly. "It was jumbled, but there was something about three brothers returning from splintered realms. I think that's where the one-third thing comes in. There were three brothers. So, this red shadow leading the collection of shadows must have been one of them."

Lannie nodded, lips pressed thin. "He also mentioned a lotus, and dragons, and something about a phoenix—"

"A phoenix?" My voice was a few octaves higher than it should have been.

My sisters stared at me a moment, before Greer answered. "Yes. It reminded me of something, too, but I can't figure out what. Why? Does any of that make sense to you?"

I shook my head a moment before Will spotted us. We each crafted a smile on our faces as we waved back at him. Dropping my voice barely above a whisper, I muttered, "I don't know what any of it means, but there's been talk about a 'Dark Phoenix' from a few different sources. I'll keep my ears open for anything further. Let's try to keep Will as happy as possible. He probably overheard some of the men discussing the attacks."

"I'm sure that's all it was." Greer swallowed.

Lannie's smile tightened. "I've already prepared more of the chamomile tea he likes. I even found some honey to add to it."

Chamomile tea was his favorite and tended to help him sleep. It didn't prevent the nightmares, but if Will was calm enough, they were less likely to get out of hand.

Will raced over to us, eagerly describing how the plant with the wide leaves was, in fact, a 'dragon' plant that had sprouted from the fallen feathers of small, playful dragons who loved to frolic in water.

He broke away, dashing a few steps ahead to tell us about another.

Will had always been prone to dreams. Most were fanciful tales, but they had been growing darker over the years.

Stronger.

He was an imaginative boy. They were dreams. Nothing more. Still, my stomach refused to settle and my sisters, though putting on a good show for Will, were on edge. It was in the slight drawback of Lannie's shoulders and the too-much-teeth showing in Greer's smile.

They were only dreams. They had to be. If only we could believe that.

CHAPTER 27

I ATE QUICKLY, SPURRED ON BY BOTH MY APPETITE AND MY eagerness to start my history lessons with Alarik. The quicker I got this over with, the quicker I could train. If that meant I'd have to sit through a few lectures, so be it.

My siblings and I bid each other goodnight. Will thoroughly enjoyed his chamomile tea with an extra spoonful of honey and insisted on sleeping in his own room. After a subtle debate, he agreed to keep his door open for Greer just in case *she* woke up afraid and needed to find him.

Sparing a few minutes to change into a comfortable pair of sweats and brush my teeth, I made my way toward the third floor. Whispers of bedtime stories drifted into the hall as I crept passed Will's room. Both of my sisters were with him. Hopefully, they'd be a soothing presence if any nightmares arose.

Gods, I missed reading stories to him. When he was a toddler, he only wanted *me* to read, but now, he mostly demanded Greer, claiming she was better at 'doing the voices.' Some days, I still viewed him as that little toddler, and others I caught glimpses of the man he would become. My heart squeezed as I realized just how fast time was moving.

Climbing the last few steps, I reached the landing. A large pair of innately carved, blue double doors were opened wide, revealing a huge foyer staged with a couch and chairs.

I stepped through, only to realize that this wasn't just a sitting room. The long walls were lined with bookshelves, complete with curved edges that allowed a ladder to glide easily along the track spanning the length of the room. A light wooden table sat against the far wall with a few books stacked beside a pair of notebooks. A dark pot of ink and two quills were placed in the center. That must be where we would study.

On the opposite side of the room, the walls of books were broken up by a grand fireplace, complete with a white marble mantle. Embroidered plush chairs and a matching sofa sat before the black netted screen, the contented flames flickering with life.

"Wow," I whispered beneath my breath. And this was just the sitting room. I spotted a hallway at the other end, branching off into various rooms. No wonder he was used to getting his way. He was a king among men.

"I'm glad you find it impressive."

A small shriek left my body as I spun, my fist lashing out of its own accord.

Alarik flinched back, but not quick enough. He groaned, bending forward as he clutched his nose.

"Gods, I'm so sorry." I bit my lip, searching for anything to mop up the thin ribbon of red dripping from his pinched nose.

He muttered something beneath his breath that definitely contained a few curse words as he stalked past me. When he reappeared from a room in the back, it was with a towel clutched to his nose.

"I really am sorry, but you can't just sneak up on people and expect them not to react."

He lifted a brow as I raised my chin. Dabbing at the slowing stream of blood, he let the silence stretch.

With one last check to ensure the bleeding had stopped, he retreated down the hall once more, exchanging the soiled towel for a stack of books. He walked over to the table, carefully lying them between the quills and ink.

"I don't blame you for..." He waved a hand at his face, still speaking toward the table. "I shouldn't have startled you."

Was that a blush on his cheeks? I wasn't sure what to say. In the end, I decided a change of topic would be best. "This room is beautiful. I can't believe you live here. A general's salary must be impressive."

He fidgeted as he turned to face me, running a hand through his growing blond locks. "Actually, most of this is owned by my family. I told you my father was part of the military. My mother's family was a descendent of one of the few human families to climb the ranks of the fae courts of old. It was centuries ago, but they were favorites of the Earth Kingdom. Together, they were very well off."

I blinked. "Wait, you're General Holt, as in Holt Academy, the owner of this entire base?"

"I've asked everyone to stop using that name. This is now Camp Bellum."

"Gods, Alarik—General Holt. You could have said something. No wonder everyone nearly fainted when I slapped you."

He grimaced. "It's not like you didn't know my name, but I liked you not making the connection. And I deserved that slap. I was being an ass."

I raised a brow. "I agree."

A little warmth crept into his eyes as he stepped toward me, his voice softening. "I liked not having to be 'General Holt' with you. I'd forgotten who I was without all of this." His hand swept the room as he took another slow, deliberate step. My stomach flipped.

"When I saw you in the forest that first day, you had no clue who I was. I couldn't bring myself to ruin that. It's been so long since someone has seen me, the real me. Not since—" His eyes grew distant a moment before he cleared his throat. "It's just been a while. And then there you were."

Another step. My heart missed a beat, and then desperately tried to make up for it.

He closed the distance between us, one of his hands reaching out to claim mine. I kept my gaze fixed to where his thumb traced circles across my palm, the small movement unleashing something foreign and wild within me.

His other hand drifted up, tilting my chin until I met his eyes. They searched mine for a moment. I swallowed, unsure what he was looking for, and scared of what he would find. His lips twitched, a small, subtle movement, and then he was leaning in, sending my heart thundering into a frenzied rhythm.

Footsteps echoed along the marble floors, snapping the spell around us. I leapt away from Alarik a moment before Vidarr strolled in carrying a stack of books. He paused, noting my flushed cheeks, before swinging his gaze toward Alarik, whose eyes still traced the lines of my face.

Vidarr shot me a wicked smirk as he deposited the books on the table. "My apologies. I didn't realize it was *that* type of study date."

My cheeks flamed as I stuttered an excuse, but Vidarr just shook his head as he retreated toward the doors.

"I only came to make sure you two weren't at each other's throats, but I can see that won't be a problem." He turned, hands poised on the doorknobs. "I'll just shut these for you two." He gave one last roguish grin before closing the doors behind him.

I buried my head in my hands. "I cannot believe that just happened."

When Alarik didn't answer, I looked up. He had a mischievous glint in his eyes. "What exactly happened?"

My answering glare shook free a wave of laughter.

"Don't worry. I trust Vidarr with my life, and my secrets."

"So, I'm a secret?"

He shot me a grin. "Not yet."

I didn't smile back. "Maybe I'm not interested in being another one of your *secrets*."

He cocked his head to the side, detecting the venom in my voice. His face grew serious as he stared. "Have you ever been in a relationship?"

My lips thinned.

"That's a no," he said, studying me a moment longer. My cheeks grew pink under his perceptive gaze. I felt exposed; vulnerable. It was an uncomfortable foreign feeling. Then his eyes grew wide, his mouth dropping open. "Oh."

"Oh?" I mocked. "What exactly does that mean?"

"Nothing, it's just, I thought you had been with others. I didn't think a kiss would be such a big deal." He ran a hand through his hair, offering a small, gentle smile.

My lungs filled with a frustrated breath as I felt a fresh wave of heat scorch my cheeks. "Just because I don't feel like kissing you doesn't mean I've never kissed anyone before."

I knew he was attempting to be kind, that his ridiculous smile was meant to be soothing, but it felt more like mocking than accepting. He lifted a brow at my outburst, but didn't rise to the challenge. He just waited, his face uncharacteristically open and devoid of teasing. Holding on to my fury, I let it shield me a moment longer. Still, he waited.

Releasing a long shaky breath, I said, "I've kissed other men, just... not many. And I haven't ever felt the need to go further."

His eyes widened at my admission.

"It's not like I didn't have opportunities. Something would always go wrong before we got to that part. Most of the guys I met were upset when they realized I could challenge them in areas like hunting or snares and stuff. Everything would be fine between us and then they'd spout some nonsense about how I should be at home helping Will, or how I should wear gloves because my hands would look nicer if they didn't have any callouses."

I needed to stop rambling, but gods, he just kept staring at me with that wide-eyed expression. "But my skills with a bow and snare kept my family alive. They are pieces of who I am. I can't change them." I bit my lip to stop the words from spiraling further.

"Alarik, please. Can you stop looking at me like that?" The plea in my voice seemed to snap him out of whatever daze he had been stuck in.

He closed the distance between us in two quick steps. I stilled, nearly forgetting to breathe. Lifting my fingers to his lips with unexpected gentleness, he brushed soft kisses across the rough skin.

"These are nothing to be ashamed of. They are a testament to your strength and resourcefulness." He pressed a single kiss to each of my palms, his eyes trained on mine, before letting our hands drift apart. "You're beautiful, El."

A flush crept up my cheeks, but I held his gaze. His eyes were a myriad of green, the bright inflections of newly sprouted leaves speckled through the darker mossy tones, much more complex than I had first thought.

My eyes dropped to his lips, full and capable of imparting such tenderness. What would they feel like against my own?

I tilted my head forward at the very moment he took a step back. Clearing his throat as he turned away, he retreated the few steps toward the table. A brutal sting of rejection sliced through me. Hadn't that been his intention just moments ago? To kiss me? Had he changed his mind already?

"There are *actual* lessons we need to get to." He gestured toward a wooden chair opposite him as he took a seat.

I forced a smile as I sat. "Of course."

Alarik selected a particularly thick volume, the binding was cracked in several places and the pages thoroughly worn. He flipped through a few chapters before turning the books toward me.

"Are you familiar with this version of Pax's history? Human history?" I took in the painting depicted across the pages. It was a map of our world, only extended. I recognized the landmass in the middle as Pax—our current world—but there were other pieces of earth surrounding it. A frozen kingdom lay far below Pax's most southern border, the painting gleaming as if it were made of icicles.

The Fire Kingdom along Pax's northwestern border was still there, but vastly expanded. Volcanos reached out for miles into the surrounding sea, the streams of lava displayed with such vibrant hues that it looked as if the page itself had caught fire.

The Dark Kingdom remained nearly untouched, the Jagged Mountains still acting as the western border with the Fire Kingdom, but the Shadowlands of the north appeared more ominous. The Air Kingdom was also pushed further into the northeastern sea, its territory mainly composed of huge islands with sharp, steep cliffs and crashing waves.

"I was shocked, too, the first time I encountered this map." Alarik's voice was soft, almost as if he was worried I would run.

"It's surprising, but I'm more curious than anything. What is this landmass here?" I pointed to a chunk of land to the east of the Light Kingdom, right in the middle of the Sea of Dreams. The word 'Scintillam' was scrawled beneath it in sprawling golden script. The land looked simple, almost peaceful compared to the complexity of Pax, with soft undertones of small flowers and flowing grasses.

"That was the original human continent, Scintillam. It means spark. Fitting, is it not? Considering how they perceive human life—no more than a quick flash in time, a mere spark, to the mighty fae." The lightness of his voice had taken on an edge. "This is a map of Ferox, a time before the fae kingdoms."

I looked over the map once more, realizing there weren't any lines dividing the land. Disbelief gave way to anger. "How did I not know about this? How does the world not know about this?"

"Humans, El, *humans* don't know of it. I'd wager the fae do, well at least the royals. From what we have learned, there was a harvesting of old stories centuries ago. All were burned, and any temples or artwork depicting them were destroyed. We discovered this," he pointed down to the detailed map of Ferox, "in a small chamber at the base of one of the ransacked temples."

"What else did you find?"

"It describes a time of mighty beings who housed the combined powers of the fae, near god-like in their strength. They were called the Merged and ruled over Ferox a few millennia ago. There may have been creatures older and even more ruthless than them, but it was a time of chaos, one without morals or ethics. The legend states that the gods of this realm crafted humans to quell the ruthlessness of their first creations, but the Merged viewed humans as nothing more than toys, something to enjoy for a time and then discard when bored—or broken."

He flipped the pages until an army of fae were poised for battle, but I couldn't tell which kingdom they belonged to. They had an array of traits: horns, fangs, shimmering skin and gills. And wings. Great wings stretched wide across the page, some with feathers as seen with air fae, but others had dark, leathery membranes stretched across sharp bones, more befitting of bats than birds.

Alarik's finger circled Scintillam. "The Goddess saw the agony her beloved mortals suffered, and warded this continent against fae, saving the surviving humans from further harm. As for the mortals who were already on this land..." he pointed to the warped version of Pax, as he continued. "Those unlucky bastards were left to the whims of the Merged—forsaken and forced to carve out a future among the bedlam surrounding them."

"We were never meant to be here in the first place." I huffed out a strangled laugh.

"No, El," his voice cut. "*They* were never meant to be so cruel. We are not the problem in this world, even the Goddess seemed to understand that."

"What does this mean? That there's a protected island where humans can live safely?" Excitement rang through my voice, but my burning hope quickly cooled when I pulled my attention from the painting back to his eyes.

He shook his head as he flipped the page to reveal a monstrous wave rising up from the Sea of Dreams, a looming wall blotting out the sun across a continent of rolling hills and gentle streams. "The Merged attacked Scintillam. Since they were unable to breach its borders, they sank the entire continent, drowning the rest of humanity along with it." My stomach twisted.

"The point of me telling you this is to make sure you understand our enemy. Most fae today may not be as ruthless as the Merged, but it would make sense that there's at least a group of extremists, like the ones who attacked us, who somehow constructed the storm."

I looped a piece of stray hair around my finger, twisting and twirling it, as I thought through all of this. "In order to understand your opponent's strategy, you must first understand your opponent. I get it, but you've already confirmed the Dark Kingdom is most interwoven with human blood, making them the least likely suspects for our current problem."

His face was grim as he nodded.

"There goes our number one suspect. The entire world thinks the dark fae are responsible for the recent attacks."

"I know," he muttered, running a hand through his hair. "They still might be responsible, or at least a faction within the

Dark Kingdom, but it seems less likely. If anything, the southern kingdoms have wanted to maintain fae bloodlines more so than the north."

My head cocked to the side as I flipped through the book, coming to another image of the Merged. This one revealed a great king with serpent-green eyes, the pupils thin, vertical slits. He had vast reptilian wings spread wide and fangs peeking out beneath a wicked smile. The light seemed to cast a luminescent glow along the skin of his neck, just beneath his ears. Could that be the hint of scales? The thinly written inscription read: *Dragcor, Tamer of Winds*.

"It looks like I *do* have a lot of catching up to do." I sighed.

His eyes were calculating. "Yes, you do."

"What is it? You look like you're debating telling me something. I need you to be honest with me."

He leveled me with a look. "There are certain things that I won't be able to tell you because of my position. Things that bleed into every aspect of my life."

I forced my breathing to remain steady and my face neutral. We were not only discussing my place among the base, but also where I fit into Alarik's world. He was warning me, testing out my interest. If we were to pursue anything further between us, there would be things we would have to deal with.

The idea of an 'us' caused my stomach to flip… and it wasn't a completely uncomfortable feeling.

After a long moment, I dipped my head in a slow nod. "I understand."

"Do you?" he asked, voice unusually small. He pushed from the table, pacing in front of the walls of books. "I'm the general, El."

"I'm aware, Al." He pinned me with a glare. I smiled with a shrug, "Thought I'd test out the nick-name."

"Don't"

"Suit yourself." I shrugged again. "I kind of like it. Al and El. El and Al."

"Stop."

I smiled, coming to stand but remaining at the table. "I get that you are the general and there are things you won't be able to share with me."

He frowned, but nodded.

"There's more?"

"There is. Much more." I watched as an array of emotions filtered across his face, each too quick to comprehend. "This base is my priority. It's the only thing I can focus on."

His words rang with a tired, sad warning. *I* could never be his focus. There was an odd crumpling of something in my chest.

"There was a time when I thought I could have both. I thought I could be the general everyone needed and also have a person to call my own." He shook his head, not meeting my gaze. "I was wrong."

I felt it then, a little crack in my armor—like a chasm opening within me, wanting to comfort him, to somehow heal his unhealable wound.

Stepping around the table, I neared. "I understand."

He looked up, the sheen of his eyes reflecting my own. "Do you?"

I nodded, because I did. He was broken from whatever horrors haunted his past. But so was I. Our stories may not be the same, but I was far from being ready to commit myself to another. My family was my priority, just as the base was his.

He needed me to understand that I could never be his everything. He wouldn't put me first over the lives of his men. He couldn't.

"I understand, but do you?"

He searched my face, and I let him. Against every comfort I had grown accustomed to, I left myself open. I left myself vulnerable, if only for a moment, so that he could see I wasn't able to be his person either.

My family was my priority, yes, but it went beyond that. I wasn't sure I knew how to peel back the layers I had constructed, even if I'd wanted to. Not anymore. I'd lived with the walls too long.

There was an unforeseen tremble of my stoic heart, as if the weakened muscle was stretching, desperately trying to recall how to run on something other than the monotonous thrum of blood. I realized that despite this being a terrible idea, despite his confession and mine, I didn't want this to end. Whatever this was between us.

"This doesn't mean we can't be honest with each other. It may take some work, or adjusting, but..." He said the words as if they escaped of their own volition, bursting from his lips without his permission. "But I'm willing to try if you are."

Try. Willing to try. To try what exactly, I don't think either of us knew. But we both somehow needed it.

"Okay," I said, a shadow of a smile gracing my lips.

He looked down at me, his eyes shimmering with an unnamed emotion. "Okay."

CHAPTER 28

"Elara, are you in there, lass?" Vidarr's deep voice sounded from the other side of the door.

I sat up with a jerk, the book I'd fallen asleep reading hitting the floor with a clash. Growling in frustration, I quickly placed it on the bedside table before dashing over to the armoire.

"Just a minute!"

I was late for my first day of training. A slew of curses left my lips as I yanked on pants and laced up my boots. Rushing to the bathroom, I brushed my teeth and swiped a hair tie off the counter before heading for the door.

"I'm ready," I breathed as I stepped into the hallway. Vidarr was leaning against the far wall, tattooed arms crossed against his chest. He gave me a quick look over, seemingly satisfied with what he found, before heading down the hall leaving me to follow.

"Late night?" He snickered over his shoulder.

I stumbled, before shooting him a glare as I rushed to catch up. Working my fingers through my knotted hair, I swiftly braided it back. "No. Well, yes, but only because I was reading."

He glanced over at me, a brow cocked. "It's been a while

since Alarik has felt comfortable enough to *read* with someone. I wouldn't take it lightly."

"We weren't—we didn't." I took a deep breath, desperately trying to quell the spike of jealousy that rose at the mention of other *reading* partners. "We were only studying. I'm expected to return to the trading market for an update on Alderidge, which shouldn't be a problem, but Alarik mentioned a mission along the Dark Kingdom's southern border. He said you'd fill me in this morning."

"It seems you two really were reading."

I rolled my eyes. Had anyone besides Vidarr implied as much, my fingers would be itching for a dagger.

"Yes, we were," I repeated as we strolled along the dirt road, turning away from the shining sun and toward the closest training facility. "Besides, it sounds like Alarik has his pick of reading buddies."

The words were sharper than I'd intended, but Vidarr's lack of denial stung far worse. A sourness coated my throat at the thought. It didn't matter, I reminded myself.

"Alderidge is important," Vidarr muttered. "But sources still point to the trading market as a possible meet up for the dark fae. They are the priority." I nodded, appreciating the change in topic.

"And the other task?"

"The other is still evolving. We've heard of a sanctuary of sorts for women and children. There may be witnesses."

My eyes widened. "Witnesses as in, survivors from the attacks?"

"That's the rumor. Up until now, it's only been burned villages and rotting bones, but survivors would change everything. If anyone could describe the assailants, how they moved between towns without leaving tracks, what they looked like, how they attacked, we may just have a chance at getting ahead of this."

We followed a line of soldiers through a set of double doors and into a vast building complete with sparring equipment, weights, weapons, and a few punching bags dangling from the ceilings.

"I thought just the two of us were training." I frowned, noting the number of men here.

"I debated it, but Evander thought you could handle the sorting." He deposited me with a wink among the clustered group in the center before taking a spot at the head of the room.

My stomach twisted with fluttering uncertainty as I took in the men surrounding me. They were a varied sort. Some looked as if they'd grown up here, laughing and joking, their toned bodies brazenly showing off years of dedicated work. Others reflected my own hesitation, their thinner frames and awkward stances pegging them as new recruits.

Vidarr's voice rumbled with low command, hushing the side conversations with ease. "Good morning, men and woman." He inclined his head in my direction, earning me a few curious stares. "We have a new student joining those who have recently passed their courses, which means that today will be a day of matches."

Cheers echoed throughout the high-ceilinged room as the men jeered and whistled. Vidarr waited for the celebration to die down before continuing. "Be aware that today will not only be assessing our new recruits, but also reevaluating each person's skill level, providing an opportunity to adjust your rank."

There was a low grumbling with those words, but Vidarr ignored them. "Your rank will decide your training groups, and therefore which missions you qualify for. We will start with some warmup drills before I announce the pairings. Those who are content to remain in their current positions may be excused from today's sorting. It's a great day to prove your worth. Take a lap."

I merged with the others, keeping pace in the middle of the pack, as we jogged around the building a few times. With a whistle from Vidarr, the herd turned toward the center, taking me with it until we formed a circle around him. He led us through simple drills and gentle stretches, walking among us until he commanded our attention, once more.

The pairings were decided, starting with the weakest and least experienced—meaning I would go first.

"Elara, Dustin, you're up. Take your positions."

I stepped into the nearest half of the circle, adrenaline pumping through my body, as a young man, probably around Lannie's age, took the position opposite me. He looked like he was about to faint.

"The first round will be hand-to-hand combat," Vidarr explained. He shifted his body closer to the two of us, dropping his tone so only we could hear. "This has been the most effective way we've found for improving skills. The purpose is not to shame but rather to understand where strengths lie, and to discover where weaknesses are, so that we may work to overcome them.

"We follow standard sparring rules? No punches to the face no blows aimed at the knees."

My opponent managed to control most of his trembling as we nodded, strapping protective gear in place and securing our gloves.

The point values flashed across my mind: one point for a landed blow to the body, two for a spinning kick to the body or bringing your opponent to the ground. Three points for landing a hit to the head, but four for a spinning kick to the head.

"First to five points wins."

We both nodded, too nervous to speak. I held my gloves out in the center of the ring, remembering Evander's advice to always show respect. Dustin smiled a little, his arms shaking as he tapped his gloves to mine.

A whistle sounded, jerking our bodies into a slow circling motion as we searched for an opening. I did my best to block the sounds of shouting and cheering around us, knowing I needed to keep this simple. All I needed to do was get to five points before he did.

Dustin balked, swinging wide with his right and throwing his entire body off balance. I was able to sidestep and land a hit to his ribs, making sure to keep it soft. This was about skill, not strength.

We regrouped in the middle of the circle, moving into action once more as the whistle blew. Dustin launched forward with little preamble, attempting to catch me off guard, but his movements were sloppy.

I turned aside, causing his gangly form to sail past. Taking advantage of his incoordination, I twisted my body around, lifting my leg as I spun. I held my foot in the air, a breath away from contact, and then completed the kick by gently tapping the cushion across his head, earning points for the move but not harming him.

"Elara wins the first round," Vidarr announced. "Nice spirit, Dustin."

Dustin's pale face broke into a bashful smile as the men around us cheered. The cluster nearest Dustin clapped him on the back, welcoming him into the fray. It looked like he had three older brothers at the base, all here to see his first match. They flashed him proud smiles, giving me a nod of thanks.

Taking up a position along the wall, I watched as the rest of the matches progressed, dropping the number of fighters to half. Vidarr read off the new set of pairs—starting with me.

I entered the ring, my eyes traveling up, as I took in the man before me. He was much larger, at least a head taller than I was, and a good deal heavier.

"Remember, light contact only," Vidarr instructed, clearly

unhappy with this pairing. Shaking his head, he said. "First to five points wins."

The whistle sounded.

"Good luck, girl." My opponent sneered.

His large fist flew toward me a moment later. His form was decent, but he was slow. I was able to deflect the first blow, causing his smirk to falter. He lashed out again and again, only to come up empty as I danced away.

His form grew wilder with each failed attempt, and I smirked, knowing the small gesture would send him over the edge. He snarled, throwing his fist forward in frenzied abandon, just as I knew he would. I spun on the balls of my feet, dodging it easily, as I came around to land a punch along his ribs.

Cheering rang around us, but my pride was short-lived. The smirk had done its job too well.

His face contorted with rage as he whipped around, not bothering to wait for the whistle to begin his assault. He swung, the force of which would've been powerful enough to knock me unconscious. I sidestepped the last just in time, landing a spinning kick to his flank before dashing to the opposite side of the circle.

Three to zero. The crowd roared as my opponent hissed. The whistle blew before I could appreciate it and he was hurling toward me once more. Form forgotten, his arms pummeled the air around me. I kept my fists up and head down, my pulse thundering in my ears as I fought to stay ahead of his deadly wrath.

There. There was my chance. He twisted back, intent on landing a kick to my face, but I slipped inside, planting a soft blow across the padding of his head.

A whistle pierced the room, calling an end to the match. My shoulders slumped and the subtle buzzing in my ears subsided, but as I turned around, I saw he was beyond hearing.

Curses tore through his throat as he closed in. I leapt back, barely staying ahead of the raging attack. Cheers turned into warnings as the crowd urged him to cease. The match was over, but he didn't seem to care. I stumbled back, arms flying wide as I tumbled to the floor.

A vicious grin flashed across his face as he cocked his arm back, fist clenched.

—crack!

Before I had a chance to react, Vidarr was standing over me. Silence rang through the room, interrupted only by the resounding thud of my opponent falling to the ground, knocked out with a single punch.

"I expect rules to be obeyed." Vidarr's fist clenched, his order made more menacing by its steady delivery. This man didn't need to yell to get his point across. He motioned for a few of the officers to carry the unconscious lump away as I righted myself.

"Elara is the winner of this match." He gave a dip of his head in my direction before addressing the silent crowd. "Next."

The second round passed quicker than the first, as more people were eliminated. The back half of the building housed the men in the losing brackets. They had two to three matches going at a time, working through the final pairings to determine their rank.

I used each minute I had to rest and gather my strength. Before I knew it, round two had finished and Vidarr was announcing the pairs for round three—only seven people left.

"Elara, Zelos, you two are next." Vidarr motioned for us to step into the circle and take our positions. Shaking out my remaining nerves, squared up to my next partner. Zelos, the name rushed over me. I had seen him around. He was always training.

Just as we stepped into the ring, the room's natural buzz hushed to a dull rumble. Everyone in the immediate vicinity quieted, spines straightening as General Alarik Holt entered the arena. He made his way over to Vidarr, muttering something too low to hear, before both turned to watch us.

A frown formed on my lips as I took in Alarik's unreadable expression. But what had I been expecting? A brief smile? A nod of encouragement? I didn't need any special treatment. We weren't even a *thing*, I reminded myself. Again.

"Elara, Zelos, take your positions," Vidarr instructed.

Okay, time to focus. I forced myself to ignore Alarik's presence. Right now, he was just another figure in the crowd, because facing Zelos was going to require all of my attention.

He was a great deal taller than me, with tanned, sculpted muscles throughout his body. He was strong, but lean enough to not be burdened by the extra weight, and those clever honey brown eyes surrounded by thick lashes were sizing me up.

I blinked. No, not sizing me up... but checking me out. His chin leaned against his thumb and forefinger as if he were working through a difficult problem. Dark lashes drifted over my body as his full lips split into a smirk. "This is the big leagues now, sweetheart. Are you sure you want to mess up that pretty face of yours?"

A few of the men behind Zelos snickered, but the whistle blew and we began to circle. Zelos still had that smirk on his face, filled with unconcerned arrogance. "Let's dance, sweetheart."

He forced us around the ring once more, toying with me as I struggled to find an opening. I stepped forward, baiting him into a quick jab. I was able to sidestep the blow—barely. He was faster than the others and quicker to recover, leaving no chance for me to retaliate.

Carefree laughter issued from him, making my pulse race, but I kept my form in check.

"Nicely done, sweetheart. You almost had me. Most women want me pounding their pussies, not their pretty little faces, but I may have to make an exception for you—"

Whack! My leg stung as I landed a solid blow to his ribs. I'd faked right, knowing that I'd favored my right side in the previous matches. I'd hoped Zelos was cocky enough to assume I couldn't deliver a blow with my left. His mistake.

He flinched with the force of the hit. I knew we were supposed to keep things to 'light contact', but his mouth had my blood boiling. He deserved to have a few bruises.

One point down.

Zelos's smirk was gone, tempered with the sting of embarrassment. His jaw ticked as he regrouped. He prowled around me letting the snickering of his friends fuel his movements and unnerve mine.

"You know, I think you'd look a lot better on your knees."

He lashed out, quick as lightning. Two stinging blows hit me, one on each side of my stomach, causing me to buckle over, knees crashing to the ground in front of him. My arms wrapped around my lungs as I desperately gasped for air.

Leaning down, he brought his lips to my ear, but made sure to speak loud enough for all to hear. "Right where you're meant to be, sweetheart. You look so pretty at my feet, mouth open and waiting for me."

My teeth slammed shut with a snarl. Shoving myself up, I made the mistake of glancing over at Alarik. His jaw ticked. He took a step toward me, fists clenched, but Vidarr halted him with a sharp glare.

Ignoring the aching throb across my lower ribs, I turned back to Zelos. No distractions. The whistle sounded.

I moved, feigning right before rounding left. He deflected the blow easily, using the opening to take a shot at my already battered center. My arm came up, just in time to take the hit. I leaned into the block, using the momentum to twist my body around as I spun into a crouch. I lashed out with my leg, sending him to the floor as I swiped his legs out from under him.

Three to two, in my favor.

The whistle had barely blown before he was on me, raining blows—right then left—each one forcing me to yield a step as I kept my head protected. Just as I thought he was tiring, he arched back, leg kicking forward to connect with my chest, throwing my body back with the force of it.

I slammed onto the floor, teething rattling as I struggled to remember how to breathe. Rolling to my stomach, I pulled in a searing gulp of much needed air. He only needed one more point, while I needed at least two.

Swallowing the sour taste in the back of my throat, I righted myself to a standing position. Refusing to meet Alarik's eyes, I took a few humiliating steps back into the sparring circle.

Fire ripped through me with each breath, but I raised my hands all the same, lowering myself into a fighting position. I gave a small nod to Vidarr, indicating that I was ready. The whistle blew. Zelos's cocky smirk was back in place as he circled me, a wolf playing with a hare.

"What's with the scowl, sweetheart?" He faked a few hits, not intending to land any. "Couldn't find anyone to take care of you? Forced to play soldier instead? Don't worry. I might be feeling charitable tonight."

His fist lashed out. I deflected the first, and the second, but wasn't fast enough to avoid the whip of his leg crashing into my ribs for the third time today. My body buckled. I was forced to bow forward. He smirked as I fell, crouching next to me as if to help me up.

Head tilting forward, his breath heated the shell of my ear as he spoke the words just for me. "I don't like hurting you, sweetheart, but it's better this way. I'd rather teach you a lesson, then have you get yourself killed."

"I can handle myself," I hissed.

"You *are* feisty, but it's best you leave the protecting to the men. Just look at you." His thumb glided over my bottom lip.

"This mouth was made for far more *sensual* things. I would hate for it to be wasted in war."

"Fuck you," I seethed, but Zelos only laughed.

"You're already on your knees for me. There's no need to beg for it—."

"Enough." Alarik's voice cut through the rumble of laughter as he came to our side.

I forced myself to stand, my battered stomach twisting further, as I took in Alarik's clenched fists.

Vidarr was there in a flash, separating the two. "Okay, the match is over. Zelos won this set. Elara, head over to the back wall and join the others. Zelos, go get some water."

"I'm not thirsty, sir," he challenged, staring up at Alarik.

"I appreciate the nerve it takes to stare down your general, but there's no contest here. Go get some fucking water before we're building you a funeral pyre."

Alarik flexed his fist, barely keeping himself in check. Zelos held eye contact for a moment longer before dropping his gaze. "Yes, sir," he said, blowing through the group along the edge of the ring and rushing from the building.

Vidarr leaned into Alarik, speaking quickly and quietly, making sure their conversation was not overheard. "What are you doing?"

"What does it look like I'm doing? You heard what he was saying."

"Yeah, I did, but that's all it was: talk. If Elara expects to join this team, she's going to hear a lot worse. Zelos may be a prick, but he's one of the best fighters we have. He was fighting clean. Elara was the one who increased the intensity of the blows. He only matched the pace she set."

Alarik barked an indecipherable reply before turning toward me. "Let's get you to the infirmary."

His hand gripped my shoulder, guiding me away from the

ring and toward the exit. Vidarr's voice called the next pair and the sparring resumed.

"Wait, what? I have to finish the matches to see where I rank."

"The matches are over. The seven participants who make it to the third round are grouped together, though they normally like to keep going until they have a winner. You're done for the day."

He tugged on my arm once more, leading me toward the doors. I looked over my shoulder at the others gathered around the rings, laughing and cheering. That's where I should be, with those I'd be fighting alongside.

"Alarik, I'm fine, really. It was just a few punches. I'm the one who increased the intensity of the hits. It was fair."

"True, but I know why you did it. The whole training facility heard him," he growled. "He's lucky he didn't get a black eye."

"You can't go around punching every jerk here. I shouldn't have let him get to me. I can handle it." I laced my hand with his, giving it a small squeeze of reassurance before letting go.

His taut shoulders released with an exhale. "Maybe, but that doesn't mean I don't want to."

He sounded bewildered by the thought. My chest expanded, buzzing with warmth as he led us toward the infirmary. I kept the smile from blooming fully, but I couldn't stifle the small tilt of my lips that surfaced.

I knew there were barriers between us, but with his words ringing in my ears and the way his arm wrapped around my waist as he led us away from the others, I allowed myself a moment to believe there wasn't.

CHAPTER 29

"I TOLD YOU, I'M FINE." I'D REPEATED THE PHRASE SO MANY TIMES that the words started to sound muddled.

"She's right, General," the healer confirmed, blanching when he caught Alarik's glare. He cleared his throat before facing me. "You suffered severe bruising on your lower ribs, with slight bruising to your left kidney. I recommend you rest for today—" Alarik cleared his throat. "Umm, for the next three days and drink a lot of water. The bruising will take a week or two to clear. If anything gets worse, come back and see me."

He ran out of the room before I could argue.

Sitting up, I pulled down my shirt before carefully working my arms through the jacket and shot Alarik a glare. "You want me to sit out of training for three days? I glared.

Alarik raised his hands in surrender. "That was the healer's advice, not mine."

"You completely influenced his decision! Three days is ridiculous. Nobody else was told to wait three days." I gestured to the surrounding beds just out of earshot beyond the flimsy curtain. There were a few others who had been treated for minor cuts and bruises. All were cleared to return to training without restrictions.

"I'll be returning with everyone else tomorrow." I stepped around his glaring form, intending to stomp from the building without so much as looking back, but faltered when I caught the chime of Lannie's voice.

Following the sounds of my sister's voice, I came to an open door, catching site of an older man seated at a desk with an official looking document hanging behind him: Horace Grant, Master of Healing, Human Studies. Listed below his name and title in bright gold letters, were the words: *inde lucem vitae.*

Lannie was sitting opposite him, turning as soon as I popped my head into view. "Ellie? What are you doing here? I was just talking to Healer Grant about the salves we could offer—oh. You brought Alarik. Does that mean he said yes?"

Grimacing, I realized I'd forgotten to ask about the healing supplies. I pinned a pleasant enough smile on my face and swiveled to face him. "My sisters create various healing supplies. They were impressed with the selection of plants available in the greenhouse and Cadoc was kind enough to give them his blessing to explore. He told them to get your permission before they started creating supplies."

"We could provide as many salves and tonics as the base needed in return for the supplies," Lannie added, dipping her chin toward Alarik's forearm. "You've already benefited from it. I know I'd be able to improve on that batch with the supplies here. Imagine if every soldier had access to a tin of their own."

Alarik brushed his fingers over the pink, nearly healed claw marks across his forearm, a permanent reminder of our encounter with the distorted fae in the woods. "Her concoction *did* speed up my healing."

Healer Grant's deep brown eyes peered up through bushy grey brows. His voice was slow, drawing out each syllable as he spoke. "If Miss Tenebris can construct the type of healing supplies she was describing, then I would be very interested."

Lannie's smile stretched wide, her deep brown eyes brightening.

"I am also in need of help around here. It is no secret that attacks have been increasing. I would like to see if you have the talents of an apprentice."

Lannie's jaw fell open.

He cocked his head to the side. "I suppose if you really don't want—"

"Yes!" She cleared her throat, dropping her voice back to a reasonable level. "I would love to. I never thought to ask. Your skills are—"

"Yes, yes. Not to worry, child," he said, waving away her praise like it was nothing. "I look forward to working with you, as well. Why don't you prepare a few of these salves over the next few days and we can put them to use this week?"

"Of course. It would be my honor."

He nodded before shooing us from his office.

"Let's discuss terms," Alarik stated as the door closed behind us. "Draft a list of the supplies you require. You will have unlimited access to the greenhouse and will keep whatever profits you make outside the base. In exchange, you will heed Healer Grant's instructions and provide whatever he requires."

"Agreed." Lannie grinned, stepping into the early evening air. "Greer will be so happy. I can't believe I get to train with Healer Grant. Did you know he learned in the Light Kingdom, meaning he trained with the light fae. The light fae!"

"I'm sure he'll be impressed with your skills. My cut hardly left a scar and it's incredible the puncture wounds on Alarik's forearm didn't fester."

Alarik ran a hand over the pink scars. "Thank you, again, for your help."

A proud smile blossomed, her cheeks the lightest tint of pink. "You're welcome."

"My brilliant sister, saving the general."

Alarik shook his head with a chuckle and walked ahead.

"I think we finally made it, El," she whispered. "After all these years of trying to keep Will safe, now we have a chance to do things for ourselves."

My heart sank a little at her words. Sometimes it was easy to forget that I wasn't the only one making sacrifices. My sisters had been beside me, every step of the way, each of us doing our part to make this life the best it could be.

Especially for Will. Greer and I cared for him often enough, but Lannie had been the one figuring out which teas would help break fevers when he was sick and which ointment to rub across his chest to help when his breathing was labored.

Now, we were offered a chance to build something else.

I glanced up, catching Alarik waiting for us a few paces ahead. "I think you're right, Lannie. I think this is the start of something good."

CHAPTER 30

"ELARA, I NEED YOU TO CHECK ON YOUR SISTERS AND WILLIAM. DO *not let them near this room. Do you understand?" Mother instructed, a slight bite to her words. Her hands trembled as she lifted them to Torin's bleeding body. She worked endlessly, attempting to reattach the skin along his arm, matching the lengths of curled flesh to the shallow gashes marring his body like some twisted puzzle. Small sputters of light flashed from her hands. The skin sealed, holding for only a moment before slouching off again, bringing with it a fresh wave of scarlet.*

I was transfixed to the spot. Mother's attention never left Torin's body but she spoke to me in the same quiet tone she used years ago, back when she spoke to the parents of ill children. "Torin is not in pain. The fever has placed him in a deep sleep, but I must heal as much as I can before he wakes."

"Yes, Mother," I murmured as I spun for the door, too much a coward to look upon Torin any longer. Jem had looked the same—and he hadn't woken up.

"And, Elara," her eerily calm voice stopped me in the hall. "Stay away from Papa's room."

I blinked the sleep from my eyes, not surprised to find a familiar dampness across my pillow. Grief was finicky. Some days the ache was buried, still lingering in the shadowy depths of my mind but muted for the most part. Other times, the memories replayed, forcing me to relive the worst moments of my life.

My body ached, protesting as I made my way to the sitting room. Deciding to settle into the settee with a book, I let the sleepy hours of the morning drift away until a gentle rapping sounded at my door.

"El, it's me," Lannie's voice called. "Can I come in?"

I leapt up to open the door, winching as my ribs throbbed with the movement. "Hey, Sis. What brings you over?"

Choosing one of the plush chairs across from my own, she answered. "I didn't see you at breakfast and figured you'd like a pastry." She set a small bag on the table where my book rested. "They're not like Sophie's but they're still delicious."

"I could go for a pastry." I grinned, biting into the flaky crust as I waited for Lannie to explain what she was after.

"I heard about the sparring matches yesterday. That's why you were at the infirmary." I swallowed a particularly sweet bite as I nodded. She frowned. "Can I see?"

The beginnings of purpling bruises peppering my ribs came into view as I lifted the edge of my shirt. I sent a silent prayer that today's training would be less physical than yesterday's.

"Gods, El. You really should have told me how banged up you were. I'll make you tea. It should help the bruising and minimize the swelling."

"Thanks, Lannie. Any plans for today?"

"Hello, sisters!" Greer called as the door flew open, unleashing a very talkative Will. "I think you two should spend more time with your brother." Will bounced through the room, looking through closets, climbing over chairs, and checking out the view from the windows.

"Training is in an hour." I protested, before snatching up the books on the table to keep them out of Will's curious hands.

"I thought we were going to work on ointments today." Lannie shot a questioning look at Greer.

"I want to, but what am I supposed to do with Will?" She gestured to where he was currently inspecting the fireplace.

"You don't need to *do* anything with me," Will quipped. "I want to train, like Ellie. I'll just go with her."

My sisters' eyes landed on me.

"Sorry, Will, but I can't have an audience and you're too young for this level of training. Maybe we could see if you can join the other apprentices."

He tilted his head to the side, considering. "I want to be a general now, like Alarik. And he said I should start with learning everything I could. He even loaned me a few books and said I could keep them in my room and everything."

"Wonderful. Let's see if there's an extra spot for you. I'll ask Vidarr today, but until then, how about you get started on reading the books Alarik brought?"

"All right," he called with renewed vigor as he dashed across the hall.

Greer sat down in a huff, massaging her temples. "We've been up for nearly two hours. He said he wanted to walk the base as the sun rose, something about the first rays of light holding hope."

Lannie giggled. "I love his imagination."

"It is fantastic, isn't it?" Greer sighed as a soft smile tugged on her lips. "Okay, I've been stuck in mommy mode. I need some sister time. El, what's going on between you and General Holt?" Her voice turned sultry as she said his name, emphasizing his title.

My heart raced as I recalled the feel of his thumb caressing my hand, the heat of his skin pressing into mine. I shrugged, trying and failing to appear uninterested.

"Oh, my gods! Something *did* happen!" She sat-up, eyes wide. Lannie looked at me as well, an excited spark swirling in her deep eyes. They pulled me over to the plush green sofa.

"Spill!" Greer was practically bouncing with anticipation.

"It's nothing, really. We were just studying and then there was this... tension. Nothing happened, but it almost did. I think we almost kissed." I could feel my cheeks flushing, as Greer let out a high-pitched squeal. "But Vidarr showed up and the moment was over. And then I started rambling about how I basically have no experience with guys."

Lannie nudged me. "That's okay though, right? Did it bother him or something?"

"No, that didn't bother him." I traced a finger over my palm, lingering along the places his lips had been. "He was sweet. I thought he would try to kiss me again but it didn't happen."

Daring a glance up, I met Lannie's wide, hopeful eyes before turning to find Greer's appraising look. Her lips were held in a firm line, chin shifted slightly down.

"Oh no, what's that look for?"

She took a small breath in, before letting the words tumble out. "I just hope you let yourself be happy."

"What do you mean? I am happy."

"I know. It's just that Alarik is a good man. And not just because he is gorgeous, but because he's actually a decent human. Did you know he's been checking in on Will? He wanted to make sure he's adjusting well. He even set me up with an official place in the kitchens. I start next week. With a salary and everything."

"He also approved my apprenticeship with Healer Grant," Lannie chimed in. "It's official at the start of next week."

"I didn't realize he'd done so much."

"He has," Greer said. "Which is why I want to make sure you give him a real chance. Don't take this the wrong way, but you don't exactly let people get to know you. Not that last guy. He was terrible. But the one before that. What was his name? Mike or something?"

"Emmitt."

"Right, Emmitt. What was wrong with him?"

"Nothing was *wrong* with him. He just didn't really want me hunting." My fingers curved, closing over the hardened skin. "He understood the necessity of it before I met him, but wanted me to stop because 'it was weird for a woman to have calluses' and 'even stranger that I could shoot a bow nearly as well as he could'."

"Okay, so maybe he was an ass too. You didn't almost match his skills with a bow, you were *better* than him. A lot better." She shook her head, clearing it of this conversation and getting back on track. "My point is, Alarik is great and so are you. There's no reason why two great people shouldn't be together."

"Neither of us really wants the pressure of labels, but I think we both want to get to know each other."

She lifted a brow. "You'd be open to an actual relationship? Physically and emotionally?"

My cheeks heated as I turned away. "That's none of your business, Greer. Just because you choose to be with guys all the time doesn't mean that I have to."

"Hey! It's not all the time! Gods, El. I've had two serious boyfriends. Two. And this isn't about me. We are talking about you and your inability to be vulnerable."

Lannie's eyes bounced between the two of us, searching for a way to be the peacekeeper, as she normally was. Taking a steadying breath, I met Greer's eyes. "I'm sorry. It doesn't matter how many people you choose to be with or how often. I don't even know why I said that."

"You were deflecting."

"True. Sorry for being a jerk. Forgive me?"

"Duh." She rolled her eyes, "You're my sister. I love you too, and that's why I'm not going to drop the subject."

My face dropped into my hands. "It's not like I'm trying to keep people back. There just hasn't been anyone I've felt comfortable around. I'll work on staying open, okay?"

Greer beamed as she wrapped me in a hug. I flinched, pulling away from the pain in my ribs. "Oh, right. Sorry about that. I only want you to be happy, sis."

"I know. I love you too."

We leaned against the counter as Lannie busied herself with tea.

"Speaking of men, how have things been going with you? It seemed like that bulky guy was into you, the one with the dark hair. Cadoc was it? Any potential?"

She wrinkled her nose. "He's all right. He seems like a decent guy and is definitely nice to look at, but I'm not getting much else out of him. He mentally checks out whenever I talk about healing or baking."

"That's disappointing."

"Yeah. Not a match. I'm still not dating. I like focusing on myself, especially with the opportunity to study in the kitchen. There will be no time for men."

I rolled my eyes, not believing her for a moment. She turned her sights on Lannie. "What about you, little sis? Anyone of interest. I know the base is pretty heavy on the testosterone but there are a few others mulling about."

"No one has caught my attention," she said, handing me a cup of healing tea.

Greer wiggled her brows at me. "It looks like you're going to be the one getting the action, El. And we expect to be told *all* the juicy details."

Shaking my head, I drained the tea in two gulps, savoring the honey-sweet taste. "I have training till about mid-afternoon and then I need to get some reading time in. Meet at dinner?"

"Sounds good. Lannie, are you good with Will?" Greer inquired.

"Yeah, perfect." Lannie said. "We'll see you two tonight."

CHAPTER 31

IGNORING THE ACHING OF MY BRUISED BODY, I HEADED OUT THE door. A quick jog to the training facility proved that Lannie's tea was already working. By the time I arrived, the swelling had considerably lessened, and the pain was minimized to a dull soreness.

Merging with the stream of men entering the building, I stepped throughout the doors to join my team. Numbers were marked through the space, matching the roster mounted near the front with the rankings of yesterday's matches.

My eyes drifted down, finding my name with the others who had made it to round three—including Zelos. I groaned at the thought of seeing him again. I'd have to figure it out, though. We were in the same group now, even if he was a prick.

I moved through the groups toward my team. The six men were chatting easily with one another as I approached. It was clear they'd grown up together, and at the center of the group stood Zelos, his obnoxious smirk firmly in place.

He caught me staring, the easy smile faltering momentarily before widening into a cold sneer. "Hello, sweetheart." The others turned with his greeting, ceasing the conversation. "If you wanted to see me again, all you had to do was ask."

Not falling for the bait, I ignored the comment, and walked past him to the weapons lining the wall. Based on the other groups, it looked like we were training with blades today.

"How are those ribs of yours? A little sore?" I flashed a sanguine smile over my shoulder, fingers drifting across various weapons

"Hardly." He shrugged, but his smile had lost some of its fire. "We all saw you yesterday, sweetheart. You don't belong here."

My spine stiffened as I selected a thin sword, slightly heavier than I would have preferred, but it would have to do. Forcing my features into a mask of confidence, I turned to face him. "I suppose that's a matter of perspective. After all, this weak, little girl managed to land two strikes against you, including the first of the match. Had it been a real battle, I assure you, that first strike would have been the last."

His sneer smoothed out, as a flash of amusement rolled through him. He stepped closer, reaching across me to choose his own blade. "If you're going to make statements like that, you need to have the skills to back it up."

"Who says I don't?"

"Prove it." His lips twitched as his arms swept toward a secluded corner of the room.

My eyes darted through the groups of men, looking for Alarik or Vidarr, but they hadn't arrived yet.

"What? Can't fight me unless the general is here to save you? Do you think he was jealous of how perfect you looked kneeling before me?"

My cheeks flushed as our group let out low whistles.

"Or is that how you *earned* your place here? I always thought the general seemed a bit prudish. Sure, he enjoys some light flirting, the occasional overnight guest, but never anything that would risk his position. Unless..."

Zelos made a show of leisurely looking down my body before his eyes made the slow ascent up. A sinister smile twisted across his face. "Tell me, sweetheart, how many times did you have to fuck him before he promised to train you?"

There was a sharp intake of breath from the men.

"I'm not fucking anyone. I deserve to be here, just as much as the rest of you."

A wicked grin lit his face as he leaned it. "Prove it."

The clash of our blades created an addictive melody as we danced. After his accusations, I expected Zelos to fight dirty, angrily even, but he stayed surprisingly honorable. We spun and ducked, steel chiming, as we dueled. He pushed and taunted, but walked the line of constructive criticism.

The pummel of his sword found the battered flash of my ribs, once again, and I flinched.

"That's the third time your form has dropped."

My lungs expanded in rapid breaths, shocks of pain pulsing across my ribs with each one.

"You say when and we can drop the swords. You know I can make that body of yours feel better."

I rolled my eyes, the last few hours acclimating me well to his particular type of motivation.

"Oh, honey," I pouted with exaggerated sadness. "It would never work between us. It's not me, it's you."

His eyes sparked as his smile grew into a toothy grin. He jerked his chin toward my side. "Do you need to rest, or can you handle a little more?"

"Let's dance," I smirked, wiping the sweat from my brow.

We increased the tempo, becoming little more than a whirl of steel and wind. I was slow to block as he spun, my lack of foresight earning a hit to my face, the pummel splitting the skin along my cheek. But I corrected my mistakes swiftly, and when he too dropped his guard a moment later, I used the same move on him.

He barked out a laugh as he swiped the back of his hand across his newly split lip. Blood trickled from the wound, staining his white teeth. He stood there in stunned silence, eyes shimmering.

"If you're waiting for me to offer to make you feel all better, it's not going to happen."

"Nice work, sweetheart. We may make a soldier out of you, yet." He laughed, the sound light.

Raising a brow, I reached for my waterskin. "Careful, Zelos, that almost sounded like a compliment."

The mirth of his voice echoed through his features, revealing that he would be considered attractive if he wasn't such a tool. I took a gulp of water, searching the area once more.

"You know they aren't coming, right?" My eyes snapped back to Zelos. "The general isn't coming. Neither is the lieutenant. They don't coach every training session. That's why they have officers."

He wiggled his brows, nearly causing me to choke.

"You have got to be joking. You're an officer?"

"The youngest, yet. Don't act like you're surprised. You know I'm talented." His chin tilted up, his brown eyes looking down at me through dark lashes in an amused challenge. Because he *was* talented, but I wasn't about to tell him that.

"Same time tomorrow?" I asked instead.

"Yeah. Get some rest, sweetheart. You're going to need it."

CHAPTER 32

A ROUTINE HAD TAKEN SHAPE OVER THE WEEKS. I'D WAKE AT dawn to join Ember in the mornings. My time with her was more cathartic than anything, composed of liberating sunrise rides or a few rounds through the archery course Vidarr composed.

Training with Zelos took up the rest of the morning, with extra sessions courtesy of Vidarr in the afternoons. Dinner was spent catching up with my siblings while evenings were reserved for history lessons with Alarik, or, at least, they were supposed to be.

We had spent the first week together, but now, most nights he was called away to deal with military matters. Ones that I was not privy to. It bothered me. I hated feeling left out, hated more that Alarik would shoot me a sympathetic look each time Cadoc, or Vidarr, or Evander called him away. Like he expected me to throw a tantrum each time he left. Though, if I was honest with myself, he wasn't too far off the mark.

I wanted to feel like I belonged, and I guess that was the worst of it. I was still an outsider. They had given me fair warning that I'd be treated like any other new recruit, but I couldn't help but wish that things were different, that I could somehow prove my worth quicker.

At least things were going well with Zelos and the others in my training group. Some of the men were still hesitant, but a little more of their stoic pretense was chipped away each day. I wasn't fully accepted, but it looked like I wasn't officially on the outskirts anymore, either.

Today was no different. Zelos's dirty mouth had the others laughing within minutes at my expense, but my responses had them laughing just a little bit harder. My chest warmed as I recalled the cocky tilt of Zelos's smile after one of my particularly crude comebacks referencing the pointy ends of swords and the ability to wield weapons effectively.

My body had grown stronger, adapting well to the new techniques. I wondered if Zelos and Vidarr had been impressed. I wondered if they told Alarik.

The echo of my feet sounded against the marbled steps as I made the routine trip to Alarik's floor. The staff had been sent away for another one of the Select's meetings, leaving the house unusually quiet. I doubted they'd still be here. After an hour or two, the men normally set off to other undisclosed locations. Still, I couldn't help the flutter of hope that hummed in my chest as I neared Alarik's floor. Maybe he'd still be here.

"It's more of the same." Vidarr's voice trickled down the stairs. My foot hovered, pausing mid-step. "Witnesses report seeing the emblem of the Dark Kingdom. The creatures appear to have a myriad of fae traits from across the seven kingdoms, but the same cold black eyes and their skin is leached of color, transfixed into a putrid grey."

Continuing my ascent at a crawling pace, my ears strained against the surrounding silence.

Evander's softer voice spoke next. "Questioning led to nothing further. More ramblings about Neith. I'll send another scout, but its stone walls are that of legends. Whatever ancient power bestowed its protection millennia ago still stands. I can't prove it, but I can feel it slinking across the stones."

"You spoke with the villagers?" Alarik asked.

"Yes," Evander answered. "They believed in the strength of Evulka's sacrifice and wished to stay."

Murmurings continued, but the sounds grew faint. I ascended the last of the stairs, creeping across the landing to the door left slightly ajar. Peeking through the narrowed opening, I found the three of them returning from the hallway in the back.

Evander shook his head. "Possibly, but I don't think we can afford the men at this point."

"It would leave us too vulnerable," Vidarr agreed.

I stretched forward, straining to hear, but my clumsy movements eased the door forward. The subtle creak of hinges was nearly imperceptible. The door had moved only a hair, but Evander's heightened hearing zeroed in on it. Before he could alert the others, I pushed into the room as if it had been my intention from the beginning.

My eyes found Alarik. "Are we still on for our study date?"

His gaze darted to the intricately carved wooden clock on the mantel. "I'm sorry, El. I didn't realize the time. Can you manage without me tonight?"

I managed last night and all of last week. Swallowing the retort, I widened my smile. "I'll survive. I couldn't help but overhear, has there been any new developments?"

Alarik grimaced. "I can't tell you that. You're still technically a recruit, though it sounds like you're flying through the steps, and our study sessions are almost complete."

I opened my mouth to insist on answers, but the quick jerk of Evander's chin told me to let it go. My nostrils flared, but I somehow forced my smile to hold. "Of course. I have plenty to catch up on."

"Wonderful." His eyes sparkled as crossed the room to my side. He lifted a hand, as if to brush back a few of my wayward curls. My breathing hitched as his fingers grew nearer, my head tilting slightly, anticipating the subtle sweep through my hair. But a moment before contact, he let his hand drop.

"Let me know if you need help. I'll try to stop by if I can. We'll have a proper review tomorrow before your mission."

The mission; the return trip to the trading market in Sonder. It wasn't me he wanted to see, not really. I should have known that would be his priority. He waited for my confirming nod, as if I could do anything else but agree. I contemplated it for a moment, considering the consequences of demanding to be included, but Vidarr was here. And Evander. And I was much too prideful to beg.

My strained smile dropped as I turned away, hating the weight that settled in my stomach at knowing he wouldn't be joining me for another night. I knew he was holding me to the same standard he would hold anyone else to. It wasn't personal, but maybe that was the problem. I found myself wishing it were.

Chiding myself at my own foolishness, I returned to my room. After a quick wash and change, I slipped beneath the cool sheets of my bed and lifted a thick volume beckoning me from the nightstand. It was the book Alarik had started with, the one displaying the origins of our world.

The stories were interlaced with stunning painted images of magnificent, lethal creatures, nearly immortal and utterly ruthless. For the powerful, the time before the seven kingdoms—the time of Ferox had been a world of beauty and magic riddled with prophecies foretelling extravagant adventures. For the weak, it had offered only torture and death.

I allowed myself a few more pages before shifting through the small stack of books yet to be read. The title, *The Dark Kingdom, an Overview*, caught my attention. Grimacing, I reached for the volume that was sure to contain blocks of boring facts and dreary documentation, but I needed to understand the dark fae as much as possible with my mission looming. Alarik had confirmed I'd be returning to the trading market in a few days' time and traveling into the Dark Kingdom soon after.

The first few chapters reviewed basic information, a little dreary, but not terribly so: dark fae were bloodthirsty creatures of war, the most skilled in battle and the most feared. But I hadn't known that certain dark fae, mainly those from a royal line, had a particularly heightened affinity for war, one that was only revealed after a fae underwent the settling.

As with most fae, the transition into maturity not only revealed the extent of a fae's powers, but also expanded them. It was around this time that aging greatly slowed. For those who knew little of their parentage, it would also serve as an indication of which kingdom they most closely were related to.

Not all those with fae blood underwent the settling. It was known in areas of human-fae relations that children often weren't able to complete it. Most could still shift, or call on their fae attributes when needed, but were unable to maintain that level of power for long. Others who had only traces of fae heritage could have inclinations toward certain affinities, such as healing, but were, for the most part, human.

Most believed it had to do with the amount of fae blood running through your veins, but, according to this book, not all pure fae lines underwent the settling and not all classes of fae had the ability to draw on the magic of Pax. The ability to shift and possibly complete the settling sounded like it was linked with both the amount of fae blood and the strength of the individual.

I absentmindedly flipped through a few more pages. The settling sounded similar to puberty, but instead of acne, you got extra powers. Wouldn't that be nice.

An image of flesh and shadows snagged my attention, my hands stilling on the page. I focused on the passage beside it: *Out of all fae, the dark fae are considered to be the most primal, their desire for war second only to their desire for pleasure.*

The dark fae are often sought for sexual pleasure. Like the tactics utilized in battle, their abilities allow them to sense the emotions of their partner or partners. This emotional bridge allows the dark fae to better understand their partner(s) response to physical pleasure, allowing for a more satisfying experience for all parties involved.

Dark fae scholars insist that there are many levels to a pleasurable release, pointing out that some are shallow, only allowing the body enjoyment, while others delve deeper, connecting with a being's essence as well as the body to achieve true euphoria. Dark fae believe others too often confuse the physical release of sex with love.

It is theorized that dark fae hold the notion of love to describe a deeper soul connection. Unlike other fae, once a bond of love is established among the dark fae, it is unlikely to waver. Many choose to remain single, avoiding such connections, while others partake in polyamory, finding it a more comprehensive and enjoyable experience. When questioned, most insist that it is rare to find only one who can meet both their physical and spiritual needs. Of note: though there are some who prefer monogamous pairings, which are viewed neither superior nor inferior to the more commonly practiced polyamorous or open relations of the north.

The next chapter will focus on the art of physical pleasure—

I slammed the book shut, puzzled by the tightening low in my belly. Despite the spark of intrigue that had ignited, I knew the dark fae were nothing more than monsters. There shouldn't be anything appealing about them. There wasn't.

Abandoning the book on my pillow, I made a cup of tea before searching through the remaining texts sprawled across the table. I had read nearly all of them. There was only one title left: *War of the Fae Kingdoms.*

Stretching wide on the sofa, I glared at the thick binding. It was sure to be useful, but I had already attempted to wade through its pages twice without success.

Instead, my eyes flickered to a smaller book with worn edges and a broken binding. I'd read it numerous times, but the playful banter of the heroine and her beautifully broken love interest never ceased to spike my interest, not to mention the aftermath of said playful banter.

We hadn't had many growing up, but I'd found a refuge in books, and in the refuge they offered. The tales enthralled me. Reading lightened the mundane burdens of reality. I looked over the particularly thick textbook once more. Well, at least most books did. Reaching my limit of studying for the night, I picked up my favorite romance novel. I was just getting comfortable when a knock sounded at the door.

"Come in," I called, surprised my sisters would bother knocking at all. I turned back to the book, marking my place with a bit of parchment as I was interrupted by another knock.

Leaving my book on the edge of the table, I made my way to the door and swung it open. "I said come in—"

Bright green eyes and sandy blond hair stared back at me. I blinked and then recovered. "Alarik? What are you doing here?"

His eyes widened as they took in my appearance, trailing down along my favorite shirt. It had been washed more times than I could count, and the thin fabric did very little to conceal the lack of undergarments beneath. My chestnut hair was loose, full of messy waves tumbling down my back, the tips falling just short of where Alarik's gaze lingered.

Crossing my arms over my chest, I fought off the hint of a smile. "Is there something you need?"

"You look beautiful."

I snorted, starting to turn away, but the gentle touch of his fingers along my arm stalled me.

He brushed a piece of hair away from my face, his hand tracing the curve of my ear before trailing along my cheek. The gesture was as soft as I had imagined, my skin left burning where his fingers had been. I willed the fluttering of my stomach to calm. He'd been clear about not being able to handle anything resembling a relationship. *We* had been. Besides, that wasn't what I wanted, anyway, I told myself. The thought sounded hollow, even to me.

"I mean it, El. I've never seen you so... relaxed."

"Maybe it wouldn't be such a shock if I'd seen you for more than a handful of minutes over these past few weeks."

He grimaced. "You know I didn't have a choice in that."

Didn't he though? The words begged to be asked, but I *had* missed him and didn't want to risk a fight. "Do you want to come in?"

"I would love to." He strolled over to the couch, zeroing in on my book of choice. His brows shot up. "I can see you were in the middle of *studying.*"

"I was just taking a break," I stammered, snatching the book back. "I've been studying all night."

"If you need help studying that particular subject, I'd be more than happy to be your tutor."

"What makes you think I need tutoring?" I flashed a sultry smile back at him, earning an intrigued but confused look. Feeling bold, I confessed, "Not every release requires a partner. I think I've *mastered* the subject quite well on my own."

His eyes grew hooded as he stepped closer. "Interesting. And if I wished to teach you, anyway?"

I couldn't stop the color rising to my cheeks, deepening as he raised his palm to the rosy tint. My breathing hitched as his thumb brushed across the stain.

"So beautiful," he whispered. "I know we agreed we had other priorities and that there could be nothing serious between us."

I nodded, unable to speak. We had agreed. He had the base to look after and made it clear he wasn't yet ready for a relationship. And me? I had never allowed myself to be open, not really. I had a few past interests but hadn't felt the need to expose more of my mind to them. And though Alarik felt somehow different, I wasn't sure I was capable of being vulnerable.

"Nothing has changed," he said. It was almost a plea.

"Nothing," I agreed. His eyes dipped, tracking the shifting of my lips as the word left. I should pull away. This wouldn't end well, but I found I didn't want to move.

He leaned in until his breath fanned my lips and the heat of his body seeped into mine. I was sure his mouth would brush against my lips, but a moment before, he paused.

"So, we are agreed?" he murmured. "To share only our nothingness?"

"Yes," I whispered, my stomach fluttering as I gave the faintest of nods. And then the space between us dissolved.

Soft lips pressed against mine in a slow, sweet kiss. He pulled back, the abrupt loss of him causing my eyes to flicker open.

"That's it?" The words were out before I could stop them.

He huffed a surprised laugh as his mouth captured mine once more, but this time it was fueled by my challenge. My heart raced as his arms came around me, pressing the small of my back into his hardened body.

Reveling in the feel of our lips meeting, I melted into him. I had been kissed before, but never like this. There had never been the urge to further it, to seek more. To *feel* more.

Electricity sparked and surged through me. I had forgotten how to breathe. How to think. And it didn't matter. All that mattered was this. Us. Our bodies pressed close and the taste of his lips on mine.

Alarik's hand trailed up my back as our breathing quickened, his fingers tangling in the loose strands of my damp hair, tugging my head back into a better angle. His tongue licked against my lips, demanding entrance.

I yielded, my lips parting of their own accord. My hands slid up his body, discovering the delicious planes of his stomach, his chest, before curving around his neck to pull him closer. The flicker of his tongue grazed my bottom lip, nipping playfully before claiming me once more. Pressing closer, the tips of my nipples brushed against his firm chest. The subtle scrape shot through my veins, pooling low in my belly.

A shiver ran up my spine as his hand slipped beneath the hem of my shirt. His fingers traced swirls along my skin, the warmth of his touch leaving scorched trails in their wake. I pressed up on to my toes, deepening the kiss, demanding more, willing his hands to continue their path. To where, I wasn't sure. I wanted to feel them everywhere. All at once.

—A loud creak sounded from my door, with a small, sleepy voice following it. "Ellie?"

Will's presence was like a bucket of ice water. Alarik and I shot apart, chests heaving, as we both fumbled to right ourselves. My shirt fell into place easily enough. Alarik turned away from the door a moment before Will pushed through.

"What's wrong, sweetie?" Kneeling by his side, I spared an apologetic look for Alarik who was hastily adjusting his pants.

Will looked up, eyes widening as he realized who was in the room with us.

"Was it a nightmare, again?" I asked, brushing back a silver curl.

He nodded, looking from Alarik and back to me. "The emptiness, it's happy right now. They killed everyone—"

"Shhh, it's okay, Will. We won't let the emptiness get you. Do you want to stay with me tonight?" He nodded his small head against my shoulder as I gathered him up in a hug. "Okay. We can leave the light on, too. Does that sound good?"

He nodded once more as I carried him to bed. After Will was tucked in and his faint snores resumed, I crept out of the room, returning to find Alarik waiting on the settee.

"Sorry. He has nightmares sometimes. I think that's why he wants to learn how to fight. Maybe it will make him feel safer."

Alarik looked to the room where Will slept, his features softening. "I'll spend more time with him."

"It's okay. I know you're busy. Greer said she got him into the apprentice classes."

"That's only schooling. He won't see fighting techniques for another few years. If he were my brother, I'd train him. I want to teach him."

Something cracked in my chest, flooding me with a soft contentment, as I sat down beside him. "Okay, I'll ask him tomorrow, but the answer is going to be yes. You're his favorite person."

I relaxed against Alarik's chest, the tension in my body easing as I breathed in the scent of sandalwood mixed with a hint of cloves. "Was there a reason you stopped by tonight?"

Emerald eyes met mine before he pressed a soft kiss to my lips. "I didn't want to end the day without seeing you, but we should both get some rest. Goodnight, Elara. Our study dates resume tomorrow evening."

I bit my lip as I watched him leave, drinking in the view. "I look forward to the lessons."

CHAPTER 33

My body felt refreshed from a dreamless sleep, and I found I was eager for the day to pass and for evening to arrive. Vidarr had given me today and tomorrow off in preparation for my mission the following day, but I doubted Zelos would make such a concession.

I was right. Training with the men flew by, and my hand-to-hand combat skills were already improving. I managed to land three blows sparring against Zelos and secured wins in two-out-of-three of my other matches.

The men wiped towels across sweat soaked foreheads as they filed out of the training ring and into the warm afternoon sun, but Zelos trailed after the others, lingering as I gathered my things.

"You're looking good out there, sweetheart. Another few weeks under me and you might just stand a chance. I'd even be willing to indulge you with a few private lessons, if you ask nicely."

I snorted. "Not going to happen, Zelos."

He stepped back, eyes lighting with mirth as his hands

clutching his chest in mock pain. "Ouch. But that's fine. I'm more than happy to keep showing you up in front of the guys."

"We'll see. As you said, I'm looking pretty good."

"That you are."

A flash of copper hair caught my eye. Evander had asked me to meet him after class, but didn't say what for.

Zelos followed my gaze. "I'll see you tomorrow, sweetheart. But don't expect me to take it easy on you just because you have a recon mission the following morning."

"I wouldn't dream of it." I smiled back.

Evander waited till Zelos passed before shooting a disbelieving look over his shoulder. "It looks like you're settling in well."

"I feel like I'm making progress."

"That makes this a little easier," he stated flatly. My brows knit together as he took a deep breath. "I know I was meant to stay for another month, but I've been called away for patrol along the Light Kingdom's western border. I'll return as soon as I can, but I have to maintain my position within the Legion of the Light."

My stomach twisted. I knew he had to go back, but I couldn't help the feeling of foreboding that swept through me. I gave his hand a squeeze. "Just... be careful."

"Always, sis." His shoulders relaxed as we started toward the door. "I'm taking Colt with me. Be sure to keep up with Ember. She's grown used to your visits."

"That won't be a problem. I love spending time with her." We stepped into the warm afternoon air, the worst of the humidity not yet here.

"Good. I caught up with Greer and Will today at lunch. She's secured a tutor, despite Will being two years younger than the other apprentices. The tutor agreed to make an exception once he met Will. He was impressed by his eagerness." Evander chuckled. "Will even asked for homework."

Of course, he did.

"Lannie was busy with Healer Grant, but I managed to say goodbye. She's thriving and Healer Grant is ecstatic. Each of her concoctions are better than the last." He released a slow contented breath. "It's nice to see everyone happy."

"I know things growing up weren't the easiest but thank you. We wouldn't be here if it wasn't for you."

"I'll always be here for you, little sis. Always."

We walked through the base, enjoying the bright afternoon sun. It was hard to believe time had passed so quickly. It felt like a mere blink, but I was due to return to Sonder the day after next.

The attacks had continued to work their way north, peppering along human settlements just outside the Border-lands, but we still didn't know who was behind the strikes. There had been no further leads, keeping the dark fae as the favored suspects.

All of Pax knew their reputation, but doubt had started to stir in my mind. I was determined to discover something of use this time at the market. At the very least, I'd be able to update the Select Guard on Alderidge's plans. From what Vidarr had shared, his speeches had only grown more vulgar, demanding an uprising of humans against fae.

Evander cleared his throat as Alarik's residence came into view, his face carefully neutral. "I've heard the study sessions with General Holt have been going well."

"They are. He's been busy, so it's been mostly me, with him checking in every few days, but I'm picking up the information quickly." I focused on the road in front of us, fighting to keep the blush from showing. "We're meeting again tonight."

His eyes narrowed, zeroing in on the faint pink sheen staining my cheeks, but he didn't press the issue. "Stay safe, El. Be smart. I'll be back in a week or two."

CHAPTER 34

IN ANTICIPATION FOR TONIGHT'S STUDY DATE, I SPENT EXTRA TIME in the shower, brushed my teeth, and selected a comfortable yet flattering pair of pants that Greer helped pick out. The shirt I'd chosen was a soft blue, which Greer assured me complimented my hazel-blue eyes. She insisted I leave my hair loose and helped shape a few of my rowdier curls until they were the perfect balance of wind-tossed and tamed.

Body humming, I ascended the last of the steps. I took a deep breath, steadying my nerves, before pushing through the doors.

They gave way easily to the dimmed space, devoid of sound. My sandaled steps echoed through the large room, the walls mocking my solo presence.

"Alarik?" I called, padding toward the back of the hall. The doors stood slightly ajar, but they too were coated in darkness. Empty.

My stomach twisted. I'd rushed through the day to get to this moment, when he and I could be together again without the pressures of base surrounding us. Had he not felt what I had last night? Gods, he probably had forgotten about our plans. If not forgotten, then he had chosen to be somewhere else. Chosen something more important.

I felt a piece of myself crumple. How could I have been so stupid. We'd agreed there was nothing between us. We'd agreed there never could be. Foolish tears threatened my eyes, springing from embarrassment and rejection, but I refused to surrender to them. We had promised nothing. If only my irrational heart had understood.

A desperate need to leave surged within. There was no need for Alarik to realize how pathetic I'd become. I raced down the steps, intending to flee into my room for the evening, but caught sight of Zelos standing before my door.

His head turned, fist hovering over the door from where he had just knocked. "El, is that you?"

Hastily wiping away the damp patches across my cheeks, I pulled together an easy smile and walked toward him. "That's the first time you've used my name."

Lifting a brow, his lips twitching. "Don't worry, I won't make it a habit. I know you like the pet name."

I shook my head, but welcomed the small smile his teasing brought. "So, what's going on? More threats for tomorrow's training?"

He attempted a light smile, but his eyes were weary. He held out a small envelope, a wax seal firmly in place. "Actually, the general wanted me to deliver this."

My face fell as I reached for it. I stared at the neat scrawl of my name, forcing a calmness to my words. "You saw him?"

"No. He left me instructions to deliver this to you. He was called away to deal with an occurrence."

"An occurrence?"

"I'm not a part of the Select Guard. I don't have information to give you. My instructions were to deliver this to your room after dinner. He gave me a recap of the mission's objectives, but I figured we'd go over those tomorrow if he wasn't back."

"Thank you. I'll see you tomorrow, then?" I could feel my mask faltering and I didn't want Zelos here when it happened.

"Wouldn't miss it, sweetheart."

Offering a grateful smile, I slipped inside my room, tearing through the seal of the letter as the door closed. A hasty scrawl awaited me, one in which Alarik explained that he was called away to investigate an ambush on a small town just inside the Borderlands. If he hadn't returned before I was due to leave, my orders were to complete the mission at Sonder.

I flipped the note over. It was blank. No goodbye or good luck. Nothing about last night or promises for the future. It was only a quick jot of instructions, something a general would issue to a subordinate.

Because that was what we were.

The prick of tears gathered at the corners of my eyes, born of my traitorous, foolish heart. I didn't bother wiping them away when they tumbled free.

The evening sky was of the softest purple with only the brightest stars winking to life, but I wanted nothing more than to crawl into bed and sleep. Tomorrow, I would package my emotions up into the carefully constructed vault they were used to residing in. But for now, I let each foreign feeling wash over me, drowning me with naïve desires for a future that was never mine to dream of.

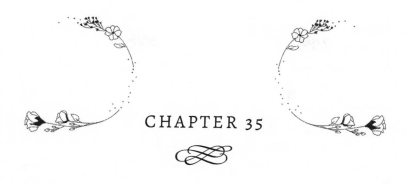

CHAPTER 35

THE ENTIRE SELECT GUARD HAD LEFT WITH ALARIK AND HAD YET to return the next day, so Zelos briefed me on my expectations for the mission: Discover any and all movements of the dark fae, particularly in regard to their rogue factions. I was also to provide an update on Alderidge's plans for possible mobilization of a human force.

The market was only a few miles from base, so we left early the next morning, reaching the large wooden barn without incident after only a few hours of travel. The crowds had picked up, meaning Alderidge would start his speech soon, if he hadn't already.

I stopped at Sophie's booth for a brief hello. She rattled off a quick update, gushing about how Lucy's belly was starting to show and how Liam couldn't be prouder. The nausea had finally left her, and she was regaining some of her strength. In return, I shared a short summary of my sisters and Will, before bidding her goodbye.

A creeping feeling of unease clawed its way up my spine as I neared the back of the hall. Though the market was packed with larger crowds than I'd seen in months, there was something missing. My eyes darted to the surrounding tables before expanding out. With a small gasp, I realized there were no fae. It would seem Alderidge's hatred for fae hadn't gone unnoticed by the southern kingdoms and precautions had been taken.

There was a sizable group around Alderidge's table. He stepped onto a small raised platform as I pressed forward, launching into a rehearsed speech while brandishing weapons as he performed. His voice boomed with the need for vengeance, calling all humans to heed his words.

I knew these words. He'd given a nearly identical speech last month. Sinking further into the shadows, I watched as others surged forth, jeering and cheering, while Alderidge urged humans to take up arms and demand freedom from fae, the dark fae, in particular.

He alluded to the tides of war changing, to the mounting surge of human resilience against the mistaken fae who thought to call themselves our masters. Alderidge's cold black eyes flashed with malice as he watched his audience descend into his carefully constructed web of unrest.

His support had grown. Despite his demand for human rights, I felt only a rising sense of dread. I watched as tensions grew, as Alderidge's words took root, sowing seeds of distrust and fear. Though he offered no proof of the dark fae's involvement, the crowd cheered, all the same. My stomach twisted as he spoke of organizing a human militia, of venturing across the Dark Kingdom's southern border and demanding justice. It would be suicide.

Having heard enough, I turned from the crowd. I doubted there would be any fae present, let alone the dark fae, but I'd still look. Perhaps I'd explore the town.

A flicker of movement caught my attention. It was nothing more than a flash of dull brown, but the movement was precise, skilled even, and heading in the opposite direction of the crowd.

I followed like a moth to a flame, slinking along the wall,

until the cloaked form settled into a seat at a corner table. A short, petite woman with silver hair and dark brown eyes launched into furious whispers with the stranger's approach. A scowl was etched across her features as she waved her hands in obscene gestures toward the mob.

Definitely *not* with Alderidge. Good.

A warm chuckle rumbled around me—through me— drawing my eyes to the back of the cloaked figure, his chest still shaking with laughter. He stood, slipping around the table. The cloak shifted, revealing thick, toned arms with dark brands trailing up his tanned skin. He reached for a bottle of what appeared to be ale, his strong hands flexing, as he opened it, before taking a seat.

I took a step away from the wall, drawn toward him. A warrior lay beneath the hood, if only I could catch a glimpse of his face.

A petite woman with large glasses stepped in my path. I was vaguely aware of her pointing to the hand-painted sign on a table piled with bath oils and salts. Glancing over my shoulder, I realized this would be the perfect vantage point to overhear the cloaked figure's conversation.

Edging as close as I dared, I drifted to the far end of the booth, allowing my eyes to wander over the pair. The woman was small but feisty, the kind of attitude that came from decades of seeing the world change. But the man, gods, the man was a giant—taller even than most fae.

He sat, straddling the stool, dwarfing it with his size. The outline of one powerful thigh strained against the black fabric of his pants, the sculpted muscle visible beneath. His hood stayed drawn, but the strength etched across every muscle of his body indicated this was a man who didn't shy away from battle.

"We killed another hundred two nights ago," he breathed, his deep voice flaming an unbidden warmth within me. "But when one group is put down, another three take its place."

I blinked. Did he just say, 'killed *another* hundred'?

The woman glared at him, her blue eyes sharp as she responded. "Same as before?"

He took a swig from the bottle, swallowing loudly before answering, "Yes. All with the Dark Kingdom's insignia."

"Any leads?"

"Nothing new. Even the creatures we've *persuaded* have revealed nothing more than an interest in the village of Neith. We're watching. It remains safe, for now."

Neith. From what Evander could find, it remained a peaceful, quaint village established for centuries just inside the southern border of the Dark Kingdom. It was surrounded by rivers and housed human and fae, alike. But I knew of nothing particularly powerful about it.

"It doesn't make sense. The attacks are sloppy. Even these idiots know something is going on." A wave of the woman's hand indicated she was talking about Alderidge's lot. "It's only a matter of time before they run off and get more people killed."

"I'm aware of the lack of time, Anita. I didn't come here for a lecture."

"You should have expected it, boy. What with folks dying off left and right, and me having to keep everything hush hush. It's a miracle there hasn't been a full-on uprising, yet."

The black cloak shook with subtle laughter. The sound was deep and strong, transforming the smooth voice into a warm embrace, before giving way to a tired sighed. "You're right."

"Of course, I am." Anita blinked. "About what?"

His answering laughter rang louder this time. "About the amount of attention. The royals would never allow this much notice, but it's too clean and involves too many troops to *not* involve the power of the royals. Each kingdom suffered losses with the initial wave, human and fae alike, but these attacks... They are focused. Strategic. I know there's a pattern to be found and yet I cannot discern what it might be."

Anita's eyes cut into the figure like freshly sharpened steel. "There have been rumors, you know."

"Oh?"

"Yes, *oh*. Rumors that say this—all of this death and suffering for the past seven years—is the work of The Dark Phoenix." His spine stiffened, but she continued, reciting a disconcertingly familiar line. "A phoenix's vengeance will rise, severe and unbending. With it, torment will reign, unchecked and unending."

My skin pebbled as a cold that had nothing to do with the temperature crawled through me. There was a tugging in the recesses of my mind, a clouded memory swirling on the periphery, just out of reach.

"That's enough." His words were like ice water splashed across burning coals. "The phoenix, the dragon, the lotus—they are all myths. Taken and distorted by the unreliable filter of time into what little information is left now."

Anita started, but he gripped her hand in a silent plea for her to hear him out.

"I believe in the word of the goddess as much as you. But there have been no indications this is the fulfillment of one of the great prophecies. Trust me when I say that I have thoroughly looked into it. That being said, I've just come from the Light Kingdom."

Anita stilled.

"I wasn't able to break through to the inner city. Most of the outer provinces were oblivious, completely unaware of the destruction surrounding them. A few of the more... open minded settlements were destroyed. No clues left for us to find, either. Everything was burned to rubble."

"Just like the others?" The hood dipped in a nod. Her lips thinned. "The settlements, were they all human?"

"Mostly. Some of the victims were fae, but from what we can tell, only fae friendly with humans or those of mixed blood have been targeted." His eyes darted toward Alderidge. "There was an attack a few nights ago, the first within the Borderlands."

Anita's eyes widened. "Why wasn't it reported? I would have thought Alderidge would pounce on that sort of news."

"Why indeed," the dark figure muttered, head turning toward the swarm hovering around Alderidge. He took a slow drink, revealing the hint of dark stubble lining a strong jaw. "The strike was different from the others. It was a group of humans this time, demanding the humans of the town free themselves from their fae oppressors. Never mind the town was home to those of mixed descent and blended families who had been peaceful for the past century."

"How bad was it?"

"A few were hurt. No lives were lost. It was more about containing the mob. The Select Guard arrived the next day. I knew they had informants; even so," his voice pitched with amusement. "Their response time was impressive."

I blinked. The Select Guard? Was that where Alarik had gone?

"The dark fae have lost the most lives, next to humans, of course. The Earth and Water Kingdom continue to feign ignorance of any such happenings. But I've seen the destruction of their territories firsthand."

"And the others?" Anita prompted after he had fallen into silence. "Has Dragcor made his decision?"

The hood nodded. "Ryuu's made sure we have the Air Kingdom's backing. The Fire Kingdom doesn't seem to be buying into the slander, either. At least not yet."

Realizing I was staring, I reached blindly for a jar of bath oils to maintain my façade, my mind buzzing with his words. Why would the Dark Kingdom be suffering losses if they were the ones responsible for the attacks?

"Those bigoted arses. They know damn well someone's killing off the humans and anyone showing us a lick of kindness," Anita snapped. The dark figure chuckled, earning him an angry glare. "Look here, boy. This is not the time for jokes."

"Why do you insist on calling me boy when I am centuries older than you, *girl*?"

Centuries? My grip loosened around the narrow vial I'd been holding. The sharp sound of breaking glass splintered around me, drawing a ring of attention from those within earshot, including the cloaked figure.

Warm cinnamon eyes streaked with darker flecks snapped to mine, peering out beneath the shadows of his hood. I froze, but my heart beat frantically.

Gods, he was huge. The cloak was fastened across his chest, but thick bands of sculpted muscle peeked through to coat every inch, forming the warrior god before me. A wave of heat flooded my cheeks as another pooled low in my stomach. His nostrils flared, lips stretching into a wicked grin.

I pulled my bottom lip between my teeth, praying to the gods that I hadn't accidentally spoken my thoughts out loud. His deep eyes released mine, dropping to track the movement of my lip, drifting to the deepening blush across my cheeks, until they captured me in their gaze once more.

Fathomless depths twinkled with mischief, daring me to come closer, tempting me to play. The tempo of my heart fluttered to a rapid hum as I took a single step forward. His smile shifted into a tantalizing taunt. Were those fangs?

If only I could see him clearer... The crunch of glass cut through the spell as I made to take another step. The small lady who was selling the oils had appeared with a broom and bucket, making quick work of cleaning my mess. I helped her with the remaining pieces, depositing coin on her table for the broken vial.

When I glanced up, the cloaked figure was gone.

CHAPTER 36

I CLUNG TO EMBER AS WE DASHED THROUGH THE THRIVING forest. The sun had only just crept past midday, leaving plenty of time for our return trip and I intended to use every moment to wrap my mind around what I'd heard.

Alarik had mentioned military operations, but gods, I doubted even he realized the extent to which all of Pax was involved. If what the cloaked figure said was true, villages in each kingdom had been destroyed.

The dark fae have lost the most lives, next to the humans.

How was that possible? They were the ones responsible for this mess, weren't they? Though, I suppose a rogue faction of fae wouldn't be bound by loyalty to a kingdom.

And what was all that talk about the humans instigating a fight within the Borderlands?

Based on the way the people of Sonder had responded to him, Alderidge could very well have been behind the altercation. The cloaked figure had studied Alderidge, as a predator would another carnivore. Not with fear, but with heedful caution. Though he seemed nothing more than a hateful human, perhaps Alderidge was someone we'd need to watch more closely.

Families across Pax continued to be slaughtered and it was glaringly obvious that humans were the target. How many had died these past seven years? How many others thought their lives had been shaped by that cursed storm, when it had been the work of much darker, vindictive forces all along?

Ember and I rushed through the forest, pushing the boundaries of speed and time, but before either of us realized, the trees started to shift. The trunks had grown wider, the underbrush thicker, and all around us there was a growing haze. Not quite fog or clouds, but a murkiness that distorted the light, throwing us into a space suspended between morning and night.

I felt it, then. It was nothing more than a twist of my gut, the minute tugging across my skin as fine strands of hair stood on end, but I knew there was something waiting for me.

A low thrum rose to greet me, emanating from the earth itself. It was calling, begging me to follow.

And I did.

Urging us onto untraveled paths, I turned away from the promise of clear skies and moved further into the warped branches that beckoned me.

Ember's ears pressed back, her gait slowing as we wove through tangled vines and gnarled roots. The forest grew thick with collecting shadows. A distant part of me knew I shouldn't be here. I sensed the charge held within the hushed silence, pleading with my body to listen, to turn back. But the draw was too great. I pushed forward.

The low, steady vibrations summoned me. We wove deeper, chasing the eerie enchantment until we came to a grove of awaiting darkness.

I vaguely remembered sliding off Ember's back. I dimly recalled her taking a few unnerved steps in retreat as I crept nearer. A barrier of crumbling stones slowed my approach, ensnared by a network of twisted vines and thorns, as if some primal part of the forest sought to hide them.

My attention was drawn beyond the ring of stones to the shrouded grove beyond. There was something else there—something within—hidden from my human eyes.

I stepped closer, my foot landing atop the nearest stone. An electric shock wrapped around my ankle, surging up through my body in painful spurts as the shadows flared to life. Marbled blue-silver swirls pulsed from toppled boulders and crumbling rock, spiraling in toward the dense center. But it remained impenetrable, nothing more than a pit of churning black.

Another blast of power tore through me, wrenching a scream from my lungs. My spine snapped back, arching with the searing current. My muscles seized, forcing my body into a warped contortion as a dark, cold presence dove into the recesses of my mind.

I was helpless to stop the invasion. Ruthless claws shredded through my memories, mercilessly digging, hunting for something, until the very center of my being was unveiled, and the assault ceased.

My eyes snapped open, pupils focusing on the ancient temple at the heart of the blackness. I wanted to enter, needed to obey her command, but before I could cross the stone circle, Ember was before me.

Frantic shrieks pierced the fog surrounding my mind. She reared up, thrusting me back with a brutal shove. I crashed against the earth, the jolt severing the remains of whatever spell had gripped me.

Heart thundering against my ribs, I snapped my attention to the temple. But I found nothing more than the twisted branches of an ancient forest. The hairs along my neck pricked as icy dread snaked down my spine. I hurled myself onto Ember's back, legs clenching as we fled.

CHAPTER 37

WE RAN. WE RAN AS IF WE COULD OUTPACE THE MADNESS BEHIND. I paid no attention to the slap of branches against my arms and legs nor the sharp stings that followed. Crouching lower, I desperately willed my body to forget the macabre kiss of darkness that had ravaged my mind. I felt it still; the lingering effects of its cold touch. The foreign presence was gone, yes. But I felt irrevocably changed.

I knew it was impossible. Nothing was able to invade the mind. No fae possessed powers like that. It must have been an illusion, or a parasite projecting images meant to incapacitate me before it struck. Thank the gods for Ember. I leaned into her, letting her bright presence ground me as we raced toward the base.

My eyes automatically sought the flash of copper hair as we returned to the stables before I remembered Evander was away. My heart sank. He would have believed me, even if it ended up being nothing more than a lower creature playing tricks on me. Evander would have taken the threat seriously. But he wasn't here.

The rest of the horses had returned, though, meaning their

riders were back as well. I raced to Alarik's residence, flying up the stairs, needing to speak to him—to hear words of reassurance—just needing to be with him.

But as I flew up the stairs and reached his doors, it was quickly apparent he was not alone.

The entire Select Guard was present, minus Evander, though Zelos pacing in the back of the room seemed to make up for his absence. They were deep in conversation, volleying ideas off one another and unaware I'd joined them. From what I could gather, they were developing plans for the next wave of evacuations.

Another strike had occurred. Another village full of lives destroyed. It had taken place only a few miles from where they had been, with no discernible traces of the enemy. It was like all the others: tracks within the town, evidence of a vast army, and then nothing.

"What of the people in the village?" Zelos asked.

Vidarr gave a tight shake of his head. There were no survivors. There never were.

The look of devastation across Alarik's face was like a serrated dagger piercing flesh. More lives lost. He would view this as a failure on his part, even though there was no way he could have known.

I took a step into the room, eyes locked on him. Someone needed to tell him this wasn't his fault.

Green eyes flashed to mine, and I could have sworn I saw the weight across his shoulders lighten, just a hair. "El, when did you get back?"

"Just now. But it sounds like you're in the middle of something." My eyes looked past him to the others who were deep in conversation. Zelos was the only one looking in our direction.

"I'm sure you've heard, but there was a strike just outside the Borderlands, a mere stone's throw from where we had been. We heard nothing, El. That area had scouts. We should have seen something. There were no signs of an army and yet an entire village was decimated." He ran a hand through his wildly tossed hair.

I had no explanation to offer and so remained silent.

"I'm sorry I wasn't able to be here before you left. How did it go? You look a little shaken. Did something happen?"

The words were spoken with concern much too intimate for our current setting. My eyes darted around the room, witnessing the most skilled warriors of the human race unravel. Alarik was their anchor. They needed him to tame the situation and construct a plan. He was the tether, the voice of reason in an otherwise reasonless world.

"El?"

I wanted nothing more than to fall into his arms, to allow someone else to shoulder this burden with me. So much of my life was me never breaking. Even with my sisters, I sought to keep the worst from them. It would have been nice to tell him about the presence in the forest, to have him calm me as he did everyone else, but he had more important priorities right now.

"It's nothing."

He nodded, too distracted by the clamor of the room to sense the lie. He led me over to a table, off to the side of the others' conversations.

"And the mission, what information did you gather at Sonder?"

"Alderidge is as terrible as ever. He's demanding humans revolt against fae. I hate the way we are treated as much as the next human, but he isn't being smart about it. There's no strategy. He's only going to get more humans killed."

"He nearly did. We were called away to stop a mob of humans from ripping a peaceful village apart. Their only goal was to end the fae. A few gave us Alderidge's name."

So, he had been behind the attack.

"What of the Dark Kingdom?"

The image of the cloaked figure flashed in my mind. "None of the normal fae were present, not with Alderidge there, but there was this one man. I'm not sure if he was fae because he kept his hood up, but he spoke of the strikes. He said every kingdom has been attacked, but dark fae have suffered the most, apart from humans. He was worried about Alderidge. Not a lot, but you could tell he was uncomfortable with the situation escalating."

Alarik nodded but maintained his mask of calm.

"There was also mention of a place called Neith."

A man with hickory skin and warm eyes turned toward us.

"Go on," Alarik prompted.

"He said it was being watched but was safe for now."

Cadoc joined the other man, attention focused on me.

"Anything else?" Alarik asked.

Two others had joined, their nearly identical sleek dark hair and broad cheekbones marking them as brothers. Even Vidarr waited for me to speak.

"Just one more. The woman he was speaking with mentioned a prophecy. In particular, she brought up a phoenix's vengeance bringing torment. There was mention of a dragon and a lotus, too..."

The room went still as my voice trailed off. That nagging feeling resurfaced, the one of a memory just out of reach.

"Did they have any idea who The Dark Phoenix was or where it could be found?" Cadoc's voice snapped me back to the present.

"No, that was it. What does it mean?"

Everyone looked to Alarik. "We're not sure."

I tilted my chin in challenge. "And if you were, you wouldn't tell me?"

"No, he wouldn't," Zelos answered, arms crossed and eyes burning.

Alarik's lips thinned. "There are still a lot of missing pieces.

But this helps. Thank you, El. Take the morning off. We'll meet tomorrow evening to finish your history lessons."

My spine stiffened at the dismissal. I bit my tongue against the retort. I wouldn't give him the satisfaction of seeing me ruffled. My eyes darted to Zelos, but his shoulder lifted in a what-did-you-expect shrug.

"Your assistance is not required, General. I'm more than capable of studying on my own."

His mouth fell open, a protest poised on his tongue, but I fled the room before he could utter it.

CHAPTER 38

AFTER A LONG SHOWER, I CRAWLED INTO BED AND SLEPT FOR hours. Visions of my brothers woke me, their lifeless bodies dragged by thorny brambles across glowing stones toward a gathering darkness. I woke with a sheen of sweat coating my body. Nausea rolled though me.

It was a dream, nothing more than the remnants of yesterday's encounter, but the slinking in my mind—in my very soul —left me feeling exposed. I needed to speak with Alarik, or perhaps Vidarr. Shrugging off the chill, I changed into a new shirt, before brewing a midnight cup of tea, courtesy of Lannie. Gratefully, I was able to fall back asleep.

When I awoke, it was nearly noon. I dragged a cushioned chair in front of a large window, and spent my day curled up inside, reading. After flipping through a few lighter texts, I turned to one that explored different fae traits and regions.

The wild fae remained a mystery, even centuries ago. They were said to live atop the mysterious Arcane Mountains, rarely venturing past the infinite fog that wove among their slopes. But there was a vast well of knowledge in relation to the other kingdoms.

I thought all fae of a particular kingdom resembled one another, with each having specific, well-known traits. The grand feathered wings belonged to those of the Air Kingdom, curved horns were seen among the earthen fae, adapted breathing vacuoles and shimmering skin were associated with water fae, allowing them to live above or below water, and a set of pointed fangs were common among dark fae. Even the light fae were known for their fair complexions and gentle features.

But my assumptions had been wrong. Sure, there were distinguishing traits among the kingdoms, but they weren't as exclusive as I had thought. Royals fit the classic idea of each fae most strictly, but the rest of the kingdom displayed fae features in varying degrees.

It was also pointed out that not *all* fae of a particular lineage possessed the same attributes. One of the top theories was discussed in *Kingdom Genealogy, A Study*, which discussed the possibility that in rare circumstances, a fae may possess traits from multiple kingdoms, as was previously common among fae predecessors, the Merged.

'It is the current belief that a single fae may possess traits from multiple lineages of the fae in question is powerful enough. Among the current blended societies, both of fae-human and fae-fae relations, no offspring to date have exhibited more than one trait. Even among fae-fae pairings, one lineage will prove to be the dominant of the two with one set of visible traits. There appears to be no rationale for how dominance is selected among fae-fae reproduction, though most believe it has to do with the affinity of the individual's genetic material to that of a specific lineage.

'Fae-human relations have proven to be more volatile with an inability to predict how powerful an offspring might be or to what degree specific fae attributes may manifest. Some appear human until the settling occurs at which time they will transition as a full blooded fae would. Some appear human, but are powerful enough to shift,

calling on the fae blessing for a short period of time, while others maintain the appearance of being human throughout their lives.'

It would appear the history of humans and fae were far more blended than the current royals of the seven kingdoms would have us believe.

A knock on my door sounded. I contemplated leaving it closed, figuring Alarik would be the only one who wouldn't let himself in, but we needed to speak eventually. Might as well get it over with.

Alarik stood in the doorway with a tray of freshly prepared macarons. "I was hoping we could talk. I've received updated information on your next mission, if you're still interested."

Of course, I was still interested, but I was also upset. Lifting a brow, I asked, "And the macarons?"

He gave a sheepish smile. "Greer said I would have better luck speaking to you with a bribe. Is it working?"

I rolled my eyes, stepping back to allow him into my room. "If she went as far as baking macarons, the least I could do is eat them."

Snatching a few of them from the plate, I sank into the chair, and listened.

"We've stationed a few men to keep an eye on the happenings of Sonder. With Alderidge gaining sway, we need to make sure he doesn't instigate further riots, let alone a war with the Dark Kingdom."

"About that, I was reading through a few books this morning. It sounded like fae-human pairings were common, at one point."

Alarik nodded. "Many humans alive today may have traces of fae blood running through their veins. Even now, most of the kingdoms choose to feign ignorance, but I've traveled extensively. Fae-human relations are much more common than the royals realize."

It made sense, but still was difficult to wrap my mind

around. We had been taught humans were scorned by the fae. We were treated as lesser creatures. The idea that many didn't suffer such oppression, that families lived together in peace, was jarring, and, yet, I found myself yearning for such a world.

"I was hoping to meet with the Select Guard tonight to go over who should accompany us through the Dark Kingdom," Alarik said. "We are considering promoting Zelos from officer to one of the Select. He has the skills and leadership abilities. My concerns are in regard to his respectability."

"You mean, you hate the way he spoke with me during the sorting." Alarik gave a tight nod as I laughed. "He was a jerk. He still is some days, but we've moved past our beginning."

Alarik lifted a brow. "You think it's a good idea?"

"I think you already know that it is. He's a skilled fighter and the men love him. He's a little rough around the edges, but he means well."

"No, he doesn't."

"Okay, no, he doesn't. But despite his protests, he's trained me well. He's pushed me harder than most and that challenge has not only increased my physical strength, but enhanced my mental strength as well. I think we might even be friends."

Alarik's jaw ticked as he pushed back from the table. "I wish I could stay longer, but I need to prepare to welcome as many refugees as possible."

"The evacuations?"

He nodded. "I expect more will accept the offer this time."

I stood, chair sliding across the marbled floors, to join him. "When do we leave?"

"The plan was to give you a few months, but..."

"But the attacks are growing closer," I finished for him. "And each day we waste is a chance for another village to fall."

"I won't send you into the Dark Kingdom before you're ready."

"Who says I'm not ready?"

His face hardened. "You haven't finished your lessons."

"We both know I've surpassed your expectations. We have what? Maybe another week or two until I've finished your requirements?"

"That's not the only requirement, El."

"Has Zelos or Vidarr voiced any concerns?" I leveled him with a look, challenging him to tell me I'd fallen short. He couldn't.

"That's not the point."

"But that *is* my point. I've passed all your tests, or nearly have. I'm ready."

The silence stretched, but the flash of anguish in his eyes extinguished my mounting flames. He searched my face, taking his time to trace the shape of my lips, the curve of my cheeks. Moments passed and still he looked, until his eyes slowed along the shadows lingering beneath my eyes.

His voice was soft as he spoke. "If there something wrong?"

"No." The word pitched unnaturally high as the eerie feeling of the glowing stones rose.

Alarik lifted a brow, waiting.

"I'm sure it's nothing, but I sort of stumbled across a temple in the woods on my way back." I attempted a light-hearted shrug but his concern didn't falter.

"A temple?"

I frowned, recalling the shadows. "I think there was a temple. There was this ring of stones that surrounded a denser part of the forest. I couldn't see, not at first, but I was drawn to it. Almost as if I was being guided there without my intention. And then, this *thing* invaded my mind."

His brows lifted. "What do you mean by 'invaded'?"

"It was as if something was combing through my mind, searching for something. Not memories, or even secrets... but hunting for something specific." I shook my head, hearing the way I sounded. "I'm sure it was nothing."

Alarik drew a deep breath. "The stones—did they pulse, like the ones at the temple we ran across near your home?"

My eyes widened. How had I not realized it? "Yes. It was just like that, only... more, somehow."

My stomach churned as a wave of unease settled over him. It was gone in a flash.

"There are no creatures I know if with that ability," Alarik said. "I'm sure it was nothing more than a trick of the mind, but I'll have Vidarr search the forest tomorrow, just to be sure."

"Thank you," I mumbled, embarrassed that I was another person he needed to worry about.

There were a few among the light fae who could bend light and I'd heard of creatures releasing hallucinogens, but there were none capable of mind manipulation... But the violation had felt real.

We hovered near the edge of the table, nothing further to discuss but not yet ready to leave. We were alone. Something that had become exceedingly more difficult to accomplish.

"I should be going," he said.

I nodded, but still we lingered. There was no one to see the way my breathing hitched as he stepped near, or the way my legs weakened as his hand cupped the back of my neck, drawing me close.

Nobody heard the small, sweet sounds that stole from my lips when he deepened the kiss. Nor was there anyone to hear the whispered words he breathed against my ear that darkened the already pink flush across my cheeks.

He pulled away too soon. "I really need to get work done, tonight."

"I thought you were my tutor. *I'm* work," I smiled against his lips, refusing to release him.

"If only it were that simple." He untangled my arms around his neck, leaning his forehead against mine. "Priorities and all that, right?"

Priorities. Priorities that did not include me. I swallowed, taking a step back. "Right."

He pressed a quick kiss to my forehead before starting toward the doors. "Until tomorrow?"

"Sounds good." I waved him off, letting my smile drop after he was out of view.

If only it were that simple.

If only.

If I were only a woman and he only a man, without the self-inflicted priorities that plagued us, would things have been different? Had the storm not occurred, had we grown up in a world where death was not a familiar foe, what could we have become?

I wasn't sure I wanted to know. That girl was a stranger. Though she may have lived a happy, contented life—one devoid of horrors—that girl was not me. Not as I was today. There was something strangely sad and oddly optimistic in such a thought.

If only.

Leaving the books on the table, I left, returning to my bedroom. I liked the person I was in this reality and wouldn't wish her away for another, but I couldn't help wondering how things may have been different. My lips remained slightly swollen from my interlude of responsibilities and I found the dull ache was a lovely incentive to forget my priorities more often.

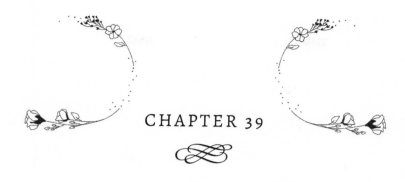

CHAPTER 39

THE NEXT DAY PASSED IN A BLUR, MY MIND PREOCCUPIED WITH the visions of the glowing stones. Vidarr left early in the morning with a small team of men. They assured me, it would take only an hour or two. If they spotted anything of concern, they would return straight away to gather a larger force.

Vidarr had only been gone for a few hours, but worry plagued me. I must have been seeing things. No creature was powerful enough to break into my mind. It was only an illusion. I repeated the thoughts over and over again as I worked through morning drills, as if the repetition alone would make them true.

It had been a source of distraction for me all morning. My stance was suffering for it and Zelos was quick to point out each flaw. He was in a particularly bad mood, picking me apart with every swing of my blade.

His words blazed through me, drowning my worries, until all that remained was the movement of my body, the clash of my blade against his. It was effective, but that didn't make me hate the method any less.

Zelos called an end to training, waving off the rest of the group, before flashing me a wicked grin.

"What?" I snapped, tired of his smug expression.

"You're welcome."

I shot him a glare as I took a sip of water.

Zelos leaned forward, his words a caress. "I don't know why you're so wound up, sweetheart, but if the general isn't seeing to your *needs*, I'd be more than happy to assist."

The water shot out of my mouth in a choked spray. I coughed and sputtered, attempting to dislodge the remainder of liquid from my lungs. Zelos leaned back with a grin, shaking his head at the mess.

"You're such a prick," I gasped between ragged breaths.

His fingers tilted my dripping chin up to meet his eyes. "Such a shame. I figured you would have been an expert in swallowing by now."

I swatted his hand away, hating the burning of my cheeks. "You're disgusting."

"I know. But I can still kick your ass in a fight."

Pushing past him, I headed toward the door. Quick steps and a heartbeat later, he was by my side.

"I mean it, though," his voice dipped to an unusual somber tone as we pushed into the sun. "It doesn't matter what's going on outside. When you're fighting, it's only you and your opponent. That's it. You have to shut everything else out."

My brow lifted, a I waited for a snide remark, but there was only a steady seriousness in his gaze. I gave a tight nod as we parted.

"Oh, and sweetheart?" he called over his shoulder, loud enough to draw the attention of the men around us. His grin turned wicked. "I meant what I said. I have a *long* list of skills I'd be happy to instruct you in. We may have to stay up late, working until we we're both satisfied, but assure you, I'm up for the challenge if you are."

I rolled my eyes as a rumble of snickers greeted his words.

He held my gaze, waiting for the color to rise along my

cheeks as the others starred. But I'd played this game often enough these past weeks and was done with blushing.

With more confidence than I felt, I let my eyes slowly trail down his bronzed frame, brazenly noting every defined muscle, before unflinchingly meeting his stare. "Pass."

Howls of laughter echoed around us. Zelos dipped his chin in my direction, a playful challenge flashing across his eyes, "It's okay, sweetheart. Not many can handle a study session with me."

"That mouth of yours never stops, does it?"

"Don't pretend like you want it to."

He wiggled his brows, causing a laugh to burst from my lips. "Gods, Zelos."

"You know you love me."

With an exacerbated shake of my head, I continued on. Even though my muscles were cramped, and my arms were striped with little nicks from when I'd been too distracted to avoid a blade, I dragged my body to the field beyond the stables where Vidarr would hopefully be waiting.

He would be back by now, unless the men had experienced the same pull I had. What if they weren't able to retreat. What if that thing had found a way to warp their minds?

I rounded the final corner, my mouth lifting into a relieved smile, as I spotted the burly lieutenant. His blond hair was secured back with intricate braids along the sides, half of it fastened with a leather tie.

"I wasn't sure of you'd be back."

"We returned an hour ago," Vidarr said. "We scoured the forest, but found nothing. No temple. No stones. It was clear, lass." He spoke softly.

My chest fell. I guess I really had been seeing things. "That's good. I'm glad there's nothing to worry about."

Vidarr's shoulder nudged mine. "The forest gets to us all at times."

I nodded, not wanting to hear excuses for my weakness. There must have been a type of hallucinogen in the air, a parasite, something. I'd ask Lannie if she knew of anything in the area with that capability.

"Are you ready to get your ass kicked?"

A ghost of a smile lifted my lips at Vidarr's obvious change of topic, but I took it. "Bring it, old man."

He grinned. "Start with the drills. Jabs first, then combos. Did you run the extra five miles this morning?"

"Six, actually." I gloated, pushing the forest from my mind. He bent his knees as he raised the pads up.

"Time?"

One-two, punch. I'd run these drills so many times over the last few weeks, they were second nature by now.

"I shaved an extra twelve seconds off per mile." *One-two, one-two.* "Not a lot, but I was sleepy this morning."

Pivot, strike. Hands up, one-two.

He snickered. "Yeah, I've been hearing about your study sessions."

My spine stiffened as his words crashed over me. A flush heated my cheeks as images of Alarik's hands drifting up, our mouths clashing, danced in my mind.

"What did he tell you?" The words held more bite than I meant as I squirmed with the idea that Alarik was discussing our relationship with others. Was that the right word? Relationship?

"Form, El. Three more, then switch sides. Make sure to keep your guard up."

I glared a moment before relenting, and raising my hands as instructed.

One-two. One-two.

"He said nothing about the two of you, personally, but he was impressed with how quickly you mastered the lessons."

That brought a smile to my face. I switched sides.

"He should be."

"Combos. Keep your form tight. Make sure you use your left side as well as your right."

I adjusted to his corrections, sweat gathering between my shoulder blades.

"The mission seemed like it went well."

"It did." My chest heaved as I worked through the set. "I'm ready for the next."

He nodded, adjusting the pad. "Good. I expect us to be moving out next week."

"Next week?"

"If you're feeling up to it. Alarik warned the Select Guard not to push—"

"No," I interrupted. "Nobody is pushing me. He mentioned it would be sooner, and riskier than the last, due to location, but I feel well prepared for the challenge."

"Good." He flashed me a proud smile before jerking his chin to my lax form. "Then we need to make sure you get all the training you can until then."

After what felt like hours, he finally called it. My body was drenched, muscles thoroughly worked, but I had gone beyond the exhausted stage and stumbled into that hazy feeling where my entire body was buzzing. I felt incredible. Exhausted but euphoric.

I gulped down fresh water, appreciating the gentle caress of a wayward breeze, before turning to Vidarr. "Did Alarik decide who would be joining me on the mission?"

"Zelos will be joining us."

I paused mid punch. "Us, as in you're coming?"

Vidarr shifted. "I am. Zelos is up for a promotion. This is an opportunity to see how he does away from the base."

"I understand the need to test Zelos, but this is just a recon mission. I assumed I'd have one or two men traveling with me."

My eyes narrowed as he continued to avoid my gaze. "Vidarr, just how many people do I need *protecting* me?"

He sighed, clearly uncomfortable with the direction this conversation had taken. "Zelos and the entire Select Guard: Kavan, the brothers Skender and Xaun, and I believe you've already met Cadoc—the tall one that usually looks like he's hovering somewhere between anger and confusion."

"Yeah, I've seen him a few times, usually hanging around Greer. He still doesn't get that she's not into him. She told him countless times, and very directly, but he thinks she will end up changing her mind for some reason."

"That's not surprising. Just make sure he doesn't lose his temper. Any problems, you tell me."

"I'll let her know," I said, surprised by the steel lacing his words.

"If he were here, Evander would join, as well."

A lump dropped into my stomach. It had been weeks without so much as a message from him. Alarik had assured me that this happened sometimes. Every once in a while, Evander would be sent further away than anticipated. He was most likely in an area where he couldn't send a message or was being watched too closely to risk it. But the presented rationale did little to quell my unease.

Pushing my worries aside, I focused on the next week's mission as Vidarr cleaned and returned the training pads. "Do I really need all seven of you for the mission? The less attention the better. Besides, I thought only I could get into the shelter. No boys allowed, right?"

"We won't be able to get in, but there's been an increase in attacks near the surrounding settlements." I blinked, surprised by the news, but Vidarr continued. "Alarik doesn't want to take any chances. We'll stay within the forest, just outside the town, so as not to blow your cover."

"Like my bodyguards?"

CHAPTER 39 | 269

"Something like that."

"I see. Tell me, is it normal for the Select—the most elite warriors among humans—to be babysitting on a basic recon mission?" He flinched with the force of my words. "Would they have joined this mission if it were anyone other than me?"

Frustration ticked along his jaw. "You know they wouldn't El. Alarik takes extra precautions when you're involved."

"Including withholding pertinent information to the mission? He mentioned an increase in overall attacks, but nothing specific to the mission. I should have been informed about the risk near our designated location."

He shrugged. "I just did."

"You know what I mean, Vidarr."

Running a hand over his face, he answered, "Yeah, I know what you mean, El. But he's the general. He's the boss. If you want to be treated like a member of this base, then you must understand that your current rank doesn't entitle you to certain information, which puts me in a tough spot. It's not my place to go above his commands. But as your friend, I won't stand by and watch you get fucked over either. So, I need you two to talk. Figure this shit out."

My lips tilted in a half smile. "We're friends?"

He rolled his eyes. "Gods, out of everything I said, that's what you focus on?"

"It seemed like the most important part." Scowling grey eyes held mine. "I'll talk with Alarik. Promise."

"Good. You are done for the day. Get some rest. Or better yet, go find Alarik and get that conversation over with."

A weight dropped into my stomach. My discomfort must have been visible because Vidarr added in a soft tone. "It's just talking, lass."

"Yeah," I scoffed. "Just some light talking about why fighting is so important to me and him explaining why the idea of me in battle is so triggering for him."

I knew my need originated from that shadowy space within myself, the one cultivated from blood, and death, and the desperate desire to never feel helpless again. It was gritty, and uncomfortable. How was I supposed to explain that to someone like Alarik?

Vidarr's face pulled into a frown, warring with some internal debate. In the end, he let out a long sigh. "This conversation has been a long time coming for him. He's seen things that no one should have to see. He's been different lately. Just small things, but there have been glimpses of the man he used to be." Vidarr trained his storm-grey eyes on me. "And I think you're the reason for that."

I blinked, and then nearly laughed. "Alarik hasn't changed. He's been the same responsible general that he's always been. In truth, I miss the playfulness he showed before we arrived here." Memories of a too-small tent played through my mind. "If anything, he's less fun."

Vidarr barked a laugh. "Partaking in hollow distractions is different than being happy."

My jaw clenched at the mentions of Alarik's previous *distractions*, but if Vidarr noticed, he kindly acted like he didn't.

"Just talk to him."

Just talk. He said it like it was an easy thing to do. Just talk. Just rehash past trauma and current toxic coping mechanisms. Just explain how training and fighting are the only things that bring peace to my twisted mind. I'd have to admit this to Alarik, the savior of humanity, the hero of the realm, and then we can get to pertinent topics like the swiftly approaching mission in the Dark Kingdom. How hard could it be?

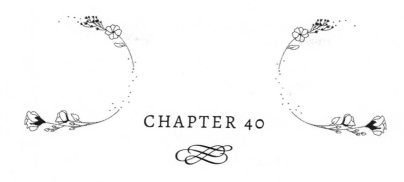

CHAPTER 40

With a deep breath, I stepped through the doors of Alarik's favorite training spot, engulfed by the sounds of a solo pair of fists pummeling the sand-filled bag. The dangling chain rattled, twisting against the ceiling, as the bag teetered with each punch Alarik threw.

I'd been avoiding him the last few days, but we were leaving for the Dark Kingdom tomorrow. Vidarr had gone as far as canceling our session, insisting we speak before we left.

My heart skipped a beat as I looked Alarik over. His shirt had been discarded, and defined muscles rippled across his chest with each powerful thrust. Sweat dripped from his face, trailing along his defined core, before ebbing into the deep V peeking out of his low-slung shorts.

I blinked, trying and failing to remember how to breathe normally. *Focus, El. You came here for a reason.* Clearing my head with a quick shake, I made my way across the room.

"Hey," I called.

Alarik turned, his face breaking into a carefree grin when he recognized it was me.

"Hey, beautiful." He leaned over, his lips grazing mine, before reaching for his water.

I licked my lips, loving the salty taste and the nonchalant way he delivered it.

"Does this mean you're ready to talk to me?" he asked.

"What do you mean? We've been talking."

"Technically, but you've kept things pretty short this week. We can delay the mission, if that's what's kept you away—"

"No. It's not that."

Alarik nodded once, taking a sip of water. "Tomorrow's a big day. It's normal to be nervous, but I don't expect it to be much different than the market. I won't let anything happen to you."

"No. I'm actually excited about the mission. I know tomorrow is recon only, but I'm ready for more." His expression hardened, fracturing my resolve. "Not more tomorrow, obviously. I only meant that I'm doing well with training—really well. And I've passed all the extra tests you've thrown my way with top marks..."

He twisted away with a scowl, taking his time adjusting his shirt before turning around. I expected his anger, but my stomach twisted at the forced calm exterior that greeted me.

We left the training ring in tight silence, heading toward the house. He waited until we'd passed through the doors before speaking. "Why don't we see how tomorrow goes and then we can worry about the next step."

"Right. I mean, tomorrow is already set, but I would like to be considered for more than recon missions." His arm stiffened along my waist as we started up the stairs. "I've gone through the steps, like anyone else would. This isn't just a phase I'm going through. I plan to be a working member of this base. You understand that, right?"

He let my words hang there, clouding the air between us. Reaching the second floor, I started toward my rooms, sure he'd follow. But he continued climbing the marbled steps without me.

"Alarik," I called, stumbling after him, but he'd already brushed past the doors, heading for his room in the back. The quiet grew thicker by the moment, interrupted only by my frantic steps, echoing across the cool stone.

Catching him before he could make his final retreat, I threw my hand forward, clasping his sleeve and tugging him to a stop. Still, he refused to face me.

"Alarik, tell me you're okay with me being a part of all of this." *With me being a part of you.*

Taking a steadying breath, I reached for his arm once more, needing him to at least meet my eyes. "Alarik—"

"No, Elara! I am not okay with this." He rounded on me and I recoiled as his voice thundered through the room. His chest shook as he fought to regain control of his crumbling façade, but he couldn't hide the terror of his voice. "You being in danger is never going to be okay with me. *Never,* and I refuse to act like it is."

I allowed the deadly quiet to stretch as my shock melted into fury. Gritting my teeth, I forced my words to hold an even tone. "Every person here is in danger at some point, Alarik. I'm no different."

"You're different to me," he snapped, something breaking in his eyes. The cutting retort died in my throat as I watched him deflate. There was nothing but worry and fear and agonizing pain staring back at me. "Can't you at least try to be happy staying out of trouble? The others, they've had years of training —*years.* You've only had a few weeks. The low-risk missions are fine, but the others..."

I bit my tongue, trying to get a grip on my temper. He was only looking out for me and what he said was true. Every other warrior had years of training, most joining the base as children. He was trying to protect me. I couldn't be mad at him for that.

"You could still be a part of the base, an essential part, but there's no need for you to willingly go into combat, at least not yet." His voice lifted with hope, urging me to see the beauty of his plan. "If things go right, you would never be in any real danger. There would be no need for you to risk your life."

"No need for me to fight?" I questioned, studying his reaction. My heart sank as a relieved smile stretched across his face.

"Yes. Gods, you understand. All of this training—it's great, but you won't need to use it. I'll protect you. I'm the general, for gods' sake. I can command the entire base to protect you. And your family. I won't let anything happen to them, either."

Tugging me close, he leaned his forehead against mine. "I'll keep us safe."

It was a vow, one that he intended to keep. One given with his whole heart. I swallowed the panic threatening to overwhelm me. I could do this. I could yield on this one point.

It didn't mean I'd have to give up other missions—not really. This was more about giving Alarik time to adjust. He hadn't been able to watch me these past few weeks. He hadn't seen how much I'd grown.

Exhaling a deep breath, I willed my body to calm as I eased into the warmth of his chest. Tomorrow I'd show him I was ready. There was no point in having this fight, because after tomorrow, he would see that I was more than capable of handling *any* mission.

His strong arms wrapped around me, holding me close as he pressed soft, sweet kisses into my hair. I pulled back, just enough to glimpse his haunted expression. Previous conversations with Vidarr and Evander played through my mind—about how Alarik had a tragic past, someone or something that had left scars much too deep to be detected on the surface.

"Did something happen before? You seem worried about me fighting..." Startled eyes snapped to mine, his face blanching.

"I've wanted to tell you. I didn't know how... the things they did to her." His breathing hitched.

"It's ok," I stammered. "You don't have to talk about it if you don't want to, but know that I'm here."

He pulled me toward him, body enveloping mine in an encompassing hug. I allowed him to fall into me as his mind wandered. He was lost in his past, and I could do nothing but brush soothing strokes across his back, assuring him he wasn't alone.

I'm not sure how long we stayed like that. My arms grew stiff, and the room grew cold. The golden rays of the sun streaming through the windows dimmed to a dark, vibrant violet, giving way to splashes of starlight winking into existence.

And still, I held him. I stayed there until he pulled away, only moving us to the nearby sofa. I waited for him, watching as he started the fire, the warmth of the flames doing little to melt his rigid countenance.

He paced before the orange glow, running a hand through his already disheveled blond hair. Bidding me a nervous glance, he sank into the vacant space beside me, letting out a weary, frustrated huff tainted by years of grief.

"It's hard to know where to start..."

"Start wherever you can," I whispered.

"I—I loved her." He glanced at me as he spoke, checking to see how I would respond to those three words.

I squeezed his hand, rubbing slow circles. This was about him, not me and I wouldn't let my insecurities prevent him from achieving whatever type of relief he could attain.

"Her name was Rhosyn. I met her while on deployment in the Earth Kingdom. I'm not sure how familiar you are with their customs, but parts of the kingdom are very... traditional. Women are meant to be beautiful and compliant." The corner of his lips lifted ever so slightly as a wash of sorrow filled his eyes. "But she was wild. She wanted to be a soldier.

"She stumbled upon our camp and followed us back. She was good—great, really. Within weeks, she had proven how skilled she was. She joined the Select Guard."

"*Your* Select Guard?" He nodded at my shock. "I didn't realize you allowed women to join."

"Plenty of fae kingdoms have female warriors fighting alongside males," he said with a frown. "I never understood why humans were against it, but I've seen women in battle. They can be just as brutal and skilled as any man."

"Oh."

"It's not because you're a woman." He took a steadying breath, holding it in a moment longer before exhaling the words, "I can't lose you the way I lost her. I won't."

His eyes blazed, but the passion was weakening, stripped away by the vast well of grief he kept locked within. I leaned into him, attempting to calm his racing heart, since I was unable to banish the ghosts haunting his mind.

"What happened?"

"I didn't protect her. Rhosyn was the daughter of a light royal, the cousin to the reigning queen, and her father was a prominent member of the aristocracy. He's currently the head of the Fae Purification and Preservation Society." He spat the words, face twisting, as if the phrase itself had tainted the surface of his tongue.

"I thought that party died out years ago."

"No, they'd been hiding, keeping a low profile until the storm hit. They have a decent following in the Earth and Light Kingdoms, even now."

I blanched, realizing the implications. "Gods, Alarik... did they find out she was dating you—a human?"

"Yes."

He gripped my hands as if drawing strength to finish this

story from them. "We were planning a wedding. She never got along with her father, but she wanted her mother's blessing. Rhosyn hadn't seen or spoken to them since she left—except to say that she was alive. She sent the final letter, confessing our love and the date of our wedding. There was no location, no guest names, but she at least wanted her mother to know. It was only the date.

"We had one last mission. It was the night before the wedding. I wanted her to stay back—I wanted her happy and resting—but she told me she wouldn't be happy until I was safe beside her. So, I let her come.

"It was a trap. Her father tracked us down. The entire mission was a setup, a sick performance to show the world what would happen to any fae that chose to pollute their blood with a human."

I could feel Alarik drifting, pulled under by the weight of the memories. His stare was vacant, skin pale as he forced the words through numbed lips. "He gave kill orders. For his own daughter."

A gasp tore from my throat, but Alarik didn't hear. He stared through me, remembering that terrible night. "We were outnumbered and outmatched. They—they made me watch as they carved her up, and then hung what was left from a great oak tree."

My stomach turned.

"I knew her father had orchestrated it—knew he was capable of horrific things... but then her mother stepped out from behind the tree. She didn't flinch—not once—as her daughter's blood dripped... as the earth grew dark with it."

"Gods," I breathed.

His fists balled as his thoughts shifted, sorrow transforming to rage. "And then that bitch cast a ward around the tree, as if everything else wasn't enough. She warded her from me, forcing her body to remain on display.

"It took me weeks to find a fae who would help me. None wanted to risk the wrath of the society, not with the Earth and the Light Kingdoms backing it." His eyes found mine. "I can't let that happen to you, El. I won't make the same mistake. I can't. I won't survive…"

A sob wracked his chest as he crumpled against me.

"I'm here," I soothed, holding him as his body shook. "I'm here. I'm not leaving you."

Pain seared through me, burning with the need to comfort him, but nothing I could say would lessen the his anguish. Nothing I could do would erase the horrific scenes he'd been forced to witness. I couldn't change the past, and I wouldn't insult him by offering hollow words he'd heard dozens of times before.

So, I held him as tight as I could, letting my body impart the emotions my words couldn't. We sank deeper into the cushions, his head coming to rest against my chest. The beat of our hearts slowed as our breathing synced, our two bodies recognizing the other as a place of safety.

After a time, he spoke, his voice as broken and as raw as he was. "Stay with me. I'll have dinner sent up." The green of his eyes was made brighter by the redness surrounding them, swirling with a vulnerability and a hint of playfulness.

I quirked a brow. "What exactly do you mean by 'stay'?"

"Not like that. I just want to be near you." He brought his full, soft lips to my knuckles, pressing gentle kisses against them. "Please?"

My small, surrendering smile answered. "I'll need to get some things first. Say goodnight to Will and my sisters, but I could come back after—"

He pulled me in for a deep kiss, stealing my breath as he pressed me further into the cushions.

Just as I'd decided a change of clothes was overrated and I'd much rather continue this, he pulled back. The hunger grew softer, transitioning into something far more sensual. Feather light kisses adorned my nose, my cheeks, a whisper of one across my lips.

"Will you reconsider your plans? Now that you understand our enemy better, will you be content with safety?"

I should've answered no. I should have explained that 'safe' wasn't a word that described me, nor would I want it to be. But Alarik had just confessed. He was broken and I knew all too well what that felt like. He had patched himself up, as I had, but our scars were still there. Ripping open again and again when the ghosts came calling, always knitting together into an alluring collage of life and death. Of sorrow and hope.

Right now, there was a budding blossom of hope peering down at me through his eyes, reaching through a wash of darkness hovering along the edges, the thick clouds waiting to smother it.

I wanted it to grow, that light, more desperately than I'd wanted anything before. Because if Alarik could hope, if he could love and allow himself to be loved after everything he'd been through, then perhaps I could too.

I'd thought we were meant to be sculptures, ones that had been chipped and poorly glued back together, but maybe we weren't broken. Maybe we were a mosaic, our exterior grey shells meant to be shattered, the pieces gathered and flipped to expose the bright, colorful coating within.

No, I wouldn't be content with a life of safety, but in that moment, with the raw exposure of his past before me, I couldn't find the will to destroy him with the truth.

Instead, I crashed back into him, my lips dancing with his as the world and all the horrors of the past fell away. I needed nothing more than this, than the taste his lips on mine, the warmth of his hands slipping under my shirt, scorching my flesh as they continued up my back.

Our breaths grew ragged, our bodies heating, as we

consumed one another. I wanted more—*needed* more. I pulled back, only long enough to yank my shirt free. Alarik wasted no time in removing his own, emerald eyes igniting as they swept over my heaving chest, my flushed skin.

And then he was on me, his body leaning over mine, as I sank into the sofa. My fingers wandered over the hard planes of his back, memorizing every shifting muscle as he moved. I arched into his touch, gasping as his hands explored my chest, his mouth never breaking from mine.

This was what I wanted—what I yearned for. This was what my starved, withered heart had been deprived of.

He pulled back, hovering above me as his eyes held mine. "I want tonight to be about you. I don't want to rush this."

Alarik pressed soft kisses to the curve of my jaw, trailing the sensitive slope of my neck. My body hummed as he continued, licking and nipping at a torturously slow pace down my chest and over the slope of my aching breasts.

His lips closed around a nipple, tongue swirling as his palm worked the other. A gasp stole from my lips as his fingers pinching the peaked tip, before drifting down. They traced the soft edge of my pants, my body tensing as they slipped beneath.

Alarik paused, making to pull away, but my hand lashed out, refusing to let him go. I'd never been with anyone in this way, never known these feelings. And yet... I wanted to. Gods, did I want to. It felt right with Alarik. Easy and uncomplicated—so different from anything else in my life. I took in the sight of him, his swollen lips, the desire tinting his cheeks, and the question looming in his deep green eyes.

"I haven't done this before. I'm not sure what to do." I flushed with the admission, knowing he'd been with others.

He seemed to read beneath the confession. "Would you like to stop?"

Would you like to stop? I was nervous, yes, but the kind of nervous where my entire body felt alive. Where I was scared and excited and… awake for what felt like the first time.

"Keep going." My voice was steady as I answered.

"Let me know if we're moving too fast." He held my gaze a moment longer before pressing a gentle kiss to my lips.

"I will," I said, lifting my hips to remove what was left of my clothing. The erratic beat of my heart thundered through my ears as I laid back, baring my trembling body before him.

Yearning and something deeper flashed across his face. "You're beautiful, El," he breathed as he drank me in.

His movements were unhurried and tender as he sank into me, always ensuring I was comfortable, letting me know it was okay if I wasn't. But I wanted him—wanted us. I wanted to feel alive, to feel beautiful and bright and good. I wanted to feel *seen*.

My mind, my fears and worries, everything quieted. I allowed myself to simply *feel*. Letting my body take over, I arched into his touch, willing him to stroke the warmth pooling low in my stomach, seeking release from this mounting tension. His hand cupped the apex of my thighs and I dropped my knees wider, wanting him—needing him. I groaned as he answered my body's plea, sinking a finger through my slick heat. My hips undulated as he added a second, tensing as that euphoric coil drew tight.

He increased the pace, his mouth lapping at my breasts as I rode him. My body was on fire, tightening around his fingers as they pumped. And when his thumb stroked that sensitive bundle, when his mouth clamped over mine, stealing the moan from my lips, as I shattered against him.

His gaze held mine as he worked the last bit of pleasure from my body. It simmered with a desire and tenderness that I'd never known. I stared back into his eyes, letting him see the vulnerability in mine… My life was a mess. I was flawed and a little broken, but as I stared up at the man before me, I let myself believe I was whole.

CHAPTER 41

LANNIE AND WILL WERE SETTLING IN FOR A BEDTIME STORY WHEN I arrived at my room. Will insisted I stay for the tale, but ended up falling asleep half-way through. Being sure to leave the light on in case his nightmares returned, we tucked him into bed before returning to the hall.

"Goodluck on the mission, tomorrow," Lannies said. "I'm guessing you'll be leaving early?"

"Before the sun rises. It should be a quick trip. Only a few days, and then we'll be back."

Lannie nodded. "I took the liberty of adding fresh salve to your supplies. I dropped off a batch earlier in the day for the Select Guard, just in case."

My lips broke into a smile as I pulled her in for a hug. "Thanks, sis."

"No problem. Try not to need it," she said, turning for her own room.

I had only started packing when Greer found me, her eyes going wide when she saw the overnight supplies. When I confessed I'd be spending the night with Alarik, she squealed and rushed me from the room, assuring me she would have everything I needed delivered to his rooms.

〜

THE SAVORY SCENT OF BUTTER AND ROSEMARY STILL CLUNG TO the air of Alarik's suite, remnants of the juicy chicken and roasted potatoes we'd consumed earlier. The reprieve of dinner faded into an awkward silence, warmth heating my cheeks as I reflected on what we'd done just hours before. Fluttering nerves swirled through me, and I couldn't help but imagine what tonight might bring. Alarik wasn't the type of man to instill expectations, but I found myself unnerved by my own longing.

A member of the kitchen staff returned to gather the plates, bringing with him a platter of pastries accompanied by a bundle of clothing and toiletries.

My brows furrowed. "Where's my pack?"

"Greer said you'd ask about that," he answered as he piled the food-stained dishes. "Said to tell you it would be sent in a few hours. Something about not wanting you to wear your uniform to sleep."

Alarik snorted, his hair still damp from his recent shower.

Shooting him a glare, I scooped up my things. "Would it be all right if I took a shower?"

"Of course," Alarik said, starting toward the back hall as the man wheeled the plates away. "It's right this way."

"Thank you," I mumbled. After retrieving new towels, he left me.

The near scalding water drifted over me in a warm embrace. It was strangely intimate to be using his shower, and I found I liked the cool blue tones of the tiles. I took liberties with his shampoo, inhaling a deep breath of his scent as I worked the suds across my body.

Insecurities and nerves plagued me at the idea of staying over. I'd thought about an excuse to leave half-a-dozen times already, but if I left now, it would seem like I was running from all that Alarik had shared. I couldn't do that to him... and I realized I liked the idea of spending tonight in his arms. It was a new feeling, to be wanted.

Toweling off, I reached into the bag of clothes, expecting to find a set of comfortable sweats and one of my oversized t-shirts, but Greer had other plans.

She'd left me the choice of a sheer nightgown with a fitted bust—the edge of the material definitely not long enough to cover my ass, a pair of white silky night shorts with a small matching tank, or a bundle of red lacy fabric that I didn't bother holding up.

A curse left my lips. I debated putting my filthy training clothes back on for a moment before sighing and selecting the shorts and top set. The material clung to my body like a second skin.

Stiffeling a groan, I brushed my damp hair, leaving the chestnut waves loose, but the ends barely covering my chest. I frowned at my reflection, rearranging my hair to provide the most coverage. Taking one last steadying breath, I tilted my chin up and walked out.

A choking sound rang from Alarik's direction, followed by a harsher-than-normal clang of his cup meeting the table. I refused to meet his gaze as I sank into the plush sofa. Leaning against the opposite arm, I swung my legs up toward the middle, my toes brushing the worn fabric of Alarik's sweats.

Failing to contain the blush staining my cheeks, I dared a glance up. Hooded eyes met mine, drinking in the effect my damp hair had across my pebbled skin.

"Greer promised to send up clothes for me. Clearly, she can't be trusted." I bit my lip as Alarik's eyes roved across my body, leaving trails of electricity in their wake. "Trust me, this was the best option."

The intensity of his gaze was searing. Flames danced across my skin as his eyes wandered along the silky material stretched tight across the slope of my breasts, down the stretch of my stomach, lower still to the small bits of material pooled at the top of my thighs.

My legs clenched under the heat of his stare. Alarik swallowed, noting the movement before dragging his eyes up.

"I can only imagine what the other options were."

My cheeks flared a bright red. I willed the frantic beating of my heart to calm as I focused on adjusting the edges of the shorts, as if they would somehow grow longer. "Yes, well, she has a funny sense of humor."

"Funny is not the word I would use to describe what you're wearing." He hesitated, but continued after a moment, forcing the words out. "But if you're uncomfortable, you can wear some of my clothes."

I twisted around, an incredulous grin threatening to break free. "You want me to put *more* clothes on?"

"What? No, I want you in less clothes. I mean, not less clothes, per se. I think you look great with any amount of clothing on." He groaned, raking a hand through his already messy hair. "Gods, what I'm trying to say is that you're beautiful no matter what you wear."

Strangely, his ramblings put me at ease. Maybe Greer was on to something. Leaning forward, I grabbed a book from the table and settled closer, allowing my thigh to graze him.

"Thank you for the offer. It's good to know I have options."

"You always have options. Many, in fact." He draped his arm across my shoulders, his fingers tracing small circles along my skin. "For instance, if *you* wanted less clothing, that would be a perfectly acceptable option."

"Ha. Ha." It was meant to be light, but the words were little more than hushed desire as images of myself bared before his surfaced.

"I promise you, I mean that with the utmost sincerity."

My mouth went dry as I lowered the book. Looking up at him, I thought that maybe I'd been more lost than I'd realized— not lost, but stunted. Maybe Greer had been right about more than one thing, tonight. I'd stopped myself from letting anyone get close, and in doing so, had prevented my heart from maturing. At some point, my circle of protection had become a cage, one in which Alarik had managed to unlock. Now, I found myself craving freedom.

Pressing up, I watched his eyes grow wide as my chest brushed against his. Willing my erratic heart to calm, I bit down on my trembling lip. We had kissed before, but this felt different —bigger somehow. His eyes dipped to my mouth, his tongue flicking out across his own at the sight.

Pushing past the frenzied emotions whirling through me, I leaned in, my lips meeting his in a bold but questioning kiss. He stilled, causing my stomach to twist in angst. I knew we'd been off earlier. He'd known my answer to his question, even if I hadn't voiced it.

"Now that you understand our enemy better, will you be content with safer missions?"

We both knew I wouldn't. I wasn't about to give up the thrill of fighting before I'd even started. Or worse—was his hesitancy about Rhosyn? Gods, if he regretted being with me... Heart sinking, I made to pull away, but his body came alive before I could retreat.

His fingers gently tipped my chin up, green eyes darting between my hazel-blue ones with a desperately harsh glint. "I meant what I said, about not being able to give you all of me."

I had listened before, but only now did I understand. "You still love her."

"Always," he breathed, face crumbling as the word left his lips. "I know there are things we need to work through, but if you can be content with only half of me, I promise to try to understand your need for training."

There was that word again. *Content.*

His heart wasn't whole and probably never would be. Mine was locked away and had been starved for years. If he could offer me the fractured pieces of his, then I could find a way to crack the cage around mine—to share in the root of our nothingness.

"To share our nothingness?"

His lips twitched. "So, we are agreed?"

My eyes dipped to his lips. I nodded. "Kiss me."

"El, I think we should set some parameters—"

"Just kiss me."

His jaw ticked, wavering between logic and lust. I tilted forward, letting my forehead lean against his.

"Please..." I didn't want to talk. I was stunted and he was splintered. We were flawed. Boundaries weren't going to change that. It was better to simply jump and enjoy the fall without being completely aware of the merciless shards waiting beneath.

My hands slid up his chest, fingers brushing across the nape of his neck, a silent request joining my pleading words. Just as I thought he would turn away, he yielded, his lips claiming mine in a swift, sensual kiss.

I gasped as heat surged through me, melting into the gentle rhythm of his mouth moving sweetly beneath mine. His lips eased, his broad, sweeping hands gliding up my spine to hold me against him in a tender embrace.

I didn't want tender. I deepened the kiss—craving his taste—needing to feel him want me as much as I wanted him. He growled, mirroring my own unquenchable thirst, as his palms gripped my thighs, his tongue sweeping between my lips. And then we were nothing more than tongues and teeth and soft lips clashing. We were two blazing bodies rocking against one another, seeking the answers to questions left unasked.

His hands left sparks of electricity in their wake as they trailed up, reaching around to cup my ass, lifting me onto him. My knees wrapping around his waist, opening the softest parts of me to his growing hardness. Fire roared through my veins as I ground against him, gripping his head to mine as our mouths fought to consume one another.

A breathy moan escaped my lips as his fingers dug into the flesh of my thighs, his hard length shamelessly pressing against my core with only the thin scraps of fabric separating us. His hands snaked under the silkiness of my top, igniting every inch of my body as he explored the curves of my back. His thumbs drifted around—just below my breasts, tracing their full outlines before stopping.

Panting, he pulled back. I couldn't help but appreciate his swollen lips, already desperate to taste them again.

"I'm not sure what you're ready for," he breathed, chest heaving.

Taking a few shallow breaths, I kept my eyes locked with his as my fingers grasped the edge of my top. His gaze latched on to the movement with reverence as I pulled the light material over my head, the silk caressing my skin, before it fell away.

"Any questions?"

His eyes met mine at the challenge, a hand darting to the back of my neck, while the other wrapped around my ass. Before the gasp left my lips, he flipped us, laying me out before him on the soft cushions.

"You're so beautiful," he said, yanking the back of his collar up and tossing his shirt aside. A wicked grin flashed across his lips as he leaned over me, holding the weight of his body so that we were nothing more than a tantalizing brush of flesh.

I gasped as he pinched my nipple, rolling the tip before his tongue flicked across it, soothing the ache with gentle, easing motions. My back arched, my hand gripping his hair, begging for more of that pleasurable pain. He answered, mouth rumbling, as he switched to the other side.

Then his lips were traveling down. I fought for breath as his hands returned to my breasts, working the hard tips until they, too, were on fire. The warmth between my thighs grew with each brush of his lips against my flesh, each caress bringing him closer to where I needed him most.

His movements slowed as he looped his fingers in the silky material of my shorts, eyes finding mine.

"Tell me to stop, if you wish."

I didn't speak.

His tongue darted out across his bottom lip as he lowered himself between my legs, slipping the last of the fabric off. A warm heat flooded my body as his hands slowly trailed up my ankles, wrapping around my knees, to press my thighs apart. My breathing hitched as Alarik hovered over my core, his golden hair mussed and messy.

He flashed me a wicked grin before pressing soft, tantalizing kisses against my inner thighs, working his way up. I arched into him, that deep coil low in my belly drawing painfully tight.

"Alarik..." It was a plea, an acknowledgement that I wanted more of him, that I needed more.

His chest rumbled as his mouth descended in answer. I gasped as he tasted me, nervous at first, but soon my knees weakened, dropping further to draw him deeper. He licked and swirled, feasting on my center, until my hands were gripping the cushions, my back arching. The wicked pressure escalated, thrusting me toward the edge.

Sensing my need, his mouth moved up, finding the sensitive bundle as he slipped a finger through my slick heat. A second joined, filling me, stretching me, as his tongue flicked. Moans poured from my lips, growing louder as my body burned. His teeth grazed the bundle of nerves as his fingers pumped harder, hurling me into oblivion.

Only after the last of the waves had ebbed and my breathing returned to normal, did I open my eyes. He licked his lips as he took in my soaking core. The sight alone nearly caused me to come again.

"Gods, you're perfect."

He rose, coming to rest beside me. I kissed him, loving the taste of myself on his lips.

"I take a tonic every month." I swallowed, hating the hint of pink that graced my cheeks, even after what we had just done.

"Are you sure?" he breathed, his thumb brushing over the color.

There were no false promises between us. No hidden agenda. We simply were. I knew his heart had followed Rhosyn beyond this realm and he knew there wasn't enough of my guarded heart to give. Neither of us was whole. This wouldn't be a fairytale, but it would be real. Flawed, and broken, and... ours.

"I'm sure."

He pressed a tender kiss to my lips as he lifted me from the sofa. My legs settled around him, tightening across his middle as he carried me down the hall. His mouth never broke from mine, each kiss delivered with a gentleness that ate away at me.

The cool press of sheets greeted my back as we tumbled onto the bed. My thumbs hooked into the band of his pants, pushing the fabric down. He shifted, disposing of the last of his clothes as he settled over me.

Our bodies fit together, his hard length pressing against me. Only then did he wait, watching my face as he nudged at my opening. I nodded my permission.

My breathing hitched as he eased in. His thickness stretched me, the burning ache increasing, until a sharp pain lashed through me, pulling a gasp from my lips.

"Should I stop?" His voice was strained as he fought against the need to move.

"Keep going," I breathed, the foreign sensation painful and thrilling all at once.

"Tell me if I hurt you."

His body started rocking within mine, the slow momentum lessening the pain. I dropped my knees a little further, relaxing into the tempo, as his hips gently worked. Alarik's lips worshiped the rest of me. They dipped to my neck, turning ravenousness when they found my breasts. Electric shocks raced through my veins, igniting wave after wave of pleasurable heat until the pain was lost and only bliss remained.

I moaned as our pace increased, the soreness between my thighs replaced by that delicious tightening I was coming to know. My fingers dug into his back as he surged forth, our bodies finding the perfect rhythm as we moved, climbing and chasing the peaks of pleasure together.

I found it first, soaring from the mountain tops as my body shuddered around his, sending Alarik over the edge to fly with me.

My breathing was still ragged when he disentangled himself, both of our bodies flushed. My head lolled against him, cradled in the nook of his arm as he pressed a sleepy kiss to my forehead.

We had agreed to share our nothingness, knowing that was all we had to give, but as we settled into bed, as the ebb and flow of his breathing evened out and the curves of our bodies sank into one another, I couldn't help but wonder if we had created something, all the same.

CHAPTER 42

I wasn't sure rest would find us with the mission looming, but sleep had come and gone. Once again, my nightmares had been absent.

My hand stretched behind me, searching for Alarik's warmth. Only cold sheets greeted me. Fabric rustled from the other side of the room as legs slid into pants, followed by a quiet click of the door. My eyes fluttered open. Could it be time already? The room was still dark, but I knew we'd be leaving before dawn.

Stifling a yawn, I rolled out of bed in search of my own clothes. My pack had been sent up, as promised, and now sat beside the chair, the scraps of silk from last night piled next to them. The soreness between my thighs confirmed I had, indeed, spent the night with Alarik. The memory was arousing, unnerving, and liberating all at once.

I slipped into a pair of crisp, brown pants, and an off-white long sleeved undershirt. Wrapping the russet leather overlay around my body, I tugged the strings to cinch in at the waist, letting the fluttering of my heart fill me with warmth. I expected to feel different, and I guess a piece of me did, but not how I'd thought I would. I was myself, only a little stronger and less inhibited than before.

As I secured my brown, knee-high boots, I contemplated the journey ahead. There was a buzzing creeping through my body, a drive to move beyond the limits of the Borderlands and the forest that surrounded it. A yearning to explore outside of this small patch of land that had been the backdrop to my entire life.

I'd realized it last night when Alarik's arms came around me. It wasn't an urge to leave, not exactly. It was more like a restlessness—the nagging feeling of being in the wrong place at the right time, of forgetting something important with the shadow of a memory stirring just beyond consciousness.

The turning of the doorknob and the sound of easy footsteps signaled Alarik's return from the washroom, pausing the reveries of my mind.

"Good morning, beautiful." Alarik smiled, sweeping across the room to place a gentle kiss on my lips. The minty aftertaste and swirling scent of spices filled the air.

"Good morning." Pressing onto my toes, I surprised both of us by deepening the kiss. Alarik's arms wrapped around me, the intimacy of last night rushing back.

"Mmm, *great* morning," he mused, a roguish grin on his face. His thumb grazed my chin, holding my face to him a moment longer before letting his hand drop. He offered no sweet words about what last night meant. Rather than a flash of disappointment, I found I was grateful he didn't fill the silence with hollow words.

"The others will meet us at the stables. Are you ready?"

"Almost," I muttered, slipping past him to the washroom.

When I returned, the lights were on, allowing me to take in his room for the first time without the cover of darkness. The bed was a swath of soft greys, complete with a few throw pillows and one fluffy off-white, knitted throw. The walls were minimalistic, a clean slate of the lightest storm clouds, mirroring the crisp chill of morning fog on an early winter's day. It was ordered, devoid of clutter, but there were hints of personal touches, like the leather-bound journal on his bedside table and a map of Pax along the far wall, marked with multicolored flags.

My eyes narrowed as I took in the small red dots concentrated throughout the northern half of Pax. The scarlet splashes trailed up, spilling over the southern portion of the Dark Kingdom. Amid the pins was a glaring, crimson circle encasing a town only a few miles west of where we'd be traveling today: Neith.

"What's this?" I asked, pointing to the circle.

Alarik looked up from pulling fresh sheets over the mattress. "Just a map cataloging the attacks."

The artificial offhandedness must have seemed forced even to him, because he released a sigh after tucking in the last corner and came to my side.

"We haven't been able to find a common ground between the attacks, not in all the strikes we've looked into in the past seven years, until this." His finger reached out to indicate the circle.

"Neith? Wasn't that the city mentioned at the trading market?"

"Yes. We've been monitoring it, but the inhabitants remain peaceful. It's known as a quaint village where the residents have given up riches and chosen to live quiet lives..."

"But," I prompted, jolting him from his thoughts.

He shifted, swallowing once before turning to me. "It's surrounded by a wall of stone. Stone that, if legends are believed, pulse with a silver-blue light in times of an attack."

My heart skipped a beat. Like the ones at the ancient temple near my home. Like the ones that had called to me while I was with Ember in the forest.

I swallowed. "What does it mean?"

"I'm not sure. I do know that Neith is an ancient village and said to be where Evulka and her human lover, Khrysaor, built their life."

"I've heard the stories," I breathed. "They were the first fae-human union. Evulka gave up her life to be with her human lover."

Greer had called it 'tragically romantic,' and though I couldn't see how *two* individuals dying rather than *one* was romantic, I found it fascinating that Evulka would give up her own unnaturally long life for another.

"Yes," Alarik continued, "but she didn't just die. Upon Khrysaor's death, Evulka chose to siphon her life force into the surrounding lands rather than live without him. It is said that with her death, the stones were blessed with the power to protect, only allowing those who hold no ill will for the town's inhabitants to cross the boundaries. To this day, it is known as a place where humans and fae are free to be with one another, without prejudice."

I turned my sights from Alarik to the blazing red circle on the map. "That doesn't sound bad."

"No, but the legend is not well understood and has not been tested by an attack over two hundred years. If it truly is protected, what power decides who is friend and who is foe?"

His face knitt together in concentration, as if he could discern the information from the circled village. It was there a moment longer before smoothing out.

"It's of no matter, at least not for this mission. Our target village is here." He pointed to a benign black dot to the right just beyond the borders of the Dark Kingdom.

"That's where we're going?"

"It is."

Bubbles of anticipation rose within me as I stared at the seemingly insignificant black dot. This was my first mission, the first real one, anyway. The trading market was familiar, but this would take me outside the boundaries deemed safe for humans.

It would be the furthest from home I'd gone—into the Dark Kingdom itself. For most, that thought alone would send a shiver of fear snaking through them.

I turned to meet Alarik's resigned expression, a smile stretching across my face. "Let the adventure begin."

CHAPTER 43

We met the others at the stables, their stallions saddled and prepared for the journey. In the dim light of dawn, I could make out Vidarr's blond hair. Small twists and braids pulled along the sides, the top half secured in a woven tie, drawing attention to his full light-blond beard. He always looked ready to destroy something, but with his thick frame covered in battle leathers and the glint of steel along his thighs and back, he looked down-right primal.

Cadoc was beside him, looking as much like a bear as ever, with his shaggy dark hair and wide jaw, his bulk only growing with the number of weapons strapped to him.

I saw Zelos next, hovering among three others working on saddles for their horses. I vaguely recognized them from training. The one with dark skin and golden eyes was exceptionally skilled at archery and the other two were brother, their sleek black hair and broad cheekbones hinting at their origins from the southern kingdoms. They all donned similar weapons and armor, the insignia classifying them as members of the Select Guard.

My eyes widened as Evander stepped from the stables with

Colt in tow. I shrieked, causing all eyes to snap toward me as I sprinted for him.

"I didn't know you were back," I choked, crashing into him with a hug.

"I returned last night. I went to see you," his eyes darted to Alarik briefly before returning to mine, the small movement heating my cheeks, "but was told that you were spending the night studying. With General Holt."

His face hardened at my confirming blush.

"Gods, El. I told you to be kind to him, not to escalate the situation. I thought you would let him down easy." His voice was stiff as he attempted to keep it low enough for the others not to hear. "He's your commanding officer. *My* commanding officer. Have you thought about how this will affect your role here? How people will doubt if you've earned any advancement or mission you receive?"

My heart stumbled at his words.

"Not to mention the strain that comes from being in an inferior position." Evander pressed his fingers against his temples. "You will need to separate your personal relationship from the professional one, because if he issues commands as General Holt, you will have to obey them, like we all do, even if you don't agree."

I swallowed past the thickness in my mouth. "Gods, I didn't think it would be this complicated."

He fixed me with a pointed stare. "Do you care for him? Is it serious?"

Did I care for him? Was it serious? Those were two very different questions, but I nodded all the same.

Evander sighed. "Alarik is not a man prone to relationships. If he voiced any type of sentiment or affection for you, it's real."

A warm glow spread through me. I glanced over Evander's shoulder, watching as Alarik mounted his horse. His eyes found mine across the distance, smirking at having caught me staring.

"I want you to be happy, El. I want him to be happy, too. Gods know you both deserve it. But commanding officer or not, you tell me if he does anything to hurt you."

My mouth twitched with Evander's earnest promise. His frame was as tall as Alarik's, but lean. I doubted a fight would sway in his favor.

His lips quirked, as if reading my mind. "He may be bigger than me, but not all battles are won with physical strength. You of all people should understand that. I have ways of defending my loved ones."

I smiled as he mounted Colt before joining the others. Ember was waiting impatiently beside Alarik. She was small compared to the battle stallions surrounding her, but just as fierce.

"I'm surprised you've been able to tame her," Alarik remarked. "She even let Evander secure a saddle for this journey."

"There's no taming Ember. I set her free and with her freedom I earned her trust and respect. We're a team, her and I."

"Whatever you did, it worked," Alarik said as he handed me a few small weapons. "These are to be used in case of emergency. The mission is still recon, but I'd rather have you over prepared than under."

He placed the blades into my outstretched hands, giving me an approving nod as I looped one along my forearm and the other along the hidden inner seam of my boot. I held an expectant hand up, but Alarik shook his head.

"That's it? I have plenty of room for others."

"Recon, El. You shouldn't need weapons." He turned toward the others, completing a final check before we left.

"Need and want are two very different things," I mumbled under my breath as I climbed into the saddle.

And then we were off.

CHAPTER 44

THE SUN BROKE OVER THE HORIZON AS WE GALLOPED THROUGH meadows, the yellows and whites of wildflowers sprinkled among swaying grasses. Small creeks gave way to large rivers as wide stretches of smooth pastures climbed into rocky slopes covered with vast pine forests.

The horses proved nimble as they maneuvered the rough terrain, ascending the foothills until we arrived at a clearing on an outstretched sheet of rock. The valley expanded beneath us in shades of evergreen pines. Great mountains pierced the sky in the west, their violet ridges capped with snow, trickling along hidden crevices to give way to the frosted lakes beneath.

"Incredible, isn't it?" Alarik asked as he dismounted. The Select Guard and Zelos followed suit, trailing in various directions for a much-deserved rest. "We'll be stopping here for a few minutes before we finish the last leg of the journey. How are you doing?"

Ember wandered with the other horses as I came to Alarik's side. "I'm excited. And nervous. This is the furthest I've ever traveled."

The wind swirled across my face as I peered over the land. It was there again. That pull, beckoning me, daring me to follow. Closing my eyes, I could almost see it. It was the promise of open skies and vast, green-covered mountains. One of dramatic cliffs and free-falling waters.

Alarik's fingers threaded through mine, their warmth grounding me to the present.

"Even before," I said, voice soft, "when I traveled with my father and brothers, we never ventured beyond the trading market. My mother had planned on taking Greer, Lannie, and me to the Light Kingdom at some point. She claimed it was to widen our horizons, but we both knew the trip would be for hunting husbands more than anything else."

He huffed a laugh, pulling out a bundle of bread and a block of cheese. "In that case, I'm glad you never got the chance to explore."

"Thank you," I said, biting into the loaf and savoring the flaky crust.

Alarik pulled out a canister of water, following my gaze back to the valley below. "Those are the Jagged Mountains in the west."

My eyes widened. The Jagged Mountains trailed through nearly all of the seven kingdoms, growing until their massive peaks reached the secluded Wild Kingdom. This far north, they were known as the marking border between the Dark Kingdom and the Fire Kingdom. "Wait, so we're almost out of the Borderlands?"

"Almost. Do you see the river that widens along the eastern edge, curving around the field of purple flowers?" He turned toward the east, pointing out a twisting brook, its waters glistening under the high sun.

"Yes."

"That's the border. Once we cross, you'll be in the Dark Kingdom. Selene is another two hours north. When we reach the town limits, the others will stay along the tree line, but I'll trail you the entire time to ensure things go according to plan."

I cocked an eyebrow in his direction. "I thought I was to go in alone. Aren't I to mingle with the other distraught females and figure out what the men of this world have been destroying lately?"

He met my snark with a glare. "I do want you to listen, specifically for anything helpful in identifying our enemy. Right now, all signs are pointing to a rogue group of dark fae."

A chill raked through me as I recalled the warped, crazed fae we met near my home—rotted creatures with cold black eyes and greying, mottled skin. My eyes flicked to the tick of his jaw. "You still don't believe the dark fae are responsible?"

He shook his head, looking out at the beauty of the forest. "Like I said, the dark fae were known for their acceptance of humans and celebrating the diversity of the fae. I know that's not what most humans have been told, but from what I've gathered from ancient texts, they've been welcoming. A few accounts even mention them accepting unwanted fae-human offspring. It doesn't make sense they would be targeting humans." Ernest, green eyes found me. "Maybe if we listen long enough, the people of this realm will reveal something to lead us to our true enemy."

I nodded, mulling over the truth of his words. "Any other leads?"

"I have a theory."

"You think the southern kingdoms are behind the attacks," I stated, guessing where his thoughts had led him—to his past, to her. "You think they somehow orchestrated the storm?"

"Both the Earth and the Light Kingdoms have a documented history of hatred." *Like with his marriage to Rhosyn.* "The Water Kingdom as well, though to a lesser extent. They are geographically isolated from the north, which puts them in a precarious position if they speak out against their neighbors."

Alarik's face was marred with a frown as he continued in a low, steady voice. "But, yes. I think the storm was a curse against humans enacted by the southern kingdoms. I still believe it to be the first attack in a list of countless others. I know it sounds like the vendetta of a scorned lover, but my reasoning has nothing to do with what happened to—to her."

"I trust you, Alarik. I'll keep my eyes and ears open."

And I did trust him, but I understood that he'd also been through a lot. Not only losing his first love, but to have her butchered in front of him... it was more than anyone should have to endure. How could that not skew his opinion?

Most of Pax feared the dark fae and looked to the light fae as our saviors. They were blessed in healing and unrivaled in their talent to construct wards. I wasn't sure about the Earth Kingdom, but it was ingrained in light fae to fix illnesses, not create them. Furthermore, their army was quaint in comparison to the other kingdoms. They weren't welcoming to outsiders, especially humans, but they lacked the physical skills and mental ruthlessness to construct something of this magnitude.

"Time to go," Alarik said, giving my hand a brief squeeze before rounding up the others.

We picked our way down the hill, one after the other, angling for the border. The forest thinned as we neared. Bright green shrubs dotted the forest floor, speckled in pale pink blossoms and patches of bright white daisies until we came to the river.

Crossing along a shallow, rocky bank, we entered the Dark Kingdom. The scent of sweet-smelling flowers filled my lungs, enveloping me like a soothing embrace. Soon, the sun was low on the horizon and the shadow of a village winked into view.

"Ember will stay with us," Alarik said as we stopped near the edge of the trees. "She's too conspicuous. Remember, you were displaced from your home along the outskirts of the Dark Kingdom after running from an attack and are seeking shelter."

I slid down as Ember huffed her disagreement. "Don't worry, I'll be back soon and then we can race these guys back to the base tomorrow morning. What do you think?"

She neighed her excitement, nudging me with her velvet nose as if insisting I hurry with the mission so we could get to the fun part.

Alarik slipped off his own horse, pointing toward a tall, pitched roof. "I'll be waiting near that building to collect you."

"I can do this," I soothed, suppressing my own nerves to give him a reassuring smile.

He frowned, looking like he might change his mind. "Actually, I think it might be best if—"

"Of course, you can do this," Vidarr's strong voice sounded as he dismounted next to us. He clasped my shoulder before meeting Alarik's hard glare. "She's smart, Alarik. She can handle herself. Not to mention she's been kicking the men's asses for days now."

The rest of the Guard voiced their agreement at Vidarr's candor, but Zelos's raucous huff was the loudest among them.

"She can handle herself, General," Zelos said, eyes never leaving mine. "Can't you, sweetheart?"

"Yes, I can." I flashed him and the Guard a grateful smile. My heart clenched as I caught sight of Evander's face, beaming with pride. He gave me a near imperceptible nod. A blessing.

"See?" I said, meeting Alarik's waiting eyes. "There's nothing to worry about. I'll see you in a few hours." Not waiting for a response, I pushed past him toward Selene.

"El," Alarik called. "Remember to be out before nightfall. The shelter closes at dusk and won't open again until dawn. If you're inside when that happens, we won't attempt to get you out. The women and children within have been through enough."

"Relax, General. It's just a recon mission."

His lips twitched. Ignoring the men's stares, I turned and headed toward the looming buildings. How hard could it be?

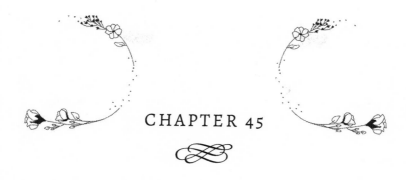

CHAPTER 45

SELENE WAS A QUAINT VILLAGE. SMALL COTTAGES COMPLETE WITH home gardens and worn dirt roads stretched before me. Tattered cotton clothing swayed in the light breeze as children scurried beneath, their giggles mixing with the growing sounds of the town beyond.

Following the gentle slope of the road, the packed dirt transitioned to cobblestone streets lined with window-front shops and petite cafes. A worn wooden sign with a fresh coat of paint greeted those entering the town: Welcome to Selene.

Passing through the main square, I skirted around the babbling fountain toward the building tucked in the far corner. The stones were a dark grey, the edges rounded with time, but the stained glass adorning each window was as majestic as ever. Following the narrow path, I approached the small door under the tower with the symbol of the triple moon goddess set atop its arched frame.

I made to enter, but drew up short when I spotted the two burly looking men in full armor standing guard. A woman with ash colored hair and kind eyes stood between them, dwarfed by their size. The lines across her face deepened into a smile as I took the last few steps forward.

"Hello, young soul. Are you in need of a safe place to rest? It's not much, but we can offer a soft pillow and a meager meal. If you have any men with you, they will need to find lodging elsewhere. Only women and children are allowed."

I glanced at the two hulking figures on either side of the steps.

"Don't mind them. These are a few of my grandsons. They are here to protect us but still not allowed to enter." Her voice softened with the small dip of my head. "Come, child. Let's get you something to eat."

The guards parted, allowing us to slip under the ancient goddess's protection as we entered. The cool stones of the hall widened into a vast room. Great wooden beams arched across the vaulted ceilings, the space illuminated by domed windows along the upper level. Ornate metal lanterns lined the walkways, their flickering candles casting small designs against the deep greys of the inner stone path. We stepped through the peaceful place toward the hallway along the far wall.

The grey-haired woman drifted down the stairs, surprisingly nimble in her movements, until we came to an expansive room, the same length as the one above, but this space was completely enclosed. Rows of make-shift beds covered the floors, composed of repaired cushions and ruffled blankets, but the few families scattered among them seemed content—happy even.

"We originally had the sleeping quarters on the main floor," the elder lady explained. "But most feel safer below. You'll find this room gets rather full as the day ends. We close the gates at sunset and open them with the dawn, but the guards will continue standing watch throughout the night."

"Thank you," I said, finding my voice.

She offered me a warm smile in return. "We do what we can."

A young woman with a child trailing after her, and another slung across her hip, passed through a side corridor, extending a bundle of blankets topped with a pillow. The old woman thanked her before guiding me to an open nook.

"You may stay here as long as you wish. Dinner is served an hour before sunset every day, so they will be preparing it now." She pressed a gnarled hand to mine, her eyes crinkling with a warm smile. "If you have any questions, come find me. My name is Flora."

Once I was sure she was out of sight, I set the blanket and pillow aside. I spared a quick glance around the mostly empty room, composed of a handful of exhausted mothers tending to their crying infants, before stepping into the shadowed hall beyond.

Women and children past, some sparing kind, hesitant smiles, while others shied away. My stomach twisted as another kept her head down. It was an uncomfortable reminder that each person here was seeking refuge. Most had presumably lost family and friends to the deadly attacks, while others were forced to relinquish their homes in an attempt to outrun the onslaught.

I kept my own eyes low as I wandered along chilled passage-ways and abandoned rooms, purposely leaving the crowds to search for anything useful. Some rooms were filled with relics of old, or bits of altars and candles meant for worshiping, but most were vacant.

A weight settled in the pit of my stomach. I'd have to find my way back to the main hall and speak with a few of the residents. I needed to find information that could help the base pinpoint our true enemy.

A looming figure along the far wall of the hallway startled a gasp from my lips as I made to return to the main passage.

"Hello." A sweet voice sounded as a young woman stepped into the light. Tight, umber curls framed her face in a beautiful mane, her deep complexion and thick ebony lashes highlighting the rich, golden hue of her eyes. They were sharp, as calculating as a panther's, but her full lips stretched into a bright smile. "Are you new here?" she asked. "You seem lost."

I fixed a carefree grin to my face as I neared. Her body was crisscrossed with lean, toned muscles, not dissimilar to what mine was becoming.

"It's my first day," I said. My gaze drifted over her long cotton top paired with black pants and boots. It was practical. Most would glance over it, but I knew the quality was too well preserved to be a hunter and too refined to adorn someone of common origin. I glanced toward where the tips of her ears would be, but the halos of curls obscured them from view.

"Would you like me to show you where the food is? Dinner should be nearly ready." Her smile tightened as I joined her side.

"Yes, thank you."

"Not a problem," she said as we started walking. "You can call me Naz. I stop by periodically to see how things are going here. I helped build the shelter, and though I'm glad its bend a place of refuge, I'm sorry for whatever circumstance brought you here."

I could have left it at that, but something about her presence felt oddly comforting and I found the words were tumbling from my lips before I thought better of it. "I lost my parents and twin older brothers."

"I'm sorry for your loss."

Hating the pang of grief that never seemed to fully heal, I shrugged. "Others have suffered greater than I have. I've been traveling on my own, trying to stay ahead of things and heard this place offered safety." Technically, not a lie. "Has there been any progress in identifying the attackers?"

Gilded eyes shot to mine, her smile slipping. I held her gaze, willing my pulse to stay even. A swarm of children darted past as we turned down another well-lit hall, their mothers offering lighthearted apologies as they trailed after.

Just as I had given up on an answer, she spoke. "Some. It sounds like another fae attack. Two more villages have been claimed to the west. Both were isolated and had not asked for additional protection from the crown."

"The crown? As in, the Dark King is offering protection?"

She quirked a brow, studying me a moment longer before responding. "Of course, but they denied the king's aid. Whether from pride or suspicion cultivated from the circulating slander, it was their undoing. I'm sure you've heard some terrible things about the Dark Kingdom yourself. You said you were traveling north?"

I controlled my features as best as I could, trying to recall if I had mentioned traveling north. I didn't think so, but she didn't wait for an answer.

"I assure you, the ruling dark royals are not responsible for the plague ravishing our lands. I know it can be difficult for those not living in the Dark Kingdom to believe, but the king does his best to protect us."

My jaw clenched. So much for blending in. "Perhaps the dark royals aren't responsible for the attacks, but that doesn't mean other dark fae aren't."

Before the words finished leaving my mouth, fingers dug into my shoulder and the world spun. My head crashed against the stone wall with a heavy thud as my vision swam.

"What are you doing here?" she hissed, face inches from mine. I blinked, discovering we were pressed into a secluded alcove just beyond the hall. "You don't seem to be running from anything; no great fear or distress is troubling you, beyond our current predicament."

My hand flew to the concealed dagger along my forearm, but she was quicker.

"Don't," she warned with the press of a blade to my throat. I hadn't even seen her move. "You smell of horses and men, and yet you're alone. You don't have the look of someone accustomed to privilege, but your clothing is new, as are the leather straps beneath holding your freshly sharpened blades. New and *expensive.*"

I swallowed, the movement causing the soft skin of my neck to stretch across the cool steel.

"Instigating fear will not be tolerated here. I will ask only once more, what is your purpose here?"

She glared at me a moment longer as my pulse raced before stepping back. We both knew she could disarm me—or worse—before I'd have a blade in my hand. I took a large breath, and then another, attempting to reign in my fear as my mind whirled, but there was no point in lying.

"I'm not from one of the nearby villages and I'm not here to seek shelter." Her eyes turned to steel, but I pressed on, words rushing from my lips. "I'm not going to hurt anyone. I meant what I said earlier about loosing members of my family. To suffer that type of loss... If I can prevent another person from having to experience that, I will."

Her chin tilted up as Naz swept an appraising gaze over me. "You plan to fight."

I nodded.

She pursed her lips but I appreciated that she hadn't dismissed me "These attacks may not be authorized by the dark royals, or from the Dark Kingdom at all, but they *are* fae attacks. No human army could match the brutality and speed at which villages are being destroyed."

Naz stepped away, deciding this conversation was over as she made to turn toward the hall.

My hand lashed out of its own accord, clasping her arm to draw her attention back to me. It was risky, but I needed answers.

"I saw them." Her head dipped with a skeptical tilt as I

continued. "The fae. At least I think I did. There were only a few when we were attacked, but I think they're the same as the ones targeting human-based villages."

She sighed, crossing her arms as she did so. "You think you saw the creatures responsible for slaughtering hundreds of villages over the last seven years?"

"They had pitch black eyes." She stilled. "But cold and lifeless. And their skin was grey, almost as if the body wanted to decompose but wasn't allowed to. They had tipped ears but they were... off."

A chill raked through me as I recalled the synchronized voices in the clearing, the ones that had predicted Alarik's failure and promised the downfall of humanity. I shook my head, looking up to find her critical gaze recovered.

"You've faced the Fractured. And lived?"

My eyes widened. They had a name. *The Fractured.* "I was with another, but yes, we lived."

"Not many can say that, but you're human. Humans cannot win this war." Though her words held no malice, they sliced deep. "Your numbers have been decimated. The storm cut the human population in half within a fortnight. Add in the ongoing massacres and inability for human infants to survive... I'm not saying this to hurt you, but if you plan to fight, you should know what you're up against. I worry you don't understand the gravity of the situation."

She shook her head as she made her way back toward the hall, leaving me little choice to follow.

"Then explain it to me," I said, my jaw ticking.

Naz raised a brow but proceeded. "Those with human blood continue to die by the thousands. The strikes are premeditated and strategically placed, but cannot be tracked or predicted by anyone—human or fae. One day there's a thriving town—the next, nothing is left but embers and ash."

"And no one has bothered looking for an alternative enemy

when all the world believes the dark fae responsible," I said, deflating as the reality of the situation closed in upon me.

Her tone softened as she took in my pale complexion. "The point is, I respect your bravery, but it's safer if you leave this to the fae."

Leave this to the fae. I narrowed my eyes but was still unable to catch a glimpse of her ears through the thick curls. "*We*—you mean. As in *we* humans, you and I, should leave this matter to the fae."

Her plump lips pulled into a tight smile. "Yes, of course. It's growing late. I'll take you to the dining hall. At the very least, you will come to understand that the dark royals are innocent in this."

We turned down another corridor, walking toward the open door at the end of the hall, the clattering of silverware and idle conversation growing.

Naz pulled up short, pinning me with a warning smile. "You are free to listen, but if I hear of you making one person seeking refuge uncomfortable, I will escort you from the premises myself."

"I'm not here to hurt anyone." I narrowed my eyes, offended she would still question my motives. "I meant what I said."

Her smile grew. "Good, because I meant what I said, too."

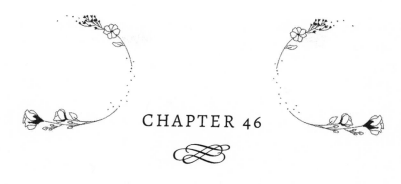

CHAPTER 46

THE BUSTLE OF THE KITCHEN DREW MY ATTENTION AS I FACED THE room. It was narrow with stout granite walls, but the warmth of the ovens and cozy conversations brought life to the small space.

The line for food shifted, drawing me with it. I decided on a bowl of leek and potato soup with a warm buttered roll before searching for a place to eat.

Benches lined either side of long wooden tables spanning the length of the room. My stomach flipped as my eyes combed through the nearly full sitting area. The thought of having to force my way into a table among the clusters of friends and families was nauseating.

"I know it can be overwhelming." I jumped with the nearness of a voice, turning to find a middle-aged woman. "Why don't you come sit near me? You look to be around the same age as my daughters. Perhaps you could be friends."

Light reflected off silver streaks in her otherwise dark hair as she signaled to a pair of girls at the far end of the nearest table, sporting the same tanned skin and ebony locks as their mother.

Muttering a thank you, I took a seat beside them. Their mother sat a small distance away, diving into conversation with the others at the table, as her daughters greeted me.

After a quick hello, her daughters turned back to their conversation with a pair of fair skinned girls across from them.

"No, it happened two nights ago, I swear. He said they would be coming back tonight." The girl with bright red hair and a splash of freckles looked to her friends for validation.

One of the daughters snorted, a cynical glint flashing in her eyes as she waved off the girl's plea. "Why would a soldier give away their plan? You probably had another nightmare, Serephina."

"I did not, Briony, and you know it!" Serephina shrieked, her fist balling as a red tint lit her cheeks. Her outburst pulled a few looks in our direction, but soon the sounds of dinner picked up again.

"He didn't know I was there. I told you, I was going to visit my cousin. I left early, running the entire distance, even though Mama told me not to go. It was before we'd heard about the town…" She stared daggers at the girl as she fought to keep her voice steady, tears pricking at her eyes. "I thought it would be safe, that—that she was safe. I didn't think…"

"I'm sorry you lost your cousin, Ser," the elder of the two daughters soothed. Rather than her sister's skepticism, her eyes imparted kindness. "We're all sorry, but the attack on her village was *just* reported. If what you claim to have heard were the truth, the soldiers scouting the surrounding area would have found the fae responsible."

Serephina flinched. "I don't know how they're staying hidden, but I wouldn't make this up. They were describing Neith, just west of my cousin's village. I've run across the length of the guarded stone bridge every summer since I was a child. There could be no other place to fit the description."

The elder daughter frowned. Ser shifted her attention to the last of the girls, her sister most likely. She had the same splash of freckles and light brown eyes, but her hair was blonde with just a hint of strawberry.

"Please," Serephina pleaded.

"It had to be a nightmare, Ser," her sister said, shaking her head. "Even small armies aren't invisible, and the entire surrounding area has been checked. If an attack was going to happen tonight, they would've been found."

"Wait." All four girls snapped their attention toward me, but I focused only on Seraphina's copper eyes shining with tears. "You heard of an attack that was to take place tonight? Did you report it?"

Briony rolled her eyes. "Great, she even has the new girl freaking out."

"I'm not freaking out, just curious."

"I did, but nobody believes me. Most don't even believe I made it to my cousin's village in the first place."

"We believe you, Ser. It's the other parts that don't add up." Ser's sister reached for her across the table, but Ser snatched her hand away.

"Why wouldn't people believe you travelled to see your cousin?"

Her lips quirked with the faintest hint of a proud smile. She shrugged. "I'm fast."

Her sister snorted, starwberry-blond hair catching the light as she shook her head. "She's not just fast, she's the fastest person we've seen. She's even tried to prove it, but the soldiers wrote it off to her cheating in some way. And she's getting faster."

I turned back to Ser. She shrugged again at the question in my eyes.

"It started picking up when I was around ten. It gets easier the more I run or if I'm frightened. That's part of the reason the soldiers don't believe me, because I made it home within two hours and the village is a little over fifteen miles from here."

A human with increased speed—speed to rival a fae. I cocked my head to the side. Weirder things had happened, but still it was unusual. "How old are you?"

"Seventeen."

Around Lannie's age. Which meant the change occurred right around the time of the storm. It had be linked. There were whispers of humans displaying fae-like abilities shortly after, but only humans with trackable fae lineage should be able to tap into them.

Evander had theorized it could happen if the humans involved housed dormant fae genes, which were somehow activated with the storm. It'd been unheard of for such diluted fae genetics to exhibit traits, but things had been changing these last seven years.

My hazel eyes locked with Ser's fierce brown ones. There was fear there, yes, but also the calm assurance of someone who knew they spoke the truth.

"Why don't you three believe her?"

Ser's sister shared a chagrined look with the elder daughter, while Briony looked at me as if I were a particularly complex puzzle she was trying to piece together. "Who are you, anyway?"

I smiled. "I'm Elara."

"Well, Elara," she drawled. "It's not that we don't believe her, but what she is saying can't be true."

"Those two things are different how?"

She bristled. "You're new here, so I'll give you a little insight. Ser always has nightmares. I, personally, just think it's a ploy for attention—"

"Bri," hissed Ser's sister, eyes darting to Ser's flaming complexion.

"Either way," Briony spat the words. "There's no army. No

tracks, no horses, nothing. Ser either made it up or she dreamed it."

"Maybe, maybe not." I met Bri's haughty look with a carefree shrug. Dismissing her with little more than a glance, I focused back on Ser. "Even soldiers make mistakes. Perhaps they missed something or perhaps it was a dream. Either way, I'm glad you warned them. If anything does happen, it won't be your fault."

"I hope I'm wrong." It was a soft whisper, directed toward her meal as her shoulders hunched. The others followed suit, diving into their own food.

After a few minutes, I muttered an excuse and took my leave. I retraced my steps, passing the sleeping quarters to ascend the stairs. My feet dashed across the ground level, the tight coil in my chest releasing as I noted the burst of color shining through the painted glass. The sun was still up.

My fingers worked the reinforced latch on the side door, swiping it open as I stepped through the arch and onto the cobblestone street. The sky was stained a bright magenta, the last surge of light before the sun yielded to the horizon.

The wind whirled and the hairs on the back of my neck stood up. My shoulders tensed as I felt the presence of an unknown entity watching me. I scrutinized the square, my eyes snagging on a cloaked figure lingering in the shadows. Could that be Alarik?

The hood was pulled low, but the breeze caught the edge, flipping it back to expose warm cinnamon eyes framed by dark lashes. His full lips twitched into a playful grin. With the subtlest of movements, his head dipped, as if daring me to follow.

I inhaled deeply, catching notes of cedar and far off places. My feet moved of their own accord, taking me closer to him, but a firm hand snagged my wrist. Repressing the urge to hiss, I spun around.

Fierce brown eyes peered out beneath silver-grey locks, the

low sun casting shadows across her face, deepening the worry lines across her brows: the grandmother who had first welcomed me.

"Child, you may stay, if you wish. I promise you, we can keep you safe. Others have tried to enter before and have failed. There is more than my grandsons protecting us here."

I shook my head, yanking my attention toward the hooded figure in the shadows. He was gone.

Another figure stepped forward from the alley, right where he promised he would be. Green eyes swept down my frame— relief, worry, anxiousness whirling together.

"I'm okay," I said, speaking to Flora and the two guards flanking her. Alarik approached slowly, extending his hand from the far side of the road.

"The choice is yours." Flora's words were low but strong, drawing my eyes to hers. Concern peered out, flashing from Alarik's poised form before her hand slipped into mine and gave a comforting squeeze.

"Thank you, but he's a good man. I wasn't sure if he would make it before nightfall and I didn't want to risk being alone, but now that he's here, I won't need to take space away from another."

Her sharp gaze pierced mine, holding it until she uncovered what she sought. She gave one more squeeze before sending me off. "If you find any women or children in need, please direct them to us."

"Of course."

Sparing a glance toward the vacant shadows where a lingering tug still called to me, I stepped forward into the descending night.

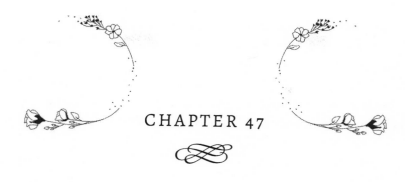

CHAPTER 47

ALARIK AND I WALKED IN SILENCE, MY HAND LINKED WITH HIS, until we were outside the village and away from any prying eyes.

"I'm glad to see you're in one piece," he said, pulling me against his chest. My arms wrapped around him, inhaling the spiced scent.

"I told you there was nothing to worry about."

"You did," he said as we started through the trees. "The others are waiting for us. We made camp about a mile in."

We walked, a peaceful contentment surrounding us as the sounds of the forest hovered with the haze of twilight. Orange flames danced in the fading light, signaling camp a few paces deeper.

Ember's crisp nicker cut through the air, followed by an annoyed huff. A giggle tumbled from my lips as I dashed to her side, undoing the tie tethering her to the branch.

"Did you miss me?" She nuzzled her velvet nose against my chest. "I missed you, too."

Alarik's deep chuckle sounded behind us. "She was furious when we fastened her to the tree."

Ember neighed and pinned him with a glare.

Alarik held his hands up with a laugh. "She kept acting like she was going to run off to find you."

"I don't think that's true. If Ember wanted to follow me, she would have." She gave a quick dip of her head in agreement, tilting into me as I scratched behind her ears. "Come on, girl. Let's join the others."

She made a gesture, not unlike rolling her eyes, but followed as Alarik and I pressed through the last of the branches, joining the men in the open glen.

Evander spotted us first. He was at my side in a flash, squishing me with a relieved hug before holding me out for inspection. Finding nothing amiss, he smiled. "I knew you'd handle it. It looks like you didn't even have to draw a weapon."

"Nope, but I think I need to reconsider where I keep them." I waved off their confused looks. "It was nothing. We need to talk."

Zelos cocked his head to the side as the others gathered near.

"A girl I met claimed she heard an attack would occur tonight." The men stilled. My eyes darted to each of them before focusing on Alarik with keen interest. "She claimed it would happen at Neith."

It was brief, but I saw the flash of stunned recognition before he turned away with a curse.

"I don't see the problem," Zelos added with a shrug.

"Zelos," Alarik warned.

"What? We can check out the town tonight instead of tomorrow morning."

"You were planning on going to Neith?" My eyes bounced from Evander's flushed face, to Vidarr's frown, and back to Zelos's confused brows.

"El—" Alarik started.

"You didn't think to tell me, even after this mor—" I bit my tongue a moment too late. The men shifted, looking anywhere but at me. Forcing the words to remain low and even, I started again. "You should have told me about Neith."

"There was no need," Alarik said cooly. "It wasn't pertinent to your mission."

A flicker of understanding snapped into place. "Is this why you insisted on the Select Guard joining me? In case Neith was attacked?"

"The Select are here because I deemed it was necessary. They have their own task for this journey, one that does not require your involvement."

Ire rose within me, snapping the limited amount of control I had left. "I should have been warned of the possibility. I would've prepared differently."

"That's exactly why I didn't tell you," Alarik said with, the harsh edge creeping through as he fought to maintain control of his temper. "You would have been distracted. It could have jeopardized your task."

"My *task*," I spat. "I can handle more than gathering information."

Even as I spoke the words, a coil of doubt twisted my gut. The woman—Naz—had managed to disarm me within seconds, before I could even draw a blade. Pushing the thoughts away, I held Alarik's glare.

"I know I need to earn my position among the men, but I already have. My skills in battle are good—great, even. I'm in the highest-ranking group—second only to him," I seethed, gesturing toward Zelos.

Zelos's dark eyes darted between the two of us before his head dipped ever so slightly. A vast warmth spread from my chest at the small movement. He agreed with me—in front of Alarik and the entire Select Guard.

"Now is not the time to have this discussion," Alarik growled. "It's not up to Zelos, or anyone else, for that matter. There are rules in place for a reason. I can't have you running off with only half of your training. You're going to get yourself killed."

I flinched, but his words didn't slow.

"This isn't personal, El. I'm the general. I can't make exceptions for you just because—"

My cheeks heated as he glanced toward the others. When he spoke again, his voice was low and laced with a sad frustration.

"I'm trying to keep everyone safe. You would be a liability to the others."

A liability. My heart clenched.

A dark form materialized from the shadows. I vaguely recognized him as the archer who'd introduced himself earlier —Kavan. His rich vibrato voice cut through the awkward silence. "The sun is fading. Most of the strikes happened at night. We should go."

The others muttered their agreement, scattering to prepare the horses and check weapons.

Alarik turned toward me, his face grim. "I don't suppose you'd be willing to stay in town for the evening while we check things out?"

I gave my head a firm shake.

He raked a hand through his hair, groaning with indecision. "El, you need—"

"I'll stay with her." Zelos stepped forward. He tilted his chin up as all eyes fell to him. "If there's any chance this could be a real attack, we can't afford a delay."

I hastily closed my mouth as Zelos's gaze found mine, his dark brown eyes swirling with an unrecognizable emotion.

"Elara wasn't exaggerating her skill level. She's tough and has worked harder than any of the other recruits." His words were stated calmly, delivered as a matter of fact and unfazed by the growing tick in Alarik's jaw.

"Zelos—" Alarik said, but his protest was cut short.

"There are things she still needs to learn, but she knows

enough to not be a *liability*." Alarik's eyes narrowed as Zelos forced a laugh. "Come on, General. You've known how talented she is from the beginning. Evander recruited her for gods' sake. Give her a chance."

Evander stilled.

My brows knit together. "No, Evander didn't recruit me. Alarik found me in the forest."

But even as the words left my lips, a crashing realization descended. Alarik found me in the woods, miles from the base and under the pretense of gathering food. *Gods*. The notion that Alarik would need to hunt—the general of the strongest human base, complete with a dinner hall and full kitchen staff—sounded ridiculous.

I swallowed past the dryness of my throat. "Evander?"

He glanced to Alarik, and with that one look, I knew the truth.

"Gods," I breathed.

"All I did was recommend you. You earned your spot on your own." I could hear the desperate notes bleeding through Evander's voice, but couldn't find the strength to comfort him.

"That's not the point," Zelos said, a frown marring his face. "The *point* is, Elara is well equipped to handle the possibility of battle. We're only following up on a lead."

"I think you've said enough, Zelos." Alarik's voice was cold.

"It's not my fault you lied to her—"

"I didn't lie."

"Please," Zelos sneered. "What else would you call—"

"Enough," I snapped, forcing a deep breath into my lungs. "We don't have time for this." My heart was still lodged somewhere in my stomach, but I'd deal with Alarik and Evander later. "We need to go. And I do mean *we*," I added with a pointed glare at Alarik.

The others hovered in the lengthening silence, waiting for their general's reaction. Just when it looked like he was about to shake his head in denial, Zelos added, "I'll take full responsibility for her. Any orders she does not obey will be at my expense."

I sucked in a breath, knowing if I did anything wrong, it would be his promotion on the line. "Zelos—"

"Agreed," Alarik said, releasing the others. They hurried toward the horses. "If you can't keep one soldier in line, then perhaps you're not ready to join the Guard."

Zelos stiffened, but refused to look away. "Yes, sir."

"He can stay with me," I snapped, swinging up onto Ember. "But I'm still going."

Neither of them acknowledged I'd spoken.

Alarik stared down from his horse, pinning Zelos with a harsh glare. "She can ride with us, but this does *not* end with her drawing a blade, do you understand? At the first signs of a threat, you two return to the base."

My eyes widened, realizing if it came down to it, I wouldn't be allowed to fight—I'd be nothing more than a spectator.

"No." I urged Ember forward, blocking Alarik's view of Zelos and forcing him to face me. "No, Alarik. I've passed all your tests. I deserve to be included in this."

"Zelos, that is a direct order," Alarik boomed, refusing to meet my eyes.

"Yes, sir." It sounded like the words were dragged from his mouth.

My heart sank as Alarik finally met my burning gaze. "Stay safe, El."

"Don't you dare. This conversation isn't over—" but he was already gone, leading the thundering collection of men through the trees and into the swiftly approaching night. Evander spared a brief shake of his head, before falling in line.

"Alarik is going to be furious," Zelos muttered as he pulled out a long, narrow bundle from his pack once the others had left. The fabric fell away to reveal a slender blade.

"My blade?" I gasped.

It wasn't my blade, not really, but I had taken to it during training. The bright silver hilt felt familiar in my hand, imprinted with woven vines stretching up and around into blooming Nightshade. I allowed myself to briefly appreciate the freshly sharpened edge and the care with which someone took to prepare it, as if it, too, were meant to see battle.

"I don't know how to thank you for this," I said, swallowing the lump in my throat.

"I figured it would come in handy." His lips tilted into a smirk. "But if you insist, I have plenty of ideas of how you could show your gratitude." He wiggled his brows at me, shattering the glare I'd shot his way as he swung onto his horse. "Alarik said you could join us, but let's hope there won't be a reason to draw your blade."

"I still can't believe you did that," I said as the two of us started after the others.

"Which part? Complimenting you or irritating your boyfriend?"

"He's not my boyfriend," I said, my smile fading. "You risked your spot in the Guard for me. Why would you do that?"

He shrugged, his cocky smile firmly in place, but his eyes grew distant. "Maybe I was wrong about you. Maybe I like what comes out of that pretty little mouth of yours almost as much as I like looking at it."

My lips tilted as I glanced over, expecting to see his familiar smirk, but his face was calm, his eyes fixated on my lips. My stomach twisted. My tongue darted out of its own accord, licking my bottom lip before pulling it back between my teeth. It was a habit born of nerves but Zelos groaned as he tracked the movement.

"Maybe I have more selfish reasons."

I yanked my eyes away from him, focusing on the road before us.

"Or maybe I just like getting under Alarik's skin and have found the perfect way to do it." Zelos laughed. It was forced, but I was grateful for the reprieve it offered.

"Whatever your reasons are, I hope you won't regret it." I leaned into Ember, urging her on as we sped through the trees. I could have sworn I heard the whispered words, 'I won't,' chasing after me.

CHAPTER 48

DESPITE THE INDIGNATION COURSING THROUGH MY VEINS, I couldn't help but admire the graceful movement of the horses and their riders as they navigated the darkening forest. We sped past overturned trees and rocks, avoiding upturned roots and potholes with ease.

The sky dimmed as the last of the sun's light faded, giving way to glittering stars winking to life. As the moon reached its pinnacle overhead, we came to a standstill hovering within the shelter of thick trees on the edge of a large clearing. Gently swaying grass shifted in the subtle night breeze, stretching out before us until it met the edge of a vast river. The rolling waters lapped along muddy banks, with a sleepy town nestled within. The only sound emanating from the island was the churning of a great watermill positioned alongside its gates. Everything else was still, as if frozen in time.

The town was connected to the field stretching before it by a great arching bridge. It reached across the waters with silver-blue stones glinting in the light of the stars. Matching stone-buildings riddled the cozy town beyond, completed with thatched roofs and squat chimneys.

A cloud passed, allowing the light of the moon to illuminate the scene before us. I had thought it a trick of the light, a refraction, or distorted perception of some kind, but the stones were glowing. All of them. Composed of the same silver-blue rock that had haunted me since that day in the forest.

"Alarik..." My voice trailed off, unsure what to ask.

"I see them," he answered. "I'm not sure what it means. Perhaps an enchantment of some sort?" The question was meant for Evander.

"Perhaps," Evander frowned. "I would need to get closer to be sure, but something feels... off." His eyes flicked to mine. "This is what you saw in the forest with Ember? The stone ring and temple Vidarr was sent to investigate?"

"Yes. They are just like the ones near our home."

Evander drew up short. "Are you referring to the ancient temple to the west?"

"Yes," I said slowly, unsure why he would need clarification. "The same ones we happened upon as children. Alarik and I stumbled upon it a few months ago—"

"Those stones don't glow, Elara. There is magic—something primal," he shook his head. "But the stones have never glowed."

Silence enveloped us as my mind whirled. "What do you mean? It's the same place Greer and I described the summer before the storm. You went back to investigate. You and Jem and Torin—"

"We did," he cut in, voice troubled. "We found a temple, but it was composed of normal, grey-slated stones."

"There was a pulse to them when I was with her," Alarik answered, eyes trained on Evander.

The two seemed to dive into a silent conversation. I meant to interrupt, to ask the dozens of questions swirling in my mind, but a strained hush had fallen. The subtle currents of the gurgling river were loud against the night, and I realized that even the normal clamor of the forest had vanished.

"Vidarr, stay with Elara and Zelos," Alarik said.

Zelos stiffened. I opened my mouth to argue, but Alarik had already turned away, dismissing my response before it was issued.

"I want us to be as silent as possible. That means everyone leaves their horse here, except for Cadoc." His eyes searched the trees, the river, the bridge. "Cadoc, you up for it?"

"I'd love to, boss," he said, his smile grizzly, even from here.

Alarik gave a nod, sending Cadoc galloping into the forest, moving parallel to the river toward the bridge. "Evander and I will take the right flank," he said. "Kavan, I want you to blend into the trees. If this becomes a fight, you know what to do."

A stallion with a midnight black coat and white spots along his front hooves came forward, bringing with him the silent archer. His black hair was shaved close, his midnight eyes locking on Alarik.

"Stay hidden," Alarik ordered. Kavan nodded, his quiet countenance providing a soothing calm to the growing tension. He dismounted swiftly before rushing into the trees, as mute as the dead.

"Skender, Xaun, left flank." The older brother, Skender, nodded, his sleek black hair secured with a tie. Xaun dipped his chin, his smooth hair grazing his shoulders with the motion before turning into the night.

I dismounted, rounding on Alarik, as Evander shook his head just behind his shoulder. "You really expect me—"

"Once we know everything is safe, I'll give the signal for you to join us. You agreed to stick with recon *only* until we reevaluated the situation at a later date."

A reproachful shake of Evander's head, had me biting my tongue. I nodded once, before Alarik and Evander stalked through the trees toward the mouth of the bridge.

"I thought you were going to call him on his overprotective bullshit for a moment there, El," Zelos said as he dismounted, tying his horse next to the others. Vidarr muttered something under his breath before purposely turning toward the glen, moving a few paces away to afford us privacy.

"I don't want you taking the fall for my actions," I grumbled. "The town looks peaceful anyway. There's no sign of an army. It makes sense to avoid an argument."

"Sometimes it's smart to avoid arguments," Zelos said, tilting his head as both of us watch Cadoc trot toward the bridge. "But other times, it's important to not let little things slip. Those little things could turn out to be much bigger. And before you know it, you're in a landslide, swept away with the current and unable to do anything about it."

"Don't let things pile up. Got it."

He chuckled, opening his mouth to speak, but a flash of blue light blared from across the glen. It was tucked in the far corner of the glen, a few hundred yards away, but growing by the second.

I blinked against the unnatural color, watching as the orb stretched until it was nearly eight feet tall. "Is...is that a—"

"Gods. That's a portal," Evander breathed as he and Alarik dashed to our side.

Alarik made a sound that echoed through the night. Cadoc jerked his head in our direction, immediately forsaking the bridge and galloping toward us.

"A portal? But I thought that craft had been lost." I dared not take my eyes from the swirling blues, but Evander answered anyway.

"I thought so, too. Only a particular branch of wild fae possessed the talent, but the last recorded portal was nearly one-thousand years ago."

Snapping branches and clipped footprints thundered nearer as Skender and Xaun burst through the trees, chests heaving.

"Did you see it? Is that what I think it is?" Skender panted.

"That's a portal, isn't it?" Cadoc's deep voice carried.

Vidarr's keen eyes tracked the flickers of silver lightning across the portal, slowing into a unified sheet. "That's how the army has been moving. That's why we haven't been able to track them. They have a portal wielder."

All eyes snapped to the nearly solid portal, watching as the last piece of the shattered mirror snapped into place and glossed over. It flashed a brilliant silver before fading into a low hum.

A tall man, body hardened with lanky muscle, stepped forward. A gasp stole from my lips as recognition crashed into me. "Alderidge."

It was a curse as much as an admission. It *was* Alderidge, I was sure of it, but his dark hair was pulled back to reveal thinly pointy ears.

Alarik swore. "Evander?"

"It's him," Evander confirmed with a tight nod. "He's wild fae, or at least partly. See the runes?"

I hadn't before, but as I squinted, I could make out the shimmering silver script across his forearms, snaking its way up his neck to cover his face. They pulsed, just as the portal had done. The stones surrounding the town of Neith flared in response, as if sensing an intruder on the brink of invasion.

Alarik must have noticed it, too, because he asked, "How is that possible? I've seen him countless times in Sonder. He was human enough then."

"Not human," Evander contradicted, "but not fully fae, either. He's like me, only with more human blood. He can shift to call on his powers but cannot sustain them."

"How long do we have before he burns out?" Vidarr growled.

Alderidge turned back to the portal, murmuring something that caused the sheet of silver to shimmer.

Evander shook his head. "Too long."

The earth shuddered as a pair of thickset boots hit the ground. Sharp rows of weapons adorned a broad chest, the glint of steel flashing as the figure straightened. He was monstrous, reaching nearly the height of the portal itself. Hands tipped into black claws flexed, stark against his alabaster skin. Long white hair hung low past his shoulders, drifting over black leather armor. His mouth twisted into a fanged sneer, but it was the malicious glint in his eyes that had me sucking in a breath. They were red, a blazing scarlet streaked with blots of black.

The air shifted, drawing my gaze from the red-eyed fae to focus on the wavering shadows just to the side of us. My eyes widened as the flickering tendrils of darkness parted. I made to scream, to warn the others, but before I could, a tall woman with a crown of tight curls and dark skin stepped forward.

"Naz?"

Evander turned first, quickly followed by the others. The slick sound of drawn blades pierced the air but she didn't flinch. She was a few paces away from us, her golden eyes fixed on the portal across the clearing.

The red-eyed fae was staring at the town with hungry eyes. Luckily, our position along the eastern edge of the forest hid us from view. He took a step back toward the swirling light, as if whispering a command. The portal shuddered once more.

And then they came.

An ebony sea opened from the pulsing silver light. One after the other, they emerged, skin tinged with a sickly grey pallor, their black eyes cold.

"The Fractured," Naz breathed.

Alarik's voice was low with forced control. "Naz, is it? I need you to speak quickly and plainly. Who are you, how did you manage to appear without us hearing you, and what in gods' name are 'the Fractured'?"

"You didn't sense me because you are not dark fae and are obnoxiously unaware of the shadow world around you."

"Who are you?" Alarik asked once more, voice clipped.

She tore her gaze from the growing throngs of Fractured to meet Alarik's. "Who I am is unimportant. All of you need to listen and listen well. There is a powerful force emanating from Neith. We haven't been able to uncover the source, but it looks like the Fractured are set on obtaining it."

"What are those things?" Cadoc growled, already growing impatient. "The Fractured you call them. They appear to be some type of fae?"

She cocked her head to the side, taking in Cadoc's measure. "The Fractured were once fae, or at least we believe so. They no longer are of this realm. Their souls have been splintered, corrupted, and manipulated into the beings you see before you. Their essence is no longer preserved, and though they have some cognitive autonomy, they've yielded their free will to another."

"My bet would be that big guy in the middle," Zelos chimed.

Naz gave a grim dip of her head. "It would appear so. We need to move quickly. Defending the town is our priority. I'll be back as soon as I can with help." She spared one last glance for me before she folded into the darkness.

Alarik's eyes bounced between the rapidly filling meadow and the bridge set just before the unsuspecting town. We were close to the bridge, only a few hundred paces as compared to the hundreds of yards standing between the Fractured and gate of Neith, but their numbers continued.

Alarik let out a curse. "Kavan, how many arrows do you have?"

"A few dozen. It won't be enough."

"No, but it will be something." Alarik's eyes darted among the group, lingering only a moment on me before the calm exterior of the general was secured in place. "We need to make a dash for the town. If we can get behind the walls, we will have a far better chance of defending it. Kavan, get to the towers, pick off as many as you can."

His eyes swung to mine. "If I thought we could outrun them, you'd already be on your way to the base, but there's no outrunning this. Alert the town once you get inside and then hide."

"I will not—"

"That is a direct order," he snapped. "You are either a part of the base or you're not, but you can't have it both ways."

My jaw ticked as I stared into his eyes, blood pounding in my ears. With a hiss, I turned away and stalked to Ember's side, urging her and the other horses to flee. There was no place for them here.

"The rest of us will be prepared to defend the city in case they breach the walls," Alarik finished.

Evander's taut voice sounded behind me. "And if the barrier around the town holds? If we are not able to retreat behind the city walls..."

"We will be sitting ducks across that bridge," Vidarr finished with a growl.

Alarik clasped Vidarr on the shoulder, bringing their eyes level with one another. "Then we will defend the town for as long as we can and pray it's enough for help to come."

Alarik met each of his men with a look of pride—of honor— a look that conveyed how grateful he was to have them by his side. Even if help never arrived. A moment later, we were off, racing through the last of the trees to the mouth of the bridge.

I should have been focusing on reaching the safety of the town, should've been noticing the way the stones of the bridge flared beneath my feet with a subtle shift, but instead, I dared a glance over my shoulder, finding the pale fae with blood-red eyes amid a sea of black.

The Fractured continued to spill from the portal, sweeping out around him to form a teeming pool in the far corner of the glen. I realized they were waiting for his instruction, like starving hounds eager to be set free. The red-eyed commander threw his head back and inhaled deeply.

His lips curled into a sinister grin, his scarlet eyes locking with mine. My stomach twisted. That was impossible. He couldn't scent me from this distance, let alone sneer at me like he was doing. It must be the adrenaline, he couldn't—

"You die first, little humans. Then we shall have our fun destroying this cursed place."

The blood drained from my face as his voice thundered across the clearing. The surrounding creatures heckled their agreements, a chorus of snickers resonating as one. I fought back the wave of nausea, forcing my attention ahead.

We crested the bridge and then sprinted down the other side. Kavan was the first to reach the walls surrounding the still sleeping town. He made to open the large wooden door, but his hand halted midair.

Evander was at his side in a flash with a curse. "It's warded."

"Then get them to unward it," Zelos growled, his fists pounding against air.

Evander's copper eyes clouded with grim resignation as he pressed a hand against the invisible barrier. "I doubt those within are even aware of what's happening. The wards feel different—wilder. Almost like it's connected to the stones themselves. The power anchoring them sinks beneath the earth. We aren't able to pass."

A deep, cruel laugh echoed across the field. It vibrated through the earth, the stones, rippling along the waters, rattling through my bones to settle like a cool weight in the pit of my gut. Alarik, Evander, and the rest of the Select Guard turned, all of us drawing our weapons as we prepared to face our fate.

"Now, we play," the commander of the Fractured teased with a white-fanged sneer. "*Framganga.*"

The Fractured shuddered under the weight of the command, bodies straightening as it washed over them. Then the tension released and the tidal wave of ebony eyes and ravenous grins descended.

Alarik cursed. "El, in the back. The width of the bridge will thin them. Steady, precise movements. Nobody takes risks."

This would be a test of endurance, slowly cutting through the herd. The portal was still shimmering, pumping hordes of warped fae toward us in a steady current intent on delivering death. They were endless. Infinite. How could a cluster of humans stand against such a force?

I was pushed to the back of the group, watching as the snap of Kavan's bow sounded with the first creatures cresting the bridge. The arrow struck, the feathers of the fletching protruding from the oozing eye-socket of the still sneering Fractured. It shook with crazed laughter a moment longer before it crumpled.

Arrows rained down, plucking off the Fractured as they came for us. Too soon, Kavan tossed his empty quiver to the side, stepping to the front with the others as he unsheathed a deadly looking blade. Weapons poised, they braced for impact.

Blades whirled as they crashed against us, the clang of metal and the slick sounds of sliced flesh filling the clearing. Alarik had been right. The Fractured fell in great heaps, forced to thin as the narrow width of the bridge bottlenecked the thundering swarm.

The Select moved as a trained unit, cutting through the onslaught. Dark liquid misted the air as the bodies piled up, the sickly-sweet scent of blood and death misting like macabre clouds. Corpses tumbled over the side, thunking off the stones to be swallowed up by the rolling waters below. The once peaceful river had turned ravenous, waters churning, engulfing each body it claimed.

A raucous cackle sounded, tremors of the noice reverberating through the swarm in eerie aftershocks. Crimson eyes smiled at me, the flecks of black within made all the more menacing by the flaring scarlet hue surrounding them. It was the only part of the wretched fae not entirely devoid of color—his eyes and the black curving claws of his hands.

"Such determination from a species so fragile," the commander sneered. "Already your bodies are weakening."

The Guard spun, rotating who was taking the brunt of the impact so as to conserve energy, but their bodies were slick with sweat. Their movements had already started to slow, and still the waves of Fractured came for us.

"How I love watching you insignificant humans fail." The commander smirked, languid steps drawing him closer. "How I bask in that moment of clarity when you realize your entire existence, everything you have been, everything you might once have achieved is lost. Such precarious creatures. Nothing more than wisps of foolish dreams sewn together in a suit of feeble muscles and brittle bones."

Squeezing the hilt of my blade, I felt the need to move rise within me, but a swirl of darkness snagged my attention. Shadows parted among the trees at the opposite end of the clearing. My heart stumbled as fear of another portal surged forth, but when the shadows calmed, there were only three beautiful, terrifying fae.

I blinked, and they were gone. Blurs of flashing blades wove through the snarling swarm with inhuman speed, cutting through the sea of black with ease. I watched in awe as bodies littered the ground in their wake, each swing of their swords drawing them closer to the bridge. These must be the warriors Naz was speaking of.

"*Drepa*," the commander growled, blood-red eyes fixated on the blurs.

The swarm split, heeding their orders but failing to neutralize their target. More and more diverged, focusing their strength on the fae warriors.

"Now's our chance," Zelos shouted over the sounds of battle.

"We need to take out the commander. Cut off the head of the snake. It's our only option."

"No," Alarik thundered, slashing through another. "We can't match his strength. Be smart, officer. Hold your ground."

Zelos's sword jerked back from a body as a sheen of blackened blood spurted from the gaping neck wound. He kicked the still twitching Fractured into the water before dropping back. He was awash with tainted grime and filth, his dark hair disheveled and chest heaving, but his eyes blazed with life as he reached me.

"This is fucking stupid, El. We need you fighting."

"Zelos," Alarik warned, yanking his sword from another's chest.

"I was wrong about you," Zelos continued, ignoring Alarik. 'I thought—it doesn't matter what I thought—because I know you can handle yourself just as well as any of the men. You're brave and addicting." His eyes dipped to my mouth. "Like a spark over kindling."

I swallowed, unsure what to say.

"I was right about one thing though." His voice dropped to a rumble as he shot me a cocky grin. "Those lips really are wasted on the battlefield."

"Zelos—" I started, but the red-eyed fae bellowed another command, a clawed hand gesturing toward the growing mounds of slaughtered Fractured and the three blurs responsible.

Zelos's gaze hardened. "We need to end this."

"Don't," I pleaded, but he was already rushing past the others and into the swarm.

Alarik cursed. "Evander, to Zelos. Provide what cover you can. Get him back."

Evander's sword lashed out, coming down across the neck of the nearest enemy in a great arch that carried through to the top half of its torso. Foaming tissue bubbled from the exposed lungs as the head slid clean, quickly overwhelmed with a flood of blackened blood. The body crumpled as Evander's russet eyes locked on Zelos carving his way down the slope of the bridge. He tore after him, ripping through bodies until he, too, was swallowed up but the swarm.

With a curse, I chased after them, slipping past Vidarr only to be halted by a firm grasp across my wrist.

"El, stop." Alarik's green eyes were dilated with the adrenaline of war, swirling with a desperate need for me to hear him. "We don't have the advantage in this fight."

"But Zelos—"

"Evander will bring him back."

"And if Zelos refuses to retreat?" Because I *knew* he would.

Alarik flinched.

My stomach twisted, but then his hold weakened. Cold black eyes and snarling, rotted fangs flew toward us. I leapt to the side, allowing my blade to do most of the work as it whipped across its chest. My pulse thundered in my ears, but I took a calm breath. Alarik shook his head as my decision hardened in my eyes.

"Don't—"

"I'm sorry." The words overlapped, both vying for understanding, but I was gone before anymore could be uttered.

Blood hummed through my veins as I entered the fray. That restless tugging in my mind stretched, eager for freedom. It had been the same in the forest when I'd first faced them—the Fractured. Where I'd expected panic to grip me, there was only an uneasy longing. When I should have been hesitant, there was only an impatient willingness.

I could feel it slinking within the shadows of my mind, as I slashed through skin and tendons, trying to reach Evander and Zelos. As my sword grew slick with blood, and the trail of bodies swelled behind me, I surrendered to that darkness.

A strange humming filled the air—blotting out the sounds of

blades clashing and bodies falling—until the only thing I could hear was the pulsating thump of my heart and the frantic whooshing of blood through my veins.

Cocking my head to the side, I took in the horrible creaturese. I could feel it now, that taint, the utter wrongness of them. It was like a layer of cooled fat smudged across soiled meat, coating their skin, seeping into the hollowed place of their centers, where their essence had once been.

They fell, staining the earth with spurts of black and red as my blade struck true, until I was at Evander's side. He was riddled with angry cuts, but the small cuts along his arms began to heal, one of the benefits of having light fae affinities.

"Where is he?" I shouted as we spun back-to-back, creating a ring of mangled bodies.

"To the south. He's almost to the commander."

"We have to stop him," I huffed, ripping my sword free from a particularly bloated gut, the contents of which gushed from the wound in a vile wave of spoiled blood and slimy organs.

"Are you up for the challenge?"

My lips quirked as three more dropped at my feet. "Always."

We blazed through the masses at a steady pace, catching glimpses of the fighting as we went. One of the fae Naz had brought was closing in on the portal and managing the brunt of the army, while the two others worked their way in our direction. No, not toward us, but toward the red-eyed commander—and Zelos, who stood before him.

My stance faltered, earning me a burning slice across my thigh. Evander spun, ending the culprit, but my attention snapped back to Zelos and the commander peering down at him with glee. We were only a hundred paces or so away, but we were too late.

The commander took a step toward him, his bone-white hair shifting in an abhorrent breeze, bringing with it the scent of wilted roses and burnt sugar. His lips peeled back in a grin as ebony claws flexed with anticipation.

"Leave the mortal alone," a deep voice rumbled.

My eyes snapped toward the sound, but he was nothing more than a flash of dark hair and cinnamon-colored eyes amid a sea of carnage.

"Or are you afraid to face a worthy opponent?"

The commander snarled as he spun, he attention divert from Zelos for the moment.

I exhaled. Only half a dozen Fractured were between us now. We'd be able to reach him and—

Zelos launched himself forward, using the taunt as a distraction. My breathing hitched as I watched Zelos fly through the air, his sword held high in a fierce grip as the red-eyed commander remained fixated on the fae before him.

It would be a killing blow, the tip poised just above the commander's throat. My heart pounded—just one joyous thump—before it stopped completely.

Black-tipped claws lashed out, plucking Zelos from the air by his neck. His body jerked, sword clattering to the ground with a useless thud. Zelos's hands raked across the claws that held him, pulling and tearing at the alabaster hand, desperate for air, but the commander only sneered, an ominous spark smoldering in his ruby eyes. His grip tightened, the cclaws piercing the tender skin along Zelos's neck. Bright red blood dripped from the punctures, running over the commander's pale fingers in long rivulets as he squeezed.

A whimper tore from Zelos and I felt something crack in my chest. I saw only him. Only the horrific red of his blood flowing freely down an alabaster arm, pooling in the earth beneath. Only the way his eyes flashed with regret and pain and… fear.

"El, move!" Evander's voice freed me from my trance.

My blade joined his as we slashed and killed in a fury of iron and blood. Too slow. Where one fell, two more rose, locking us in an endless loop of maiming and killing. Gods, there were so many of them. Too many.

I looked back at Zelos, willing him to find a way out of this, to hold on a little longer. The commander saw, choosing then to pull free a curved dagger. Zelos's deep brown eyes found mine, but there was no hope. No fight left in them. Only a resounding, gut wrenching resignation.

"No," I breathed, the chaos around me dulling as I held his gaze.

The edge of his Zelos's lips tugged into a small, sad smile. I shook my head. We'd find a way—we were almost there.

The commander sneered as he poised the blade over Zelos's chest. He waited until I met his blood-red gaze. I was only a few paces away—only a few moment—but it didn't matter.

Cruel, crimson eyes held mine, the commander's sneer stretching into a sickening smile, as he sank the steel between Zelos's ribs. Maddening laughter issued from him as he savored each ragged breath, each shudder, until the hilt was flush and Zelos's chest was still.

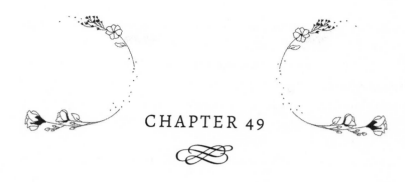

CHAPTER 49

My heart slowed as an eerie hush settled over the world. I vaguely recalled a blistering burn raking down my back, but the pain was muted. Like everything else was: the thud of Zelos's body as it met the earth, the commander's sneer as he stalked away to meet the now enraged fae who thought to challenge him—it was all numbed.

Pricks of electricity singed my skin as my vision refocused. I blinked, but the soft hints of light clinging to Zelos's broken body remained—a mist of gold hovering in a sea of black. My eyes darted to his face, twisted at an unnatural angle. The welcoming browns were now cold, but that ghost of a soul remained.

A ragged breath sounded from my lungs as feeling returned to my body, shattering the serene silence of my mind. The battle came crashing back in a thunderous wave—grunts, clashing metal, and the distinct metallic tang of blood. He was dead—I knew he was—but something, some part of him waited for me. And I wouldn't let him down, again.

My sword became an extension of myself as I launched forward, letting anger flood my veins—holding off the frigid pangs of grief. Mourning would come, as it always did, but right now, they would pay. All of them.

The monster within me purred as we sliced through the Fractured. They were nothing more than hollowed sacks of bone and skin. I could see that now. That's all they were. Decay. Dead flesh reanimated.

I deflected blade after blade that came for me, my own flying through the air, releasing diseased souls from their stagnant animation, from their perpetual state of undead. The pounding of my pulse increased—a tempo, a chant—urging me on and carrying me through the last of them, until the whirl of battle stalled.

I could sense the Fractured scrambling, still pouring from the portal. I could feel the red eyes of the commander tracking my movements, but nothing else mattered in this moment.

My knees sank onto the earth slick with Zelos's blood as I gathered his head into my lap, brushing flecks of dirt from his brow.

"I'm here now. Gods, I—I'm so sorry. I should have saved you, but I'm here now. You won't have to leave this world alone. I'll stay with you until you're ready."

The gold shimmer flared to life at my words, rising through his chest. It swirled around me, the whisper of a kiss across my cheek before it released, fading into the moonlight.

"It can't be," the commander snarled. I snapped my head to the side, stiffening as his crimson gaze darted from my spine to my eyes. "The Dark Phoenix."

Some distant part of myself trembled at his words, the same part that shuddered at what I'd done. What I had seen—Zelos's essence, his soul, the one bright spot among a swarm of darkness. I saw them still, the black shadows of the Fractured, vacant pits where their essence should be. Alarm blared deep within, but my body still hummed with blissful detachment, anesthetized by adrenaline... and something more.

I met the commander's eyes and grinned. It stretched into a deranged smirk, as warped and as twisted as my soul. His fear coated the air as he fell back, nearly tripping over the mounds of bodies in his haste to be rid of me, he retreated across the glen to the portal and Alderidge standing before it.

Tension released from my shoulders, despite the battle still raging. I blinked, watching as the black clouds surrounding the Fractured dimmed and then dispersed, like smoke being carried away on a breeze.

The fae who had tried to save Zelos, the one with dark hair and cinnamon eyes ringed in silver along the edge of his irises, came to my side. Puzzlement cinched his brows as he watched the commander retreat. He opened his mouth to speak as he took in the state of me, but I looked away, staring across the battlefield toward the fleeing monster and the traitorous half-fae that stood beside him.

"Another time," he promised, before slipping through the swirling silver. Alderidge spared the town one last look, rage warping his features, before he too disappeared, the portal vanishing along with him.

CHAPTER 50

THE FAE BATTALION ARRIVED MOMENTS LATER. NAZ LED THE charge, sweeping through the rest of the Fractured within issue. It was jarring, switching from the thundering clash of steel and wailing screams of the dying to an emptied silence. The squelching of corpses being dragged across damp earth were the only sounds as the fae started the tedious task of arranging bodies into great mounds for burning.

I wasn't sure how long I sat with Zelos, but I couldn't find it in me to move. The searing drive that allowed me to reach his had gone, leaving behind only the bitter taste of guilt and anguish.

The dark-haired fae had stayed, not speaking but remaining close, until Alarik found me. He drifted away then, and for some strange reason I had the urger to ask him to stay.

"Gods, El," he cried, crumpling to the ground beside me. "I couldn't see you. I didn't know…" Alarik took a deep breath, words stalling as he noticed Zelos's limp form clasped in my lap. When he spoke next, it was with forced calm, as if I were a child on the verge of fleeing. "You can let go now."

Evander appeared, flanked by Vidarr. Both held pained

expressions, resigned to the unyielding truth presented before them.

Alarik brushed back a tangled stand of my bloodstained hair. "Zelos is gone, El. You can let him go."

And he was, I knew he was. I'd felt the shimmering haze of his essence pass from this world. A fresh wave of agony, unleashed another torrent of tears tumbling down my cheeks, but I gave a small, nearly imperceptible nod.

Kavan stepped forward first, flanked by the brothers Skender and Xaun. In slow, powerful movements, they gently lifted Zelos and carried him away from the carnage.

"Do you follow the blessing of the goddess for your warriors?"

I blinked, searching the field for the subdued voice.

Naz stepped forward, her tight curls and black fighting gear just as bloody as the rest of us. "We carry shrouds with us, if you would like a burial pyre..."

My stomach clenched at the implication. They carried shrouds because there were always bodies to fill them.

I looked to Alarik, realizing that I didn't know what Zelos would've preferred. He gave a tight nod, his hand closing around my shoulder to draw me close.

"Zelos did. Thank you for your kindness."

"No, thank you, General." Her golden eyes graced each of us. "Thank you all. I'll see to your warrior."

The coldness that had settled over me began to thaw, leaving me all too aware of the ache in my bones, of the pricks of tenderness along my spine, as if fire had lashed across it.

Before I could contemplate leaving, the fine hairs on the back of my neck stood on end as a subtle shift of energy whirled through the air.

I pushed to my feet, pulling away from Alarik as I spun toward the southern end of the clearing. Evander and Vidarr must have felt it too because they were there within moments, ushering me behind as Alarik stepped in front of us. I allowed it, but unfastened a dagger, just in case.

Two fae stepped forward, flanking a taller one with dark-hair as they approached. Their thick, muscular frames gleamed with countless weapons attached to leather straps and scabbards, all speckled with varying shades of gore.

One had perfectly styled blond hair despite the battle, shorter along the sides and swept back across the top. Light-blue eyes the color of frozen waters and raging storms were set above a straight nose and full, pink lips. Moonlight brightened his luminescent skin and long tipped ears—most likely a light fae.

The other had dark skin, stark against the molten gold of his eyes. Great horns sat atop his head, arching back against a thin layer of jet-black hair. His ears were pointed, though smaller and slightly more rounded than the others. My stomach fluttered. He must be an earth fae.

They were both stunning, but the one in the center nearly made my heart stop. I recognized him now, though I couldn't believe I hadn't sooner. There was no hood to hide his features and the hints of a beard had been shaved, but those knowing eyes pulled a gasp from my lips. The shimmering silver ring around his eyes had faded completely, giving way to the familiar cinnamon with hints of midnight flecks. He radiated the same self-assured presence as the first day I'd looked upon him in the trading market.

Pointed ears showed through tousled umber hair, the bright rays of the moon reflecting hints of auburn. The fae's somber gaze burned with the reflected grief I was feeling, as if he could sense the ebbing hollowness clashing with the sharp sting of loss within me. A flash of starlight caught the curves of his lips as they tilted into a small, sad smile, revealing the tips of sharp canines. "Hello, love."

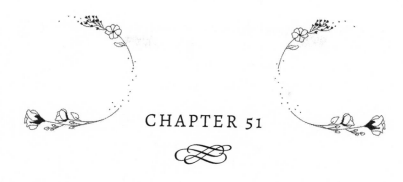

CHAPTER 51

"She's not your 'love'," Alarik snapped, a low warning lacing his words. His grip tightened on the hilt of his sword, despite how exhausted he must have been.

The fae's lips quirked, lingering on me a moment longer, before meeting Alarik's scowl. "General, is it?"

The light fae beside him nodded.

Alarik stiffened as the dark-haired fae turned, wading through the stained field. He knelt beside one of the many bodies, examining the insignia over its chest.

"Jarek, is this the same as the others?"

The blond fae stepped forward, glancing at the crescent moon and stars. "Exactly the same."

The dark-haired fae stood, letting out an exasperated sigh, before turning toward Alarik.

"It seems we have a common enemy, General Holt. My name is Zaethrian. This is Jarek." The blond smiled. "And Soter." The earth fae remained quiet, but his golden eyes seemed to grow a little brighter. "We have been tracking and killing off these impersonators for some time, now."

Impersonators?

"They aren't from the Dark Kingdom?" I asked. Zaethrian's eyes snapped to mine, causing Alarik's spine to straighten.

Zaethrian gave a slow shake of his head. "No. These monsters are not of the Dark Kingdom."

"But you are?"

"El, please," Alarik said. "Let me handle this."

I knew I should heed my general's request—but the fae's cinnamon eyes stayed locked on me. Shame crept across my cheeks. We'd all killed, but Zaethrian had seen me during battle. I hadn't just killed, I'd enjoyed it. I knew what he saw when he looked at me—a murderer, a monster, no better than the creatures piled around us.

This darkness of mine needed to be contained, as it had been for most of my life, but gods, it was hard to lock it away after I'd yielded so fully. Even now, I felt no remorse, no guilt. There was only an unrelenting fury coursing through my veins. Loss and grief were present, and an emptiness that had fissured through me when Zelos fell, but stronger than that was the insatiable yearning for revenge.

I was already thinking of ways to track down the commander—already looking forward to severing the red-eyed fae limb from pale limb, and any others who thought to stand in my way.

Who would wish for that? Who could stand covered in the coagulated splatters of flesh and blood and want more?

Only me. Only a monster.

Zaethrian's jaw clenched. He gave a quick jerk of his head. "None of that, love. I assure you, these creatures have no essence left to grieve. I'll not have you condemning yourself for their sake."

Alarik took a step forward. "Zaethrian—"

"Please, call me Zaeth," he interrupted with a grin, flashing a pair of gleaming fangs.

Alarik scowled, but started again. "Zaeth. Do you mean to say you've been hunting this group of dark fae?"

"I don't mean to say anything more than what I do. These impersonators are not dark fae. Unfortunately, they have taken to wearing the Dark Kingdom's insignia." Zaeth cocked his head to the side. "Surely, you realized there was something wrong with them?"

"Yes, I noticed. They're fae, but different—slower, clumsier, and more ruthless than I've seen before." He nodded to where Naz and the others were returning. "I was informed they're called the Fractured."

"Yes, though, I don't consider them fae any longer. They don't even bleed as we do." He waved toward the puddles of black tarry substance surrounding the already bloating corpses.

Alarik frowned, looking closely at the decomposing bodies. "It's almost as if they've been killed and reanimated."

"Something like that. Though, no creature of this world has the power to command legions of the reborn." He nudged one with a thick, black boot, the gash in the stomach spilling curdled chunks. "Their very essence is splintered, twisted and distorted, and then reawakened to give you this."

Zaeth's hand swept out toward the field of greying corpses. He then took slow, measured steps toward us—toward me— keeping his gaze locked with mine, heedless of Alarik's scowl. "There is nothing left inside of them besides warped pieces, too weak and too wicked to feel remorse or pain. I had hoped it was merely a radical group of dark fae. That would have been simple and easy to disband, but these creatures, they seek nothing but death."

My heart thundered as my mind raced. Had that been what I'd seen? Zelos had a golden shimmer as he passed. I wasn't sure how, but I knew it was an imprint of his soul. These things— there had only been a cold, black haze.

The blond—Jarek—tilted his head looking past us toward Neith. "It would seem they had a different priority tonight."

Zaeth followed his gaze before returning to our group. "Yes. There is something about this town they wished to claim. Do any of you know what that could have been?"

Silence answered him. A stone dropped in my stomach as his face fell, provoking an irresistible urge to dispel the disappointment etched into his features.

"There was a ward around the town," I offered, feeling the eyes of the Select heat my back as Zaeth's attention returned to me. "We weren't allowed to pass." My eyes flashed to Evander. "It was stronger than a normal warding."

Jarek's eyes followed my line of sight, landing on Evander. "Is that what you felt?"

"Yes," Evander answered reluctantly. "There was something off about it. It didn't feel like a casting. More like the barrier rose from the ground itself, connecting to something... else."

"Interesting." Jarek's eyes dragged along Evander's frame before languidly returning to his face, his cheeks now a rosy pink. "Very interesting."

"Either way," I said. "I doubt the Fractured would've gotten past it."

Zaeth's lips twitched. "Perhaps, but a skilled enemy can find ways of shattering wards if they want in badly enough. It looked like the Fractured wouldn't have stopped."

"But they did," Alarik cut in.

Zaeth's eyes drifted to me. "Yes, they did. I wonder why that was."

My cheeks burned. The commander had called me The Dark Phoenix, but the only phoenix I knew of was the one from legends, spoken only in whispers. A memory rose to the surface, a flash of young Greer dancing as Mother sang, but the image was gone before I could make sense of it.

For one horrible moment, it looked like Zaeth was going to

elaborate. I gave a nearly imperceptible shake of my head, a plea to not speak of what he overheard, and his lips stilled.

"What is it you want from us?" Alarik asked, stepping nearer. He swayed, wincing as my arm grazed his ribs.

My brows furrowed, roving over his body until I found the red-stained slit across the side of his chest. "You're hurt. Why didn't you—"

"I'm fine, El."

I flinched.

His eyes softened, his voice growing lighter. "It's nothing, I promise. Only a flesh wound."

He wove his fingers through mine as if to prove how well he felt, but I could see how ashy his complexion had grown. There was a faint sheen of sweat coating his brow despite the cool night. He needed to see a healer.

Zaeth's eyes flicked from me to Alarik, the hint of a frown marring his beautiful face before answering. "Despite my many talents, I am unable to be in multiple locations at once. We have been doing our best to keep the citizens of the Dark Kingdom safe, dispelling rogue groups and heading off attacks before they occur. Still, our efforts have fallen short."

Vidarr took a step toward Alarik, steadying him as Zaeth continued. "These vile creatures have grown bold, slaughtering most of our smaller villages and starting on some of the larger ones. The Dark Kingdom will manage, as will the Air and Fire Kingdoms, but I need help defending those with human occupants south of our borders. The dark royals have offered assistance to humans, but most have come to distrust fae, the dark fae in particular."

He surveyed the field once more, fury rising as a tint of silver flared briefly along the outer ring of his eyes. "After watching you fight, I believe you could be the army we've been looking for. I suggest we train together, share knowledge of our common enemy and in return, I'll teach you how to effectively defend against fae and the Fractured."

Kavan drew a sharp breath as the others froze. It was Vidarr who spoke first, glancing briefly to Jarek and Soter, before turning toward Zaeth. His voice hovered between tight control and disbelief as he asked, "You would divulge fae fighting techniques to humans?"

"Dark fae techniques," Zaeth corrected. "Fighting, certain weaknesses, I'd even disclose information on our southern territories to help with scouting. The world as we know it is ending, reverting to a time without morals. A time without humanity. If this madness is to end, we must work together, as we once did long ago. Even then, it may not be enough. Their commander, the one with the red eyes, he is something different."

A swell of vengeance and pain rose within me. The pale fae, the one that killed Zelos, the one leading the slaughter of thousands of fae and humans across Pax—he was our true enemy.

Zaeth offered me a curious look, noting my clenched fists and gritted teeth.

I tilted my chin up. "He isn't fae?"

He inhaled as if to speak, but it was the earth fae, Soter, with the liquid gold eyes and striking ram horns who answered. "He is not fae in the modern use of the term." All eyes swung to him, his deep voice reverberating through the clearing as the rest of their army continued with piling bodies. "He is older, more powerful, and tainted with a viciousness I cannot place."

The Select looked to each other, communicating with glances before Alarik spoke. "Where would we train? I can't risk dividing my men across the kingdoms. It would weaken what little strength we have left."

Zaeth conceded that point. "We would have to create a new camp, something close to the border."

The two of them volleyed various known locations, each one proving to be problematic.

"What about Fort Dhara?" Soter suggested.

"The old horse stables?" Jarek questioned.

"Yes. It was a fort before it was used to board horses. Repairs would need to be made, but it's in the heart of the recent attacks, maybe a half a day's ride from the border."

"Perfect, Soter. Saving the day, as always," Jarek jested, nudging his shoulder. Soter shifted uncomfortably.

Zaeth's lips quirked as he nodded. "It would be a full day's ride from the human base, possibly needing to be broken up into two."

Alarik nodded as his grip on my hand tightened to prevent him from swaying. Zaeth's eyes dipped to the small movement, his smile faltering as he took in the worry pinching my brows.

"Go. The town has adequate healers, not nearly as talented as those at your base if rumors are to be believed, but they will manage." He glanced at the sky, the dark blues fading into the deepest shade of violet with the approaching dawn. "I'll send a messenger this evening with information of Fort Dhara. We can decide on a commencement date then."

Alarik nodded. "Agreed. Until this evening."

We turned toward the bridge as the fae drifted into the forest. This time when we approached the gates, we were allowed to pass. I made to follow, but a nagging sort of pull urged me to pause. I glanced over my shoulder, looking past the dozen or so burning piles of bodies and into the trees beyond.

I felt him there, hovering just within the forest. My eyes searched until they found what they were looking for. His face was half hidden in shadows, but his eyes remained as piercing as ever. He dipped his head as his lips tilted up into a lopsided smirk.

"Until next time, love," he whispered before slipping into darkness.

CHAPTER 52

A YOUNG BOY, NO OLDER THAN WILL, STOOD TRANSFIXED IN THE middle of the road, staring at the bloodied field beyond. His mouth dropped as we pushed past the gates.

"Hello," Evander said, kneeling beside him. "My friends and I are in need of a healer. Would you be able to find us one?"

The boy nodded before racing off through cobblestone streets. He returned within minutes with a group of people who looked to be a group of both fae and humans. I relinquished my hold on Alarik, allowing Vidarr and Evander to escort him as we were led to the healing quarters.

After what felt like hours of being fussed over, the healer released us. Evander remained with Alarik as they tended to his wounds, but the rest of us were guided to a cozy inn sitting atop a hill.

It overlooked narrowed streets wrapping around small, worn homes. The inn was no different. Its shingles were slanted and the shutters could use a fresh coat of paint, but the glow of candles within and the plumes of pink and purple flowers amidst narrow troughs framing the windows were welcoming.

I inhaled the sweet scent of petunias as we entered, guided

by a stout, grey-haired lady. Her ears had a slight tip to them, and though I could see the effects of time in the creases of her brow, she moved as nimbly as ever.

"It would seem you've had quite the night." She glanced over her shoulder. "You may not know, but this town is protected by the blessing of Evulka. When night falls, the city is sealed. We were unable to hear you, and even if we had, the wards wouldn't dissipate until dawn."

"That sounds a lot like prison," Cadoc bit out.

She lifted a brow, pausing on the foot of the stairs. "That's a matter of perception. Those who choose to reside here view it as a form of sanctuary."

Cadoc rolled his eyes, earning a shoulder nudge from Kavan, just as the young boy from earlier stepped forward. He had long limbs and wide ears, but he tilted his chin up as he approached Vidarr.

"We have men searching for the horses, sir, but we've only found the copper stallion and the young mare as of now. The mare was injured, but she's being treated as we speak."

I gasped. "You found Ember? Is she all right?"

The young boy nodded, his fluff of brown hair bobbing as he did. "I think so. I'm not a healer, but the man tending to her said the wound was shallow. With her fighting spirit, he doubted even Death would be brave enough to claim her."

"That's Ember, all right. May I see her?"

"Sorry, miss," he mumbled. "She had to be given a sleeping drought in order to clean her wounds."

I nodded. "Thank you for checking in on her."

He answered with a gap-toothed grin. "I had your bags brought up as well. Figured you would be looking for them."

"That was very kind of you." His energy was reminiscent of Will's, and I couldn't help but smile.

Vidarr laid his large hand on the boy's shoulder. "Thank you, lad. Do not fret about the horses. They are used to battle and know how to find their owners. We were mostly worried about young Ember."

The boy nodded before running off.

"Right this way, if you please," the grey-haired lady called as she started her ascent. "I'm afraid we are a small town and do not have the largest selection. We have five rooms available, so the men will have to share. The room at the end of the hall is the smallest with just the one bed. I've placed the belongings from the mare along with a fresh set of nightclothes in there for you, dear."

Cadoc grumbled something about women always sticking up for each other as we turned down the second-floor hallway.

"There are showers in each of your rooms and fresh linens have been brought up. The chef was informed of your arrival and will have food sent within the hour." Her brown eyes warmed as she addressed Vidarr. "The items retrieved from the stallion were placed in the second room on the left. Thank you, all. I shudder to think what may have happened had you not risked your lives for us."

"Would the wards not have protected you?" I asked.

"I'm not sure. This is a small, peaceful town. Most of us live meager lives. We haven't been attacked in my lifetime, though I can see times are changing." She shook her head. "Either way, we are grateful for all you've done and all you have sacrificed."

My stomach twisted as a vision of Zelos flashed through my mind.

She pressed a hand to my shoulder. "You may stay as long as you like, free of charge." With that, she departed.

We filed down the hall. Skender and Xaun took the first room, with Cadoc and Kavan taking the next.

"Hey," Vidarr called, halting my progress down the hall. "Today must have been a lot."

My breathing hitched as the fresh sting of grief rose.

"The first battle is always hard, but losing Zelos—"

"We didn't lose him," I growled. "He was murdered. Like countless others. And for what? Because some twisted fae decided he could? Decided that Zelos didn't deserve to live?" My voice cracked on the last word.

Hating the dampness coating my cheeks, I dropped my head into my hands, unable to look Vidarr in the eyes. What I found was worse. Blood was caked beneath my nails, dried flakes of it chipping across the crease of my knuckles. Death clung to me.

A sour taste burned the back of my throat as the tears fell. Zelos was gone. The barb of that truth muddled with the sting of fury, as I focused on my bloodied, soiled hands. These hands —my hands—were that of a killer. I *should* feel guilty. The sane part of me understood that—the part that was rational and responsible—but the piece of me that had roared to the surface today, the monster within, it had enjoyed the bloodshed.

"I wish there was something I could say to dull the pain," Vidarr murmured.

I shook my head, stopping him before he could go on. "There's not." I brought my eyes level to his, my lips twisting into a sad, bitter façade of a smile. "I've been through this before. I've been through worse, but it still hurts, all the same."

"I'll bunk with Evander tonight." *Leaving a room open for Alarik if you wanted space.*

I gave a tight nod as Vidarr walked away, the gentle click of his door sounding through the empty hall as it shut.

CHAPTER 53

IF IT WEREN'T FOR THE BLACK SLUDGE COATING MY BODY, I would've passed out on the bed within moments. As it was, I peeled off the layers of stained clothing and dumped them in a pile on the bathroom floor.

Steam filled the narrow room as I worked the shampoo into a lather, pulling bits of flesh and tissue out of my hair. I repeated the process until the suds remained white as they washed down the drain, leaving my hair with a soft floral scent.

Wrapping a towel around myself, I padded across the wooden floor toward the bed but was brought up short.

Alarik was leaning against the door, his hair slightly damp. Smooth, strong planes of sculpted muscle tapered into a fresh pair of loose-fitting pants. The chiseled plains of his chest were on display, their perfection tarnished by a white bandage looping across his middle.

His eyes widened as they drifted over me, taking in my flushed skin still pink from the shower. He cleared his throat, as if remembering why he was here, and dragged his eyes back to mine. "How are you doing?"

I sighed, too exhausted to answer. Instead, I made my way

over to the pile of clothes left for me, not bothering to sort through them. Lifting the thin nightgown on top, I raised an expectant brow toward Alarik, waiting for him to turn around.

He pushed off the wall, heeding my request.

"I didn't want you to be alone tonight, unless that's what you wanted, but there are things we need to talk about."

I slipped the thin cotton gown over my head, the ends falling just above my knees, and gave my damp hair one last squeeze with the towel, before turning toward him. There were so many things we needed to talk about. My disobedience, the Fractured, training plans with the dark fae, and... Zelos.

There were also a more pressing concern: what the commander had called me—The Dark Phoenix. My brows furrowed. Many had mentioned it, Evander included. But Anita, the woman at the market, had quoted a line that danced along their periphery of my mind. She had claimed the Phoenix would be the bringer of death and destruction.

And Zaeth knew. Of all the beings in this realm to have overheard such an outlandish accusation, it was none other than a dark fae, the leader of an army who *enjoyed* death and destruction. Unease slithered in the pit of my stomach. At least he hadn't exposed me. It didn't mean he wouldn't. Kindness wasn't free.

I shook my head, dispelling the thoughts. I didn't want to think about him, or The Dark Phoenix and what the future held. Instead, I focused on Alarik's silent form, still facing the wall. My lips parted, breath filling my lungs.

No words came. I should speak, should say something, anything—everything.

But I wasn't ready to talk. I wasn't even ready to *think*. I just wanted to *be*—to focus on getting through this one moment and let that be enough.

Exhaling slowly, I crossed the room to Alarik. The muscles of his back tensed as my head dipped against him, the damp chill of my hair sending ripples of raised flesh across his spine. Careful to avoid his wound, I wrapped my arms around him, unable to help myself from breathing in a large gulp. Sandalwood and spice was tinged with the minty effects of his recent shower, but they were calming all the same.

He pulled back, twisting around to see me. "El, we should talk—"

"Please. Just—just can you hold me?" I pleaded, arms falling to my sides. So many things had changed tonight, but I wasn't ready to acknowledge what had happened or what it meant. I wasn't ready to try to understand.

He held my eyes, and for a moment, I feared he would force a conversation, but then his strong arms wrapped around me, pulling me against his chest. A shuddering sob escaped my lips as I fell into him, sinking into the warmth his body offered.

I wanted to erase the last few hours, to forget what we'd lost. To forget what I had become, because I didn't think I could conceal the darker part of myself any longer. I had allowed her freedom and I feared there was no going back.

Silent tears rolled down my cheeks, gathering and building until raw cries shook my body. He let me fall apart, holding me as the tears fell. After a time, my chest stilled and the dampness across my face dried.

Still, Alarik's arms cradled me, his hands tracing slow, languid strokes across my back. "It's okay, El. What you went through tonight with Zelos..." His voice trailed off as I drew in a ragged breath.

"It's not just Zelos. It's—gods—it's everything else, too." It was how I couldn't separate the sadness from the smoldering anger. How I needed to make the scarlet-eyed fae pay for what he'd done.

"I know what you're feeling and it's okay," he whispered into my hair, stroking back stray pieces.

I pulled back a little, just enough to study his reaction, as hope laced my voice. "You do?"

His head dipped in a slow, heartbreaking nod. "No matter how terrible the enemy, it still weighs on us. In war, there is always the risk of physical harm, but people are constantly underestimating the toll it takes on your soul, on the pieces of you that your enemy drags to death along with them."

The splash of hope evaporated. "Alarik, I think you were right." I swallowed, cowardly burying my face into his chest once more. "I—I think there is something wrong with me. I should never have been allowed to fight."

He lifted his hand to my chin, tugging my tear-streaked face up to meet his. His green eyes were full of misplaced understanding as he spoke. "Whatever you're feeling, El, it's okay. It's normal to feel sad, even a little broken. There's nothing wrong with you."

His voice was so sure, so confident. I couldn't bear to explain the devastating truth to him. I couldn't risk losing him. Alarik was everything decent and honest and good in this world. How would he ever be able to understand someone like me?

I pressed my face against him, not bothering to hold back the tears as sobs racked my chest. He held me there as I cried, pressing soothing kisses to my head.

Being the despicable person I was, I let him. Even knowing that I was a fraud, a wolf in sheep's clothing—I let him hold me. And as we shifted to the bed, as my breathing calmed and sleep beckoned me, I let Alarik convince me everything was going to be all right.

CHAPTER 54

MAYBE THERE WASN'T SOMETHING WRONG WITH ME. MAYBE I WAS trapped in that numb phase soldiers sometimes described. The aftermath, the feeling of relief that poured through my soul, maybe that was just a side effect of adrenaline, of surviving my first battle.

I groaned, unable to believe the lie. Last night had brought with it nightmares of the past, visions of my brother's rotted corpses, but resurrected with depthless, black pits for eyes. They heeded the command of the scarlet-eyed fae, laughing as their blades tore through my flesh.

My body shuddered. The need for vengeance was just as potent now as it had been last night, like a primal drive pushing me toward violence. Sparing a glance at Alarik's steady chest, I dragged a hand across my face. There was no way he would want to be with me if he knew the truth.

No one would.

I needed to hide this diseased part of myself, but tt had grown more powerful, like an infection taking hold. Maybe that was my problem. I had been suppressing it for years, but what I needed to do was find a way to eradicate it.

Battle was my trigger. So, I'd have to give it up, at least until I figured out how to fix this rotting part of myself.

I would have to give up my dream of being a member of the base. My heart cracked a little more, but I couldn't become a monster. I wouldn't.

Alarik shifted, throwing a lazy arm over my middle. A sleepy moan sounded from his chest as his eyes fluttered open.

"Good morning." His blond hair was framed by the late afternoon sun as he pressed a soft kiss to my lips. Golden hints of a beard dotted his jaw, causing a rough scrape. I brought a hand up, exploring the texture further.

"Mmm, you may need to keep this," I cooed, forcing a light-ness to my tone.

His deep chuckle rumbled against me as he leaned in once more. All worries faded to the background, replaced by the feel of his lips against mine, the heat of his hands drifting up along my thighs, the warmth of his touch sending shocks across my flesh.

This was the cure I craved. My body responded, a needy groan escaping my lips as he rolled, pulling me on top. The scratchy feel of his bandage grated against my leg, snapping me out of the spell.

"Alarik, your wound!" I shrieked as I leapt off him. "Gods, you can't just throw bodies at it. You're going to rip it open." I dashed for my pack, snagging the healing kit within. Amused laughter greeted me as I knelt beside him.

"I hardly consider what we were doing to be 'throwing bodies' at it."

"You know exactly what I mean," I said as my fingers worked the dressing free. I braced for the flow of blood that was sure to come, but when I pulled the final piece away, only a thin, shallow cut remained, the sutures poking through healed skin.

Alarik twisted to see. "Is it okay? I used one of Lannie's salves. Figured it was best."

"It's great, actually." I blinked. "Little more than a scratch, but I don't think the healer was expecting it to mend so quickly. Your sutures should've been removed hours ago."

Alarik stilled as I reached for the scissors, carefully clipping the stitches free. After donning a small application of Lannie's salve, I secured a light bandage over top.

"There."

"Thanks, El." He stared at me for a moment with open adoration.

I shrugged. "Lannie's taught me a few things."

Reality crept back in as we dressed and when I met his gaze once more, there was an added weight to his shoulders. "We need to meet the others. It's nearly dinner time. Zaeth will have sent a messenger by now."

I nodded as I finished securing my hair in a braid. After Alarik had changed, we made our way to the tavern at the back of the inn to join the others. With only a little pestering, I was able to convince him to stop by the stables on the way.

The rest of the horses had returned, safe and whole, and were now resting. I made my way to Ember, happy to find that her wound was much shallower than I'd thought. I pulled the salve out regardless, sending a plea to the gods that Lannie's skills would extend to horses.

Ember stomped the dirt once I was finished, already eager for her freedom. After a lot of promises of sunrise adventures and a bushel of apples, she conceded to rest for the evening while we met with the fae.

My stomach fluttered as I fell into step behind Alarik as he pushed through the crowd gathered around the large table in the back. A pair of cinnamon eyes flashed through my mind as I wondered which fae would show. Banishing the dark fae from my mind, I focused on Skender and Xaun. They were recounting the battle at the bar with exaggerated details, but the huamns and fae gathered around didn't seem to mind.

Alarik and I brushed passed the crowd and took a seat next to Vidarr with the rest of the Select. Discussions of what the new alliance with the dark fae entailed as well as what it meant for our future rang heavy through the air. Thankfully, Skender and Xaun had the town captivated, which afforded us some much-needed privacy.

"We would be fools not to seize the chance to learn coveted dark fae fighting techniques, Cadoc." Evander's voice rang with poorly controlled annoyance. "Not to mention the possibility of ending the attacks focused on humans."

"They are fae," Cadoc sneered, his grip flexing around his pint of ale. "They cannot be trusted."

Evander's face flared, his eyes narrowing as he leaned in. "If you have something to say about my genetics, then I suggest you say it. I know words can be difficult for you, but I'm sure if you try really hard, you'll be able to manage a few sentences."

Cadoc's fist slammed onto the table as he launched his body forward. Evander smirked, but Vidarr's knife sliced through the tension, his blade nearly catching Cadoc's nose, as it wedged into the wooden table between them.

"Enough," Vidarr growled, low and controlled. "Cadoc, you need to adapt, brother. There is no room for hatred here. Fear can lead you down a path of destruction. I suggest you redirect."

He pinned Cadoc with a glare before turning toward Evander."Evander, you know he's double your weight. He may be an asshole, but he's your brother-in-arms. Help educate rather than exacerbate the situation."

"Why does it fall on me to enlighten him? I'm to be the target of his ignorance and also expected to correct it?"

Vidarr's silver eyes swirled with sadness. "I know it's not fair, but—"

"Or Cadoc could stop being a selfish prick and take some responsibility," I interrupted, hearing enough. I held my chin high. "Maybe try to see life from a different perspective? Fae can

368 | STORM OF CHAOS AND SHADOWS

be dicks, but so can humans. There are assholes in every species."

Vidarr's lips twitched. "That there are. Despite his actions today, I believe there is still hope for Cadoc."

I shrugged, reaching for the pitcher of water. "It doesn't mean he should be given a pass."

"I'm right here. Stop talking about me like I don't exist." Cadoc's gaze seared into mine before he released a long breath. "Look," he gritted, meeting Evander's guarded look. "I'm a prick. I know that. You know my history. I'm working on my issues."

Greer had mentioned something about Cadoc's home being one of the first villages claimed by the attacks. Cadoc had been at the base, as he always was, but his family hadn't been as fortunate. She said that was the reason he was always angry, always eager for a fight.

The rest of us remained silent, watching as Evander weighed his admission, not quite an apology, but probably the closest he'd get to one. He must have come to the same conclusion, because Evander gave the slightest of nods before the two went back to eating.

"Now that that's over," Alarik said, "we need to discuss our next steps. Has the messenger arrived from the fae?"

"Yes, about an hour ago," Vidarr said. "She dropped off a map to Fort Dhara with an agreed upon date." His voice grew grim as his eyes darted to me. "Zelos's body has been prepared. The burial pyre has been constructed and will be lit with the setting sun."

My stomach twisted as a wave of nausea rolled through me. It was traditional to light the pyres at either dawn or dusk. It was thought to mimic the transition from this life into the next. Some wished to be sent with the sun, its heat burning through the ties of this world and allowing the soul freedom. But others still clung to the old ways, choosing to be greeted by the darkness in a welcoming embrace. I liked to think Zelos would have sought the tranquility the night offered as much as I did.

Alarik frowned. "I would have preferred to speak with the messenger directly."

Vidarr's eyes bounced from Alarik to me. "I thought it best not to wake you. My apologies."

Alarik cleared his throat as he turned to the table. "We need to discuss who will join us at the training camp. And yes, we will be allies with the dark fae. I believe Zaethrian's intent to stop the attacks is genuine. We won't waste this opportunity."

Alarik waited until Cadoc's head dipped before they proceeded to review candidates joining us at Fort Dhara. *Them*, I reminded myself, not *us*, because I'd made up my mind to step back from the allure of battle.

Skender and Xaun returned to the table as the conversation transitioned. Theories about the Fractured circulated. No one knew of an entity powerful enough to splinter a soul.

My mind raced with everything I'd learned about the creatures, returning to the first encounter near my childhood home. "Are there any fae who can communicate telepathically?"

The conversation stalled as the men stared at me, clearly surprised I was joining in.

I shifted in my seat as their eyes bored into me. "Telepathy, it means to communicate psychically, like without words."

"We know what it means," Cadoc snapped.

"But what made you ask that?" Vidarr cut in, his shrewd, storm-grey eyes boring into mine.

I sat up straighter, eyes flicking briefly to Alarik before answering. "When Alarik and I fought them—the Fractured—the first time, near my home, there was a moment when the voices sort of blended and synced. And then with the attack last night, clusters of them moved with such familiarity, almost like they were coordinated."

Cadoc scoffed. "That's what happens when you train together for years, not that you would know."

"This wasn't something you could learn," I snapped. "It was as if someone was controlling them from afar. Instinctual rather than developed."

I recalled the tarnished feel of the Fractured. They were identical. I felt it. I saw it, the cold, black fog where their essence had once been, but it wasn't like I could admit to seeing visions of splintered souls while in a bloodthirsty haze.

"Is there anything you know of that can link beings?" I asked instead. The men each shook their heads, though Vidarr's eyes stayed sharp.

"I'll look into the theory when we return," he answered.

"Which needs to be soon." Alarik looked out of the window. "It's nearly time. We'll have tonight to mourn but be prepared to leave tomorrow before the sun rises."

CHAPTER 55

THE MEADOW HAD BEEN CLEARED OF BODIES, ALL BUT ONE. A grand funeral pyre stood proudly in the center, surrounded by wreaths from the town, tokens of appreciation and safe passage from this life to the next.

A short, squat man stood up from having placed an additional bundle of flowers among the largest of the wreaths. He turned to face me.

"Hello, Ellie." Recognition washed over me with his thick accent.

"Mr. Sapo? What are you doing here?"

His chin tipped up, gesturing to the town behind me. "I came to pay my respects to the warriors who defended my home. I'm sorry for your loss."

I let the last sentence slip through me. I'd heard similar phrases in the past. Not once did they quell the brutal sting of loss. "Your home? But I thought…"

"This is my true home. Sonder is a second residence, but Neith is where I grew up. It's where my nieces and nephews live. Where I donate most of my earnings. Thank you for keeping it safe. I know it's not much, but this is how we show gratitude." He gestured to the dozens of trinkets decorating the pyre.

It was grand, a tribute worthy of kings. My gaze flicked to the bundle of flesh sitting atop, bound by a death shroud. Swallowing back the lash of grief, I gave a short nod.

"I'll leave you to it," Mr. Sapo said, placing a warm hand on my shoulder before retreating.

My spine stiffened as tears welled. The town saw Zelos as a great sacrifice, a hero. He was honored, but he was still gone.

I didn't want to hear their praises, their thanks. I didn't want his death to be glossed over as some tragic outcome orchestrated by fate. I wanted them, the town—the world—to feel the anger and sorrow pumping through my veins. I wanted to slice through hordes of the Fractured, to see bodies littering the floor where my feet touched. I wanted to watch as the commander's red eyes flared with fear.

My blade would pierce his heart, maliciously slow, allowing me to savor each and every burst of agony that he felt—just as he had done to Zelos.

I blanched. *Just as he had done to Zelos.*

I wasn't him. I wasn't *evil*, at least not yet.

I couldn't allow myself to become one of the creatures I was trying to destroy.

The bitter scent of smoke stung my nostrils as a torch was thrust into the base. My eyes prickled as the flames caught, climbing up the sides.

I wouldn't give in to this need, this *sickness*.

The flames stretched, ravenous in their consumption, needing more—reaching for Zelos. They were nearly there.

I wouldn't abandon him, or my family, or the countless others who had been slaughtered.

The first of my tears fell as the flames caught, the shroud set ablaze.

I'd find a way to enact my revenge without losing myself.

The vow echoed through my soul as Zelos's body burned, but as the last scraps of cloth were ingested by flames, as I forced myself to watch the layers of skin and fat and muscle melt away, I knew that I was already lost.

CHAPTER 56

THE JOURNEY TO THE BASE WAS QUICK AND WITHOUT INCIDENT. Ember and I flew through the trees, letting the chill of the early morning wash over us as the moon sank low in the sky. She was back to her full strength and eager to prove herself, just I was eager to forget the events of the past few days. The wind whipped against my cheeks as the sun rose, the brilliant array of colors mocking the tumultuous nature of my thoughts.

We stuck near the others for most of the ride, stopping to rest when needed, but as the sun started on her descent once more, we pulled ahead. My thighs clenched as we flew through the lively forest. We paused, only once, as the gate along the walls of the base was opened, and then we were off again.

My thighs burned as we splashed through the shallow stream and up the familiar slope. Ember whinnied as we tore through the last of the trees and into the meadow, now spotted with bursts of yellow flowers among the soft, swaying grasses.

I slipped from her back as we came to the stables, setting her loose on a flock of pixies. Ember chased them mercilessly through the flowers, causing a small smile to to bloom as I turned toward the base.

The dirt across my boots left a trail up the cool marble stones of Alarik's residence. Slipping them off in the foyer before climbing the steps, I turned down the hallway, searching for my sisters. Disappointment coiled in my chest as I found each of their rooms empty. I pushed through my door, eyes snagging on the clock. My siblings were probably at dinner. I could take a quick shower and meet up with them... but how would I explain everything?

Bile burned the back of my throat. I wasn't ready to relive what had happened. Instead, I set my sights on the large claw-footed bathtub across the hall in Greer's room.

Sprinkling bath salts into the rising water, I relished the eucalyptus-scented steam filling the room. Slipping out of my travel-worn clothes, I sank into the near scalding waters, letting the heat seep into my sore muscles. I urged my mind to follow suit, to relax, but the memories of the past few days refused to quiet.

Despite the dismissal of the others, I still believed the Fractured were coordinated somehow. Their movements were clumsy and slow but synchronized enough to prove deadly—as if strings were linking them together, all of which were controlled by a faceless puppeteer—probably the same dark force that had shredded their souls.

Could it be the same darkness that was now in me? Was that how it worked? Like some sickness that spread, a wickedness that corrupted the very essence of who a person was until they were unrecognizable?

My heart raced, thrashing inside my chest as I fought against acknowledging the similarities. The Fractured didn't care about who they killed. They felt no remorse and—if their hideous cackles were anything to go by—they enjoyed ending lives nearly as much as *I* had enjoyed reaping theirs.

Cursing, I sat up, splashing water with my hasty movements. Is this how it started? The splintering of a soul? I gritted my teeth against the thought. I wouldn't become some mindless monster. I refused. Even if that meant giving up fighting forever.

My stomach twisted. Gods, the thought of not training, of not fighting... I'd have to be okay with it.

I pulled the drain, watching as the warm water swirled down, taking the last of the bubbles with it. I stepped onto the cold stone, toweling off my hair before wrapping the soft, fluffy fabric around my body.

Small puddles trailed me as I padded across the hall and into my room. My stomach fluttered as the sound of voices carrying from the hall. I'd just finished slipping into a pair of loose sweats and my favorite worn top when my door opened.

"You're back!" Greer's gleeful voice called as she swept through the door and gathered me in a tight hug. "We missed you."

I hugged her, swallowing the fresh wave of guilt. "It's only been a few days, but gods am I happy to see you too."

She tugged us over to the couch as Lannie and Will appeared in the hall.

Will sprinted into my arms, knocking me against the cushions. "Ellie! I have so much to tell you! I started a new class today with the other kids my age. Well, they're a little bigger than I am, but I'm going to show them I belong. I've decided that I'm going to be the best general ever. Even better than Alarik! But don't tell him that. I don't want to hurt his feelings."

A small chuckle escaped me. "So, you're to be a general, are you?"

"Yes, but don't worry." He patted my hand as he spoke. "I'll be nice to Alarik once I'm his superior."

The three of us fought to contain our smiles.

"That sounds like a wonderful dream, Will." I pressed a proud kiss to his mop of blond curls as he squirmed.

"Generals don't need kisses from their sisters," he said, wiping it away.

Greer snorted as Lannie giggled.

"You're right, I'm sorry."

"And it's not just a dream, Ellie." He tilted his small chin up. There was a stubborn glint in his eyes, begging me to believe him. "I'm going to do it. I—I know that Greer says my dreams aren't real, but this one is. I'm going to be a general."

"I believe you," I said, shooting Greer a questioning look.

She leaned forward, the cushions of the couch dipping with her shifting weight. "I only meant that the bad dreams can't hurt you because the monsters in dreams aren't real. The good dreams, the ones you want to happen, those can be real."

Will's brows furrowed as he glanced between Lannie and me for clarification. "Why would I be able to pick which dreams were real and which ones aren't? That doesn't make sense. And if I can't pick which ones I want, that means all of them are real or none of them are."

The soft melody of Lannie's voice responded first. "She means that it's good to have ideas about what you want to do for your future. If you work hard enough, those things will come true. The dreams that you have, the stories that play out in your mind when you're asleep, those aren't real."

Will nodded his understanding a moment before hopping down and heading for the door.

"Where are you going?" I called after him.

He paused, turning to me with surprised confusion. "To go study. I want to be the best general ever. That's going to take a lot of hard work, Ellie."

"Yeah, Ellie," Greer teased. "The general needs his study time."

I suppressed the urge to laugh as I held Will's stare. "Yes, of course. Have a good night."

He shook his head as he sauntered off.

"When did he grow up? I feel like just yesterday we were lighting all the candles we owned to keep the monsters away at night and now he's studying to be a general."

"So grown up these days." Greer sighed, her soft words overflowing with pride for our baby brother. "You should have seen him, El. He was so excited to go to class. Afterwards, we spent the rest of the afternoon watching the men train, not that I minded that part. With the warmer weather, most of them chose to train without their shirts. They just leave all of that muscle glistening in the sun for anyone to see."

My lips twitched. "I thought you weren't dating?"

"Who said anything about dating? I'm merely appreciating their hard work." She gave a not so innocent shrug. "But really, I'm happy being single. It's nice not worrying about anyone else's opinion."

"You know their opinion never mattered anyway, right?" Lannie questioned.

"Yeah, I know that logically, but I still wanted to impress whoever I was with. Without that pressure, I've been able to figure things out. Learn what I want to do for my own happiness."

"That's good." I said, reflecting on how far we'd come. "It's nice not having to worry where our next meal is coming from, too. Takes the edge off."

"It does a lot more than take the edge off," Greer said, her hand gripping mine. "I hope you know how grateful we are that you figured out how to properly hunt. We would have starved if it hadn't been for you."

"I know we don't say it often," Lannie added, "but we always knew what you were sacrificing. I did my best with keeping us healthy through plants, but, well, you remember when I tried to go hunting." Her cheeks flared a bright pink as a wave of giggles poured from Greer.

"We all remember, Lannie. You almost killed her!"

I failed to stifle my own snickers. "The arrow barely grazed my thigh. And she had me bandaged up within the hour."

Greer scoffed as Lannie's blush turned crimson. "I really am sorry about that."

"It was an accident, and I know you two are grateful. I'm grateful too. Lannie, without you, we'd have all died from some type of infection or fever and Greer, you were the backbone of our family—still are. You're so good with Will, even when he was a toddler. Gods, those days were hard, but we managed it. And now we've got a future general on our hands."

Their smiles met my own as the three of us sank into a deep hug. I was surrounded by my family, safe and protected and *happy*—while Zelos was forever gone from this world. Tension crawled along my spine, clogging my throat as the blissful reprieve of the evening waned. This time yesterday, the flames had only just begun to lick at his bones and here I was, *smiling*.

Nausea threatened to turn my stomach as I pulled back from my sisters.

"What's wrong? You look like you're going to be sick." Greer pressed the back of her hand to my forehead as Lannie frowned, taking in my measure.

"I'm not sick." I prayed to the gods that was true—that I hadn't been poisoned by the same darkness that created the Fractured. "The mission I went on, it didn't go well."

My sisters shared a look, but it was Greer who answered. "I thought it was just a scouting mission, right? Low risk, high reward type of thing?"

"It started out that way, but there were rumors of an attack on a nearby town. We went to check, and—and it turned into a battle."

Lannie was able to maintain a controlled exterior, but Greer's face twisted with worry as she reached for my hand.

The all-consuming weight of guilt pressed against me, my throat burning with the need to confess. "Zelos was killed."

Greer gasped as I blinked away the sheen of tears.

"I couldn't reach him in time. Evander and I tried, but there were too many of them, of the Fractured. They're the creatures that have been mounting the attacks. They're fae, but not. The dark fae we met said their very essence was splintered and twisted—"

"It's okay." Lannie leaned in, drawing me close for a hug. "You've clearly been through a lot. There will be time to explain everything when you are ready. For now, know that we love you and are here for you."

I wiped my cheeks. "I guess I'm still processing, but you're right. I'm not up for talking just yet. I—I think I might put the fighting thing on hold… just for a bit."

Greer's eyes shot up. "Really?"

"There are other things that interest me," I said defiantly. Greer couldn't help the quirk of her brow as she stared. "Well, there could be. With everything that's happened, it's best if I take a step back."

"We understand," Lannie said as she stood, silencing Greer with a quick shake of her head. "I should get to bed. Healer Grant has me working on creating tonics that can purify the blood after poisoning."

"That sounds interesting. I wouldn't think poisoning was a common occurrence," I muttered as we headed for the door.

"It's not, but this black substance is the oddest thing. It binds to the cells of the body, latching on as if it were about to destroy it, but it doesn't take anything from the host—just controls it."

The hairs on the back of my neck stood on end. "A black substance?"

She nodded, stepping into the hall after Greer.

"Where did Healer Grant find it?" I asked, trying to ignore the tendrils of dread coiling in my center.

Could this be related to the Fractured? It would make sense for Alarik to want to learn about their weaknesses. If so, did that mean I was infected, that the hordes of Fractured were subjected to the same disease? More importantly, could it be cured?

"I have no idea. But it's a difficult mystery to solve. It has similar properties to a parasite and some components to an infectious disease, but not enough of either to be classified as such. I'll figure it out." Lannie stretched into a yawn, her voice distorted as she answered. "I'm just next door if you need me."

"I should get to bed too. I'm showing the staff how to make macarons tomorrow." Greer smirked as my eyes lit up. Macarons were my favorite. "I thought that might take your mind off things." Her arms pulled me close, holding me until some o the tension eased from shoulder. "I know you're going through a lot of emotions that I can't understand, but I hope you know you're not alone. You're never alone."

CHAPTER 57

I COULDN'T RELAX. MY BODY WAS EXHAUSTED, AND MY emotional energy was beyond empty, but my mind continued to play Zelos's death over and over again. He was there each time I closed my eyes, his head tilted at an unnatural angle, his neck riddled with five deep puncture wounds.

Giving up on sleep, I returned to the sitting room intent on distracting myself with a good book. I had just reclined on the settee when hesitant knuckles rapped against the door. Already knowing who it would be, I groaned as I strolled to the door, not surprised to find Alarik waiting on the other side.

"I tried to come earlier, but I heard you with your sisters. So, I left and went to shower."

"Thank you."

His face hardened. Was that the wrong response? I knew we hadn't had a chance to talk yet, but I'd hoped to put it off a little longer.

He took a deep breath, but the angry quiver lacing his words carried through. "You rode ahead of us."

"Yes."

"Through the very forest where we first encountered those

creatures." He pushed past me into my room, running a hand through his slightly damp hair. "You decided to ride ahead. Alone. Weren't you afraid of encountering them again?"

I took my time closing the door before facing him. He wouldn't understand. It wasn't fear that propelled me through the forest. I wasn't afraid of them... but of myself. Pushing thoughts of murder and bloodshed away, I finally turned to meet his searing gaze.

"No."

He stared at me through narrowed eyes. I held my breath as I watched warring emotions flicker across his face: anger, disbelief, but it was his all-consuming worry that won.

"El, I know the first time you kill can be difficult. I've been through it myself. I feel the weight of each life I've claimed, even the terrible ones." Alarik's words were gentle, desperately attempting to reach me. He took a hesitant step. "It only means you're human. I promise, you won't ever be put in that position again."

"I don't think I should fight anymore." His body straightened, stunned into stone. The words left a gritty, bitter taste in my mouth, but I willed myself to continue. "A lot has happened. It's safer for everyone if I stay away from the battlefield."

He closed the distance between us, stopping just in front of me. I could feel the heat pouring off his body as his strong, steady hands came to rest on my shoulders. I risked a glance up. He was perfect, all tenderness and concern, but the small, brittle pieces of my heart broke a little more at the hint of pity underlying it all.

"If anything happened to you..." His words hitched, his fingers sweeping long strokes over my arms. "Gods, El, I'm so relieved to hear you'll be safe—I really am—but this doesn't seem like you. Are you sure you'll be happy?"

I bit my lip as I reached a hand up, tracing the now smooth skin across his jaw. I let my fingers wander to brush the short blond tips of his hair, still hinted with traces of his late-night shower, the scent of cloves and sandalwood scenting the air. "I thought that's what you wanted."

"It is, but it's your decision." His hand covered mine, holding it to his cheek, the intensity of his gaze searing through my core. "Do you really not know?"

It was little more than a whisper, a musing given voice. The soft sincerity released a multitude of emotions, all crashing through my body in a beautiful, chaotic storm.

"I know that my heart isn't whole," he said, his other hand coming around my waist, pressing his body into mine. The worn fabric of his sweats did little to shroud the muscular form beneath, and I couldn't help but lean in. "It probably never will be. I can't promise myself to you because half of me is still with her."

With Rhosyn.

"But," he continued, giving voice to that deliciously wretched word that caused my heart to flutter. "But I care for you. More than I thought I was capable of."

His eyes widened as if a confession had been pulled from his lips. Taking a few shallow breaths, I met his gaze. Gods, he was worried about not being good enough for me—that his broken heart was not worthy of my blackened one.

I pressed onto my toes, slamming my lips against his. Because he was more than worthy. He was the hero of this world. He was everything good and right and strong.

So, I kissed him.

I kissed him like I was falling into an endless abyss of wickedness with Alarik as my only chance for salvation. I kissed him like his lips could somehow eradicate the sinister soul inside of me.

He pulled back. "El, I still can't promise—"

"Please." The word rushed from me, breathless and needy. "Please, just kiss me."

Something in my tone, or perhaps the desperate plea in my eyes must have convinced him that words could wait—that in this moment, all we needed was each other.

His hand drifted up to cradle my neck, tilting my face toward his, before his mouth met mine with a hunger I wasn't expecting. The kiss was harsh and frantic, his lips moving with relentless abandon.

And I let him have me. I needed him. Needed this. Needed to lose myself to everything he was and everything I wasn't.

His fingers sent waves of electricity through my body, racing through my veins and coiling low in my center. I moaned as his fingers knotted in the soft curls at the base of my neck, tugging down with just enough force to open my mouth to his.

I met his challenge with a ferocity of my own, tugging the cotton shirt over his head in a clumsy, desperate motion before ripping mine off as well.

His breathing was ragged, his eyes smoldering as they took in my bare chest, nipples growing taut under his hooded gaze. He licked his already swollen lips, transfixed as I slowly started to slipped down my pants.

Alarik looked at me in wonder, the clear desire burning in his gaze. I realized there was strength in that look, a different type of power, one of passion and desire. It was new to me.

Our first time had been soft touches and sweet kisses, but the man before me now promised fire.

Stepping out of the pile of fabric, I relished the way his eyes feasted on the thin scraps of black lace adorning my body. I held my hand up against the broad expanse of his chest, flashing him a wicked grin as I did so.

I wanted to savor this. My fingers dragged across the hard planes of muscle as I circled him, curving over his shoulder, dipping among the chiseled bands of his back. I stalked him like the predator I was, unable to help but admire the multitude of

scars across his skin. He was a warrior, a defender of the innocent. And right now, he wanted me.

My breasts pressed against his back, drawing a hiss from
him, as I leaned forward, pressing small kisses to his neck. I
savored the taste of him, leaving a trail of nips and kisses until I
came to a jagged pink scar in the exact location of where his
wound was yesterday.

It was completely healed. Good. There was nothing left to
hold me back.

I came around to face him, hooking my thumbs in his sweats
as I pressed my lips to his. The thick length of him strained
against the soft material, the tantalizing pressure against my
body urging me on. My hands worked the fabric down to
expose the deep cut of his abs trailing into an enticing vee
before they fell away completely.

His hand curved around the soft skin of my hips, pressing
my near naked flesh against him. My hands locked around his
neck, a moan escaping me as he cupped my ass, grinding his
impressive length against my heated core.

We kissed and licked, devouring each other, slamming
against chairs and walls as we slowly made our way toward the
bed. We fell against the sheets, unwilling to part from one
another for even a moment.

His hand slipped beneath the thin fabric between my legs,
groaning as he felt how ready I was for him. I lifted my hips,
barely feeling the scratch of lace, as he disposed of it before my
legs parted.

His fingers worked my flesh, pumping and stretching until
the coil low in my belly grew taut.

"Alarik." I moaned, needing more of him.

Nipped the tip of my breast as he pulled back, his knees
nudging my legs further apart as he settled between them. He
slowed then, allowing my body time to adjust. And then we
were moving.

Our bodies rocked, the gentle motion giving way to a heated tempo.

We had both been trapped in the frigid loneliness of our lives. But together we burned. It wasn't love, not exactly, but it was real.

Our bodies grew slick with sweat as the fire raged, until my fingers scraping down his back and we detonated together.

We came together again and again, neither of us willing to give up our inferno of refuge. It was an escape as much as a release and we reveled in it, in each other, until the moon was low in the sky and we could evade sleep no longer.

CHAPTER 58

THE DOOR SWUNG OPEN WITH A CRASH, YANKING ME FROM A peaceful dream. My eyes blinked open, locking on the hard planes of Alarik's tanned chest as a set of self-assured footsteps grew louder.

I gasped, sitting up and shoved Alarik awake. My eyes bounced from him to my open bedroom door and the nearing strides, but before I could tell him to hide, Greer came into view.

Her soft blue dress swayed as she strolled in. "Hey, I figured if you were serious about the not-fighting-thing you could join—"

She froze as Alarik sat up, the sheets drifting down to pool in his lap. Greer gawked at the expanse of his chest, her mouth dropping open as she caught sight of the scratches along his back. I flushed scarlet, covering my own exposed body.

"Good morning." Alarik grinned, having the decency to look bashful.

Greer's mouth snapped shut, pulling into a scandalous smile. "It does appear to be a good morning. A *very* good morning."

I groaned.

"Sorry, El. I can see that you have other plans for today." Her eyes burned with questions and a hint of satisfaction as she stepped toward the door. "I'll just be in the kitchens if anyone needs me."

With one last wiggle of her brows she left, shutting the door behind her.

I flung myself into the pillows.

"That wasn't how I pictured our day starting," Alarik smirked.

I threw the comforter over my face, too embarrassed to speak.

Alarik's rumble of laughter shook the bed, his frame sliding down next to mine to join me under the covers. "It wasn't that bad."

"It was terrible! How could it have been any worse?"

"At least we weren't in the middle of anything." A wicked grin spread across his cheeks at the suggestion. He brought his lips to mine, his hand trailing down my stomach to settle just above my hips. "How are you feeling?"

"A little sore," I admitted.

His hand stilled, but I tilted my hips, urging him to continue. A hungry groan escaped him, igniting my own desire.

"Then let me ease that ache for you," He breathed, slipping his fingers between my thighs.

The rest of the world could wait. At least for today.

I knew we'd have to address everything, eventually. Our alliance with the dark fae was fragile at best, and there was so much we didn't know about the Fractured, or the mysterious force responsible for unleashing them.

Then there was me. The darkness hadn't dissipated, but Lannie was already working on a cure. It was only a matter of time until I was free.

His lips brushed over mine as his fingers gently explored. "Are you sure you're feeling up to this?"

I answered him with a kiss, forcing my mind to clear. Reality could wait. Right now, in this moment—with the feel of his hands on my body, with the taste of his lips against mine—I allowed myself to stay in the beautiful haven we'd created.

"Do your worst, General."

BONUS CONTENT: ZAETH

GODS, SHE WAS INCREDIBLE. THE SCENT OF BLOOD MISTED THE air as her sword burst through the bodies of her enemies, each defeated monster a testament to her strength.

To her power.

She didn't stop. Never faltered. There was no hesitancy, no remorse. This was a warrior goddess, delivering vengeance while relishing the thrill of death.

A groan built in the back of my throat as I cut down my own share of monsters, my blood heating for an entirely different reason as I watched her revel in the gore around her.

She was glorious, so different than the fae I'd encountered. This was a being who saw the beauty in blood, one who recognized that killing soulless creatures wasn't something to be ashamed of. We were keeping this word safe. Purging the plague of the Fractured from Pax's shores in order to protect innocents.

I wondered if she could see into their essences the way I could. If she knew they weren't alive—not really. They'd given themselves over to the red-eyed commander, or another, greater entity controlling him.

"Leave the mortal alone," I shouted, feeling a spike of anxiety rock through me as the monstrous commander descended on the cocky mortal before him.

Red eyes turned toward my voice, tracking my movements as I flitted through the throngs of Fractured. Relief not of my own making surged within, flickering before vanishing as the warrior launched himself at the commander, sword held high.

Foolish boy.

There was no time to reach him. No way to prevent the mortal's death. It shouldn't have bothered me. Mortals died all the time, especially with the growing number of attacks, but that sense of unease—almost pain—wouldn't abate.

Through the mess of battle, I caught glimpses of the commander heading toward the warrior goddess with chestnut curls and skin streaked with blood.

No, I thought. He couldn't have her.

I slashed my way through the black haze of the Fractured, my sword finding the next body before the others had time to fall, but when I'd finally reached her, the commander was retreating.

My brows furrowed, trying to make sense of the red-eyed fae's decision to flee, but the girl's large, hazel-blue gaze met mine, swirling with anger and loss, her hands cradling the bloodied body of the fallen soldier.

I left my questions unasked, remaining by her side until the rest of her guards joined her. There would be other days to seek answers.

For now, I yielded to the overwhelming desire to *protect* her. She was a stranger, a mortal if the rounded tips of her ears were any indication, but there was an undeniable urge to keep her near. To keep hee safe.

I cocked my head to the side, assessing her as she stared at the boy, helping his spirit pass from this world. She *was* human... but something other lurked beneath.

Tendrils of soft shadows stretched under my command, brushing against her essence. There was darkness within, primal and chaotic. Wild. And all of it—all that power—was trapped.

Inhaling deeply, I bypassed the tang of blood and concentrated on the scent of lavender and citrus mingling with the rich undertones of ambrosia, trying to discern what sat before me. Notes of sandalwood clashed with the sweetness, twisting my gut as I realized she was involved with another.

"Gods, El. I couldn't see you. I didn't know…"

My lips press thin as I took in the stammering human. This was the source of the smell lingering on the woman before me. He could be easily dealt with. His pulse hummed, his blood and others staining his clothes.

One flick of my wrist and his chest would still. I could steal her away, scrub every inch of her body until his unworthy scent was gone. Until mine took its place.

But she was mortal.

And I was cursed.

We could never be. Ignoring the pang of jealousy, I turned from her and faded into the darkness.

ACKNOWLEDGMENTS

Thank you to everyone who had a part in making this story a reality.

To my husband, Jake. Words cannot describe how grateful I am to have you in my life. Thank you for the countless nights you took care of our girls, of singing lullabies and reading dozens of bedtime stories, so that I could write. Thank you for all of the dirty dishes you've cleaned and all of the meals you've made; for walking our dog every day, regardless of the weather, and remembering to always refill his water bowl when I, inevitably, forget. Thank you for not letting me give up, even on those rough days; for knowing when to comfort me and when to push. You not only gave me strength when I needed it most, but helped me discover my own resilience. I love you more than I will ever be able to describe.

To the wonderful supportive authors I'm lucky enough to call friends, thank you. To my fantastic editors at Second Pass Editing, Claire Wright and Darby Cupid. This book would not have been finished without you two. Thank you for working with me through multiple rewrites, and for helping me craft this story into the best version of itself.

Lastly, to the readers: thank you for all of your love and support.

Thank you.

ABOUT THE AUTHOR

C.L. Briar is a graduate of San Diego State University. In her spare time, she likes to participate in impromptu dance parties with her little girls, and to look for "nice bugs" in the backyard, when the weather allows. She lives in Northern Virginia with her husband, three daughters, and dog.

Made in the USA
Middletown, DE
17 February 2024